To Maxin
Enjoy — and what
It's a pleasure to meet a
non-boring man!
Linda

THE IRISH AFFAIR

LINDA CHRISTIAN DIVER

FriesenPress

Suite 300 - 990 Fort St
Victoria, BC, V8V 3K2
Canada

www.friesenpress.com

First Edition — 2018

This is a work of fiction. Names, characters, businesses, places, events, locales, and incidents are either the products of the author's imagination or used in a fictitious manner. Any resemblance to actual persons, living or dead, or actual events is purely coincidental.

ISBN
978-1-5255-2673-2 (Hardcover)
978-1-5255-2674-9 (Paperback)
978-1-5255-2675-6 (eBook)

1. FICTION

Distributed to the trade by The Ingram Book Company

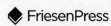

To David.

My husband, friend and companion.
You always believed I could write a book.
Well here it is with my endless love, and gratitude for your patience and humour.
Without you this book would have remained a figment of my imagination.

Time shall unfold what plaited cunning hides: Who covers faults, at last shame them derides.

—William Shakespeare

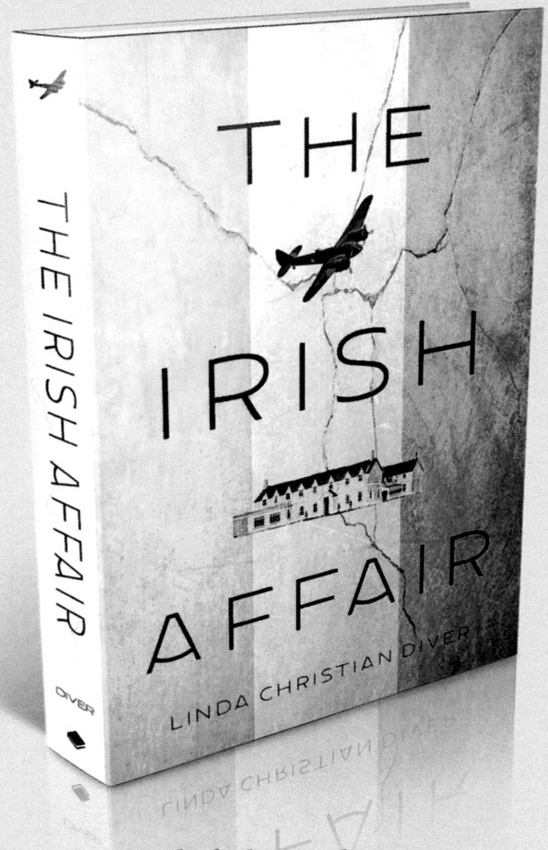

www.lindachristiandiver.com

CONSUMER REVIEWS

"Dating the chapters was brilliant. For anybody with even a smattering of knowledge of 20th-century European history, the dating was quite evocative. It immediately set the context and conjured images of the era against which The Irish Affair plays out. That's especially effective in a book with the grand, four-decade sweep of this one. The author artfully weaved the threads of the Irish situation, WWll, and the McKellan family story together into whole cloth. The characters are wonderfully drawn. The book never lagged; it kept my interest throughout."

- Rick Husband

"Bravo to Linda Christian Diver for creating this marvellous page-turner."

-Elaine Prodor

"I enjoyed reading The Irish Affair very much because historical fiction has always appealed to me more than straight fiction. The author obviously did a lot of research."

Don Howlett

"The characters in The Irish Affair hooked me. They were engaging, funny, and genuine. It mattered to me what choices they made, and how they made their way."

-Dale Graham

"It has a nice quick start; I like that!"

-Frank Mott

"This novel is a delightful and engaging story from start to finish. When I hear 'period piece' I brace myself for dry and tedious. This is neither of those. The author transports us to rural Ireland and grooms her characters masterfully. I loved sharing the journey of Helen and while this story involves love and betrayal, tragedy and triumph, all set in WW2, this story inexplicably gave me comfort."

-Annette Moore

Killala Bay
River Moy Estuary
Enniscrone
Ballina
Ballinrobe
Castlebar
CO. MAYO
SCOTLAND
Edinburgh
N. IRELAND
Belfast
IRISH SEA
Dublin
ENGLAND
REP. OF IRELAND
Bletchley Park
WALES
London
ATLANTIC

CHAPTER 1

1916-1920

COOPER O'NEIL, NOT yet ten, held a gun for the first time when he and his sister, Sophie, were playing hide-and-seek. Scrunched inside his parent's wardrobe, he saw the Luger—a semi-automatic pistol—wedged behind a pair of his da's mud-caked boots.

He needed both hands to tug it free. Dry-mouthed, he squinted down the barrel. The action caught him rabbit-like, as if in a car's headlights, before footsteps on the landing broke the spell. Clutching the gun, he scrabbled from his hiding place, and crouched the way British soldiers did on Belfast's streets. Holding his breath, he aimed the Luger through the open door.

"Cooper!" Sophie screamed. "Are ya dense? Put that down."

Her body filled the gunsight. Cooper fell back from the dread thrall that gripped him and lowered the pistol. "Is it Da's?"

"It is, but it's not for you to touch. Put it back. Now. Afore Ma comes. Not a word to anyone—not even to your best pal. Promise, or I'll tell Da, and there's not a saint will save you."

"You're my best pal."

"Swear," she said, her face redder than her hair.

Cooper stuffed the gun back. "I promise." *What a sissy. When I'm older, I'll get me own gun.*

The O'Neil's house squatted in a redbrick row hemmed in by streets that reeked of boiled cabbages and outhouses. It was a typical two-up-two-down dwelling, with an outside shack serving as a latrine—a rank object of envy for in the Falls one privy served an entire street. Nothing else identified the house, except for Sophie's pot of weed-strangled flowers by the front door.

Beneath the rain-hammered roof, three straw mattresses covered Cooper's bedroom floor. Sophie's suspended sheet divided her from him and his older brother, Eamon. His parents' room across the landing boasted nothing but the wardrobe and a sagging bed. Many nights, Cooper braced for bouts of cursing and crashing furniture after Da staggered home from the pub. At the sound of his footsteps on the creaky stairs, Cooper would cover his ears—he'd seen enough dogs hooked together to understand the urgent twanging of his parents' bed springs that followed soon after.

A handful of days after the gun incident, Cooper dawdled in the kitchen doodling on the steamed up windows while Ma shortened Eamon's castoff pants for him. The pot was on the boil, and Sophie groused as she peeled potatoes over the chipped sink. He was set to mutter that he didn't appreciate waiting in his drawers, when Da burst in trailing stale pub smells behind him, his face dark with a day's stubble and his hair straggling lank on his collar.

"The stinking Brits have murdered James Connolly," he yelled.

Fed-up from listening to Da gab on about the Irish Republican leader—the man's courage and hard work—Cooper wondered if he was just plain jealous. But not today. Today, Da had the look of a kicked dog.

Ma slewed her eyes in his direction. "Murdered, did you say? The man is invincible, Liam. Didn't he and his men hold Dublin's General Post Office against thousands of them Brits over Easter week?" She thrust the altered pants at Cooper. "Here. Put 'em on."

Liam sagged against the sink. "He's dead, Nora. Tried in secret he was, lashed to a prison chair and shot point blank—him and them others who signed the Irish Proclamation—slaughtered.

Cooper hauled on the altered pants and skulked towards the door. "Where do you think you're going?" Ma barked, before she moved behind Da and kneaded his back. "The killing can't be undone, love. But there'll be no stopping us. Even when our brave lads get shipped to British prisons, there'll be plenty more itching to scrape British shite off our land. We'll be a Republic one day."

"Our Ma has the third eye," Sophie whispered to Cooper, later that night. "She sees into the future." Hearing that, the hairs on the back of his neck prickled.

Within a month of the rising, Eamon and Da regularly stumbled home, blood-splattered and knuckles skinned. From their private mumblings in the parlour, Cooper learned they had become foot soldiers for the movement, and dedicated themselves to the growing popularity of Michael Collins, who had fought alongside Connolly. All this before a single prison ship had sailed beyond the bluffs of Ireland. That third eye of Ma's was a rare gift, Cooper decided.

§

"Cooper, don't be taking after Da and Eamon when it comes to missing church," Ma said, eyeing the three of them eating their supper one Sunday. "The lot of you should be on bended knees, praying them Protestants don't always get the best of everything ... work, houses, doctors, and schools."

Cooper scowled. He'd choose cuffs to his head before he'd quit playing Sunday kick-the-can and hopscotch in the Falls' idle streets.

"Ach now, Nora," Da chided, between forkfuls of potato and cabbage mash, "the saints change nothing. Confession and penance are sops for the gullible." Hearing that, Cooper grinned and jabbed the air with a fist. It earned him a swift kick under the table from Sophie, but to him the nod from Da was worth it.

"The devil will get you, Liam O'Neil for saying that in this house," Ma retorted.

With that third eye of hers, Cooper was worried, especially when Da landed a job in a Protestant-controlled welding shop. Sure enough, six weeks in, he limped home early, his clothes in tatters and his skin lacerated from broken glass.

"The proddies goaded me into a fight," he mumbled.

"And you an innocent, were you?" she asked.

Cooper gnawed his thumbnail. There'd be no more playing now. He'd have to earn money—stand on street corners shouting newspaper headlines, and follow coal trucks for fallen lumps to peddle. Was there nothing better? Retreating into himself, he schemed on how to hook proddies out of cash.

§

The Sinn Fein nationalists won their first election two years after the Easter Uprising, the same day Eamon turned seventeen. Cooper and the family crowded into the parlour to munch on Poor Man's Cake, made from flour, clarified pig's fat, baking soda, and scrounged sugar and raisins. Between mouthfuls hard enough to break a tooth, Cooper eyed his brother. "What's it like, being seventeen?"

"I'd be asking his girlfriend, not him," Sophie giggled, her flirty eyes setting Cooper to wondering if his sister had blown a man's pipe yet. 'It's what girls do,'

Eamon had told him, giving him a man-talk after catching him early one morning pulling on his flute.

Eamon grinned and straightened, as if on parade. "Being the grand age I am now, I can take the oath and join the Irish Republican Army."

"The volunteers? Did ya hear that, Da?" Cooper warbled.

Liam puffed up like a rooster. "About time an O'Neil helped the cause. King Georgie's boys won't know what's hit 'em when my boys split their arses."

"Liam! Mind your tongue!" Nora shouted, and waved the cake knife under his nose. "As for you, Eamon, you'll get nowt sympathy from me if you end up in prison or worse. By the by," she said, knife on the table and fingers now gripping the nape of Cooper's neck, "don't be recruiting this one for messenger jobs or worse, or you'll be stoking the devil's fires."

Hot to challenge, Cooper caught Sophie's warning look and shut his mouth. He'd form his own gang—arm his pals with slingshots, and practice until bottles and cans toppled with a single strike.

Within the month, his lads were swarming improvised proddy barricades, shattering glass-fronted shops, and pelting stones at proddy school boys. Each raid confirmed to him that he, Cooper O'Neil, needed no IRA to fight *his* battles.

CHAPTER 2

DECEMBER 1938

TWO HUNDRED MILES east of Cooper's world, Helen McKellan sat tapping her teeth with a pencil in the resplendent living room of the family home in Edinburgh. Attempting a cryptic crossword in a fog of frustration was futile. What was Lawrence doing? Her husband had finished the puzzle within minutes, then decamped to his study to revise one of his architectural designs, she supposed. What a boring Christmas, especially when Harry, her brother-in-law, had resorted to a liquor-induced snooze on the end of the sofa to her. She gave a loud sigh, leaned over, and poked him in the ribs.

He started upright and eyed her crossword. "What? You want help?"

"Help? You're worse than I am with these. I'm mad as hell. Fine company you and Lawrence make."

"Oh dear, you *are* upset. Doesn't bode well for the rest of the evening."

She didn't respond, thinking instead of how she missed the easy-going Lawrence—the one who sang off-key and took her on wild midnight spins in his Jaguar sports car. If only she could turn back the clock, or give Lawrence a dollop of Harry's disposition, and Harry a dollop of his.

Just then the kitchen door opened, and Lawrence strolled in munching a sandwich. Harry downed the remains of his drink, rolled off the sofa, and placed a fresh log amongst the fire's dying embers.

Helen sat up and put the puzzle on her lap. "Welcome back. I thought you were busy in the study."

"I was, but not for long. I've been in the kitchen preparing a surprise but first I've things to discuss." He dropped into his leather-studded armchair and jiggled a foot, waiting while Harry crossed to the side-table and refilled his glass of scotch.

After a mouthful, Harry returned, glass and decanter in hand. Helen watched his jaunty walk, thinking he hadn't a deferential bone in his body, despite Lawrence bailing him out of debt and letting him occupy their guest room. Not that she minded, Harry's humour was a blessed relief these days.

"Are you ready? Comfortable?" Lawrence asked, "Then I'll begin. You both read the papers so you're aware of the upheaval in Europe with Germany on the march. We need Churchill to curb Hitler's treacherous ambitions. Chamberlain's 'Peace for our time' declaration is pitiful. In my estimation, Britain will be at war with Germany before year end."

With Lawrence's voice droning in the background, Helen pushed at the cuticles of her right hand. A nervous habit. *There he goes, upsetting us with his politics and embroidering facts. Ah! The crossword.* Dropping her eyes, she filled in the remaining blanks. *H-y-p-e-r-b-o-l-e.* The last clue had alluded to embroidery.

"So Hitler is now war minister," Lawrence said, then stopped. "Are either of you remotely interested?"

Helen let her pencil fall to the floor. "Trying, but why the history lesson?"

"Because, my dear, we're moving. I've bought a hotel and farm on the west coast of Ireland."

"Bloody hell, old man!" Harry blurted, "we're moving?"

Helen looked at Lawrence, unblinking for eternal seconds, gripping her glass hard, in case it flew at him from her fingers, before forcing herself to stay calm. "So, you're going to chain gang me and our two children, including Harry, and march us off to wherever you choose, without so much as a *what do you think of the idea* to your *wife?*"

Lawrence leaned forward, elbows on his knees. "I couldn't risk someone else snapping up the property, or deal with your *whys* and *what ifs*. War is coming. Ireland is safer."

"Discussing plans with *me* does not risk a damned thing," Helen shot back with a flash of anger. Her mother's Boston accent twanged in her head. *You're marrying a Scot. Are you mad? They're a taciturn, misogynist lot.* Right now, she had to agree. After a decade of marriage, hers and Lawrence's innermost confidences had congealed into colourless facts related to household, money, and newspaper headlines. If they weren't careful, the derailment of their marriage could flatten them, and leave the children floundering in their parents' wake—Margaret not yet ten and Alex eight. She reached behind her and pummelled the cushion. *Why*

Ireland with its history of famine, civil war, and partition into North and South? What a decision for a conservative Scot to make.

"Will we get to watch the Irish Republican Army and the British military have at each other?" she asked.

"Don't be disingenuous, my dear. The IRA operates in Northern Ireland. The west coast is perfect, and Ireland's insistence on staying neutral helps since it will deter British invasion *and* German bombing."

Harry seized the decanter like a parched man, filled his glass again, and resurrected his voice. "Wonderful, but you haven't given a toss about dropping your bomb on us, have you?"

Helen gave him a shake of her head. Any opposition on his or her part was wasted effort.

"Quit guzzling the scotch, Harry," Lawrence said, throwing him a look. "We don't need you pie-eyed a second night."

Aware Harry would argue, Helen escaped by glancing over to a grouping of family photographs on the Steinway piano. The central one showed the McKellans in stiff collars, their women in over-sized hats, and their children primed to quell their exuberant selves. *A second war will change those pretensions,* she thought. Another photograph displayed her father, Eldon Sullivan, with a Cunard steamship in the background. He had made a fortune improving a desalinization process for the company, but the Great Depression brought him financial ruin. It took weeks for Helen and her mother to accept his untimely death—a death he brought upon himself by inhaling carbon monoxide inside his Rolls Royce in the family garage. After the tragedy, Helen became wary of men's ambitions. The last photo showed her parents standing with The Honourable Charles McKellan and Mrs McKellan at Oxford University's recognition ceremony for benefactors. With Lawrence's pedigree, she sometimes wondered what he'd seen in her. Maybe her piano skills and her fluency in French had impressed him, or was it her father's international connections?

Harry said that his brother had found her an invigorating breeze compared to the parochial types in Edinburgh—a surprising statement she thought, since Lawrence had been anything but adventurous with her at first. These days, it seemed her 'invigorating breeze' had become a bitter downdraft.

A lull in the men's conversation pulled her back. With the proposed move, Lawrence was exercising an antiquated sense of entitlement as the eldest son of a Scottish Laird. There was no breaching that wall—Scottish Inheritance laws scuppered Harry and protocol foiled her. Catching Lawrence's eye, she asked him why a hotel and farm had attracted him.

"Because, when I join the navy, which I prefer to the air force or military, both properties will give us a safe haven and extra income."

Harry butted in. "Where exactly is this haven of yours?"

"In Killala Bay, County Mayo, Harry."

Feeling none the wiser, Helen determined to study the family atlas. At least Lawrence's plans for Harry suited him well. He had the common touch and would make a good farmer—the insurance job Lawrence had pushed him into had never suited. Nice that the farm neighboured the hotel.

"I hope the hotel isn't one of those buildings you claim has unique character—blistering paint, leaky roofs, and discoloured floors," she said. "Is my husband, the architect, to become the hotelier?"

"No. That will be your job, and when I'm called to serve, my partner, the worthy George Drummond, will keep the firm on course."

Had her husband gone mad? She knew nothing about hotels beyond being a paying guest, let alone accounting. *I should speak up ... tell him I don't want to be a bloody hotel manager.* Apart from organizing sixty Edinburgh women into soup kitchen teams around town, she had never supervised staff. And, although she knew how to entertain a household of guests, thanks to her parents' high society life, New York and Paris were a far cry from the west coast of Ireland. She loathed the business world, not that anyone would guess. She should have been an actress, and to judge from her husband's subterfuge, he should have been an Alfred Hitchcock spy.

She let out a heavy sigh. "How did you plan this without Harry or me knowing?"

Harry snorted. "That's easy. My brother takes after our father, who preached to never let the right hand know what the left hand was doing."

"Good advice too, Harry," Lawrence said. "Don't tell me you haven't used it."

And very dodgy, Helen thought, recalling how, despite his honoured position as Lord Lieutenant of Stirlingshire, her father-in-law had often imbibed whiskey to the point of being sodden, and pinched female bottoms. "What about schools for Margaret and Alex?" she asked. "I don't see you, a true-blue Presbyterian, approving Catholic influences."

"Schools are not churches, Helen. I'll find a good one."

She held her tongue. When had Lawrence stopped saying 'we' and when had that special smile, reserved just for her, fallen away? Harry gave her a surreptitious wink, before Lawrence fastened his attention on him.

"To answer your earlier question, being an asthmatic will likely prevent you from fighting, but Britain will need Ireland's farm produce, and that's how you will serve. The Irish countryside and your love of horses will be just the thing for you, Harry. Look upon the move as a fine chance for a new life."

"I see. Harry rising from the ashes, so to speak."

Lawrence waved a dismissive hand. "You never know. Now for my surprise, which I left in the kitchen. I'll be back before you can count to ten." True to his word, he reappeared with his prized Remy Martin cognac, a plate of biscuits and Stilton cheese, plus a self-satisfied smile. "I've been saving this for a special occasion. Let's drink to celebrate our future."

"That's the best thing you've said in the last hour," Harry said, holding his hand out for the glass.

Helen took hers in silence. *There, done. Game. Set. Match. Loose ends tied and family in tow.* But she had a million questions. How reliable would Harry be—a known gambler, too fond of his drink, and a notorious womanizer? And what of Ireland? How secure was Killala Bay from hothead nationals to the North? Could she find the right staff? And what of the children? Where would she find the time to give them the love and attention they deserved? Would she be lonely? Being resilient and smart was no armour against that.

Lawrence, with an uncharacteristic appeal in his eyes, lifted his glass high. "Let's toast to our future success."

"Success," Helen said, raising her glass slowly, and giving him what she hoped was a winning smile.

CHAPTER 3

1919-1929

AT THE AGE of thirteen, when Cooper could knock an opponent unconscious with a one-two punch, he cornered Sophie on her way home from school.

"I don't much like the way them proddy dogs gawk at you. Their school's within spitting distance of ours. You need protecting. I'll be walking you home after school by way of our turf. No shortcuts."

Sophie's face coloured. "You're daft. I'd not let them scum cop a feel."

"They're not the asking kind. Eamon says sex ain't got no manners, and makes men steam for pouty lips."

"Is that what he calls our private parts? Been talking the birds and the bees to you, eh?" But her eyes softened. "Ach, Cooper, it's me used to look out for you. Still, your company is grand."

The new routine suited them fine, until one afternoon a teacher hauled Cooper into the classroom by the ear for starting a brawl. Forced to write 300 lines, *I promise not to start fights in the schoolyard,* he squirmed on his well-caned backside and worried about Sophie.

§

Patience was no friend of Sophie's—not with summer heat coiling around her and sweat soaking her armpits. With plans for an ice cream with her chums, she cussed Cooper's non-show and took the forbidden shortcut. A half mile out, the thud of feet landing on the ground caused a backward look. Two Protestant girls stood glowering at her, and ahead, three more jumped off a wall. The leader, a bully with pudding bowl breasts, brandished a stick. A foul taste swamped Sophie's mouth. There was no escaping Maisie Ferguson and her slags.

"Sophie O'Neil, ya Fenian cow, did ya think ya could have it off with me boyfriend and me none the wiser?"

Sophie gave her a cold stare. "Your wanker sweet-talked me, but I wasn't having none of it. I know about him and his pals trapping Catholic girls for gang shags."

Maisie swore. "Shut yer cake-hole. Grab her."

Sophie's heart thumped so hard she thought her ribs would crack. "You bitches!" she screamed, launching herself into the oncoming girls, her feet kicking, and her hands grabbing fistfuls of hair. When she hit the ground, one of them straddled her chest and stuffed a urine-soaked rag into her mouth, while the others yanked off her knickers.

Unable to scream, Sophie felt something gritty rubbed between her legs, followed by a terrible burning. Around her, the air broiled with savagery, then collapsed into silence.

§

When Cooper let himself in the back door, sounds of whimpering drew him towards the parlour. He peered through the half-opened door and froze. Sophie was huddled on Ma's lap—the two of them crowding Da's tatty armchair. Tears rolled into blood oozing from Sophie's lip, and her balled hands were pushed between her thighs.

"It kills me to pee, Ma," she sobbed.

"The pig fat will take the sting from the salt, my precious."

"Them slags should get it," Sophie said.

Cooper's ears burned as raw details tumbled out. He seethed at his stroppy ways, even blamed Sophie—the way she tossed her hair and eyeballed the fellas—until he realized the slags could have killed her. He'd start no fights. That was a promise. Instead, he'd use stealth and cunning. *There'll be no slappers messing with her again,* he vowed and tiptoed away.

A week later, while gnawing a heel of bread in the kitchen, Ma jabbed a flour-caked finger at the newspaper. "You don't know nothing about this, I suppose?"

Five teenage Protestant girls have been brutally beaten on Shankill Road. They were not defiled, but had their heads shaved and one had the letter 'P' carved across her chest. The perpetrators are still at large. An unnamed source said the leader was 'a small, wiry fellow with boxer's hands, and fast on his feet.

Cooper took a satisfying bite of his bread. "Nah. Don't know nothing."

It didn't surprise him when Sophie quit school and took a job at the linen mill. At sunrise, when the mill-horn blasted, he would hear her tiptoe down the stairs and leave home to work a twelve-hour shift. One morning, he caught her smearing grease in her armpits.

"The mill's so hot, my skin is raw from sweat."

"Can you not open the windows?"

Sophie scoffed, and arms folded, imitated her boss. "Sophie O'Neil, the needs of the flax come first. There'll be no opening windows. We don't want the flax getting brittle."

Cooper laughed. "You should be a movie star. Get yourself another job."

"No need. I've got plans, but I ain't telling you yet."

She told him a week later, when he walked her home, "My boyfriend Brendan and me, we're away to Derry. I can't abide this town, with Brit soldiers looking for trouble. Brendan has asked to marry me. Derry's shirt mills pay good, and work finds him like fleas to a dog."

"You're marrying the plumber? That was fast. What's the real pull?"

Sophie ignored the question. "Ma's upset ... says Derry's no paradise."

"Well, she's right. A border town don't make sense if you want away from soldier-boys." Was there nothing he could do or say to change her mind?

She gripped his arm. "Cooper, I love Brendan. Besides, he owns a house in Derry."

So that was it. There was no fighting a house. "How did he come by a *house*?"

"From his parents. They got killed in them Derry riots but the IRA squared off against them proddies and a truce came afore they grabbed the place."

§

Sophie married less than a month later. Wind plucked at the wildflowers braided through her hair as she hurried into the church. Dressed in a muslin gown of traditional blue—paid for by Aunt Mauve from Dublin, Sophie floated down the aisle on Da's arm—him spruced up and proud as a strutting cob horse. The groom beamed at her with a sappy look that made Cooper breathe easy—no question, Brendan loved Sophie. Ma snuffled into a lace hanky, and Cooper hoped the expression on his face passed for a smile. Beside him, Eamon grinned, no doubt his head clogged with thoughts of the *Ceilidh* to follow. Moments before the church doors reopened, the weather cleared—a grand omen everyone thought, until an hour later, when the rain returned.

§

To Cooper, Sophie's absence felt like a canker eating at him and making him irritable and lonely. He had lost his confidant, his pal, his supporter. To block these feelings, he sought girls for quick relief, but he couldn't stand their giggling or jealous ways, so he swatted them away like flies. Resorting to work, he started up a business that had been germinating since the proddies had bullied Da at the welding shop.

Using distracting tactics—a fire within a rubbish heap, a cat inside a chicken coop, a girl showing more flesh than was proper—he filched vegetables, shanks of ham, and clothing from market stalls. Within a year, he grew bolder and twice nicked arms and ammo from British trucks. There were buyers a-plenty for his hauls and the raids led to establishing a protection business. With Da not working, and Eamon often on the run from police and soldiers, he knew Ma would squelch her doubts and take his offerings of food, money, and clothes.

§

Towards the end of 1927, Cooper, now twenty-one, came home in the small hours to find Ma pacing the parlour, a frantic look in her eyes.

"Your da is never this late. His gun's gone. I've got a bad feeling, Cooper. Get Eamon. He's holed up at Sheelagh's place."

Cooper raced through the dark streets, and at the back of a run-down house, threw pebbles against the top window. Sheelagh peered out from behind the curtains.

When Eamon unlatched the door, and heard Da was missing, he pulled on a coat. "We'll rouse Quinn," he said. "For a few quid, he always has tip-offs."

They found the snitch holed up in a one-room squat behind the pub. "Nasty business," he said, after Eamon forked over the money. "I heard your da and pals were plastered and made a run for it at a roadblock. Daft apes. Bloody antique, your da's gun. Wouldn't fire. The soldiers were all over them. Punched them until they puked. Threw your da's pals in a wagon but treated him different. Whipped him with a belt studded with upturned bottle caps, poor bugger."

"Jaysus! Where'd they take him?"

"Likely dumped him out Divis Mountain way."

It was Da's boots gave him away—those and the blowflies and smell. The crows had already pecked out his eyes. Bent double, Eamon vomited, but Cooper remained cold-eyed and grim.

Smudged clouds gave the dawn a bruised look before the brothers succeeded in rounding up help. They brought their da home through the Falls in a wheelbarrow, his body shrouded in old sheets. Word had spread and neighbours crowded in front of the house, when Ma, white-faced and unmoving as stone, stood at the front door to receive her husband's broken body.

Tears streaked Eamon's face, but Cooper choked his back. What use were tears? Their da was dead—fecking murdered. If he bided his time, one day he'd get his revenge—the cunning kind that brought his targets to their knees wherever he found them.

For months, Nora refused to leave the house, or attend church. "Prayers aren't helping, Cooper. Me man's gone." Then, after a visit from Sophie, she left her bedroom and came into the kitchen, hair brushed and dress ironed. "Cooper, will you come with me to Aunt Mauve in Dublin? The memories here are driving me crazy. Your auntie has been lonesome since your uncle got shot in the Easter Rising and her son, Daecon, bought a piggery on the west coast. She says she can find good paying work for you."

Cooper smiled. Top dogs in the IRA were nagging him to join the movement. Best leave while he could. Dublin provided a grand escape, a grand stepping-stone—new recruits, new marks, and new shakedowns. His top man would tend to his Belfast business. And Eamon? He'd stay, and for a small fee, be a fine strong arm if trouble brewed.

CHAPTER 4

MARCH 1939

Enniscrone village lay on the eastern side of the River Moy—a short distance from the hotel—and Harry loved the miles of sandy beach and bracing ocean air almost as much as horse sweat and foaming Guinness.

The village pub mirrored the whitewashed cottages that stitched the main street, but inside a stained, gouged bar counter reflected hard drinking. Decades of peat smoke from a blackened hearth seasoned the ceiling. Playing Lawrence's on-site overseer for the hotel's renovations *and* learning basic farm skills had seriously taxed him, but Harry was canny and a fast learner. To avoid village gossip, he steered clear of the race tracks and the heat and tumble of local female lovelies. Dublin's fair city bloomed with both when he had the need.

Secluded in a corner, he cradled his second pint and scanned the want ads in the *Killala Echo*. Soon, a noisy mix of workers, turf cutters, farmers, and fishermen poured through the door, bantering amongst themselves. Harry screened himself behind the paper. Who knew what useful morsels of gossip might fall into his lap?

"The new owners be daecent folk, to be using you layabouts," the waitress joked—the only female in the place. She shimmied between tables, balancing loaded trays with the ease of a juggler.

"Has anyone laid eyes on them yet?" asked a round-faced fellow, who was a Ballina out-of-work chef.

"Calls himself Harry, I've heard tell," a glass cutter said. "Me pal says he don't know it's the hammer to the nail head, not the nail to the thumb."

"And whitewash for walls, not clothes," shouted a painter, above the laughter. "So, tell us, are you looking to tempt them with your rabbit stew, chef?"

"I am, along with chunks of my brown soda bread soaked in a broth of cockles and mussels, or my name's not Murphy O'Brian."

Helen will need a good chef, Harry thought, scribbling the name down.

A stooped fellow with shreds of turf stuck to his jacket piped up, "I hear tell, once them new windows are in, Father Gareth plans a walkabout."

"Blessings is it? Ain't that something, them being non-Catholic and from over the water," a sullen-faced lout sneered. "Maybe the new hotel needs boycotting." He slouched at the counter, engulfing a beer mug in a meaty hand.

So much for Lawrence thinking there won't be mischief-makers. Good thing Helen sees through them. Hadn't taken her long to get the measure of me.

"I think you're the black sheep of the family," she had told him in his parents' garden soon after her marriage.

"Doesn't every family have one?" Amused, Harry told her how he outsmarted his brother in many diverse ways, having smoked before he was into long trousers, and sampled the softness of girls' lips and good scotch before he was fourteen.

"Then you might find marriage a settling influence—cures boasting," she had teased.

"I'm saved from that life sentence. My loves never outlast mother's interrogations. Besides, what woman would put up with my gambling, my late nights, and patch me up after a brawl or two?"

Helen's laughter had stayed with him ever since. *Lawrence should make her laugh more often.* She had brought liveliness to the McKellan staid doorstep. *God knows how she will cope with the likes of the lout at the counter though.*

"What sez you, Cooper? Your protection business would soon have the hotel back in good Irish hands, don't ya think?" said the lout, elbowing the man beside him.

"You're a fecking busybody, Joe" said Cooper, and dumped the full contents of his glass in the fellow's lap. "You'll lose your bleeding tongue next. My business ain't none of yours."

Joe roared to his feet and chopped sideways at Cooper with mallet-sized fists. A table overturned. Bottles rattled across the floor. One skittered towards Harry. He pushed it aside with his foot. From the shocked looks of the surrounding faces, he knew the brawlers weren't local.

Cooper came in fast and low, and slammed an empty bottle against Joe's forehead. The blow sent Joe staggering backward into the counter. A vicious knee delivered to the groin, and he crashed to the floor. Every man there gulped from phantom pain. With Joe's outstretched hand pinned hard under his boot, Cooper drained his glass, threw money on the counter, and after a final kick to Joe's ribs, left, banging the door behind him.

"Oh, my sainted mother!" Murphy exclaimed, "Who the hell was that?"

Joe struggled upright and pawed his forehead. His shirtsleeve came away bloodied. "He's Belfast born and got a reputation tougher than I reckoned. Don't be asking."

"Well, we don't want the likes of him, or you, bringing the North's bleeding troubles here," Murphy said in high scorn. "As to the new folk—who gives a rat's ass what faith brings them to their knees? They're giving us jobs, aren't they?"

Joe threw Murphy a baleful look and stumbled away. Harry, feeling he'd gained enough insight for one night, tucked the paper under his arm and dropped a shilling on the table. Another week and he'd be meeting the family in Dublin. He threw a quick nod of approval towards Murphy and opened the door just as two old regulars lifted fiddles to their shoulders.

"A lively jig will soon bring these hotheads to heel," one chortled to the other. Bows poised, they down-bowed into the spirited street ballad, *The Wearin' of the Green.*

CHAPTER 5

MAY - DECEMBER 1939

HELEN HEAVED INTO the toilet bowl and choked on the acid burning the back of her throat. The storm had been savage—heavy clouds darkening the sky and raging winds flinging the ship into canyons of foaming water. A green isle beyond the horizon defied imagination. She hauled herself upright, hair hanging in limp tangles, thankful that in two hours the ship would dock.

She could hear impatience in Lawrence's voice when she re-entered the cabin. "Margaret, do as I say: Put the ice chips in your mouth and let them melt."

"I don't *want* them Daddy," Margaret whined, shoving his hand away.

Helen knelt beside her. "He's only trying to help you. The ice will settle your tummy and stop you feeling sick. Pretend I'm a nurse, and you're the patient." Margaret opened her mouth and took two. She loved playing nurse.

Blessed with the stomach of a seasoned sailor, Alex waved a drawing at them from the bottom bunk. "It's a ship and those are lifeboats. The stick people fell out."

Helen ruffled his hair. "Good thing stick people can float." The picture reminded her of an inkblot test. Was his drawing showing suppressed worry for the future? She had a touch of that herself. The sale of the Edinburgh house had not proved profitable, the children's schooling remained elusive, and right now, managing a hotel was farcical.

After the ship arrived and sidled up to the wharf, Lawrence organized his documentation for customs while dockworkers secured the mooring and unloaded passengers and cargo. Alex spat gobs of spit over the railing and watched them fall towards the water. Ignoring him, Helen and Margaret scanned the quayside for Harry. Helen glimpsed him first, standing beside a Wolsey sedan waving a bright red scarf. "There! There he is."

Once on firm ground, she cocooned Margaret in the back seat under a blanket. "You'll feel better soon, if you have a nap. Alex, let's inspect the new car."

Adopting a horse dealer's stance, Alex ran his hand along the car's flanks, patted the hood, and then gave the front tires decisive kicks. "Looks tip-top, Uncle Harry, how fast does it go?"

"Faster than nags at the races. It's a thoroughbred amongst cars. I bought it from a Dublin car dealer on your Dad's instructions, and here he is. Are we landed immigrants now, brother?" he asked.

"Landed visitors, not immigrants. I need to find a newsagent. Load the car, and Helen, settle Alex in with Margaret." Helen watched him disappear into a sea of arrivals and red-capped porters and shook her head. For Lawrence, being deprived of a newspaper was a torture. When he returned, he commended Harry on the car and told him to drive.

Harry nodded and steered the car onto Dublin's now rain-sluiced streets, soaked by a cloudburst. From the odd word drifting back—upgrade, barn, livestock—Helen knew Lawrence was being clued in on the farm. As the car sped past rows of tenements, she glimpsed two children as thin as Alex's stick people playing in the street, their faces dirt-smudged. Everywhere, poverty confronted her eyes. She had seen the same thing in Edinburgh during the Great Depression.

From the rear-view mirror, Harry gave her a rueful smile. "You're getting the educational tour. Take heart, it gets better." Even as he spoke, the sun broke through the clouds and the tenements gave way to copper domes, red-bricked townhouses, and sparkling vistas of Dublin's River Liffey. Playing the guide, Harry took the O'Connell street route, and pointed to the General Post Office, which was still pock-marked with bullets from the 1916 Easter Uprising.

Twenty minutes later, Dublin yielded to open pastures, donkeys with peat loads, and drovers with working dogs urging sheep and cows into grassland. Stone walls bounded every field and weather-beaten cottages with straw-thatched roofs dotted the greenery. The thought of being marooned on a spit of land, surrounded by ploughed ground, mooing cows, and crowing roosters stabbed Helen with panic. She lost count of the times Harry halted on the brink of a muddy ditch to give way to an oncoming cart. The parade of church spires thrusting skyward above the trees dumbfounded her. How could Ireland's impoverished areas support such edifices? Bake sales and church offerings from the ragged pockets she'd seen would garner slim pickings. Images of mud-booted farmers stomping through the hotel made her shudder.

Beside her, the children slept, oblivious to what she had seen, but they had shown a natural excitement at what lay ahead. She should do the same: grip this new venture and use it to reclaim her independence. Maybe if she...

§

She awoke to Harry's voice and saw he had parked in the cobbled courtyard of a roadside tavern. Beside her, the children yawned and stretched.

"Pit stop, sleepy heads," he said. "Welcome to the pub that claims its food and Guinness are the best for miles."

A waitress, with chestnut hair rippling in waves around her shoulders, greeted him with a wide smile. "Mister Harry, a pleasure to see you again, and to meet your family." She guided them to a window table. "Nary a drop of rain now, so it's a grand view you'll enjoy." She blushed under Harry's gaze and the brush of his fingers against hers.

Best to keep Harry far removed from my female employees, otherwise they will be ceiling-watchers in no time, Helen thought.

Margaret and Alex tucked into leek and potato soup, dipping fingers of soda bread into their bowls. Helen chose the same as the men and relished the beef-and-Guinness pie. To her far right, she noticed women dressed in fine lace shawls and long skirts sitting at a round table. Their menfolk wore heavy lace-up boots and rough clothing, and talked amongst themselves, ignoring the women and their troupe of children. She queried Harry on their 'quaint' language, anxious as to how she would communicate with her staff.

"It's just English smattered with Irish colloquialisms. These are rural people. They don't all speak that way. You'll get tuned to it. After our meal, we'll take a walk along the top of the cliffs."

The air, thick with the smell of seaweed, thrummed to the roar of Atlantic breakers, and in the distance, Helen saw a horse and rider cantering along the edge of the surf. Seagulls sailed the wind currents, and Alex and Margaret cheered when the birds swooped for bread crusts.

A surge of excitement made her grab Lawrence's hand. "Ireland might be a grand place after all."

"I told you so," he said. "Harry, I'm sleepy from the Guinness. Continue driving."

By mid-afternoon, Harry nosed the car down the hotel's sloping driveway.

"Look, Mummy! It's a fairy palace!" Margaret gasped.

Helen agreed. It *was* magical. Sunlight hitting the glass in the dormer windows formed prisms of light and made rainbows on the white walls. Close by gleamed the silvered body of the estuary. In the way life can change without warning, Helen felt the predictability of her old life fall away. Here was her future, offering the challenge to start afresh. She hugged Margaret and touched Lawrence's shoulder. "Our hotel will be the pride of County Mayo," she said.

§

At her first management meeting, Helen made Harry responsible for publicity. "Put your friendly manner to good use. Talk our hotel up. Tell everyone to come and see for themselves how great it is. And, Lawrence, don't think you're getting off Scot-free. You have to teach me the essentials of bookkeeping."

"No, no, we'll get a reputable accountant. Just keep track of the receipts."

We're not in Edinburgh anymore. My hotel, new rules. "Lawrence, you won't be here. Teach me bookkeeping, or I'll go on strike." She gave a small laugh, but looked him unwaveringly in the eye.

Over breakfast the next day, she involved the children. "What outside activities do you think our guests would enjoy?"

"Horseback riding," said Margaret.

"Fishing," chirped Alex.

"That's easy; anything else?" Helen asked.

"Croquet and tennis," Lawrence added.

"Good, we've got the lawns available for both, and the estuary will offer fishing. All we need is a horse in the paddock."

"I can arrange that," Harry said.

Later that day, Helen stood outside and watched dense clouds gather in formidable domes to the west. They threatened to obscure the sun. Crossing her arms over her chest, she wondered what pitfalls would befall her family while Lawrence fought in a godforsaken war.

§

On opening day, Deidre—the front-desk clerk who had been lured from a Dublin hotel by Harry—managed reservations and allocation of rooms, while Helen welcomed guests. Half of the rooms, which led off to either side of the central staircase, were booked by noon.

To the left of the foyer was the dining room, which dazzled with white linen tablecloths and sparkling dinnerware. Murphy, the out-of-work chef Harry had found in Enniscrone, ruled the kitchen. Fragrant aromas of baked salmon and rabbit stew enticed those with appetites into the dining room. Others who preferred a liquid lunch, Helen directed down a well-lit corridor to the bar. The panelled walls showed off pictures of historic buildings, horses, red setters, and deer. A marble counter ran the entire length of one wall. Facing the counter were red-leather stools. Chairs and tables filled the floor space.

In the evening, Helen checked in on Brigid, a plump farm girl she had asked to look after Margaret and Alex in the family suite.

"They're being as good as calves," Brigid said.

"Briggie is telling us stories," Margaret trilled.

A smile bloomed on Brigid's apple-cheeked face. "Fairy stories, Ma'am. Them good witches always win against the warty ones with their pointy hats."

Reassured, Helen returned to the foyer to find Lawrence surrounded by new arrivals. She ran a caressing hand down his back. "I think you've done enough meet-and-greet. How about checking in with Harry? He's in the bar. I'll join you once the dining room closes." When he smiled, a wave of happiness washed over her. *This is better. We've become more appreciative of each other.*

Grateful to her mother for teaching her how to entertain guests, Helen knew where to linger and chat with the diners and where to be attentive yet unobtrusive. After the diners reached the coffee and liqueur stage, she disappeared into the kitchen and kicked off her shoes.

"Murphy, you're a miracle-worker. If we have days like this, we won't have much to worry about, will we?"

"Right enough, Ma'am, it's been a rare day," but he looked apprehensive.

"Did we slip up somewhere?"

"No, Ma'am, it's just when I took a breather, I spotted a dog known for its vicious bite slip into the bar from the side entrance."

"Oh, my goodness, who let the dog in?"

"Faith Ma'am, it wasn't the four-legged kind. Calls himself Cooper O'Neil. Has a cur's nose, and an appetite for sniffing out a person's weaknesses, so I'm told."

Oh Lord, I hope Harry isn't back to gambling. "Let's not worry. I'm sure our bar won't appeal to the rough types, but I'm glad you told me."

Prepared to close the kitchen for the night, Murphy hung his chef's apron on a hook and jammed on his cap. "I'll be back afore the cock crows, Ma'am," he said and touched his cap to Lawrence who stood in the doorway. Lawrence nodded and waited until Murphy had left, then advanced holding two glasses of champagne.

"Helen, we've had an excellent opening! Congratulations! Come and meet the locals. Harry has introduced his Black Velvets, and now everyone is drinking them."

"That's because he claims cider and Guinness steady jangled nerves and uneasy stomachs. We'd be smart to steer him away from the bar though, or he'll become a permanent fixture."

"Don't fuss; the farm will keep him out of mischief."

Helen ran her teeth along her bottom lip. *Does Lawrence really believe farm work will deter Harry from anything?*

Sounds of lively voices, the clink of glasses, and a woodsy smell of tobacco streamed towards them as they entered. Customers were clustered around the counter, while others perched on stools. Tables and booths were full, and there was little standing room. The hubbub made her thankful the bar was set well away from the hotel's sleeping quarters.

She waved at Harry and watched him break off from a group and push towards her. Turning sideways to Lawrence, she gave him her empty glass. "I'd love one of those Black Velvets now." Obliging her, he threaded his way to the counter. When Harry closed in, she lowered her voice. "Murphy said someone called Cooper is here—a dangerous man from all accounts. Do you know him?"

Harry, his face a picture of painful concentration, shook his head. "Never heard of him." His voice rose when Lawrence returned. "I met an amusing fellow this evening. Says he's a pig farmer, but he's also into racehorses. He's promised me a tour of his piggery and the Ballinrobe racetracks sometime."

"Forget pigs and horses. Think crops and cows."

"Right, sir, and if I get waylaid by a poultry farmer, I'll explain that I prefer birds of a different plumage. Now, it's time you met our local bank manager. He's making eyes our way."

As they left, Helen threw a glance towards the side entrance to where a handful of boisterous locals were leaving. A second glance showed a sinewy man leaning against the wall. He had a derisive expression on his face. Was that Cooper? She dropped her gaze, but not before the stranger's shrewd eyes nailed hers.

§

Three days into September, Hitler's army invaded Poland, and Britain and France declared war. Before the old year limped away from the new, a letter arrived from the British Admiralty summoning Lawrence to London. After the hotel staff had gathered in the foyer to see him off, Helen and the children walked with him to where Harry waited by the car.

"You mustn't worry about me, Helen. I will probably be stuck behind a desk pushing a pen. The main thing is that *here* you and the family are safe."

Margaret sobbed and hung onto his arm, pleading for him not to go. "I have no choice, dear," he said. "Be a good girl and look after your brother." He kissed her tear-streaked face and then gave Alex a hug.

Helen stood by, regretting every snipe and short-tempered word she had ever said to him. When he pulled her close, she buried her head against his chest, and inhaled the rich pine smell of him then inched away and took a deep breath. The last few months had felt like a second honeymoon. They had shared work and laughter, and even reawakened half-forgotten intimacies.

Competing with raucous seagulls overhead, Harry called out, "Come on, brother, war beckons; you can't miss the plane's departure."

Aware that war changes everything, Helen stood with an arm around each child, and as the car bore Lawrence away, wondered how long before they would see their father again. At least Lawrence was not an enlisted man, so they would not endure long separations. But communications between them would be difficult. Deidre had told her that local exchanges were delaying extensions to their automatic systems, and Lawrence said letters were already censored. But, now was not the time for niggly worries; she had a hotel to run.

CHAPTER 6

JANUARY-JUNE 1940

LAWRENCE LIKENED HIMSELF to a mole that lived underground. His office was a small cubicle, among a maze of others beneath the Admiralty complex—a three level, U-shaped structure in Whitehall. Tunnels snaked from his working space to communication systems, civil defense, and military facilities. Armed guards stood before metal doors, and trespassing between areas resulted in rigorous interrogation.

Monty Phelps offered Lawrence the guest room in his lavish Chelsea flat that overlooked the Thames—a convenience Lawrence appreciated, since he worked three consecutive twelve-hour stints. He and Monty had met as undergraduates. It was Monty's flair for mathematics that lifted him from his father's East London bakery and took him to Oxford. A diligent man, he now held the coveted position of financial analyst at *The Daily Telegraph*.

Relishing one of Monty's duck dinners one evening in March, Lawrence said, "Any bright ideas how I might get out of the admiralty's rabbit warren? It's a claustrophobic, bureaucratic nightmare."

"Crossword puzzles. You're a whiz at solving cryptic stuff. The government has asked our paper to organize competitions. The aim is to get the brightest minds working in Intelligence. Tomorrow, you'll find the first crossword competition in the middle section. Promise you'll do it." Lawrence agreed.

Five days later, he found himself being escorted by a young petty officer Wren through the main admiralty building to the sparse office of Captain Butler—a man with an air of repressed energy. Butler pointed him to one of two well-worn wooden chairs.

"Congratulations, McKellan, your entry in the recent Telegraph crossword competition has qualified you for the next step."

Well pleased, Lawrence smiled. *Good old Monty, and farewell rabbit warren.* "That's welcome news, Captain. What happens next?"

"An exam designed to assess you for work vital to the war effort. Do you wish to continue?" Lawrence nodded, and Butler pushed a copy of the Official Secrets Act across the desk. "Then you must sign this. Be aware, any breach of confidentiality will bring severe penalties."

Wondering whether this meant wooden stocks, thumbscrews, or being hung, drawn, and quartered, Lawrence penned his signature.

The exam was held in a windowless room. Pencils, scratch pads, and a letter-sized sheet of paper laid facedown on each desk. Lawrence and twelve other entrants—*unlucky thirteen,* he thought—sat before a stern-faced man. Armed with a stop watch, he told them they had six minutes. Checking his time piece with a wall clock reminiscent of those in train stations, he barked, "Begin."

Two weeks later, Lawrence again waited outside Captain Butler's office, but this time, with six others. When his turn came, he learned that he was destined for Bletchley Park's Government Code and Cypher School. "Divulge nothing to family or friends. Blame operational security if asked. You have forty-eight hours before assuming your new posting."

He doesn't know Helen—a stickler for details, Lawrence thought, taking the Bletchley train-pass pushed towards him, while calculating that there wasn't enough time to get to Ireland and back.

Outside, Whitehall bristled with bicycles, handcarts, horses, and buses, but few cars, because of petrol rationing. Above the noise and bustle, Big Ben thundered the noon hour. Lawrence hurried past a newsboy yelling the latest headlines and headed to the Charring Cross underground—the quickest route to the flat. Monty had refrained from asking how he'd done in the competition—maybe because he already knew? Most of the men and women exiting the shops and offices for lunch, carried gas masks in cardboard boxes suspended with string straps from their shoulders. He missed seeing children, but the government had evacuated them to the countryside. Sandbags dozed along the embankment, and in the park nearby, anti-aircraft guns poked through the trees. Poor London had developed a split personality—half its brain submerged in slumber, the other half watchful and vigilant.

When Monty heard Lawrence's news, he splashed aged Calvados into glasses and suggested dining out. "Perhaps a risqué variety show at the Windmill Theatre afterwards?"

§

Lawrence knew the town of Bletchley from his university days, when he'd hiked the trails in the Chiltern Hills. Bletchley Park dated back to the mid-nineteenth century, but when he arrived, there were no signs of its refined sophistication other than a croquet lawn and a large, well-treed lake harbouring swans. His credentials checked and cleared by a sentry at an imposing wrought iron gate, Lawrence proceeded to the main building. It was a clutter of Gothic, Tudor, and Baroque design, and he thought it the ugliest mansion he had ever seen. A short, uniformed man with clipped brown hair, a moustache, and a fighter's stance waited beneath an arched portal.

"Lawrence McKellan? I'm Lieutenant Commander Yarrow, Commodore Dwyer's second in command. Another fly caught in our crossword web, eh? Done in no seconds flat?"

Typical little strutter, Lawrence thought, hearing the Liverpool accent. "Not quite, but nice that a commissioned officer would think so."

In a don't-mess-with-me look, Yarrow said. "I'll give you a quick tour, but first you have more forms to sign. Follow me."

Beyond the portal, a small office guarded the entrance. Lawrence signed a second copy of the Official Secrets Act—bulkier than the first. "Is the Act based on different security levels?"

"Yes, and you'll be signing a third soon."

After climbing two steep flights of stairs at Yarrow's pace, sweat beaded Lawrence's forehead, and he vowed to follow an exercise regime. Confronting him was a maze of passageways.

"Most of the rooms are dormitories for shift-work professionals. You won't be on this floor," Yarrow said. "I understand you know the commodore."

"We met at Oxford."

"Commodore Dwyer is tops, but don't expect special treatment. Few of his sort come through Bletchley's doors these days."

"Maybe that's why you use civilians," Lawrence said, and got a blank stare.

A low hum met them as they descended to the commodore's section. Yarrow flashed a pass at an armed guard. Once through, an air of urgent energy prickled Lawrence's skin. He rubbed sweaty hands on his trousers.

Wall maps flagged by pins displayed troop and naval movements, and uniformed personnel and civilians hurried back and forth between rooms.

"They're carrying decoded enemy transmissions or rerouting messages to various command posts," Yarrow explained in answer to Lawrence's enquiring look.

"And what about the air force?"

"The navy uses Coastal Air Command. Our planes fly counter-strikes on German subs—that is if you cryptographers can get your collective arses together fast enough to make it happen. Early detection of enemy escort ships and U-boat wolf packs is our mission. You'll find the commodore in that office over there. When you're done—usually takes fifteen to twenty minutes—meet me at the main entrance."

Second Officer Anita Jones, a Wren with a manner as starched as her uniform, looked up from her desk when he approached. "Commodore Dwyer is expecting you. Go in."

The commodore stood with hands clasped behind his back, looking at a map flanked by floor-to-ceiling bookshelves. He turned as Lawrence entered. "Good to see you, Lawrence. You haven't changed. How long has it been? Fourteen years?"

"Closer to nineteen," Lawrence replied, biting back the "sir." He shook hands and returned the commodore's smile. They had been part of the same Oxford rowing team, had frequented the same boathouse parties, and often played chess. Their friendship dwindled when Helen hove into sight. Quoting the familiar saying 'three's a crowd', Dwyer had moved on, taking with him his known misogynist views, and his love of things related to the sea. They had not seen each other since.

"Yarrow showing you around all right?"

"Yes, sir. With precision," Lawrence replied, stifling old memories. "What does Yarrow do?"

"Security. Used to be with Coastal Command, but no promotion because he couldn't handle night vision. Their loss, my gain. By chance, do you know Alan Turing? He heads your section.

"No, sir. He was at Cambridge. I'm looking forward to meeting him. A brilliant mathematician, from what I've heard."

Dwyer nodded and pointed Lawrence to a chair. "Yes, a genius. Not a social chap, but who cares? He's a logician, a philosopher, and a marathon runner to boot. He invented a miraculous device we've christened The Bombe."

"That has the sound of a tasty crème-glacé—of explosive quality," Lawrence said.

The commodore laughed. "Ah, still a humorist, I see. No, this bombe is an electro-mechanical device that deciphers complex German-encrypted messages. It's been revised since its inception. You'll learn more when you've signed these. I know you've signed earlier copies, but this one reflects a higher level. Take your time, and be sure to read the small print."

From the words, *counter-espionage, surveillance, informants,* and *operational territory,* Lawrence realized that, once he signed, there could be no backtracking. "Signing my life away, am I?" he asked, uncapping his pen.

"Only if you break our Ten Commandments," Dwyer said, but something in his tone registered a warning. "Regarding leave entitlement. You're permitted forty-eight-hour leaves every six to eight weeks. Anything longer will be at the discretion of your superiors." Judging from his poker-face expression, Lawrence guessed longer leaves were as rare as Londoners eating haggis. "Another thing, cryptographers fall under special scrutiny."

"We're not trustworthy?"

"You are, but cryptographers handle vital information first. We can't afford leaks."

Lawrence heard his father's admonishment: 'Keep people guessing. Always be prepared.' He had embraced that advice throughout school and university. Bletchley now joined the list. "Am I off leash during leaves?"

"Never. You're a bloodhound, Lawrence. Hunt the enemy, but don't stray from the kennel." The commodore glanced at his watch and rose to his feet. "Good to have you on board."

Lawrence found Yarrow pacing the front entrance. "Twenty-five minutes. Old boys club, eh? Time to see your workstation."

Without further ado, they hurried through a dismal ghetto of converted cottages, prefabricated wooden huts, and miscellaneous buildings squatting on the park's lawns. At Hut 8, Yarrow opened the door and pushed it wide with his foot. "Go in. They're expecting you."

A cheerful fellow, looking more like a cricket player than a code-breaker, sauntered over as if accepting applause at the Oval, and stuck out his hand. "Lawrence McKellan? I'm Dennis Watson. Let me introduce you to the chaps."

The 'chaps,' huddled around a central table made him think of lions crouched over their prey. After brief introductions, Watson gestured to the machine on the table. It resembled an odd-looking typewriter but with three rotating drums banded around with the letters of the alphabet. "Meet Enigma. All German ships carry one of these blighters. We captured this one from the Italians. We also managed to get our thieving hands on a few current code and cipher books."

Lawrence nodded. "How does it work?"

"Similar to mixing cake batter," said a lanky fellow. "The Bosch feeds the letters of his message into a machine comparable to this, then these rotating drums garble them. To unscramble everything from one bloody cipher setting can take us a month. At best, we break one down in two to three days. Turing is working on a device to decipher codes in hours—still a wet dream though."

An untidy, rotund fellow grinned. "I'm John Beswick. That means we've still got our pants down in stopping the U-boats from sinking our convoys. It's getting worse. Their attacks are on the increase."

"It sounds tough. Yarrow intimated as much."

Dennis gave a dry laugh. "Called us a bunch of slow arses, did he? He's always watching for missteps; that's why we call him Auntie."

"The sod should know the main problem is the Admiralty's big wigs wasting valuable time translating German into English. We've got chaps fluent in bloody German right here."

Lawrence kept quiet. He had met several translators at the Admiralty, and they were exceptional. The real problem was the bureaucratic chain of command. Changing the subject, he asked Beswick, "Will I be meeting Alan Turing?"

"You can't miss him; he's everywhere, upgrading machines, networks, streamlining different systems."

Dennis touched his shoulder. "Let's get you started. Bletchley intercepts hundreds of messages a day, so you can jump in now."

At his workstation, which contained a beat-up desk and a wooden chair beneath a black-curtained window, Lawrence faced a meaningless jumble of characters scrawled on paper. He reached for a pencil and notepad and set to work.

§

In early June, a raffish Dennis, sporting a tweed suit, with his hair slicked back, and clean-shaven—though he had clearly overdone the cologne—arrived at Lawrence's digs.

"How about a little love thy neighbour tonight?" he grinned. "To hell with this war and slogging over mysterious messages. Who knows? There may be no tomorrow. Let's go to Old Smokey and tie one on."

Lawrence shouldered into his jacket. He enjoyed Dennis. He made for amusing conversation and a break in London would be good. "Should we be worried about Auntie Yarrow dogging our footsteps?"

"No worries—he's in the village having a drink with Beswick at the Swan."

They went by train. Dennis, oblivious to all sounds, settled down for a snooze in the compartment's upholstered seats. To escape his snores, Lawrence moved into the swaying corridor. It surprised him to see so many back gardens dug up to accommodate Anderson air-raid shelters.

A military man next to him explained that the sunken, galvanized-steel structures were big enough to sleep six. "Creative owners crown them with rockeries, others store root vegetables—very resourceful. Do you know London?

"Not well," Lawrence lied.

The man shrugged. "No sign of war yet."

"That's why it's called a phony war."

"Yeah. Like many, my mum believes it won't happen." He looked down at his army boots and polished each one against the back of his trouser legs. "She'll be convinced soon enough."

Lawrence nodded, before the train plunged into a tunnel. Darkness coalesced around him—the air thick and rank. When the train re-emerged, he returned to his compartment to find Dennis awake.

Twenty minutes later, they entered a well-frequented Mayfair pub and ordered copious amounts of beer. Enjoying themselves, they shared stories about their misspent youth and recalled bawdy limericks. Security posters in strategic spots, such as the men's washroom, reminded everyone that *Walls have ears*, but Dennis pointed out that no posters demanded *Keep your eyes to yourself*. A good thing too, they agreed, seeing the lovely ladies around them.

"Which reminds me, I've had enough male companionship, ole chum," and taking his glass, Dennis crossed the crowded room to chat one of the lovelies up.

Left alone, Lawrence nursed his drink. Bars were not his scene. He should leave, but across from him, a lone woman caught his attention. Her legs were long and athletic, but it was the bored expression on her angular face that piqued his interest. Helen should be here and he should not be intrigued by a stranger. Again, the woman caught his eye, and this time gave a faint smile. Lawrence picked up his drink and walked towards her, thinking, *this could be interesting*.

CHAPTER 7

JULY-SEPTEMBER 1940

HELEN MASSAGED HER aching shoulders and glared at the accounts on her desk. They demanded attention, but Lawrence was coming home on a short leave, and each car that arrived pulled her eyes to the window.

Seven months apart was a long time, and sparse letters between them hadn't helped—Lawrence becoming more removed and the changes in herself disconcerting. She had to curb her dislike of haughty guests, practice patience in the face of parents who were unkind to their children, and on children who ran wild. And yet, she found managing the hotel exhilarating. She no longer knew the meaning of boredom, although she lamented the piano standing idle, books unread, and that time with Margaret and Alex was limited.

A question nagged her. Lawrence was a civilian, so what did he do on his weekends? She couldn't imagine him in a state of endless celibacy. Her own libido was dormant, but erotic images of women beguiling Lawrence plagued her so much that she had finally cornered Harry for advice.

She chose a summer's afternoon. Once the children had scampered off in search of hen eggs, she and Harry leaned over the split-railed paddock to admire his new cart horse. She offered it a carrot, and it ambled over, white fetlocks fluttering. Keeping her eyes on the horse, she said, "Harry, how do husbands cope with long separations from their wives?"

"That's a hell of a question," he said, and ever the clown, trilled, "*Shine on, shine on, harvest moon. Up in the sky. I ain't had no lovin' since January, February, June, or July.*"

"Stop it. I'm not in a joking mood."

He coughed, and swatted flies off the horse's nose. "To put it crudely, a lot of men just want to have at it, but not my brother. Can you see him putting work aside to wine and dine a winsome lass? He doesn't have time for romantic dilly dallying. Stop worrying. He's not one for casual sex."

Helen sighed. His evaluation hadn't helped much, but at least he'd given her the truth as he saw it. It was true, Lawrence was no philanderer. Squeezing Harry's arm, she switched the conversation to horse racing and promised herself never to raise the matter again.

To shake off her present mood, Helen closed the ledger and sought the outdoors. It felt good to stretch. Above her, house martins soared skywards searching for insects. She stood marvelling at their aerial acrobatics until she heard the clunk of a car door.

It was Lawrence. His lean features still caught her breath—a strong jaw that inspired confidence, brown intelligent eyes, and now just a touch of distinguished grey at the temples. "I didn't hear the car until you got out," she said. "Welcome home." In his arms, she inhaled the familiar whiff of pine and cigars, and yet sensed a difference too nebulous to name. *Have to get reacquainted that's all.* "I've missed you," she said.

Before he could respond, Margaret appeared from nowhere and hurled herself at him. "Daddy!" she whooped. "I was in the paddock feeding Uncle Harry's new horse. Come and see him! He has hooves big as dinner plates!"

"I would like that, but later, Margaret. Where's your brother?"

The corners of her mouth pulled down. "He's in the barn learning how to milk cows. You don't have to see him now, do you? Can't it wait?"

Helen dropped an arm over her shoulder. *Poor Margaret, she still hasn't learned that, for a McKellan, a son always supplants a daughter.* "Best you fetch him, Margaret, and please remind your uncle to join us for dinner."

§

Harry headed for his usual place at the head of the table when he arrived, but at the last moment wheeled past Lawrence and sat across from the children.

"Why are you sitting there?" Margaret asked.

"Because I've eyes all the better to watch you with," he growled, mimicking the wolf from *Little Red Riding Hood.*

Helen circulated the gravy boat and condiments and listened while conversation lurched forward in haphazard fashion. Lawrence's only contribution was to describe to the children how everyone covered windows and doors at night to block light. "It's called a blackout. You're lucky you're in your home. British children have been evacuated from theirs."

Harry finished his pork chops and said, tongue-in-cheek, "Well Lawrence, this dinner must be tastier than the navy fodder, eh? The chops came from my pal, Deacon, by the way. He's the pig farmer I mentioned to you before you went off to war. When you tour the farm don't let my hens and roosters surprise you. Deacon suggested I diversify."

Behind a spiral of cigarette smoke, Lawrence shrugged, but his set face suggested annoyance, so Helen turned to Harry. "Daecon and you have become quite chummy, but perhaps we should discourage his bar visits for a while. We don't want his smelly boots emptying the place."

"Oink, oink," Alex chirped.

"Oink, oink," repeated Margaret, and both convulsed into giggles.

Harry frowned at them. "Don't be rude. Daecon is okay. Should we put a bucket of water and a scrubbing brush outside the bar's side entrance, Mrs McKellan?"

Helen made a sheepish face at him and tried to draw Lawrence out. "You would find it interesting how the Irish treat each other in the bar. Accountants and lawyers chat and play darts with farmers and shopkeepers, just like old friends. Can you imagine such a thing happening in Edinburgh society?"

Lawrence folded his napkin. "So, you're a devotee of Irish culture now, are you?"

"I suppose I am. There are two kinds of culture. The urban and the rural. I'm getting to understand the latter, but for urban culture, Dublin is impressive."

"Who took you so far afield?"

"My new friend, Jill Armitage. She spent two weeks with us in February. We hit it off right away and went to a zany show at Dublin's Abbey Theatre. You and I should go."

"My visits don't allow time for that."

Helen worried her cuticle. It was as if she and Lawrence stood on opposite sides of a river without the means to cross.

"Jill is a handsome wench," Harry said, filling the silence. "With her looks, I bet she packs her place with customers just about as well as Helen does."

Flustered at his inept compliment, Helen fell back on telling a silly story about a donkey that ambled into the dining room during breakfast one morning, and how Jill had coaxed the poor creature out through the foyer with flowers from the table vases. The story aroused little more than a mild smile, and she lapsed into embarrassed silence.

"Brigid told us the donkey was a Pooka in disguise, Daddy," Margaret said. She glared at Alex. "At night, Pookas turn into black horses or hairy bogeymen and eat naughty boys."

"Pookas don't scare me, but the devil does."

"Margaret is teasing you, Alex. They're just fantasy creatures." *I must caution Brigid about monsters and demons.*

For the first time, Lawrence laughed. "That's enough make-believe. Bedtime for you two. I'll read to you from *The Camels Are Coming.*"

Margaret clapped. "I like camels. They're ships of the desert."

"True, but this story involves a pilot called Biggles, who flew secret missions. His plane was called a Sopwith Camel. In the last war, it was a whiz for shooting down enemy planes."

Margaret pulled a face, "Phooey! I think I'll read *Anne of Green Gables.*"

"Good idea," Alex crowed. "Leave the men's stuff to Dad and me."

Lawrence left with the children to retrieve the book from his suitcase. Harry left too. "I'll just check in on the bar. Be back in a tick."

Helen cleared the table. The entire family had run for cover. What a fractious meal. With luck, adult interaction would improve without the children. To help her and Lawrence unwind later, she must ask Brigid to leave wine and glasses in their room.

Following a tradition started before the hotel opened, Helen and the two brothers reconvened in the reading room. Playing host, Harry strengthened Murphy's anaemic coffee with shots of Irish whiskey and poured it into cups. "We're ten months into a war, Lawrence, but no bombing—seems like a sham pregnancy to me. Were we premature to move, not that I'm complaining; farming beats the hell out of insurance?"

"If you will lift your head away from female cleavages, Harry, you will discover that the Luftwaffe is now attacking our airfields as a prelude to bombing our ports and cities, so don't jump to conclusions."

"You're forgetting that news is lousy here. Fill us in."

"It's not good. Although we miraculously evacuated thousands of soldiers from Dunkirk, sadly Belgium, Holland, and Norway have fallen, and last month Paris fell, so France is also collapsing."

Dismayed, Helen pushed back her chair. "Lawrence, listen to yourself. My mother is in France. Remember? She moved there after father died. What's going to happen to her?"

His pat on her knee was no help. "Isobel is in Lyon. She's safe. Germany needs soldiers elsewhere so it will cut corners and only occupy Northern France."

"That's no comfort. Can't we get her out?"

"Too risky and unnecessary."

His words stung with such finality, that Helen swallowed her alarm. What she must do somehow, is warn her mother not to stray north. She looked towards the estuary. Lights sparkled on the water—the moon oblivious to the combative world. War talk was crushing.

"Lawrence, please share something of your life away from us, your free time: rowing, chess, new friends—things of that nature."

"It's work, eat, and fall exhausted into bed, Helen. No rowing and no friends—other than colleagues." He rummaged for his cheroots, lit one, and blew smoke into angry clouds.

Chastened, she reached across and took his hand. "Let's you and I take a walk by the estuary. Harry, will you excuse us, please?"

Harry gulped the remains of his coffee but showed truculence in every move as he elbowed into his jacket. *Poor Harry, he has fallen too comfortably into hiking across the fields from the farmhouse for supper and breakfast.* Sometimes his encouragement—and criticism—came across as if she and the children belonged to him. She raised her hand in a conciliatory goodbye as he departed.

She took Lawrence along the footpath that angled towards the shoreline. Muffled voices and laughter drifted from the bar to mingle with the slap of water, while they crunched along the wet, pebbly strand.

Lawrence found a flat stone and skipped it across the water. "This place is idyllic. One can almost drink the sea air."

Helen counted the skips—five—and clapped her hands. "You should teach Alex that trick. Let's have a picnic with the children tomorrow."

"No, I'm sorry. I need to tour the farm, and then check the hotel accounts."

"Why the hurry? Can't it wait a day?"

Instead of replying, he turned his collar up against the night air and suggested they go upstairs.

Brigid had done as asked. Two glasses stood alongside a bottle of wine on the side table, but the walk had not turned out well. Helen found it hard to talk. "Lawrence, why are we being so awkward? It's sad."

"I expect plenty of servicemen and their wives experience the same self-consciousness after months apart," he said, uncorking the bottle.

But he's a civilian. He should find it easier to come home. "I suppose." Emptying her glass in three quick gulps, she joined him where he now stood at the window, humming, *A Nightingale Sang in Berkeley Square*. Still humming, he put an arm around her waist and danced her towards their bed.

Later, between sips, Helen said, "I wish you were as bold with sharing what you do as you are with your love-making—separation has added a surprising nuance to that."

There was a moment's silence, before he said, "Helen, my work involves protecting shipping lanes, and that's it. I can't enlighten you further. Security forbids it."

"Have you been to London? You can't have forsaken the city altogether since that mystery posting of yours. Jill's hotel, The Hermitage, is within walking distance of your Arts Club. Please drop in for a drink. She might even give you one on the house."

"Do you think so?

She circled the rim of her glass with her index finger, then sprang her next question: "Why do your letters carry London postmarks, since London is no longer your home away from home?"

"Because censorship demands it. It's a way of never revealing where we work. Think of it as national security. Why are you so suspicious? What treachery have I committed?"

She tapped his nose. "My dear husband, you are altogether too adept at obfuscation. Your father would be proud."

"He was good at other things too," he murmured, drawing her to him.

§

On his return to Bletchley, Lawrence took a walk around the ornamental lake. Despite the threat of storm clouds, he needed space to himself. Since the swans were not around, he tossed away the bread crusts from his pocket. Sitting on a dilapidated bench, he watched scarves of clouds unravel in the wind and wondered, if in an insidious way, the war was unravelling his world one day at a time.

Troubled, he stood and paced between the bench and the lake. Although he and Helen had bridged their initial awkwardness, something alien lay between them. He recalled her sharp intake of breath when he finally made love to her. As a moth can scent its mate from miles away, had she discerned something new? An imperceptible change in the way he held her ... his *boldness* striking an unfamiliar resonance equivalent to a damaged tuning fork? Thoughts of Molly made him restive. Since their first encounter, the night he and Dennis made their escape to London, she had become a delightful dalliance. They spent most of his two-day passes together, and her intellect and cool manner brought a refreshing change from the expectancies of his marriage.

Suppose he had never uprooted the family? Likely none of his infidelity would have happened. With Edinburgh a day's reach of London, two-day furloughs were possible. But, although air raids on Scotland were non-existent and the firm chugged along, he still believed moving the family to have been a wise choice.

The swans, now making their appearance, squabbled over the discarded bread. *Swans might be monogamous,* Lawrence thought, *but they can squawk and bicker with the best of married couples.* One hissed and beat its wings at him, forcing a retreat to safer ground.

Safer ground? Was there such a place, with Hitler's armies staring across the English Channel to the cliffs of Dover? At least the move assured long-term security. The children bloomed, and thanks to Helen, so did the hotel. The farm earned its way too, and kept Harry safely occupied. To hell with absences and transgressions. He wasn't a monk. He would write more to Helen though, and work towards another extended leave.

§

As Lawrence had forecast, when the Luftwaffe failed to destroy the R.A.F. airfields and planes, it turned to severe daytime bombardment of London for three months. Molly told him people watched the aerial dogfights from doorways as if they had been put on especially for their entertainment. To his relief, she remained safe, as did he and his colleagues, since the push to decrypt German marine codes kept them in Bletchley, although it purloined their sleep.

CHAPTER 8

SEPTEMBER 1940

HELEN GRIPPED HER pen with forced cheerfulness. The notepaper looked as white and sterile as a laundered sheet. But she must write and put warmth in her words, despite Lawrence's long silence.

September 15, 1940
Darling,

How are you? Other than word-of-mouth information from overseas guests, we have no war news. A few days ago, Harry's radio chum received a warning for reporting, 'It's a sunny day here in Dublin for the football match.' The world has gone mad. It's unbelievable such a simple comment would influence the flight paths of enemy bombers. Visitors are arriving in droves from the north, dodging blackouts and food rationing. Even for us, tea and fresh bananas are just memories. We're fortunate Harry supplies us with milk, and his hens are bountiful. Horse traps are in style again, and Murphy keeps the range fueled with endless supplies of peat. I don't ask where he gets it.

Last week, Harry took us on an outing to Newport. We picnicked by the river, and saw lots of salmon and trout. I should buy us all fishing rods. A group of jack-booted, Defence Force soldiers paraded past wearing tin-pot helmets. Alex copied their swagger, but Harry stopped him and said that the soldiers were there to remind us to respect Ireland's neutrality. We now own a dozen second-hand bicycles for the guests to rent, and for a small fee, the local gypsies keep them in tip-top condition. I've also started a Friday night singsong in the bar, and thanks to Harry spreading the word, it's taken off like a salmon run. Margaret loves riding Harry's second horse. She's called it Smoke. Your brother has become a handyman. He enlarged the stables, made a fort for Alex's lead soldiers, and knocked together a dog kennel for a mutt we've adopted. We've christened the pooch Mr Flynn.

Enclosed is a note from Margaret about the horses, and I found a drawing by Alex, showing his stick people now fleshed out! He said his first lot couldn't bleed! Have you visited Jill's bar yet? She's seen a photo of you, so you won't be a complete stranger. Is Christmas a possibility? Love, Helen.

§

The swans were in their usual matrimonial angst, when Lawrence parked himself on his favourite bench. Intent on writing a long overdue reply to Helen, he balanced a writing pad on his knees.

November 20, 1940
Dearest Helen,

I'm a bit tardy but here I am. Good to get your news. I did as you asked and dropped in on Jill. Very busy place. She was friendly enough—maybe because I'm your husband, but I believe both of us sensed our views would clash. But at least I've fulfilled my obligation to you. As you know, work is taboo and censorship reigns, but it's common news that the incendiary bombing of Coventry was devastating. They had no warning. Remember the cathedral? You should see it now, it's a skeleton—walls flattened and everything blackened with smoke. Although our air force sent the German Luftwaffe packing after three months of non-stop aerial dogfights, the nightly Blitz still continues. London's underground has become a haven for thousands but nowhere is safe. It's a question of everyone soldiering on, doing the best they can to survive. Your fears that we won't be together soon are understandable. I will try to keep in touch. Give the children a kiss for me and don't fret; Harry is right—no news is good news. Lawrence.

Helen imagined Britain's sky turned into a patchwork of contrails, and homes and streets in London shattered beyond recognition. Had any bombs fallen near Jill? Given the dismal history of wars, what did they accomplish other than inflate war chests and military egos? A pity Lawrence and Jill had been wary.

On the heels of Lawrence's letter, Helen received one from Jill.

Hullo Helen, guess who walked into my bar? Lawrence! An intelligent, striking man, but one not to upset. Our conversation was polite, but we didn't click. After he left, I realized I'd seen him only the other evening in a mixed party of four at a restaurant near here.

I have to cancel my February visit. I've joined the Women's Voluntary Service! We give exhausted firefighters hot tea and biscuits. Poor devils, no sooner do they douse one fire than another bursts out. Dangerous too, with walls collapsing into the streets. Remember the photos of the park opposite my place? Well, now it's a sandbag depot. Still, the hotel thrives.

Must dash. New people arriving, politicians from the starched look of them! Hugs to Harry, and tell the children 'Auntie Jill' promises to bring them chocolate on my next-time visit. Tons of love, Jill.

Helen stewed over Jill's letter and read it twice. 'A mixed party of four'? Was Jill sending her a not-so-subtle warning? Maybe they were Lawrence's colleagues, but then why would he not share that with her? Most likely, because in the sodding party of four, there were two women. So, how often did Lawrence visit London?

She crumpled Jill's letter into a ball and tossed it in the wastepaper basket. What could she do? Nothing.

§

When Lawrence failed to come for Christmas, Helen immersed herself in planning a staff party, and had Margaret and Alex help Harry decorate the towering tree in the foyer. On December 24, Father Gareth came by and invited the family to midnight mass at Enniscrone's Catholic church. Pleased, Helen packed the children into the car and collected a slightly inebriated Harry from the farm. But once the family had crowded into a pew, he sang the carols with as much gusto as the villagers.

Guests from both sides of the border filled the hotel and Murphy's traditional Irish dinner of roast goose, and stuffed turkey were both hits. The only complaints came from Alex and Margaret because Helen rationed them to half a slice each of the cake since Murphy had drenched it in Irish whiskey.

On Boxing Day, she stood checking the guest register with Deidre when Harry arrived looking exuberant. "Helen, my new girlfriend, a Dublin lass, has invited me to ring the New Year in with her. Can you manage without me for a few days?"

"Of course I can," she said, and reached up to kiss his cheek just as a couple entered the foyer from the dining room. The man was large-boned and balding. In comparison, his wife reminded Helen of a small bird with big blue eyes.

"Mr and Mrs McKellan," hailed the man, "this Christmas is one of the best we've enjoyed. You make a grand couple and run a fine hotel."

Before Helen could stop him, Harry thrust out his hand, "We're glad to hear that. Thank you. We hope you will visit us again. May the New Year bring better times."

Deidre looked up in astonishment, but quelled her laughter as the couple approached to pay their bill. Helen jabbed a thumb into the base of Harry's back, and propelled him into her office.

"Harry McKellan, our hotel is not the Abbey Theatre. You are uproarious, but don't play that game with me again. What if they return next year, and Lawrence is here?"

"Well, Miss Firebrand, if they return, it's because they liked the hotel and the happy, married couple running it. I told a white lie because they saw you kiss me. Besides, the likelihood of Lawrence getting time off is optimistic." He delivered a swashbuckling bow and left.

Helen sank into her office chair, wondering if every laugh from Harry could ever outweigh her anxieties about his roguish ways. Not that she'd seen much evidence of his gambling and drinking recently. Maybe he'd reformed. Harry was full of surprises.

CHAPTER 9

JANUARY-DECEMBER 1941

January's fog and sleet caused a slow-down in reservations, and it took the Maxwell couple fleeing the Blitz to raise Helen's energies and make her doubly grateful for where she lived.

Their faces were creviced with exhaustion, so Deidre gave them one of the best rooms at half price overlooking the estuary and sand dunes.

Helen ordered tea and sat with them in the reading room. "Air raids are destroying acres of London," they told her, "and the current low tides of the Thames make it difficult for firefighters to draw up enough water. Housing areas near the docks are in ruins. Our flat, too, although it was within walking distance of St. Paul's Cathedral. We were sheltering in the Underground when it happened. We can't go back."

"I'm glad you're safe," Helen said. "Over fifteen hundred women and children evacuees from London have arrived in Dublin since last year. Each month we deliver food baskets to one of the dioceses. People are living in desperate times. What are you going to do?"

"We're heading south. Our married nephew lives in Limerick."

"That's a lovely town. It has a beautiful, medieval Cathedral. The stained-glass windows and stone arches are exquisite. It's not St. Paul's, but you will love it." Talk of London made her chafe for news of Lawrence, and Jill. She hadn't heard a word from either one for over a month.

§

In early April a letter with unfamiliar writing arrived from France. Harry and Murphy's voices floated from the kitchen into the office, as Helen sat on the sofa and slit the envelope open. She read the single page twice, and then uttered a high-pitched cry of distress.

"What's happened?" Harry said, rushing in with Brigid on his heels.

Helen struggled for breath as the letter fluttered to the floor. "Mother is dead, Harry. She was shot."

He mouthed the word 'tea' to Brigid, sat down, and retrieved the letter which was dated the third week in Mach.

Dear Mrs McKellan, I am deeply distressed to tell you that your mother has died. A resistance fighter was exchanging shots with German Polizei just as Isobel came out from her favourite bakery. In the crossfire, a stray bullet struck her in the temple. Her death was instantaneous.

Your mother was a wonderful woman and spoke of you with wholehearted affection. My family and I loved her. We buried her in a small church on the outskirts of town and burned a candle in your name. She made me the executor of her will, and I will communicate again when her affairs are in order. Yours with sincere sympathy, Philip Castello.

After he'd finished reading, Harry held Helen against him until Brigid appeared with the tea. "I'm sorry for your sadness, Ma'am," she said, putting a consoling hand on her shoulder.

Helen gave a weak smile and eased away from Harry. Using his handkerchief, she blew her nose and took a deep breath. "We could have rescued her, Harry. If only Lawrence had listened—probably didn't like her." She clapped a hand over her mouth. "I'm sorry. What a poisonous thing to say."

"It's okay. You're upset. If Lawrence had believed Isobel was in real danger, he would have acted. You know that."

"You're right. I'm not in my right mind. I should phone him. Mother would say, 'Helen, straighten that backbone of yours.'"

After Harry had gone, she left Lawrence a message at the special number he'd given her. He called back two hours later. "What a tragic accident. I've wangled a two-day leave. Tell Harry I'll arrive 2.00 p.m. Saturday, Easter weekend."

He arrived bearing chocolate Easter eggs. Since Ireland's drinking establishments remained closed over Easter, the hotel was quiet. They skirted any reference to the war but two days together after eight months apart made it difficult to adjust, and Helen found she and Lawrence acted more like polite acquaintances than husband and wife.

On his last day, she arranged an Easter egg hunt for Margaret, Alex, and young guests, and a traditional dinner of spring lamb with mint sauce and garden peas. It was a favourite meal of Lawrence's. She supposed it was a good day, but he was asleep when she climbed into bed, and did not stir until the alarm went off the next morning.

§

At the beginning of June, Helen overheard Deidre telling Murphy that four bombs had fallen on Dublin, and one had landed in her family's neighbourhood. "My auntie is beside herself. Thirty people were killed, others injured, and a whole block of houses destroyed."

Helen stepped into the kitchen and hurried to her. "That's terrible news, Deidre. I'll have Harry drive you there tomorrow morning. Murphy, please fill a dozen care baskets with food and blankets. I'm sure Brigid will be glad to help. Did your family escape injury, Deidre?"

"Bless you, Ma'am. My parents and auntie escaped, but not my cousin John. He suffered a fractured leg from a fallen beam."

Harry needed no persuasion when Helen told him, "I called Father Gareth, who said the local church will distribute the baskets, so you're to leave them there. With luck, you'll have time to charm one of your Dublin tootsies overnight before you bring Deidre back."

"There's a good idea. Glad to see you looking better."

"Yes, although I see mother everywhere." She changed the topic. "I understand the blitz is tapering off but I can't see life returning to normal yet. Do you?"

Harry shook his head while smothering sausages with HP sauce. "Nope, and my BBC oracle, Richard, says Greece and Yugoslavia have fallen."

Helen grimaced. "I wish we could get good news from somewhere. I haven't heard from Lawrence since Easter. Anyway, time you and Deidre left."

§

In July, Lawrence turned up in a rented car. "I wangled another two-day pass. I'm hungry. Could do with a good meal." He bounded up the stairs, leaving Helen speechless. Murphy rustled up a lavish lunch while she corralled the children. Afterwards, they begged Lawrence to come to a local fairground, where Margaret was competing in a gymkhana on Harry's new horse. Helen said she and their father would form a cheering team.

The tented field swarmed with competitors, hopeful bookies, anxious parents, and spectators. Margaret won a third-place ribbon, and Alex got paid for mucking out the horse stalls.

Later, when the children were in bed, Harry quizzed Lawrence for news. "Tell us about this scorched-earth policy of Russia's."

Lawrence wrinkled his brow. "It's not new. Lord Kitchener did it in the Boer war. Try to imagine Churchill ordering factories, homes, farms, and churches burned to the ground to stop an advancing enemy. That's what Stalin has done."

Horror spread across Harry's face. Helen bowed her head. "I can't imagine the terror. We're so safe here, despite the Belfast and Dublin bombing."

"I'll second that," Harry said. "Care for a nightcap, brother?"

"Please, but only one. I want an early night."

Later in their room, Helen found their lovemaking incomplete and blamed the too-short leaves. "I wish a third of your passes wasn't spent travelling."

"I know, but I'm due a longer one in December."

"Over four days?"

"Maybe. Now, let's see if we can improve matters, yes?"

After Lawrence left, the family settled into the last of the summer before school started.

But now, Lawrence's Christmas assurance made in July, motivated Helen to write him a brief reminder. He hadn't written since October.

Dearest Lawrence, only a few weeks now before you're home for Christmas. We are so excited that you will be with us this year. She wrote a few more lines, then finished with "*hugs and kisses, Helen.*"

§

With Helen's letter in front of him, Lawrence attempted a reply. Bletchley was notorious for changing its mind regarding leaves, and worse, he did not share her enthusiasm at coming home. He also lacked Harry's easy camaraderie with Margaret and Alex.

He broached the subject with Molly, but she had no advice. "It must be difficult finding a balance between family and service life. When I'm not with you, I walk, read books, and pretend I'm having a lovely time, but honestly, I count the hours until I can get back to my work. I'm relieved I don't have your dilemma."

She never discussed work, although once she had alluded to Whitehall and let slip the word 'security'. How incongruous that war had brought Molly to him. He didn't have to juggle truth and lies with her. Fed-up with introspection, he reached for the writing paper, but Dennis burst through the door, his shock of hair on end, and his voice shrill with excitement.

"Lawrence! The Japs have just bombed the hell out of Pearl Harbour! Ships sinking everywhere and—"

"What the hell? Talk slower, for chrissake!"

"They're floundering as we speak."

"How did you find out?"

"Over the shortwave radio. It looks as though the Japs caught the U.S. napping."

"Shit," muttered Lawrence, looking at his inked words, *December 7, 1941*, drying on the page. "Well, Dennis, President Roosevelt has his war now."

Dennis slumped into a chair. "Bets on he imagined nothing this dreadful happening."

"Blind if he didn't. Can't expect to cut off Japan's oil supplies—as much as seventy-five percent I've heard—and not provoke retaliation."

"Well, it's a dead cert our Christmas leaves are buggered. Thank the gods I'm not a married man. I sure as hell wouldn't want the worry of a lonely wife on my hands."

Lawrence didn't know whether to weep or throttle him. No point in sending a letter to Helen now. "Thanks, Dennis. You've cheered my day."

"Oops! Sorry, old man," Dennis said, red-faced, "stupid remark."

Within hours, America and Britain declared war on Japan. The men in Hut 8 cheered—hoping with Lawrence that, with America's resources, the Battle of the Atlantic would swing in Britain's favour. As he surmised, Lawrence found himself and Dennis amongst those required to stay.

Exhausted from spending a night in a dormitory that Yarrow had said he would never use, Lawrence dragged himself to an outside telephone. The volume of calls between America and Britain made the connection erratic.

"Hello, are you there? Helen? Japan has attacked the United States ... leaves cancelled." *Damn the static.*

"Lawrence? Yes, I'm here. We're not American, so ... are your ... cancelled? Harry says the catastrophe is a blessing in disguise, because now the Americans are involved. I say it's more senseless deaths."

He noted the connection had righted itself. "Are you all right?"

"No, I'm frustrated as hell. The children will take this second Christmas let-down hard; they don't understand. Nor do I sometimes. I suppose you'll have Christmas dinner with your colleagues?"

"War doesn't stop hungry servicemen."

"Any entertainment?"

"Maybe a cabaret."

"Well, that's something. Will your female counterparts be there, WAAFs or WAACs—whatever they're called?"

"WRENs you mean?" His thoughts slid to Molly...

"Maybe I should work in a factory, melting pots and pans for Spitfires; then I could have Christmas dinner with our brave and dashing pilots."

Lawrence winced. Sometimes her comments cut too fine. "Don't tell me you won't have a drink with the boys in your bar. Stop goading me. You're doing a great job at the hotel."

Helen's voice exploded through the phone. "Don't spout platitudes at me! I'm sick of them!"

Her words hit home. The situation was lousy, and topping it off was him—evasive because he preferred Molly's company. Molly understood what was happening. No need for questions. They and their colleagues had bonded in the same way firemen did, or sailors, or hospital staff for that matter. It couldn't be helped. Family members were outsiders.

Helen's next comment landed like a whip. "Frankly, I've forgotten what it's like to be a wife. Our marriage is falling apart, in case that's escaped you."

She's bloody clairvoyant. "Not a chance. Look, the war is putting a strain on everyone. I'll be home for my birthday."

"Watch you don't make promises to your wife you can't keep."

The phone clicked, and Lawrence, his coat now powdered with snow, plunged his hands into the warmth of his pockets, and wondered which was tougher: fighting the Bosch or grappling with Helen. But as usual, when he arrived at Hut 8, his mind cleared and codes became his adversary.

CHAPTER 10

DECEMBER 1941

HELEN STROVE TO keep her voice calm during breakfast as she broke the news to Margaret and Alex. Well-worn phrases fell from her lips. 'It's not his fault.' 'He has no choice.' 'It's the horrible war that keeps him from being with us.' But from their glazed expressions, she knew how false she sounded.

She started again. "Look, pretend you're on a ship and without warning enemy warplanes drop bombs, hundreds of them. That's what happened to the American sailors in Hawaii. America can't ignore that, so they've declared war against Japan. This means America will fight with us. You must remember that your father, and others like him, try to outwit the enemy *before* they strike. They do that even as enemy fighter planes fly overhead with their bombs."

"I guess it's bad where he is," Alex muttered, biting his nails.

Margaret plucked a homemade card for her father off the dining-room dresser and ran from the room in tears. When she reappeared, she placed the card in front of all the others. It now featured a black border.

Brigid entered behind her. "Good morning, Ma'am. Can the youngsters come for a sleepover at my family's farm tonight? We're building a nativity scene in the barn. Neighbours come, and afterwards we have a potlach. It's a grand time."

Seeing the children's expectant faces, Helen needed no convincing. "Brigid, where do you hide your angel wings?"

Harry heard the news when he arrived for his meal that evening and found Helen on her own. "Leave cancelled? What an unlucky devil."

"Unlucky? Not him. In fact, he confessed to a cabaret after the dinner."

Harry waggled his finger. "Troubled with birds of the WREN variety flitting around are you? Personally, I'd prefer two turtledoves or three French hens."

She aimed a cardboard coaster and managed to clip his hair. "I would have thought 'tits' were more in your line. If you don't stop ribbing me, I'll sprinkle arsenic in your rabbit stew." Pulling a face, Harry cautiously sampled a forkful.

Helen chewed her lip, mortified that both her children had accepted the news with better grace than she had. "Are your turkeys fattened up for the guests' dinners, Harry?"

He held his arms out like an angler exaggerating a catch. "They're at the waddling stage. I've also smaller ones for the staff."

"Excellent. I'll leave you and Murphy to distribute them when they're ready—after all, they are *your* turkeys."

"Isn't that breaking with tradition?"

"To hell with tradition; it's flown the coop in this family. I'm sorry, Harry. I'm not good company. It's unfair to take it out on you. Let's pass on coffee. I've presents to wrap."

Harry patted his stomach, by way of thanks for the meal and retreated.

Seated at her dressing table, Helen swept a brush through her hair in hard, angry strokes. She hated being the cheerful, efficient bloody hotelier. She wanted to shrug off responsibilities, be happy and alive, and interesting in someone's eyes, not a dissatisfied, resentful woman.

Kicking aside the wrapping paper, she pulled on a Merino wool jacket, knotted a scarf under her chin, and left the hotel. Crunching along the shoreline, she searched for the wet gleam of periwinkles. When she had a handful, she perched on a large rock and teased them from their shells with a hairpin.

By now, twilight had deepened the sand dunes to an indigo hue, and the shifting scene reminded her of a landscape she had coveted at the London Tate Gallery. To her, life was like that—a canvas upon which one painted impressions, dreams, and visions. The trouble was, Lawrence wanted everyone to conform to his design. Her mother had always insisted, "Look to yourself. You came into this world alone, and alone you will leave it." She missed Isobel's hard truths.

Depressed by her thoughts, Helen put the uneaten periwinkles back amongst the wet sand and pebbles, and decided to help Patrick in the bar. She needed the company of cheerful people.

§

Intent on removing dried beer stains from the counter, Helen sensed someone watching her. She looked up into the face of a tall, rangy fellow with unruly reddish hair. He wore a green sweater, which sported a holly design around the collar and cuffs. *Must have been a doting wife or relative who knitted that item,* she thought. He had grey eyes.

"Well now, it's glad I am to be standing here. A friend pointed you out, saying you were the owner of this fine establishment." His cheeky, unhurried manner reminded her of Harry. "I'm Kenneth Inglis. I suppose you could say we're neighbours, although I'm a good hike away. Now that I've met you, I wish I'd dropped in sooner."

"That's a fine example of Irish blarney, if ever I heard one," Helen said, tucking an errant strand of hair behind her ear. "What can I pour you, Mr Inglis?"

He pointed to the Guinness tap. "A pint of that, please, and call me Kenneth." He rested his hands on the counter. "I've been practising my baritone. I hear these singsongs of yours are grand, so I'm looking forward to joining the choristers; although right now I could go for a game of darts."

Helen flicked her head toward a group of men heckling each other around the dartboard. "In that case, you'll have no trouble." She drew off his pint. *Those hands of his are no farmer's.* She pushed the pint to him. "Here you are."

He took a mouthful just as Harry approached, forever nosy. Leaning against the counter, he asked Patrick's advice on how close a dart player should be to the dartboard. *As if he doesn't know,* Helen thought, speculating that Harry wasn't above hustling newcomers. Patrick, preparing an order of gin and tonic, didn't hear him or pretended he hadn't. *Maybe he's in on Harry's hustles,* she thought.

"There's a line on the floor to show you where to stand," Kenneth said, introducing himself. "If you're a beginner, you can stand closer. But the line is where the good players stand."

"That's what the chaps over there say, though I'm thinking to edge closer for a good throw-in gives an advantage."

What nonsense is he talking now? "Goodness me, are you trying to hoodwink our new guest, Harry? You know the rules—you're no beginner, so stop pretending."

Kenneth looked from one to the other. "Am I stepping into the middle of something?"

"Hell, no," Harry said, a Cheshire-cat grin plastered on his face. "We often fire potshots at each other. Helen thinks she's my minder while my brother, her husband, fights the good fight in England. In reality, I'm the minder."

"Don't believe him; he's just trying to bait me."

Harry held up a hand in mock surrender. "What, me? So, Kenneth, let's have a game. You win, I'll buy the drinks. I win, everything you own is mine."

Kenneth laughed. "That's a wild bet for sure. Let's see how good you are, but don't be edging a toe over the standing-line." Holding his drink, he threw Helen an amused look, before he followed Harry to the dartboard.

It splintered her self-control not to find out how the newcomer was faring. Instinct told her he would have Harry figured out in no time. Despite serving drinks, chatting to regulars, and welcoming newcomers, it didn't stop her from hearing Kenneth's laughter or feeling the heat in her face whenever she caught him looking at her.

§

As Christmas approached, Kenneth became a frequent visitor, and Helen watched the friendship between Harry and him take root. She played darts with them once, but rebuffed further games, since Kenneth flirted—the lingering touch of his fingers whenever she handed him the darts, served his drink, or presented his tab. The safest times were the singsong evenings when Kenneth conducted with a wooden spoon, and she linked arms with Harry and happily added her voice to that of the choristers. At night though, she had erotic fantasies, and it was thoughts of Kenneth that aroused her.

One evening in the bar, she asked him what he did for a living. His pause made her wonder if he used the same evasive techniques as Lawrence in response to questions. "I'm a journalist for the *Mayo Daily Leader*, but don't expect me to comment on the war or Irish affairs. For that, I'd have to be as tipsy as a happy drunk on the last bus home."

She laughed. *No wonder he and Harry get along. They have the same kind of humour*. "Harry says your arguments make his head dizzy. I wouldn't want to be interviewed by you."

"You never know; you might like it."

She turned quickly away. There was that blarney again.

§

The night before Christmas Eve, after an impromptu singsong, Harry staggered off on the arm of a glossy-haired brunette, leaving Kenneth on his own. Helen noticed that he stayed, nursing the last of his drink, after Patrick closed the bar. Careful to avoid eye contact, she busied herself in the farthest part of the room, straightening tables and chairs. Her lungs seemed incapable of drawing a breath when he approached. *Why doesn't he leave?*

"You look like a wild creature ready to take flight," he said. "Am I that frightening?"

She made a vague motion of her head, but didn't move. He came closer and put his warm, strong hands on her arms, sliding them up to her shoulders, and then bent his head and kissed her eyes, her nose, her lips. She stood in a molten state, then pushed her hand against his chest. "Please stop, I can't do this."

He immediately stepped back but his eyes searched her face. "I'm sorry, Helen, I can't help that I want you. Are you not battling the same emotions? Am I that wrong? If I'm not, I'm hoping our friendship will grow deeper. I know this is happening quickly but you can set the boundaries, and I won't cross them." He stroked her cheek then turned and left without another word.

Shaken, she sank into a chair, her mind and body in turmoil.

Next morning, when Harry came into her office, she thought that, if there were any truth to the notion that a woman casts sunshine in a bachelor's life, then Harry had been sunning himself royally. He had combed his hair, his clothes were free of hay, and he wore a smile to light a room. Unlike him, she felt bewildered and knew shadows darkened her eyes.

"I've just delivered five turkeys to Murphy," he said, then stopped. "You look gobsmacked. You need fresh air. Come for a hayride this afternoon. Bring Alex and Margaret, or are they at Brigid's again?"

"They are. I'm picking them up in an hour."

"Let me get them. They can help pitchfork hay into my cart, and then we'll fetch you. After that, we'll decorate the tree in the foyer and get drunk on Murphy's cake. He says he has everything fixed for tomorrow, so come to my place for Christmas dinner. Murphy told me what to do, and I have a grand recipe for stuffing."

"Good heavens, Harry, such energy. Will your lady love be there too?"

"No, Maureen will be with her family, but she and I are looking forward to a spot of togetherness on Boxing Day."

When he left, she puffed her cheeks out in alarm. She would need all her skills to head off Harry's curiosity and sixth sense.

§

She loved the farmhouse. The beamed ceiling and stone walls gave the living room a rustic feel, and the kitchen, which opened into the back half of the room, had a wood stove, pine dresser, and a table big enough to seat eight.

"Look! Uncle's tree touches the ceiling," Margaret said, in wonder. Alex glanced up, then squatted on his haunches to see who was getting what present.

"Eyes off, Alex. We'll open presents after the meal," Harry said, and guided everyone to the table, bedecked with holly and Christmas crackers. "Helen, today you relax. Margaret, you help serve while I carve the turkey. Alex, you fill the glasses—sparkling wine for your mum and me, lemonade for Margaret and you."

Helen's plum pudding, with sixpences hidden in waxed paper, ended the meal. When they finished she raised her glass. "Let's toast Daddy now."

"To Daddy, fighting the enemy, wherever you are," Alex said, "and a Merry Christmas to Uncle Harry, our second daddy."

"You can't have two daddies, stupid."

"Margaret, Alex was only being nice."

"No, Mum. I wasn't. Absent daddies should write or telephone. Uncle Harry does what daddies are supposed to do. He looks after us. Has Christmas with us. Takes us places."

With an amused look at Helen, Harry said, "I don't do everything daddies do. Smarten up, Alex; yours is at war. Remember that. Let's toast to his safety and the war ending ... good. Now let's open our presents."

Stifling her laughter, Helen gave Harry a cable-knit sweater, plus a rare bottle of Bushmills Whiskey, while Margaret and Alex received a snakes and ladders board game and fishing rods. For her there was a sketch book and a box of Irish linen handkerchiefs from Harry and the children.

"Mummy, where are Daddy's presents? Didn't he send us any?"

Thinking fast, she said, "Sending letters is difficult during wartime, Margaret, let alone parcels. So, Daddy was clever. He asked me to take you both to Dublin on a surprise-shopping spree in the new year." Her reward for telling such a whopper was Margaret exclaiming to Alex, "See! I told you he would remember!" But Alex did not look convinced. Helen improvised further. "We'll stay at the Shelbourne for the night."

Alex grabbed the new board game. "Come on, Margaret ... let's go play."

Left to themselves, Helen and Harry relaxed before the peat fire and swirled brandy in balloon snifters. Harry lit a cigarette with his battered Zippo lighter and gave her a perplexed look. "So, what's up, Helen? You seem a little pensive."

"Stop fishing, Harry. I just feel rotten for badgering Lawrence. It's not his fault Pearl Harbour was bombed." *Surely my turmoil over Kenneth doesn't show that much?* She warmed the brandy glass between her hands and hoped her partial truth was enough. "I'm also aware we're drifting apart and I ... oh, never mind."

"Maybe cold baths might help."

"What makes you say that?"

"You're a desirable-looking woman, Helen. Men want to touch you, bring you alive, hear you laugh, soak up your company. And you? You'd be abnormal if you didn't want those things too. It's not your fault. It's in your blood. I know you. Forgive me saying this, but my brother has never met those needs, has he?"

His words tripped over themselves in her head. Had she and Kenneth, with a look or smile, alerted him? "Harry, let it alone. I suspect Lawrence has his own demons."

"We all have. Wartime neglect plagues many wives. My advice is to avoid being rash."

She sipped her brandy. Of course, Harry knew her. Once, years ago, when Margaret was still at the toddling stage, an architectural project in London had kept Lawrence away unusually long—paltry compared to now. Harry had taken her on a bike ride. After lunch and pints of strong, homemade cider at a country Inn, they had stopped at a creek to cool their feet. Suddenly, with no warning, Harry leaned in and kissed her, and she responded—their fevered moment only halted because hikers came along the trail. They both pretended nothing had happened, but that scalding moment left an unspoken affinity between them.

"Advice noted. Now, since I don't want to bore Lawrence, give me a few interesting tidbits to tell him. But, before you do, may I have another splash of brandy?"

Harry replenished her glass and threw a chunk of peat on the fire. "Tell him we avoided the Tipperary foot-and-mouth outbreak that could have wiped us out. Tell him about the government's Compulsory Tillage Order."

"Is that the one forcing farmers to produce crops on a part of their land?"

"Yes. Mention I find diversification a good idea."

"How dull. Maybe I should add that the outbreak affected county fairs and race tracks, and prevented you from losing money on the horses."

"We'll have no smart-arse comments, thank you."

"How about your girlfriends? Can't you settle on one? Get married. Have children." His alarmed expression made her burst out laughing. "Alex and Margaret adore you, so why not two of your own?"

"Babies? I don't think so, and why settle for one girlfriend when I can play with several?"

Helen gave his arm a playful slap, relieved she had steered him away from touchy queries. But, still having no solution what to do about Kenneth, she spent another restless night.

CHAPTER 11

JANUARY-JUNE 1942

THE ROAD HELEN drove rose over a watershed and wound its way through chocolate-coloured peat fields. To the east, snow crowned the Ox Mountains, and also graced the Nephin Beg Range to the west.

The panorama was calming, but at this moment, wildness seized her rational mind. She turned into a rutted lane, flanked by grassy banks awaiting the golden blaze of gorse. It led her downwards to a whitewashed cottage with a thatched roof and sparkling windows. She parked beside a dog-rose hedge, then picked her way across moss-swaddled paving stones to the door. Lifting the iron doorknocker, she noted the nameplate above it.

"Benevolence is an unusual name," she said, when the door opened.

Kenneth drew her inside. "Blame the cottage. Its ambience settles me."

"I'm envious."

"Then you're in the right place." Taking her hand, he led her past a kitchen into a bright, stone-flagged room. Braided rugs warmed the floor, and a chintz-covered window seat overlooked the front garden. Helen looked about, wanting every detail held captive, like pressed flowers. Above her, a shelf encircled the room, displaying pewter mugs, ceramic horses and earthenware jugs. She liked that he was a collector. Through an archway, she recognized a Royal Standard typewriter dominating a paper-littered desk. A notebook leaned against a mug.

"The open fireplace and books everywhere make the room so inviting, Kenneth." Catching her breath, she seated herself in one of two wing-backed armchairs which flanked the fireplace. Could he hear her kettledrum heart?

He put a hand on her shoulder. "Relax. There's that wild-creature look again. I'll fix drinks for us." He moved to a small glassed-in cabinet.

Helen collected her thoughts and talked to his back. "I have no experience with a situation like this, Kenneth. None. My marriage is unhappy—a controlling husband expecting compliance and dedication to the family's name—and then there's Harry, with the nose of a terrier. This is moving so fast. And yet I can't help myself, I'm ..."

Drinks forgotten, Kenneth was beside her in two strides. "Do you think I don't know this? Time takes no account of what has happened to us, Helen. I'm in need too. I can't sleep, can't work, to the point of becoming unhinged. Whatever Harry suspects, he will never do or say anything to harm you. I'm sure he's half in love with you himself." He drew her up and into his arms. "Come with me." Holding her hand, he led her down a short corridor and into his bedroom.

Rays of light, through a curtained window, fell across a white ocean of pillows and sheets. Consumed by a sweet hunger, they dropped their clothes in soft heaps on the naked floor and fell onto the bed, arms and legs entwining.

§

During the days and weeks that followed, the delicious extravagances of her awakened body kindled a new sense of herself. Other people noticed. Brigid said the Irish air had taken a 'grand liking to her face' and Murphy asked if she'd been learning Irish jigs with that 'skip' to her feet. Even Alex and Margaret sought her out to join in their games. But, when Harry showed up with a basket of farm eggs, his cryptic comments sent her skidding to a standstill.

"Good morning! I shouldn't have put these in one basket—mixing the old with the new never works. They have different yolks and shells, you see. You can scramble the broken ones, but bits of shell can still fall into the mix."

Helen shook her head. "I see. So, what's the remedy? What should one do?"

"The Golden Rule is to keep the old and new apart—well, as much as possible."

He certainly has novel ways of approaching thorny topics. I wonder what he thinks he knows? "Well, thank you, Chef Harry, I'll try to follow that."

§

With Kenneth, even a simple walk became an adventure. He showed her where gannets and stormy petrels nestled on sea-cliff ledges, and how to freeze until timorous rabbits hopped so close she could touch them. On all things Irish, he became her patient guide and laced his stories with history.

Her first significant insight into him came during an excursion to Nephin peat bog, when he pointed out a bump on the side of a hillock. "That's a cutter's dwelling."

The twelve-foot-square hovel had a turf doorway and a basket above ground that covered a hole in the roof. How could anyone awaken each morning to brown wastes of heath and a black bog, she wondered. "Who lived in them?"

"Homeless Irishmen, after King Henry stole our land and gave it to his cronies," he said. Bitterness clouded his eyes. "There are homeless who still use them."

"England has brought a lot of misery to your country, hasn't it?"

"Yes, and when Henry hatched the Church of England, Protestant migration and Catholic oppression followed. That black mark has spawned resentment to this day."

She opened her mouth, then closed it. Lawrence would label Kenneth a radical, but if she were Irish, she thought that she would be one too. On their return to Benevolence, she remarked upon the thickness of the many hedgerows they had seen.

"Those hedges concealed schools in hard times. Generations of my family went to hedge schools. It's thanks to them that Irish bards kept our language and history alive, and our music."

"Which explains your splendid baritone voice."

"Spicing your words with Irish blarney now are you, Mrs McKellan? You being a pianist, have you played any Celtic music, or read our fine literature?"

"Ploughing through Ulysses finished me, and I have yet to try your music."

"Well, I've grand books less trying than James Joyce—and sheet music for you to play."

"Mournful Irish ballads? I can't have my guests crying in their soup."

"Your guests aren't all English, are they?"

"All right, I'll play a few, provided no one runs away. What else can you teach me today?"

"That's a very leading question, Ma'am. I sense a lesson coming up."

§

When the gorse along Kenneth's lane turned to gold, he took her for a drive to the top of Partry Mountains near Castlebar. Bog cotton and rhododendrons lined the narrow roads, and black-eared sheep watched them pass. At the summit, Helen squinted into the distance and pointed to a sparkling body of water.

"That's Lough Mask, well-stocked with trout and arctic char," he said, putting an arm around her shoulders. "I'll cook you a fine fat trout one evening."

"We could all go fishing together. Harry, the children and I got brand new rods and fishing tackle at Christmas."

"Perhaps," he said, moving away to retrieve their picnic basket from the car.

His lack of enthusiasm brought home Harry's bizarre egg comments. On the way to the summit, she pointed to the ancient ruins of stone cottages. "I've seen so many of these. What happened?"

"The potato famine."

Helen crossed her arms against a chill breeze. "Why do you never mention your family?"

"Too painful. My father was a teacher in Castlebar. I helped out sometimes. Cancer took him early, and Mother followed soon after—I suspect of a broken heart. I had a sister, two years older than me who ..." He looked away. "That's not one to share. Enough."

The anguish on his face pained her to see. She must stop with her questions. "I'm famished. Where's that river you mentioned?"

He pointed to a wide ribbon of water below them. "Twenty minutes should get us there."

§

In writing to Lawrence, Helen agonized that her pen might run away with confessions.

Hello, Lawrence,

I hope you're granted leave soon. It's been ages. A brawl erupted in the bar the other night, so I've hired a retired policeman named Seamus for Friday and Saturday nights. He found a tipsy woman sleeping it off in our reading room—didn't say whether she was dressed or undressed! Incidentally, Harry says Seamus is a great mechanic. I think your brother wants to keep on the right side of him and the law! The children are doing well, although Margaret was caught smoking. The headmistress threatened to expel her, so I stopped Margaret's allowance for the rest of the term and made her promise the headmistress in writing that she would stay out of trouble. She needs her father. Please bear that in mind. Alex is less trouble—thanks to Harry's presence. Stay safe, love Helen.

She sealed the letter, hoping he would heed her last comments but that the general tone gave nothing away.

§

Towards the end of June, after planning an afternoon and evening off, Helen suggested to Kenneth that they get away from the local scene. "I need to discuss something with you."

"Nothing ominous, I hope?"

"No, I hadn't thought of it in that light. How about we go to that retreat of yours near Belmullet?"

They took the coastal road in Kenneth's car, the day cool and overcast, the air thick with mist. During the journey, Helen tussled with how best to broach what was on her mind. Glancing at Kenneth, she caught his quizzical eye. To forestall questions, she shifted closer to him and battened down her worries as they drove past cattle huddled together in the fields, and windswept trees bent in submission to the Atlantic storms.

To reach the pub, they crossed a rustic bridge that spanned a small moat. Inside, Kenneth led the way to a window seat set back from the bar counter.

"Best place I know when I can't stand my company or want a change of scene."

Helen glanced at the heavy-beamed ceiling, the iron studs in the front door, and the Tiffany windows depicting a forest scene through which diffused light daubed the walls with splashes of red and green. "It looks an odd place, a fortress ... a sanctuary ... or maybe both. Reminds me of your articles."

"Is that good or bad?"

"Neither, just frustrating. I don't understand how you can write passionately about the present and yet be stranded in the past."

"That's because Ireland's past and future create a regular tug-of-war. We're great procrastinators. We take refuge in dreaming of what might have been, and what if so-and-so had never happened."

Helen laughed. "No wonder the bulldog English don't understand you. I imagine you would like them cornered in their kennel and—" She stopped, aware that they were not alone.

"Will you be having the usual, Mister Kenneth?"

"I will, Maureen, but make it two, please."

"Two of what?" Helen asked, looking up into a smiling face framed by red hair.

"House cider, guaranteed the best in the world," Kenneth said.

The girl flashed a smile at him and left to fill the order. Helen felt a jab of jealousy and dropped her gaze. She hated feeling this way. Why shouldn't Kenneth have female friends? It was absurd and naive of her to think otherwise.

The weather had changed and rain dulled the windows. *Probably an omen,* she thought despondently. But when Maureen returned with the drinks, Helen nodded her pleasure at the clean, fresh taste. "I'm glad you like it," Kenneth said. "Here's a puzzle for you. I'm wondering, if an Irishman is all blarney, a Frenchman all charm, and a Scotsman like Harry all affability, what is a woman raised in America, married in Scotland, and running an Irish hotel bar?"

"Desirable?" When he stopped laughing, she said, "This isn't a puzzle, more of an observation. You, Harry, and Lawrence are all very different in how you respond to people. Harry wags his tail like a friendly dog to humour them. Lawrence uses logic and reasoning to persuade them. You use blarney and charm to confuse them—even dangerous people I expect."

Kenneth put his drink down none too gently. "Well, Helen, I didn't know you for a psychologist. Are you fishing, or is Harry stirring the pot? Dangerous people? I can hardly write about old ladies and tea parties."

"Have I irritated you? I didn't mean to. You started this."

"I concede. So, tell me, why are we here?"

She sighed and dabbed her lips. "Lawrence will be home on leave in a few days. It means you and I must put some distance between us for a while."

Kenneth rolled his eyes and tilted his glass at her. Helen felt her cheeks flush. "That doesn't seem a friendly gesture. You knew he'd be home sometime. What did you expect?"

"Expect? For you to welcome your dear husband with open arms. Be the good dutiful wife, but understand that I'm a man who doesn't like sharing his woman."

His dispassionate expression was so unnerving that she thought she was facing a stranger. Her mouth went dry. Neither of them had walked into this relationship blind. If Kenneth could not achieve balance, and dropped one false word, her marriage could collapse and her family be harmed. She grabbed her handbag and pushed away from the table.

"To use your crass word, we both have to *share*. I doubt you live the lily-pure life when you're not with me. You men and your double standards. I want to leave."

Close-mouthed, Kenneth yanked his wallet from his back pocket and waved Maureen over. "Sudden emergency," he said.

In the car, Helen stared at the mist that still wrapped the landscape in gloom. The threat of losing Kenneth made her eyes tear. Lawrence had never turned her inside out like this. She drew her raincoat tighter about her and endured the silence until the car came to a standstill at Benevolence. Before she could get out, Kenneth put a restraining hand on her arm.

"Helen, you can't just drive off. I never thought of myself as a possessive man. Is this what love does? Make the heart hammer and the stomach cramp. To make life easier, I'll bugger off to Dublin or Belfast for a while. I won't cause you trouble, I promise. Now, for the love of God, let me hold you."

They were barely through the door before their fingers were tearing at their clothes. It was a long time before they fell apart, sweating and exhausted.

It was past midnight when she returned to the hotel. No lights shone from the windows, and she was certain no one saw her. She crawled into bed and fell into a deep asleep. As dawn broke, she awoke with a prickling sense of apprehension. Muttering "Please, no ... please, no," she retrieved her handbag, slung on the bedpost, and scattered its contents on the blanket.

Her breath caught in her throat as her eyes fixed on a pale-blue oval compact. Inside, like an elfin skullcap, nestled her unused diaphragm.

CHAPTER 12

JUNE 1942

HELEN POSITIONED HERSELF beside a flower arrangement on Deidre's front desk and waited. The location allowed a view of the entrance but the flowers obscured her image in the foyer's mirror. She didn't want to see the full-lipped mouth, the flawless dress that covered shameless flesh, and the wide eyes that camouflaged an adulterous wife.

She was not there long before brisk footsteps prompted her to step forward. Lawrence's mouth broke into a smile, which she returned, but she held back and gestured to where Margaret was nudging Alex down the stairs.

"Welcome home, Daddy," Margaret simpered, arriving in front of him, her smiling face guileless—showing no hint of her slip from grace.

"Well, princess, how are you," King Lawrence exclaimed, kissing her fingertips.

Alex flicked his hair back and waited until Lawrence attempted to hug him. "Dad, I'm eleven. I'm not a kid anymore. It's been a long time since you saw me."

"You're right. I hope this will make amends," and withdrew two parcels from his suitcase. "This one is for you, and this," he said, turning to Margaret, "is yours."

Margaret opened the parcel and gasped, "Wow! Mum, look what I've got!" She slipped on a nurse's uniform, swirled a blue cape onto her shoulders, and slung a stethoscope around her neck.

"Now, sir, stay still," she ordered her father. "Where does it hurt?"

Lawrence pressed his hand to his chest. "My heart, nurse. It's a-flutter from seeing you." Margaret giggled and flung her arms around him.

Alex gave a low whistle. "Wow, Dad, a train set. This is a *collector's* set. Will you show me how to put it together?"

"Come with me." Crossing to the side of the foyer, he helped Alex assemble ten feet of railway tracks. "You can set the full line of tracks out later in the table-tennis room."

"What else did Daddy bring?" Helen asked, seeing Margaret leafing through a large book.

"Cut-out paper dolls and their clothing," she beamed. "It's all the craze at school."

On the back cover, Helen saw *Selfridges Emporium, Oxford Street* stamped in gold lettering. Lawrence detested shopping—who'd helped him? That dinner date? *But who am I to question?*

"Watch out!" Alex shouted, as the train raced towards the reading room and stopped at the feet of a portly man. Mumbling apologies, Alex scooped the engine and tracks into his arms and disappeared up the stairs.

The guest laughed and cast Lawrence an approving glance. "How's the war going, Mr McKellan? Your wife told me you were arriving today."

"Not good news, I'm afraid. The North African Campaign is still ongoing, and although Churchill retaliated with a devastating raid on Cologne, it hasn't knocked the enemy out."

"That's too bad. I'm keen to hear your views, but I see my wife beckoning at the front door. Perhaps in the bar later?"

Lawrence nodded and looked at Margaret, standing impatiently beside him. "So, nurse, what now?"

"One of Uncle Harry's cows is calving today. I should be there to help." Throwing him a quick smile, she hurried off with nurse-like authority.

"My turn," Helen said and kissed him on the cheek. "You chose clever gifts for the children. Are you tired?"

"Not a bit."

"Good. Then let's take a walk, shall we?"

Over dinner, Harry told a comical story of a horse that escaped its tethers and gobbled a cake cooling on a neighbour's windowsill. Margaret chatted about her school play, and her princess's role, disguised as a gypsy, fortune-teller, and Lawrence gave vivid descriptions of the 1940 aerial dogfights over Britain. Alex pestered him with questions, and announced maybe he'd be a pilot one day. The spirited chatter with no awkward silences was such a relief to Helen, she forgot her worries.

Later in bed, relieved at Lawrence's satisfied breath against her cheek, she wondered why she had felt so submissive in his arms, as if being so might rout her wanton self. Asleep, he looked boyish. It comforted her having him home, despite Kenneth lingering in her thoughts. What compelling reason took him to Belfast so often? Perhaps it was political. The city *was* IRA turf. From overhearing Seamus and Harry chatting after the bar emptied, she'd learned the organization was rearming itself. *But that's not my concern,* she thought, more worried about Lawrence and Kenneth meeting. Weary, she curled spoon-fashion against Lawrence and counted backward, but sleep was a long time in coming.

With the sky showing no sign of rain the next day, Lawrence announced over breakfast that he and Harry would tuck in a golf game that afternoon. "We'll stop off in Castlebar for supper."

"Castlebar? I hear that there's good trout fishing there. On your return, come to the bar—it's singsong night."

"Daddy, can Alex and I come with you? We could caddy."

"Thank you, Margaret, but Uncle Harry and I will be out all day. Incidentally, what do you do on *your* days off, Helen?"

"Day's off? You're joking." She brushed crumbs from her lap. "When school is out we might go into Enniscrone for iced buns, swim at Killala Bay, or bike over to the farm."

"Sometimes Margaret and I chase rats from Uncle Harry's wheat stacks, with the help of Mr Flynn," Alex said.

"And Murphy taught us how to pitchfork for flounders in the estuary," Margaret added.

Helen smiled. "As you can see, we stay busy. Sometimes I steal time for the piano."

"Well, that's good, Helen; keeps your hands in."

"I also spend time wondering what *you* do."

His only response was to shake his head.

§

"The place is rowdy tonight," Patrick said, when Helen showed up.

She gave him a take-it-easy-look, and after mixing drinks, wiped the counter free of spills. Adept at keeping friendly banter going with the locals, she kept a casual eye open for Lawrence and Harry. But, when the door opened, her breath stopped, as if she had plummeted from a great height. To keep her hands from shaking, she wiped the counter again.

"Tired of Belfast so quickly?" she asked, icily.

Kenneth grinned and looked around, "Where's the master of the house?"

The bloody cheek of him. "With Harry," she muttered, "they'll be here soon. You should leave."

"You can't ask that of a journalist. We're naturally curious creatures."

"And it appears ones that break promises. Someday, your curiosity will kill the cat."

"Not this cat. May I have a draught of your finest, Ma'am? It helps tune up the singing voice." Once his Guinness had developed a good head of foam, he took a mouthful, winked, and swung away.

Helen turned her back and had gained enough composure to wave Lawrence and Harry to her when they arrived. "Sorry for the noise!" she shouted, with a breezy smile. With the expertise of a champion shuffleboard player, she slid two pints of the bar's best towards them. A quick glance showed Kenneth ready to lead the next song. Harry cuffed Lawrence in chummy fashion, and took up the song's bawdy refrain. She knew it wouldn't be long before he introduced Kenneth. Sure enough, when the singers caught their breath, Harry clapped Lawrence on the back.

"Bet the boys you know can't harmonize like that."

"I wouldn't know. There's nothing to sing about over there," he said, and puffed smoke rings from a cheroot into the blue-tinged air.

Harry pulled a glum face and raised his voice. "Hey, Kenneth, have you come for another dart fight? He beats the hell out of me at darts every time, Lawrence. He's our resident journalist."

In the half beat of silence, Lawrence raised a questioning eyebrow, and Helen thought, *Resident? What a god-awful word to use.* "I mean," Harry said, "he's homegrown. He writes for the *Mayo Daily Leader*. Come and meet him."

Pasting a smile on her lips, Helen moved out from behind the counter. "I haven't seen either of you much today. I'll join you." Harry cast her an odd look—anxious, or conspiratorial, she wasn't sure—as he steered Lawrence over to Kenneth's table. Had Harry confirmed his suspicions about her and Kenneth? But surely not; they had been ultra-careful. She even covered her hair with a scarf and wore dark glasses if they met in Ballina. She came up alongside Lawrence, just as Patrick arrived with glasses of Guinness, and Harry made the introductions.

"Lawrence, meet my friend, Kenneth Inglis. You two intellectuals will have more in common to discuss than I do."

"Why would that be?" Lawrence asked, ignoring Kenneth.

"Because both of you believe history and politics are more exciting than the horses, but it's the gee-gees that stir *my* blood—they make money. Have you ever seen a rich historian?"

Watching Lawrence and Kenneth shake hands, Helen could see that generations of colonial mentality governed Lawrence, while generations of resentment towards British colonization governed Kenneth. Her husband and her lover were both root-bound in their separate cultures. That spelled trouble.

"Chair or bar stool?" Harry asked her.

"The stool would be best. That way I can keep a close eye on the bar." She swallowed the lie with a gulp of Guinness.

"Well, Lawrence, it's about time I met the brother fighting the good fight across the water. You have a great fan in Harry," Kenneth said. "He's forever quoting you when we discuss issues, so it's an honour to meet the Lord of the Manor."

"Elevated to a peerage, am I? It's enough to go to one's head. Harry tells me that, apart from being a journalist, you are an exacting dart player."

"Well, although it's true the pen is mightier than the sword, I have been known to sling a mean dart from time to time."

Lawrence ducked, and Helen buried her nose in her glass. Mercifully, Seamus, on his trouble-patrol, arrived and thrust out a meaty paw.

"A pleasure to meet you, Mr McKellan. Wouldn't have wanted to be in your shoes, experiencing the London bombing."

Lawrence winced and extricated his crushed hand. "It was nightmarish, but the British are unshakable. I expect reporting news for you must be boring, Kenneth, Ireland being neutral.

"No. The war is not all-consuming. Journalists go everywhere."

"With a paper of your size? That's surprising."

Kenneth looked ready to give tit for tat, but Seamus cut in fast again. "I'll wager Kenneth's articles have politicians stewing, here *and* in Westminster, Mr McKellan. But on another matter, your wife told us that Coventry Cathedral only has a couple of walls standing? I went there once."

"Then it will sadden you to know that the famous stained-glass windows have been shattered beyond saving."

Kenneth raised his glass high, as if giving thanks to a deity. "There's a positive for being neutral. Our institutions are safe."

Helen coughed and cleared her throat. *Lawrence won't ignore that little comment.* From the way Harry tapped his foot on the floor, she suspected he thought so too.

Lawrence tipped forward in his chair. "So, Kenneth, you support being neutral, do you, but being a journalist, you must know that there are plenty of good, solid Irishmen with a more principled viewpoint."

"Principled viewpoint? There's an upstanding, high-minded attitude. I expect many of your *solid Irishmen* aren't homegrown. Our external affairs secretary said no government should court destruction for its people. That's why this country is a haven for many, *including* you and your family." He smiled an apology to Harry and took a drink of his Guinness.

"With that thinking, do you truly believe your precious country would turn a blind eye if Germany invaded England?"

"Well now, being the Irishman I am, here's what I believe: Ireland is for the Irish. It's not for the Germans to occupy, and it's not for the British to handcuff."

Seamus nudged Lawrence's elbow. "That's Kenneth. Spoken like a rabid reporter who doesn't know one end of a gun from the other."

"Careful, Lawrence," Harry urged, "you'll have Kenneth telling you how Ireland has been screwed by the English for centuries. King Henry VIII and then the atrocities under Oliver Cromwell come to mind."

"I might find that interesting."

"What? Our history or Ireland being screwed? Aren't they the same?" Kenneth asked.

"Last call coming up. Another round?" Helen asked quickly, catching Patrick's attention, and circling her hand around the table.

"Provided we don't talk politics," Harry cautioned.

"Helen, put the round on my tab, please."

"Not tonight," Lawrence said, "you're in *my* bailiwick."

Kenneth shrugged and turned to Harry. "So, who do you see winning the Grand National?"

"Is there any doubt? Foolhardy, of course."

"Away with you, Harry. The poor horse can't walk, let alone run," Seamus spluttered.

There followed lively speculation on horse racing, before Kenneth drained his glass and got to his feet. "Well, that's it for me. I enjoyed our sparring, Lawrence. No doubt we'll attempt to enlighten each other further when next we meet. Good night all." He nodded to Helen, and Seamus followed him out.

Leaving Patrick to turn off the main lights, Helen cleared the table and toted a tray of dirty glasses into the kitchen. She felt weary but relieved. Neither Kenneth nor Harry had fanned the sparks into flames. Encouraged, she waited for the kettle to boil, and realized that the intangibles of her life were shaping her into a less compliant person than her Edinburgh days.

Lawrence and Harry were still engaged in conversation and didn't spare her a glance when she returned with tea and settled into Kenneth's vacated seat.

"A good thing you warned me off further political talk, Harry," Lawrence said, gruffly. "Your friend irked me. I didn't like his opinion of Britain, nor his lofty Irish ideals."

"As we saw, but he's not wrong, brother. We're here, safe and sound, because of Ireland's neutrality."

"Don't you think we'd share opinions similar to Kenneth's, if a foreign power had occupied Britain for centuries and continued to do so?"

"Perhaps we shouldn't belabour politics, Helen."

"Not we, *you*, Lawrence. Take a hint from Harry. Enthusiasts of British policy are scarce around here."

To her surprise, he backed off, even flashed a teasing smile. "Point taken, madam. You and I have much better things to do than argue, and it *is* getting late. Right, Harry? Not too long before your cows need milking?"

"Jaysus, can't a man finish his tea?"

§

Next day, June 28th, was Lawrence's forty-second birthday. To surprise him, Helen had planned a family picnic on the grounds of a ruined castle, and a sleepover for Margaret and Alex at the farm. She had also made dinner reservations at a new place in Ballina, overlooking the River Moy.

The day was spectacular. Spires of white lupines and purple foxgloves brightened the landscape, and at the castle, both Alex and Margaret ran off to explore a bottle dungeon and climb the highest parapet. "Yoo-hoo!" they shouted from the top.

Lawrence waved, then shading his eyes, looked across the ocean. Helen spread a blanket on the ground and unpacked wedges of homemade bread, glossy tomatoes, and thick slices of ham. When Lawrence walked over and sprawled on the blanket beside her, she gave him a light kiss on the cheek. "I wish you didn't have to go back. These separations harm us."

"We must try to manage—find a remedy to help us."

"I'm not sure what you mean," she said, wondering what *remedy* Lawrence had found, and unsure if she was relieved or not that her own was not around.

"It's hard to believe that the Atlantic has become such a graveyard for merchant ships," he said, as he waved a beckoning hand towards the children.

"Lawrence, it's your birthday. Let's keep the illusion going, for twenty-four hours, that there's no war out there." When the children appeared, flushed and breathless, she passed around the sandwiches. "After we've finished, we'll explore the beach caves, and then it's off to Uncle Harry's farm for you two."

§

The moon was tracing its nightly arc high above them when Helen and Lawrence returned from dining out. Together, they tiptoed like drunken thieves into the dim foyer.

Lawrence hiccupped. "I'm going to get a bottle of champagne from the bar."

"Okay, but don't come upstairs. You're in for a surprise."

In her room, she wriggled out of her jersey-silk dress. Wearing only a narrow band of satin lingerie clinging to her rounded bottom, she slipped her feet into black patent heels, then tied a red-ribbon bow around her neck. *Let Lawrence carry this image back with him*. But a subconscious worry wormed its way into her mind, as she removed her diaphragm from its compact. Without analyzing the ramifications, she returned it to the compact. After making sure no guests were prowling the corridors, she perched side-saddle on the banisters, gave a low whistle, and descended the mahogany trail into Lawrence's arms.

"Happy Birthday," she giggled.

Somewhere a door banged. They staggered into the reading room, pushed a chair against the door, then sloshing champagne, dropped in a tangled heap to the floor.

CHAPTER 13

JUNE - JULY 1942

WHEN LAWRENCE RETURNED to Bletchley, he found a letter waiting for him at his digs. He recognized the handwriting. With the instincts of someone tuned to bad news, he stuffed it into his pocket to read later while sitting by the lake.

June 28, 1942.
Dearest Lawrence,

Just after you left for Ireland, I accepted a promotion. It involves a new posting, so the Dover Street flat has been sublet. The sensitive nature of my work demands I distance myself from you. I can't disclose where I'm going or what I will be doing, but then you are no stranger to this game. I recall you saying your work has alienated you from your wife and family, but you enjoy the intellectual freedom and being with others of like mind. You never told me how you came to marry Helen.

§

Lawrence stopped reading as a scene in his mother's living room returned to badger him.

"A wife's duty means being attentive to her husband," his mother remonstrated upon learning of his wish to marry Helen. "Your father and I believe she is more suited to an *artiste's* life. All those moves from pillar to post, due to her father's business, must have been *so* unsettling. Poor child. Lord knows how many schools she attended with no opportunity to cultivate *proper* friends. She does *try* holding her tongue, but we feel her contrariness."

Harry would have slammed out of the room at this, but he was not Harry. He knew how to play their mother. "But Mother, being so cultured in the arts, Helen's family might not give a fig for the McKellan lineage."

"Don't be absurd."

Lawrence frowned and stirred a sugar lump into his tea. "*Scottish* gentry doesn't hold status in European circles, Mother. Wouldn't surprise me if Helen's parents believe I might stifle their daughter's creativity *and* self-worth. She *is* a pianist of concert quality, besides being fluent in French."

The air in his mother's drawing room swirled with Scottish indignation. "What upstarts! Dear boy, stop frowning. It's lineage and upbringing that counts. No one spurns my son."

§

Knowing how Helen could dazzle a roomful of people, he compared her to Molly. Molly didn't come close to having the same charm, but he was sure that when she spoke to a roomful of academics, she dazzled them. It would take a bloody goddess to have the qualities of both women. His mind somersaulted to Helen, and then to her theatrical slide down the banisters. The danger of being caught had been a heady aphrodisiac, but why so reckless? Visions of his mother's horror at *that* performance made him laugh. But comparisons were unsettling. To hell with them. Enough to know he enjoyed Molly's uncluttered thinking. Still, her letter stung. He continued reading.

At this juncture in my life, I feel liberated. It pleases me to join the select world of knowledgeable men and women and manoeuvre in their currents. I shall miss our late night games of chess and debates—to say nothing of the rewards we enjoyed afterwards. Ambition is cold comfort sometimes, but I am warmed by many delightful memories of you. Perhaps our paths will cross again under more favourable circumstances, when we can share more of ourselves. Stranger things have happened, no? With much affection. Yours, Molly.

The suddenness of her departure made him think she had joined the world of spies. Once, groping for his shoes under her bed, he found two books, one in Arabic script, the other in Cyrillic. In answer to his querulous look she said, "The derivation of language and writing have always interested me." Maybe so, but he never saw those books again. Where could she be now? Russia? Iraq? Saudi Arabia?

Wherever she was, rather than being discouraged he felt a curious optimism that they would meet again.

A sudden rain-squall drove him to seek shelter in the crowded canteen. Because of increased traffic in messages being intercepted and analysed, cryptographers were everywhere.

One night, when sleep evaded him, he recorded in his notebook ideas on how to hamper U-boat operations since enemy submarines called Milch Cows, now outfitted with bakeries and refrigeration units, could support U-boat wolf packs longer at sea.

CHAPTER 14

AUGUST 1942

On a rain-swept Saturday, armed with a flashlight and metal pick, Harry crouched on the floor of Helen's office. He felt lousy. He should melt into the shadows and leave instead of staring at the safe which resembled an innocuous filing cabinet behind Helen's desk. But right now, it held the riches of Aladdin's lamp.

Caws from the rookery warned of dawn, and with its arrival, the sound of clanging pots and pans in the kitchen. But there was no evading the wrath of an unpaid Belfast bookie, unless he completed the present mission. If he didn't pay up, he would be singing falsetto quicker than he could see a knife edge. But what did that make him, stealing from his sister-in-law?

"A loser," his father growled from the grave. "You're the McKellan black sheep. Forget university—you're not Lawrence. Join the workforce."

And so he did. First as a house builder and then as a horse groomer, until asthma forced him into the sterile world of insurance. But his addiction to gambling at the tracks had finally caught up with him.

Mopping sweat from his forehead with his shirt cuff, he scrunched his eyes and examined the intricacies of the safe's lock. Remembering how he had practised on similar locks at the farm, he inserted the pick and eased it a fraction this way and that. Picking a lock needed delicacy. Seconds ticked by and the rookery grew louder. With rising panic, he started again. This time the lock clicked. He fist-pumped the air, swung the door open, and groped inside. *Nothing. Empty as Mother Hubbard's fucking cupboard.* He rocked back on his haunches. Had Helen foiled him by finding a new hiding place? It wouldn't surprise him.

She had rescued him often enough in Edinburgh: paying off small debts, loaning him her car, and when the Depression struck, cajoling Lawrence into giving over their spare room. But the debt hanging over him now was too steep. His sweat-soaked shirt stuck to him as he clamped the flashlight between his teeth, and this time, flattened himself on the floor. He waited, letting his eyes adjust to the light and saw, high on the back wall of the safe, a metal-shelf. He reached in, stretching his arm until his fingers closed on tidy rolls of money. He tumbled the rolls to the floor and exhaled a ragged breath. *Must be over two hundred quid here!* A kiss to the god of sinners that Helen only made one weekly run to the bank. He stuffed his pockets, dreaming of doubling the money at the Ballinrobe racetracks. He was a smart punter. Harness his skills to a tip from a knowledgeable tout, and he'd be in clover. Helen's original take back in the safe, her none the wiser, and his bookie's threats a puff of smoke. He might even get to pocket some of his winnings.

§

For the umpteenth time, Helen sat up and dragged the tangle of bedclothes around her before giving in to the appointments crowding her mind. She pulled on her dressing gown and padded downstairs to retrieve her desk diary.

In the corridor, a light flickered from beneath her office door. Noiselessly, she stole into the kitchen, grabbed a meat cleaver, returned, eased the door ajar and flipped on the light.

Caught in the light's glare, Harry let out an uncomfortable laugh. "Jaysus! Helen! You scared me." He levered himself onto his feet.

"So I see. What in hell are you doing?" Angrier than shocked, she hid the cleaver behind her back.

Resentment clouded his face. "I'm flat broke. I've been trying to raise funds for two months, but I'm a wheelbarrow short. If I don't pay up, my life won't be worth this," and snapped his fingers.

"I'm bloody tempted to clobber you," she said, and dropped the meat cleaver onto a nearby chair. "You've got a fine way of *raising* funds. I can't plug your leaky dam this time, and neither can the hotel. If I did help, like clockwork, you would only get in debt again."

Harry looked at his hands, as if they were to blame. "I'd planned to return the money before you noticed."

"Really? Just turn the safe's contents into Harry's private little bank whenever he chooses, because he'll replace it."

"This was a one-time act of desperation."

"Hogwash. Had I not wanted my diary, you'd be long gone. And if I had called the police, I doubt you would have come forward. How could you steal from *me,* Harry?"

"Helen, the word is *borrow.*"

"So, what do you call those fivers you filch from the bar?"

"That pittance is well-earned for the public relations work I do to keep customers drinking."

"And lost through the free drinks you take, Harry McKellan. But this is not about skimming the profits. This is out-and-out theft." She looked pointedly at his money-stuffed pockets. "Go sell one of your horses, for heaven's sake."

"I tried. It's not an easy market. Look, I'm sorry. It won't happen again."

She took the meat cleaver back into her hands and waggled it at him. "You're damn right. There's no changing you, Harry. You drink, you gamble, and I'm sure half my chambermaids suffer carpet burn thanks to you. I can't help you this time. Put starch in your backbone. Get Lawrence's help." She pointed to the telephone. "Ask him now."

"Helen, can't we pretend nothing happened? I'll replace the money."

"No, Harry, that's no good. I'd always be watching and waiting." *God, what a mess.*

Sighing, he parked himself on the edge of her desk and fiddled with a paperclip. "I'll lose the farm. Lawrence will stop financing it, if you tattletale. You don't want that, do you?"

"Of course I don't, but you won't lose the farm. He'll be mad and tell you the bar is off limits. That's all." But the sudden resolve in Harry's eyes made her wonder where he got the brass balls to fight back.

"I wish you hadn't pushed, luv," he said, shaking his finger at her. "Lawrence will continue in blissful ignorance, because, my dear, suppression of hard truths is the nature of this game, and that's how we'll play it." He looked apologetic. "I know about you and Kenneth—the sparks between you both are too bloody obvious."

Her mouth went dry. "My goodness, Harry, has alcohol addled your brain? Stop seeing goblins where none exist."

Harry shrugged and tossed the paperclip aside. "Luv, your body language gives you away. Still, you get full marks for your acting the night your husband and lover tangled. It so happens that a few nights before your Oscar performance, I departed from the amorous clutches of a guest in the wee, small hours, and what do I see but my dear sister-in-law sneaking into the hotel—hair in disarray and high heels in hand. I bet even she had a touch of a carpet burn." He clicked his tongue against his teeth. "So amateurish. You need lessons from your brother-in-law."

Helen thought of brazening it out, but then abandoned the idea. His odd remarks that night in the bar now made sense. "So, that's why your introduction of Kenneth went over the top. You stunned me when you called him our resident journalist."

"I figured if Lawrence knew the three of us were friends, it would throw him off the scent. I was only looking out for you." He pushed away from the desk and unloaded his pockets—lining the rolled bills up like soldiers. "Take the bloody money. If you say nothing to Lawrence about tonight, I won't alert him to you and Kenneth. In case you've never heard of it, this tit-for-tat is called a Mexican standoff. Remember it. I'll get my money from somewhere else. Call it Plan B."

"Is Plan B dangerous?"

"Shouldn't be."

"So, guns loaded, but no shots fired?"

"Exactly."

"Oh, for chrissake, Harry! Go home, but before you do, empty your pockets of the *loose* bills you found. Those are mine. Stay away from my bar for a week."

§

Harry put Plan 'B' into action that afternoon. It meant buttonholing his pal Daecon at the piggery. A cockfight was under way in the barn when he arrived. The lust in the eyes of the crowd, the raucous voices, the gore, and coppery smell of blood drove him outside within minutes. Fighting for air, and vowing not another cigarette would pass his lips, he flushed his lungs with deep breaths, and then took a walk to steady his nerves. Rounding the corner of the barn, he found Daecon pissing up against the wall.

"Are you about to heave your guts, Harry?" Daecon asked, buttoning his pants. "All you have to do is slap your money on the table and shut your eyes."

"I don't have the stomach for cockfights. I need to talk to you."

"About what?"

"About that recruitment list you waved in my face some time back."

"Ah, so you're needing a job now, are you?" Daecon asked, with the confidence of a man about to net a fish. "We could do with the likes of you. If my cousin approves, the money is easy, but don't be blabbing. Talk and you'll lose your kneecaps. The last fellow with a loose tongue was found bleeding out in a ditch."

Harry blanched. "I won't blab. When can I see him? If I don't have the money in forty-eight hours, I'll be joining the ladies choir and warbling in the upper register."

Daecon lifted his brows. "Like that, is it? Okay. Be at Nosens Pub tonight. That good enough for ya?" Harry nodded. "Eight o'clock, Harry. It ain't worth your life to be late."

§

The pub squatted on the outskirts of Ballina. It was a poky place with wobbly tables and hard wooden chairs. There were a dozen people or more. Two leaned against the counter, others sat on stools. Four played poker. Harry found Daecon at the billiard table. Next to him, sizing up a shot, was a lean, muscled man.

"Take the fiver off my pay," Deacon said ruefully, as his opponent slammed the last ball into the end pocket. Catching sight of Harry, he added. "This here is Harry."

Harry looked into eyes as uncompromising as stone. *Those Belfast, pie-faced thugs are wimps compared to this guy.*

"Harry, is it? My name's Cooper."

Harry stared, suddenly remembering the long-ago scuffle in Enniscrone's pub. *What the hell ... no turning back now.*

Cooper straddled a chair at the nearest table. "How's your toffee-nosed brother? Fighting the good fight, is he? Sit."

Harry chose the farthest chair. "What's my brother to do with you?" Cooper's hard-nosed look warned him to bite his tongue.

"Answer my question; that's what you'll do. Is your brother a flunky to the English?"

"I don't know. I'm here; he's there."

Cooper pushed his chair back and rubbed his hands. "Quit acting the gom. What's his job?"

"He's an architect."

"Are you dumb? I'm talking about in the war."

"He doesn't tell me. He tells no one."

"Why not?"

"Maybe because Ireland is riddled with spies." Harry made to rise. *Fuck this guy.*

Cooper waggled his forefinger. "Stay put. Daecon, what does he know?"

"Nothing—he's a good bloke. He's no chancer."

"Right you are then." Reaching inside his jacket, Cooper withdrew a slim envelope and slid it across the table. "Here's for your Belfast bookie—he's one of my boyos." He laughed. "Sized you up at the hotel opening. Twigged you'd be useful one day. We'll deduct a percentage from each job you do until you've paid me back plus ten percent interest. Just remember, I own you now." He flicked his eyes to Daecon. "Give him the details after I'm gone, and Harry, don't fecking cross me."

Harry rubbed sweating palms on his pant legs, then gingerly took the envelope. He was boxed in, but right now the weight of the envelope felt good.

"Remember, squeal and I'll have you reefed so bad you'll be a walking bruise from head to toe," Cooper added, squeezing Harry's shoulder hard as he left.

"Whew! He's a regular sweetheart, your cousin."

Daecon winked. "Has his moments, but do as he says, Harry, and you'll stay in one piece. Now, it's a Guinness on me, and I'll tell you what you need to know."

Harry slumped lower in his seat. "Make it a double whiskey, please.

§

Harry's sphincter was as tight as a spinster's knickers when he made his first run for Cooper at the end of August. His men hadn't let him get out of his truck. They'd just appeared out of the dark, unloaded his homegrown goods, told him to beat it, and like mules, staggered off with their loads around a sharp bend in the trail.

He'd never reckoned on traffic coming or going that time of night, but a mile after leaving Dunegan Bay, a single headlight on high beam came up behind him. Dimming his lights, he recognized Murphy's Leyland lorry as it lumbered past. Had Murphy seen him? But, what if he had? *No doubt reckons I've been gallivanting.* He chuckled. More than likely Murphy himself was heading home full of piss and vinegar after banging a muff in the next village.

Back home, Harry reached for the scotch like an old friend and poured a drink. There'd been no hitches, and he'd soon whittle away his debt to Cooper. Heck, with more runs coming, he could spruce up the farm, increase his crops, and buy another horse—not that he'd go hog-wild mind you. He didn't want Lawrence asking tricky questions.

Pity the cute chambermaid from the hotel couldn't share his good feelings. Feet propped on a footstool, he topped up his drink and dangled a cigarette between his fingers. He wasn't about to quit smoking yet. That first hit at the back of his throat had him snared. The cat landed on his lap and kneaded his thighs. By the third top-up of whiskey, the sharp edge of his triumph had blunted. Nothing wrong with trading veggies and dairy goods—wherever they ended up wasn't his business. He couldn't be convicted of a heinous crime, could he? Best not to look in dark corners. Imagine Lawrence's surprise when the farm prospered. Reassured by these thoughts, he wavered to his feet. Disgruntled, the cat stalked off to a corner behind the wood stove, leaving Harry to stumble upstairs to bed.

CHAPTER 15

AUGUST 1942

HELEN PINCHED HER cheeks—they were too sallow. She should get back in the car, but Kenneth was at the front door.

"Well, what a grand surprise for a midsummer's morning." He paused, eyeing her. "Or does this herald trouble?"

"Will you make me a cup of tea?"

"By the looks of you, you need brandy in warm milk. Is it the children, Lawrence, Harry ... ?"

"No, they're fine."

Kenneth heated the milk on the range, then took two china cups and a bottle of Hennessy Cognac from a cupboard and placed them on the kitchen table. He poured healthy measures into both cups before adding the milk. "Here you are. Yours is medicinal, but mine is because I enjoy the taste."

Helen inhaled the rising vapours from Kenneth's concoction. "I've had this 'medicine' before, although the Scots prefer whiskey. They claim it conquers colds and worries." The concern on his face made her swallow the drink, and then stammer, "I'm pregnant."

"Pregnant?" He laughed, his expression changing to relief. "So, it's the morning heaves I'm witnessing, not something terrible."

Men are so adept at distancing themselves when pregnancy crops up. "You don't understand ... I'm in a quandary."

"Why? Husbands on leave get their wives pregnant. What's wrong with that?"

Can't he guess? "Stop being flippant."

"I'm just saying pregnancy is a natural occurrence in marriage. You need Lawrence to coddle you."

"Lawrence? Coddle me? This child could be yours."

"Mine? That's a leap."

"Not considering what we've been doing. You're not impotent, are you?"

"No, but I doubt it's mine. Lawrence was home within days of our last tryst, and we've always been careful." He rocked back in his chair. "You didn't play the role of a nun while he was home, did you?"

"That's of no account. You're forgetting how you and I ended our quarrel. We were frantic. Remember?"

"You mean you didn't take precautions?

"We were on a roller-coaster of emotions, Kenneth. I won't play the penitent here."

Kenneth reached out, but she shifted away. "Are you telling me there were no 'frantic' moments between you and Lawrence? No omissions, no forgetfulness?" he asked

The choice she made the night of Lawrence's birthday still confused her. She couldn't meet his eyes.

"Your silence speaks volumes, Helen. Was your omission an insurance in case you were pregnant by me?"

"You make it sound so premeditated."

"Was it?"

"I didn't reason it out." She stood up and crossed to the window. "Premeditated or not, instinct tells me this child is yours." Her head throbbed.

"Why do you think that?"

"Because I was the only one involved on both occasions."

"That's no proof."

She sat and faced him again. "What if the child takes after you?"

"Margaret and Alex aren't peas in a pod."

"It's a risk. There must be a way to sort this out."

The bang of his hand on the table rattled the cups and made her jump. "Don't bloody think of abortion."

"What? I didn't mean—" But Kenneth was at full throttle.

"I'm not a practising Catholic, but abortions are offensive and illegal ones are bloody criminal. I told my unmarried sister that when she came looking for money. She didn't listen and died from being pierced with a knitting needle or some other device in a back alley." With shaking hands, he spilled more brandy into his cup.

Helen felt her face flush with dismay. "You mean you *lectured* her? She needed your help for god's sake! Maybe she'd been abused! Did you even ask? With your help, the child could have been born in seclusion and adopted. I doubt your convictions have comforted you since." His bleak look made her stumble to her feet. "Kenneth, I'm sorry. It's best I leave."

Stunned by his thinking and her reaction, she hurried out. She couldn't take back the words she'd dished out, but before she'd reached the top of his driveway, she promised never to question the baby's paternity again. When the baby was born, though, she would instill in the child all things Irish.

§

"What splendid news, if a little surprising," Lawrence enthused, when Helen telephoned him later. "We were quite tipsy that night. I don't know how you didn't fall off the banister." He chuckled. "Maybe we'll have another son."

"Or daughter. What am I supposed to do now?"

"Have the baby."

"Lawrence, I'm managing a hotel. Margaret gets at horrible odds with Alex, and ... well, Harry comes into the bar too much." She waited, unaware of holding her breath.

"Is there anything else worrying you?"

"No, other than I need help. Thank goodness you're not on the front lines. You can plan being home for the baby's birth, can't you?"

"Yes, but meantime, hire a nanny and change Margaret's boarding to full time. Also remember Alex attends school in Athlone in September. That should help, don't you think?"

"Yes, it will."

"It's reassuring for me that Harry is there for you. Now I must go. A staff meeting calls."

The phone clicked and Helen shook her head. Lawrence's response was miraculous, but the more kind and constructive he became, the more shame enveloped her.

The next morning, while she attempted to eat dry toast, Harry appeared. She hid the damp cloth she'd been holding to her head and forced a smile.

"Hello, you look relaxed," she said. "Money troubles sorted?"

He loaded a plate with scrambled eggs, sausages, and pancakes, then sat beside her. She thought she would gag. "I'm happy to report they are, me darlin'. Deacon came to my rescue, bless his wicked heart, so all's well." Between mouthfuls hastened down with tea, he looked at her sideways. "What's wrong, luv, you're looking queasy. Should you be seeing a doctor?"

"No, he can wait another few months." She looked down and touched her belly.

Harry stopped his fork midway to his mouth and gave a low whistle. "My goodness, are congratulations in order?"

"Well, it wasn't planned, but yes, and Lawrence is pleased."

"And our friend?"

Helen shook her head. "We're not talking, and I'll thank you to mind your own business."

"Anything I can do for you?"

"Yes. Is there a woman you know who is not in love with you and would make a good nanny?"

"Such gems are not in my usual cast of friends, but I'll see what I can do." He lifted the tea cozy off the pot, filled her cup, and added two teaspoons of sugar. "Drink this. I don't imagine hangovers differ much from morning sickness. Buck up, old thing, you're not alone."

CHAPTER 16

OCTOBER 1942

TOWARDS THE END of the month, Cooper and Daecon sat at Cooper's kitchen table, Daecon balancing profit-and-loss columns in a ledger, and Cooper writing secret codes in a notebook. Beside the letters 'FP' coded two down, three up, Cooper entered a number and grinned. *This will stump any nosy-parker, including the Belfast boyos.*

Sunlight slanted across the table's scarred surface. The gouges reminded him of his mother's Belfast kitchen. He missed Ma—already gone two years from a heart attack and buried near Da in the Falls at St. Paul's Church. At least her Dublin years had been worry-free, with no Ulster Constabulary roadblocks or violent scenes to upset her. After a runaway horse killed Aunt Mauve, he'd bought Ma her own house.

She had laughed when he waltzed her around the grand kitchen. "Sophie and Brendan should be here with us," she'd said, catching her breath, "but they won't move. Eamon neither."

Now, with Sophie 38, and childless from the proddy beating years back, he wished he had pushed harder. At least he sent money when he could. Shame Eamon had stayed put, but then, he was an IRA man.

Whenever they caught up at Da's old watering hole, blokes touched their caps to them out of respect. Eamon always looked as if he'd climbed out of a bog, and himself the boss man, strolling in dressed like a banker. And yet, when Eamon tried recruiting him for the Cause, Eamon had poked a finger in his chest and their roles had changed. "You're a wasted man, Cooper. 'Tis a shame. The Brotherhood needs men with your know-how."

Eamon was always quick to boil, so Cooper had taken care answering. "Being on the outside makes me useful—the boyos should know that. Trouble is them new council fellas ain't helping your Northern campaign, Eamon. Your friends are still getting killed, captured, or executed." On seeing the angry glint in his brother's eyes, he added, "Not that I'm against the movement, mind. Tell your comrades, if they need more ammo or explosives, I'm their man." He pointed to Eamon's empty glass. "Want another?"

"Aye. I'm right glad you'll help. Them Brits got terrier snouts, and many of our stash places ain't around no more."

Cooper made steeples of his fingers, thinking of the benefits to be gained from Eamon's complaint. "That's a shame. Have you and your pals forgotten the carrying capacity of ladies' knickers?"

Eamon sniggered. "I ain't heard that one."

Cooper reached into his wallet and put a fiver on the table. "Here you are. I have to go. I've a crooked politician to fleece within the hour, and a bed-battle to arrange for later. If you're looking for new hiding places, I'm your man."

Eamon gave a brief nod and covered the note with his hand.

A crow dropping a hazelnut on the pavement outside the kitchen window ended Cooper's reminiscences. He watched the bird swoop for the broken pieces. *Cunning bastards. Like me, they know how to nick booty and hide it. Thanks to Eamon's wagging tongue, maybe I've got myself a new caper.*

"Catching cobwebs are you, Cooper?" Daecon bantered, sliding the ledger along the table. "I'm ready with the numbers."

From the rise of his voice, Cooper sensed good news. He scanned the entries and flicked his cousin a grin. "You're a smart fella, so you are. We're in clover—money in the bank and suppliers aplenty feeding our coastal racket."

Daecon wandered over to the sink, and dumped the remains of his tea. "We'll get good mileage out of Harry. With him from an uppity family, the constabulary ain't likely to be looking his way. Keep him flush, and he'll give us other fish to fry. Did I tell you he's chummy with that journalist bloke, Kenneth Inglis?"

"Is that a fact?" Cooper asked, glancing at his watch. "Jaysus. Kathy will clip your ear if you don't get home for supper. It's a long drive."

Left to himself, he fried two eggs and bread, liking the egg whites curled at the edges and the bread crisped on both sides. He slid the lot onto a plate and wolfed it down. Satisfied, he poured a second cup of tea and propped the *Mayo Daily*

Leader against the teapot. On scanning the local news an article grabbed his eye. *What damn-fool Irishman fills his head with the fecking English war and doesn't get to the rights of his own people?* Fuming, he flung the paper to the floor just as the phone rang. It was Sophie.

"Cooper, its Brendan; he's dying. Not a soul in that stinking Crumlin Road Gaol will let me see him. I'm at my wit's end." Listening to her, Cooper clenched and unclenched his hands, imagining his fingers squeezing a scraggy neck. After hanging up, he stared at the paper and hawked a string of phlegm at the article's byline. *Well, Mister Clever-arse Reporter, reckon it's time we had us a cozy chat.*

§

The newspaper's head office stood a hundred yards from a small park. Cooper leaned against a pillar of the vacant bandstand and checked his watch. Two schoolboys—skipping school, he reckoned—cross-passed a football on the grass. Closer in, a playful black lab sniffed the shrubs and ignored the tugs of its leash by the owner—a young woman bundled in winter clothing. To his left, an elderly couple with canes poked along the path. No one else around—no cops, nosy-parkers, or layabouts—which made it a grand place for confronting a newspaperman.

Cooper prided himself on his patience, which he was exercising now, as well as his vigilance, which clung to him like dandruff, and his judge of character, which more than once had saved his hide. He could assess a person's temperament just by the slant of their mouth, the shift of their eyes, and their body language. Best though was the walk—Eamon's tough-guy strut, Deacon's heavy tread, or the loping stride of the right-honourable Kenneth Inglis approaching him now. One look and you knew this wanker viewed the world from a high perch. He'd be pitching headfirst into his arms by the end of this meeting or his name wasn't Cooper. The bugger's face nagged him. He straightened and ground his cigarette stub underfoot.

"You must be news hungry; you're on time."

The face staring at him never cracked a smile. "I know you. Didn't you run afoul of the law way back?"

So that's it. "I was in a wee jam, and you were just a nosy cub scrounging stories for the rewrite boys if I recall." He reached into his pocket for another cigarette, and lit it with a flick of his thumbnail against the match head. "A fecking small world, ain't it? Drop the niceties. Let's take a stroll."

"I've not come for a stroll."

"Suit yourself," Cooper said, and patted a space beside him on the stage steps. "Why are you being a holy Joe about the Brits' war when our IRA boys battle for our rights?"

"Because a world war supplants the IRA's cause."

"That ain't no reason to ditch the Movement. Bugger foreign powers. You should concentrate on Ireland's troubles; that's what matters."

"So, you're a Belfast radical. I'm yet to see violence achieve change."

A chilling wind cut through a copse of black alder and swirled leaves and debris against the bandstand. Cooper shrugged deeper into his jacket and sucked smoke into his lungs. "Scared shitless to do your bit, are you?"

"I don't promote personal agendas. I inform readers, so they can make educated choices."

Cooper picked a flake of tobacco off his lip with a yellow-stained finger. "You starry-eyed wonder. Don't you understand politicians are double-faced and shaft our people at every turn? Have you forgotten your history, boyo?"

"Your blinkered view stops you seeing both sides of the coin, Cooper. Don't preach to me. I know Ireland's history."

"There's only one side for free Irishmen, or have you sold yourself off like a street slag? It's about time you stood up for us." Cooper laughed at the curled hand ready to strike and pulled a piece of paper from his overcoat pocket. "Let's see if you can write on what them bastards up north are doing to our imprisoned IRA men. Phone Sophie at this number."

"Who's Sophie?"

"My sister. She lives in Derry. Her husband is dying in Belfast's Crumlin Road Gaol from the treatment they're doling out."

"You want me to stir the pot to spring your brother-in-law? Jaysus."

Cooper scowled and watched a flight of white-fronted geese fly overhead in tight formation, honking as they passed. "Do it. If you succeed, your newspaper will treat you proud. If you don't I'll be dropping by the hotel to take another gander at your girlfriend."

He didn't get to see Kenneth's reaction, because the black lab, now trailing its leash, lifted his leg against the bandstand, then darted at the old couple nearby. The man rained blows before the leash tangled around his ankles.

"Stop with the cane!" Kenneth shouted, bounding off the steps, and grabbing the lab by its collar.

The dog's mistress yelled at the old man. "It's only a puppy, ya old git. Quit your squawking!" She knelt and comforted the dog. "There, there, Brandy. Not your fault you got loose." The dog licked her face. Mouthing her 'thanks' to Kenneth, she led the lab away.

"Ya skinny hoor!" the old man yelled after her.

"Shut your mouth. Canes are for walking, not hitting playful dogs," Kenneth said. "Try saying 'Sit' or 'Stay,' next time."

"Who are you for telling us what to do?"

The old woman tugged his arm. "Padraig, let's away for a cuppa tea."

Cooper watched them limp off and clapped his hands at Kenneth. "I didn't think you had it in you."

"Learn from it, Cooper. It's hard enough keeping the peace between our own kind, let alone taking on Belfast prison officials. I'll call your sister, but don't expect miracles. Stay away from the hotel."

"How so?"

"Because you don't want me spreading your mud on the front page. If there's a story, I'll write it, but leave the McKellan family and my personal life alone."

"Touchy, touchy. You're getting your knickers in a twist. I'll be watching for your article—maybe become one of your fans—but don't tell me where I bloody want to drink."

§

A week later, Cooper arrived at Daecon's house for lunch. Kathy waved a newspaper at him. "That columnist of yours has stirred the sewer rats."

Planting himself at the kitchen table, Cooper read to the end of the article, and then held up four fingers and bent them one at a time. "Sleep deprived. No privacy. No communications. Captives treated worse than common murderers. I'm thinking we have ourselves a grand new mouthpiece. Wait 'til Eamon gets wind of this."

"Do you think Brendan will be released now?" Kathy asked, as she passed plates of mutton stew around. "I've been praying for him—and Sophie."

Same as Ma, always praying and scurrying to church. "Yeah, I'm hoping. Deacon, anything further on Inglis? The IRA boys will want him giving them newspaper space, so we got to keep the pressure on him."

"Aye, we're holding a royal flush. Seems the McKellan missus is in the family way. Harry has the word out for a nanny. Bloody miracle the long reach the husband's third leg has."

"Yeah, it takes some beating," Cooper smirked, while soaking a crust in the gravy. "I'm thinking Inglis is the odds-on favourite there. What if we got a nanny of our choosing into that nest? No telling what she might find out."

CHAPTER 17
NOVEMBER 1942

THE LAST PERSON Helen expected to see walking towards her on the estuary's shingle was Kenneth—his long-limbed body leaning into the wind, his hair as unruly as the Marram grass dotting the shoreline. She stuck her hands in her raincoat pockets, took long breaths, and waited until his crunching footsteps halted in front of her.

"I've been trying to muster the courage to see you for a good hour."

"Am I that daunting?" she asked.

"Sometimes. It's a grey world without you, though. Can we forgive each other?" He gave a tentative smile and frowned at the dark shadows under her eyes. "Are both of you keeping well?"

She'd forgotten how much she loved the mellow timbre of his voice. She spread her fingers over her belly. "I'm not sleeping much, but we're managing and I'm not showing notably yet." She pointed to a small boathouse set back from the estuary bank. "Harry converted that into an art studio for me. Let's get out of the wind and talk there."

A wood stove, a trestle table made from a plywood door, two canvas-backed chairs, and a cupboard furnished the space. She watched him take in everything—cups on hooks, canisters holding paintbrushes, unfinished canvasses leaning against the wall, and two shelves crammed with books. He nodded at the framed picture of Alex and Margaret, and admired her watercolour of the estuary and sand dunes. Trite apologies weren't needed, for she knew forgiveness embraced them both.

"This is my Benevolence," she said.

"When I'm away, I picture you in a place like this."

So, I'm there ... in his thoughts. The words warmed her. She gestured towards her work table. "Alex helped Harry make that. Margaret and I painted the studio."

He walked over to the books and trailed his fingers across the titles. "You've discovered Irish authors: the great novelist and playwright, Brendan Behan, and Padraic Colum. Did you know he was one of the Abbey Theatre founders? And you're reading Oscar Wilde too. You'll be quoting Irish poetry and singing ballads soon."

"Do you love me?" she asked, unable to stop herself.

"That mighty question deserves more than a one-word answer. Too often men use the word love for their own ends, and women use it as barter. You and I have never done that to each other, but we're not free." He came close and stroked the side of her face. "You're beautiful. There's a shining core within us that will survive, whatever happens. I'm committed to you and that will never change."

She put her arms around him and buried her face in his neck. "I wish we could—"

"Hush. I know. I see you have a bottle of Murphy's homemade mead. Shall we break it open?"

While he nudged two chairs closer together, she filled their glasses. "With the baby coming, we can't return to the way it was, Kenneth. Can you accept that?"

"I can, and if doubts bedevil you later, remember this evening."

For a while, they sat in companionable silence and watched twilight bring its magic to the dunes and water. When she had finished her drink, Helen looked at her watch and sighed. "It's getting late. I can't linger. It's singsong night. Will you come and play a game of darts with Harry? He misses you."

"I will, but first, I have to warn you about someone. He goes by the name of Cooper. Although he's not a big man, he's—"

"That name sounds familiar. Murphy mentioned him when we first opened. Called him a vicious dog. I believe I saw him. He was lounging at the side entrance. Something about him made me uncomfortable."

"He was probably sizing up the bar and its customers. Cooper is an opportunist. He looks for marks. If he shows his face again, avoid him, and contact me at Benevolence or at work. Promise?"

Helen faltered, remembering Harry's debt with the Belfast bookie and his raid on her safe. She wanted to tell Kenneth, but she couldn't break her pact with Harry. "Yes. I promise."

Kenneth handed her a wallet-sized card. "Ryan works at head office. Here's his number. He can always reach me, even if I'm away. Am I allowed to kiss you before you go?"

"Allowed? Since when have you needed to ask?"

He helped her to her feet, kissed her, and whispered in her ear, "You didn't hear this, Mrs McKellan, but I love you."

CHAPTER 18

JANUARY-FEBRUARY 1943

AT PRECISELY ONE-THIRTY in the afternoon, Big Ben chimed the half hour. Lawrence checked his watch—thirty minutes before his presentation. To avoid the sight of shattered buildings, he chose a route through St. James's Park to reach Admiralty House.

The park bordered Buckingham Palace, and its lake had been a sanctuary for pelicans for over a century. The first time Helen saw the birds, they had delighted her. He took her there during their courtship days, and one had preened its rose-tinted feathers beside her on a bench, while another had perched on the backrest and peered over her shoulder, as if reading her newspaper. Helen was a typical flapper of the time—ropes of beads, short skirts, and cloche hats—and loved dancing the Charleston. Even now, twelve-weeks shy of giving birth for the third time, her energy surprised him.

His short Christmas leave had gone well. No sign of the detestable journalist. Margaret, still horse mad, had developed curves, and Alex, a gangly adolescent, had completed his first term at Athlone's boarding school. Harry had even invited them over for lunch after Christmas. The renovated barn to house extra cows and the thatched roof had pleased him, but where had he found the money?

"Well, we farmers are a close-knit bunch, so we are," Harry told him in an Irish brogue. "Farming techniques have changed, which means costly upgrading, so we give each other a helping hand. Call it barter. For example, we lend equipment, plough fields, build barns, and harvest crops."

"Who buys your produce?"

"Shops, markets, hotels, the public. Which reminds me, I must cancel our business chat tomorrow. I have an exchange transaction for petrol. Can't cancel it."

That left Helen driving him to Dublin to catch the plane. Behind him, Alex and Margaret playing 'I Spy' had given him a private chuckle.

Now, in sunlight devoid of warmth, he watched a gaggle of geese splash-land on the park's lake and realized he should quicken his pace. He had Yarrow's snooping skills to thank for the upcoming meeting. Auntie had found and read his notebook at his work station while he was away, and told Commodore Dwyer the salient details.

He arrived at Admiralty House with minutes to spare. A middle-aged woman led him to a conference room, where he set up his visual aids. Once the attendees had taken their seats, Commodore Dyer appeared, nodded to him and gave a short introduction. Lawrence thanked him, and versed in verbal communication, launched into his presentation, varying his tone, and maintaining eye contact.

"To halt the U-boat's tactics in the Atlantic, we must target their Milch Cows," he said and pointed to an illuminated wall map behind him, which showed Ireland's west coast. He tapped the coastline bordering County Sligo and County Mayo. "This is where we should focus our efforts." A civilian scribbling in a notebook beside the commodore caught his attention. Dennis had warned him that no meeting was complete without Intelligence making an appearance. "The IRA wants arms and money. In return, the enemy wants food, water, oil, and medical supplies," he continued. "It's a win-win for both parties. The U-boat wolf packs stay longer at sea, and a well-armed IRA hampers the British." He emphasized his remarks with nautical charts, which showed tidal information and indentations of the shoreline, and concluded with a recommendation that west-coast farms be put on watch.

"If farmers and IRA smugglers *are* collaborating, then our surveillance should tell us when and where a Milch Cow will surface. A night raid on the submarine will cut the wolf packs lifeline *and* leave Ireland's neutrality intact."

A small group of uniformed men argued amongst themselves, before one of them raised his hand. "Despite U-boat successes, America's anti-U-boat campaign will turn the Battle of the Atlantic in our favour," he said. "Your suggestion seems ill-advised in the face of Ireland's neutrality."

Lawrence shook his head. "It could be a year before what you suggest happens, sir. We can't afford to wait. The Americans have their own troubles to solve on *their* side of the Atlantic. Putting aside Ireland's neutrality, if we cripple a Milch Cow *now*, we can stop the U-boats momentum, so I stand by my recommendations."

From the corner of his eye, he saw Commodore Dwyer draw his hand across his throat in a 'kill' sign. He thanked the Admiralty for their time, put away his papers, and wondered how long his report would languish in a wait-bin. As he donned his jacket, he looked up to see the commodore approaching.

"You overstepped the mark, Lawrence. You brought in politics, but you managed your exit well enough. The Admiralty will review your proposal. Now follow me." They entered an adjoining room, where a man stood at the window looking at the overcast sky. "Admiral Ewen Montagu wants a word with you. We'll talk later."

The admiral walked over and shook Lawrence's hand. "Let's sit, shall we? More informal. The commodore tells me you see angles to solving problems that others don't. We need people with your mental agility, McKellan." He checked the room, frowned at the opened door, and lowered his voice. "I'm having you transferred and inducted into Naval Intelligence straight away. We're not as generous with leaves as Bletchley. You'll need to tell your wife it's unlikely you'll be home for your child's birth. I trust this doesn't present problems?"

Untold problems. "None I can't solve."

"Good, then walk with me towards my club. Don't mind my driver following behind us. He'll drive you to the station once we're done. As we go, I'll fill you in on aspects of MI5. We're the domestic arm of Intelligence, although crossovers with MI6 do occur. You'll find it intriguing, to use a pun."

On the train back to Bletchley, Lawrence knew there'd be fireworks from Helen, but Montague would not have appreciated a demonstration of self-interest. He had suggested, during their walk to his club, that he refer to MI5 as The Service. "It says nothing but stops questions." As Dennis had sermonized over drinks one evening, "Those who serve their masters know full-well they walk through the valley of subservience until the light doth shine from within." *Amen to that,* thought Lawrence, as the train pulled into the Bletchley railway station.

He braced himself for the call to Helen the next day. "You mean you will be incommunicado for an *unknown* length of time, and you *won't* be home for our child's birth?" she asked. "Are you incarcerated in a concentration camp?"

"Helen, I have no control over the war. It's that way for enlisted men."

"I'm losing count of the times I remind you that you are not an enlisted man."

"I'm an Oxford graduate, not a private. The Service is a specialized division. Don't let's quarrel. How are you since I saw you at Christmas?"

"Sticking out a mile and waddling like a duck."

"A duck? I saw ducks in a park yesterday." *Good thing I substituted ducks for pelicans. That was close.* "Are the children behaving themselves?"

"Alex is enjoying school, but since Harry bought him an air-gun during a weekend break, he takes pot-shots at the crows. I've told him to practice on empty bottles instead."

"Boys will be boys."

"That's an excuse for plenty of things, isn't it? As to Margaret, she has inveigled Murphy into giving her cooking lessons, for when she lives on her own. Nothing else to report, other than Harry has promised your son driving lessons, once he can plough a straight line, and I have hired a nanny."

"Who is she?"

"Mary Flanagan. Harry found her. She's from Dublin and reminds me of an English nanny—hair plaited into a coronet, a blue serge dress, and an embroidered apron. She's widowed, childless, and has no family ties. Nice Irish lilt to her voice."

"I'm glad Harry helped. You're don't sound so anxious about him now."

"That's because he's busy and not in the bar much. He's breeding sheep—better than pigs I suppose."

"Not gambling at the race tracks, is he?"

"I'm not his keeper. Have you a number where we can reach you?"

"Use the same number. They'll route you through or you can leave a message. I'm not on the moon."

"You might as well be."

CHAPTER 19

MARCH 1943

HELEN WATCHED THE rain flog the estuary with the fury of a cat-of-nine-tails and longed for sunshine to shrivel the bleakness of March. The weather reminded her of a nursery rhyme, *Rain, rain, go away. Come back another day,* but the word *nursery* brought a smile.

Margaret and Alex had helped Mary alter a guest room into a nursery, down the hallway from the parental suite. And Alex, asked to look after his mother by Lawrence, plumped cushions, ran errands, and persuaded Harry to take them into Ballina for sticky buns and toffees. He did not take kindly to being teased that those were his favourites.

"So what, Mum? It's not right that Dad isn't looking after you," he'd said, staring at her with the resentment of a twelve year-old.

In letters to Jill, she admitted sleep escaped her, but since she had bedclothes to keep her warm, food and clothes, and the loudest bang was a car backfiring, she must count her blessings despite Lawrence's unexplained absences.

Disheartened by the water-logged landscape, and rain clouds that billowed in vast waves above the sand dunes, Helen turned and went into the dining room, which stayed locked between meals. Seated at the piano, she flexed her fingers and let the light textures of Mozart's *Fantasy in D. Minor* fill the room. In the adagio section, a spasm of pain shot through her. She stood up, but a second spasm caused her to double over and call for help.

Brigid ran in from the kitchen, followed by Mary, who had been having tea with Murphy. "Put water on the boil, Murphy, and phone the doctor!" Brigid shouted. "Mary, grab that chair. You need to support the missus under the armpits. Good! Now Ma'am, hook your arms over Mary's knees. That's it."

Helen clenched her teeth in a haze of sweat and pain, as tablecloths were pushed under her and she felt herself being hoisted into a crouching position. "This babby will slip out nice and easy," Brigid told her, checking the dilation.

"Can't you help me upstairs or into my office?"

"No time, Ma'am, but don't worry, no one is getting through them doors. Watch me now, and breath in ... that's it. Hold it ... and out."

Someone wiped her forehead, and made her sip water. *Was that Margaret?* "Push, Ma'am. Push." Helen strained and a sharp contraction made her shriek, and then Brigid, kneeling on the floor, guided the baby, blood-streaked, into the world. It gasped and cried but Brigid, accustomed to birthing calves and foals, waited two minutes then clamped and cut the umbilical cord. Mary eased Helen into a different position, then cleaned and swaddled the infant in a soft blanket. The afterbirth came soon after and Brigid removed it and the soiled linen.

She returned with Dr. Flattery, who hurried to Mary and checked the baby's vitals. Five minutes later, he beamed and placed the infant in Helen's arms. "Respiration, muscle tone, and reflexes appear normal, Mrs McKellan. Let's help you to your room. Your little girl was certainly impatient to arrive. Brigid, you'd make a grand midwife."

Brigid giggled. "Thank you, doctor. I hope to be a wife of *some* kind one fine day."

§

A week later, sitting in an oversized armchair Harry had found and placed in her office, Helen shifted her new daughter within the bend of her arm. "You don't know it, little miss, but you've been a small earthquake around here. I'm left wondering what after-shocks are to come."

That morning, Harry had presented the baby with a set of Beatrix Potter books. "She's a little beauty. Remarkable red hair, very Irish ... What are you going to call her?"

"Kelsey. Brigid says it means female warrior. If her hair stays red, she'll have my father's Sullivan genes to thank."

"Sullivan genes? Well, fancy that." Giving her an amused smile, he kissed her on the cheek and said he had to hurry off to an auction.

Spring sunshine streamed through the window and highlighted a vase of daffodils and orchids on her desk. They were from Lawrence. He'd sounded subdued on the phone and apologized for his absence. Despite Kelsey's name not being Scottish, he said he liked it, but only after learning it had Celtic origins. Helen had sighed relief. She had spent hours trying to find a name he would accept.

Hearing a discreet tap on the office door, she expected Mary, but Kenneth walked in carrying a hand-carved cradle, complete with bedding. "I'm here to pay my respects to mother and daughter," he said.

"Are you, really? I thought you'd forgotten Kelsey and me."

"Kelsey? That's a grand Gaelic name. May I hold her? You sound irritable. Postpartum blues, is it?"

"The baby is blameless, but *you* are another story. You're here, you're there, you will, you won't—I don't know where I am." Tears rolled down her cheeks.

He kissed the top of her head. "Don't be raining on the wee mite. May I pick her up and see how she likes her new bed?" He lifted the baby into his arms, rocked and crooned to her, then lowered her to the cradle, placing her gently on her back. "I'm sorry for my silence. I was in England to report on the airfields the Americans need for their bombers. They're ruining the countryside. Hedgerows have gone and thousands of trees uprooted, because the planes need long runways." He put a foot to the cradle and rocked it. "You and I will have a grand time, Kelsey. I will be your very own special Irish uncle."

Helen looked at him askance. *Uncle?* Could he not see his likeness? The red tinge to her hair, the shape of her head? Was he pretending blindness? Or did she see a likeness where none existed? "For a man who says he's inexperienced with babies, you handle her well."

"It's easy. She's just a smaller, wondrous edition of you."

"Flatterer. Where did you find the cradle?"

"In Derry—through a good fellow who spent too long in prison for the unthinkable crime of wanting Ireland's independence. He made it for me because I reported his maltreatment at the hands of the authorities. They let him go. When is Kelsey's father coming home?"

"He's here now, or do you mean Lawrence?" A slight draft made her look past him to the door. It was Mary, her face bright red.

"Begging your pardon, Ma'am. I hope I'm not interrupting, but I'm thinking the baby needs changing."

Helen, hoping Mary had not overheard, put on her brightest smile. "Mary come and meet Kelsey's Irish 'uncle', Kenneth Inglis. He's a good friend of the family. Look at the lovely cradle he's given her."

"Well now, Miss Kelsey, you'll sleep well in that," Mary said. "You have the kiss of Ireland on you, right enough."

"The kiss of Ireland? That's a lovely expression, but what does it mean?"

"Well, Ma'am, if you'll pardon me, the baby was conceived in Ireland, drew her first breath in this land, and now she's blessed with an Irish uncle and a traditional handmade cradle. What could be more Irish than that?"

What indeed? Helen thought, pushing away a pocket of worry.

§

During the afternoon, Mary mixed bread dough in the kitchen and gossiped to Murphy. "It's a crying shame the war is keeping the master in England. He's that close, you have to wonder why he missed the birth of his child. Is he a nice man, the master?"

Murphy sipped his tea, then said with slow deliberation, "He's the brains in the family and no mistake. Easy to see why the missus married him. When he walks by, he moves a man to bend a knee and bow. Not one you'd warm to compared to our Harry, though. You'll decide for yourself when you meet him."

"I've not been here long enough, so I don't know the family well, but from Margaret's ways, I'm thinking she takes after her da, and Alex after his ma. It will be interesting to see whose looks the baby takes on, don't you think?"

"If I was you, woman," Murphy growled, agitating a cauldron of potato-leek soup into a whirlpool, "I'd be filling me noggin with better things than puzzling out the baby's looks. Best you dote on the little one and look after her—that's why you was hired."

CHAPTER 20

JUNE 1943

HARRY STRIVED TO coax more speed from his old, three-ton Austin, but it had the mind of a stubborn mule. He dragged on his unfiltered cigarette, and cursed the unseasonal rain and mud-filled channels which threatened to push him towards the cliffs.

Should have bought a new truck, he thought. Now it was too late. Daecon said that there'd be no more runs because Cooper suspected they were being watched. But watched by whom? There'd been no busybodies snooping around his farm, except for Lawrence. *Didn't take half a brain to know he was fishing as to how I'd financed the farm's improvements, but why the claptrap about respecting Ireland's neutrality for chrissake?*

He hunched over the steering wheel and peered ahead. He was running late. Daecon would be at the top of the trail, cursing him, but at least the rain had stopped. He rolled down the window and inhaled the sharp iodine smell of the sea. The hairs in his nose dried. Up ahead, a light blinked. Daecon.

Harry dimmed his headlights, and slowing the truck to a crawl, inched down a steep incline. He pulled in under the lee of a rocky outcrop and waited for the unloading of another vehicle ahead of him. Once it had laboured back up the slope, he manoeuvred into the vacant spot. Like routine, three men emerged from the shadows, and working in silence, unhooked the truck's tarpaulins and hefted his freight onto skids.

Harry checked the time: 12:30 a.m. He waited until Deacon and the men had disappeared beyond the sharp bend in the trail. Since this was the last run, why not find out what happened to his produce, where it went and who paid for it? He reversed into his original space under the rocky outcrop, then got out and followed the trail which cut between wind-blown sand dunes until it widened onto the beach.

Daecon was overseeing the transfer of goods to men in rowboats. The only sounds were the crunch of boots moving back and forth across the shingle and the slap of paddles as the loaded boats pulled away.

Harry crouched behind a tumble of rocks, which extended into the surf, and scrunched his eyes. Who the heck owned the boats? He followed them as they paddled towards something that hunkered in the water. Was he going nuts? A whale? No—a conning tower! *Jaysus! A big, fucking German submarine!* Cooper was bloody-well aiding the enemy, and he, Harry McKellan, was helping fill the fuckers' bellies!

But even as the truth sunk in, his imagination flared. Think of being submerged for days in one of those behemoths—the weight of the Atlantic pressing against the hull and depth charges threatening to split the sub open. He shivered and pulled his jacket tighter. He should leave, but a man moving towards the sand dunes unbuttoned his fly, bent on taking a piss. It was Deacon.

§

Group Captain Andrew Macklin and his navigator, Nathan Coles, climbed into the cockpit of a Bristol Beaufighter. The twin-engine plane was armed with a 4x20 cannon, a machine gun, and carried a torpedo attached to its belly. Due to the quietness of its engines, the plane was used for night operations and painted matte-black. It earned the name "Whispering Death".

As a boy of six, Macklin had made paper planes, which he floated from his bedroom window. At twelve, he hung balsa models on fishing line from his bedroom ceiling. By fifteen, he was a full-fledged air cadet, and at nineteen earned his wings from the R.A.F. Pilot Training School in Surrey. After flying de Havilland Tiger Moths, and an American Harvard, he arrived at Scotland's R.A.F. Coastal Command and flew missions for the Admiralty. Gifted at flying low-level night missions, Coastal Command selected him for undercover assignments.

"Let's get cracking! We've got a two-hour window before the weather closes in again!" Macklin shouted above the revving engines.

Coles gave the thumbs up. "I'll give you a fresh course when we reach Tory Island," he yelled. When Macklin got the 'go-ahead,' he pushed the throttle forward, made minor adjustments to the trim and flaps, and the plane, moving with increased speed, was airborne. They were over the Irish Sea, heading south-west by midnight, and would reach the target at the precise time recommended by Naval Intelligence. The rain clouds had dispersed, making visibility excellent. At an altitude of 5,000 feet, Macklin throttled back to cruising speed.

At 12:40 a.m., Coles tapped Macklin's arm and pointed port side. A light flashed from the headlands. Macklin banked hard to the left, and the Beaufighter dropped altitude fast along the shoreline.

At one hundred feet, he straightened the plane out, skimmed over a beach, and headed towards the sea. Seconds later, he released the Beaufighter's solitary torpedo and banked as the 'fish' hurtled towards its target, now illuminated by the plane's Leigh searchlight.

§

Harry heard the plane moments before it whooshed overhead. Daecon and two men raced for cover and Harry tried to escape too, but he trapped his leg in a narrow cleft and could do nothing but watch the submarine's tracer fire light the sky. A ferocious explosion split the air, followed by flames shooting skyward from erupting fuel tanks. Red-hot metal hurtled onto the beach. Deafened by the noise and unaware of blood leaking through his jacket, Harry gaped at the oil-slicked sea, now strewn with human wreckage under an impassive moon.

§

Wakened from a drunken slumber, Cooper staggered to the front door. It was Deacon. "Can't a man get a decent shut-eye around here?" he grumbled. "Come in." Deacon slumped into a chair and rubbed a swollen jaw. "Got in a fight, did you? What brings you *here*? This is my *bolt hole* from Dublin."

"Fecking quit the bellyaching, Cooper. I've been trying to reach you for twenty-four hours. Our job came unglued. We'd just got paid when a warplane comes from nowhere and bombs the shite out of the submarine. The fecking thing blew apart right afore our eyes. There were no Germans on the beach. They was rowing back with a load of crates. Bloody miracle me and our boyos are still standing. We found Harry taking a sneak peek. Got wounded and leg jammed in the rocks, poor bugger. We carted him back to his farm, and the vet came over and picked a load of shrapnel out of his shoulder. Harry will be a limping, one-armed drinker for a while now. Nosy eejit, he'll have to think up a grand story for that."

"Will our boyos talk?"

"Not them. Harry neither. He won't want his brother and the English bloody army up his arse."

Cooper frowned, thought for a moment, then said, "Okay. Pay the lads, but nothing for Harry. He broke the rules. Now if we—" The phone jangled and cut him off.

"Cooper? There's a meeting. Noon today. My place," the caller said, and hung up. *Paddy, the messenger? Jaysus, what now?*

"Daecon, let yourself out. We'll talk later ... and stay away from Harry."

§

He arrived on time, knowing it didn't pay to be late. Paddy and two IRA fellows were already there: Frank the heavy and Sweeney the talker. Sweeney thrust a newspaper at him and pointed to a photograph, and the column below it. "Read it—aloud."

Could the bugger not read for himself? Cooper glared at the photo and skip-read. *"Four bodies found washed up on the beach at Dunegan Bay. Shoreline debris includes broken crates and farm produce. The beach approach was churned to mud from heavy vehicles but tire tracks are still visible. The area is cordoned off until further notice."*

"So, what you got to say, Cooper?"

"Quit with the bully-tone, Sweeney. You don't like what happened? Me neither, but we've arms and money for the Brotherhood. The Belfast boyos won't whine about that, will they? Tell them there'll be no wagging tongues from my men. None of us got injured, and it was our last run, so get off me back." *Jaysus, if the fuckers get wind of Harry, I'm a goner.*

"Thing is, Cooper, you've drawn attention to us. We ain't partial to that. Take a gander at the second page."

He read fast, all the time feeling his face redden. *"If smuggling incidents continue along Ireland's coastline, there will be far-reaching ramifications. Blundering ... Greed ... Small men with grandiose ideas ... "*

He ripped the paper in half. *Who the hell is Inglis to pass judgment?*

"Gets under your craw, does he?"

"I'll set him right."

"You won't; we need him. Keep to your corner of the pen, Cooper."

Frank weighed in, all two hundred and twenty pounds of him. "One warning is all you get, boyo; you understand?"

Cooper flashed a confident smile. *Fuck 'em*. "You can trust me."

Paddy produced an opened whiskey bottle, and everyone took a swig to pledge their agreement.

Once outside, Cooper scrunched his eyes in the sunshine. Not such a bad day. He could have been meeting his maker. As to Inglis ... *Plenty of time to set that bugger right.*

CHAPTER 21

JUNE 1943

LAWRENCE SUPPOSED MI5 had John Churchill, the first Duke of Marlborough, to thank for their grandiose home at Blenheim Palace. He learned that Winston Churchill, the duke's descendant, had transferred MI5 to the palace when bombs fell on its Wormwood Scrubs headquarters, and the fire hoses were as holey as Swiss cheese. What a rag to riches story that had proved. A call from Dennis, impersonating a BBC announcer, broke the quiet.

"Good morning! Here is the 10:00 a.m. news. Lieutenant Commander Lawrence McKellan is to receive a bottle of Napoleon Brandy from the boys of Hut 8. Due to McKellan's brilliant presentation, the big cheeses at Admiralty got off their arses, and Coastal Command destroyed a Milch Cow off Ireland's west coast."

Lawrence dropped the document he'd been reading. They'd listened to him. "Are we at war with Ireland now?"

"No, but there's stink for violating neutral territory. What were we supposed to do? Send a perfumed invitation to de Valera? *Dear sir, kindly vacate the beaches before we remove a blot on the landscape.*"

Lawrence yanked a map from his desk drawer and spread it open. "Where exactly did this happen?"

"Dunegan Bay. A few inlets south of your hotel."

"That's close. Okay, we'll share the bottle later. Right now, I've work to do." He closed his eyes and ran probabilities through his mind, then telephoned Helen on the pretext of missing her.

"Are you a mind-reader, Lawrence? I was about to call you. Harry's had an accident. He heard noises in the paddock so he investigated, but without a torch. Says he tripped over a rusty scythe. He's on crutches and has a bandaged shoulder—sliced open he said. I doubt he'd have told me had I not popped in for eggs.

"Had he been drinking?"

"I didn't notice empty bottles."

"How did he manage to raise a doctor that late?"

"Not a doctor, a vet."

"A vet?" *Bloody hell.* "How is he now?"

"Said I wasn't to bother you, but I felt I should. He'll be fine. I'm relieved, since Margaret's school play is today and we'll be in Dublin for two nights. Kelsey is in Mary's care."

"Good, good. Enjoy Dublin. Must go. It's hectic here." Making a kissing sound, he replaced the receiver.

§

Hours later, Lawrence stormed through Harry's front door to find him easing his pain with a glass of scotch before the fire. Crutches lay on the floor, and the cat snoozed on his lap.

Seeing him, Harry struggled to stand but winced and slumped back. "Jaysus, can't you knock first? What the hell are you doing here?"

"You know damn well why I'm here."

"Rats to Helen. I told her not ring alarm bells."

Lawrence gritted his teeth. "For once in your sorry life, stop playing the fool. A submarine gets blown to smithereens at Dunegan Bay the night you're injured, and I'm supposed to believe it was a rusty, fucking *scythe?*" Harry took a large gulp of scotch but said nothing. "You never stop to think, do you, Harry? Well consider this—your farm renovations have come at the cost of hundreds of dead, merchant sailors. Your actions are bloody treasonous! My problem is what to do now."

Harry flushed. "You mean you're here because you believe I've betrayed our side? For chrissake, I'm not the enemy, Lawrence!"

"No? But you *helped* them. A vet sees you in the middle of the night, and when Helen turns up, you spin a cockeyed story. I always wondered how you were financing those farm upgrades. Come clean, Harry, or you'll regret it."

"Get off your lofty perch, Lawrence. What do you know about debt or how it can make a man desperate? You've had it easy, dear brother. A fat inheritance. Best of everything. No kowtowing for you. I did it because I had money problems I couldn't solve. Someone steered me to a fellow called Cooper, who bought my debt. To pay it off, I had to work for him. That's the sum of it."

"Is Cooper from the village?"

Harry shrugged and gave a garbled account of seeing him in a pub brawl, and that he was a dangerous man to cross. "I had no fucking choice—or should I have robbed a bank?"

"You should have called me. Stay put. I'll make tea."

In the kitchen, Lawrence stirred sugar into the tea's impenetrable brew and looked through the window into a jungle of shadows. Despite his exasperation, he understood Harry's resentment and reluctance to seek help from him. The problem now was how to conceal the truth from MI5 and prevent further trouble from Harry. Grimacing at what he must do, he returned to confront him.

"Here, drink this." He waited until Harry had sipped a quarter of the cup, and then said, "You're out, Harry. I'm calling in my loan. There are farmers who will gladly take on this farm."

Harry spluttered. "Lease this farm to another farmer? You must be nuts! You think I'm the only one who smuggled goods?" He pulled a handkerchief from his pocket and honked his nose. "Look, I've lost my appetite for easy pickings. I just wanted to pay my debt, save extra money, and show you what I could do with the farm."

"Spare me the justifications."

"Have some faith. In a handful of years, I hope to pay this lease off—and *not* with ill-gotten gains."

"It won't work if you continue hanging out with delinquents." *Why am I even arguing with him?*

"That's just it, I don't hang out with them. Once they've reeled you in, it's hard to wriggle off the hook, but if Cooper approaches me again, I'll tell him I can't take a shit without you knowing. That should put the wind up him."

Lawrence sighed—trust was forever at arm's length once you uncovered someone's deceit, even a brother's. "I don't like it. Does Helen know? Does anyone else?"

"Helen? Don't be daft." Harry turned away and fumbled a pack of cigarettes from his back pocket. "Help me light one of these. Thanks. Kenneth might know. He meets plenty of scum in his business, and there's always gossip."

"Has he talked?"

"No, although during a dart game, he once warned me to look out for odd business deals, because they could be IRA related. But his advice came too late."

Lawrence took one of Harry's cigarettes. Sometimes the distinction between right and wrong *could* become blurred. Harry wasn't a dangerous criminal. He was merely hostage to his own habits, but he was a *McKellan,* and he was right about leasing to another farmer. *The devil you know is better than the devil you don't.* "All right. You can continue with the farm, but one false move and I'll pull this place out from under you faster than you can place a bet."

Looking like a fish that has escaped the net, Harry gulped and reached for the scotch. "Can we ditch the tea now and have a drink together?"

"No. Since Helen and Margaret are in Dublin, there's no reason for me to stay. Lay off the booze and drink the tea." At the door, he gave one final instruction. "Don't tell Helen, or anyone, that I've been here. Is that clear?

Harry gave a two-finger salute. "Scouts honour, guv."

CHAPTER 22

AUGUST 1943

EIGHT WEEKS LATER, Lawrence, with suitcase in hand, returned to Ireland and climbed into a Dublin taxi. "The Shelbourne Hotel, please."

"Are you from London, sir?" the driver asked, flipping on the meter. "I've heard tell the city suffered something awful."

"For weeks it looked like an inferno. The outskirts didn't get it to the same extent as the docks and business areas, but at least half of London needs rebuilding. That's not all bad though, since the city's infrastructure needs modernizing."

"It must have been a terrible sight. I've got a cousin missing in action. It's a crazy world—Irishmen fighting alongside Englishmen." Clearing his throat, the driver swung into the traffic.

How many Dubliners shared that sentiment, Lawrence wondered? Working for MI5, he must watch what he said.

"Are you new to the Shelbourne, sir? Did you know the hotel hosted the 1922 drafting of the Irish Constitution under Michael Collins?"

Pretending interest, Lawrence let him launch into further morsels of Irish politics, while he relived his recent catch-up with Dennis at Oxford's White Horse Tavern.

The tavern's burgundy walls, plastered with local scenes, politicians, and caricatures, gave no sign war besieged Britain. Dennis sat at a table beneath oak beams displaying beer tankards hanging from hooks.

He stood the first round. "How's the secret life, old chap, with its hidden entrances and exits, disguises, and people answering to 'M' or 'C'?"

"You've been reading too many spy stories, but you're right. We wear deception as casually as an overcoat these days."

Dennis nodded. “Have you seen Molly?”

He had, but that wasn’t for Dennis to know—not yet. At a briefing for a Montagu scheme, she walked in after an eighth-month absence. She didn’t acknowledge him, and taking her cue, he followed suit. It helped that the complex plot kept them apart. The deception involved giving a tramp who had died of rat poisoning false documents, dressing him up as an officer of the Royal Marines, then setting him adrift from a submarine in currents off the coast of southern Spain.

Molly’s team fabricated the dead man’s life—education and dental records, as well as receipts and a personal letter. Lawrence’s team created a bogus ID, including fictitious parents, a faked birth certificate, a fiancée called Pam, and a dog.

The body of ‘Major Martin’ washed up on a beach, and the Germans, acting on the documents’ false information that the Allies would invade Greece and Sardinia since Sicily was too obvious, moved their troops from France to Greece when in fact, the Allies invaded Sicily the second week of July.

After the invasion commenced, Molly appeared in his office and dropped a file on his desk. Inside, he found a folded note. *Let’s celebrate—8:00 p.m. if you’re free. I’m back in my Dover-street flat.*

Lawrence refilled Dennis’s glass. “Setting Molly aside for now, tell me, do you think our deceptive ways will cease at war’s end, or become habitual?”

Dennis licked his fingers clean of crumbs from a small, savoury pie. “You remind me of a deflowered virgin trying to get it back, old chap. Since we don’t know the answer, there’s no point in worrying.” He dabbed his mouth, and with a ‘may I’, filched a cigar from Lawrence’s cigar case.

“So, there’s no hope?” Lawrence asked, passing him the guillotine cutter.

Dennis decapitated the cigar and waited until the end glowed. “My worry is how we pick up our lives again after the war. What if our old jobs are kaput?”

“There’ll be new jobs. Technology never ceases, and you’re smart.”

Dennis made a mock salute. “Whew, that’s a relief. Are you secure?”

Lawrence grinned. “I’ll have no problems—I’m smarter than you. But yes, I suspect I will have plenty of work.”

A change in the taxi driver’s monologue returned Lawrence to Dublin, and he saw they were now travelling along O’Connell Street. “I thought I’d take you this way,” the driver said. “The River Liffey is grand this time of the morning.”

Sunlight glanced off the dome of Dublin’s Customs House, rebuilt following an IRA fire ignited two decades ago, and the way the Liffey meandered through the city reminded Lawrence of the Thames. He noticed that the population lacked the pinched look of their London counterparts. Good to see mothers with children in tow—a sure sign enemy planes were not patrolling Dublin's skies.

When the taxi pulled up at the hotel, he gave the amateur historian a fat tip. Aware Harry had to drive the distance from Killala Bay, he left his suitcase with the hotel porter and decided a walk would do him good.

A bookstore two blocks from the hotel lured him inside. Nothing pleased him more than the smell of books and leafing through antique collections. He headed towards that section, but a familiar face on a book jacket caught his attention. Flinty eyes and an austere cut to the mouth had replaced the man's easy-going look, but it was Kenneth Inglis all right. Lawrence skimmed through the book's essays and stopped at one that compared the relationship of Ireland and Scotland to Westminster. According to Inglis, Ireland being separated from England by the Irish Sea gave its people a sense of independence; whereas Scotland, joined at the neck, was more susceptible to Westminster's influence. Grudgingly, Lawrence agreed.

A sales girl, with her red hair twined into a braid, approached him. "That author is a savvy writer," she said.

He handed her the book. "Have you met him?"

"I have. I used to work at Hough's Pub near Belmullet, and Mr Inglis was a regular. He's a fine, generous man with a smile that knocks the ladies over. He helped me get a loan."

"Is that so?" While the girl rang up the sale, he recalled how Helen had defended Inglis's views the first time he met the man. Irritated, he fumbled the change from a pound note and hurried to leave.

"Sir? Don't forget your book."

Outside, cars crunched past, and the pavement now teemed with Dubliners. He tossed a coin into a vagrant's cap—Inglis wasn't the only generous man in Ireland.

Settled in a comfortable chair in the Shelbourne's lounge, Lawrence delved further into the book. Inglis's views on Ireland being united with a greater voice abroad were radical, and worse, implied fewer relations with Britain. A waiter clicked cups and saucers onto a tray, while a bluebottle buzzed among the ferns. Everywhere the air moved to the monotonous hum of pontoon fans. Despite Inglis's incendiary opinions, Lawrence yawned and let his eyelids fall.

§

"Hello, old chap, still the classic academic, I see, book in lap and eyes closed?"

Lawrence started awake and cast Harry a mock-scowl. "What do you expect? You're late."

Harry clapped him on the shoulder. "Irritable, are we? I soft-pedalled here because of petrol shortages, so kindly shut up. A pint and a ploughman's lunch would go down a treat."

"Good idea," Lawrence said, and pushed himself out of the chair. He hadn't seen his brother since the surprise visit, but Harry showed no embarrassment, and he was still a consummate flirt. The exaggerated swish of the barmaid's hips, as she brought their order, proved his rangy looks still stirred the women.

"In case you're wondering," Harry said, before sinking his teeth into a slab of cheese and bread, "I've expanded the dairy again, by eight head."

"By legal means I hope?"

"A widowed farmer's wife had a distressed sale, so I put my oar in, so to speak."

Lawrence shook his head. He'd caught the double entendre, and wanted to pursue livestock costs but changed his mind. Instead he asked, "Is the hotel doing well?

"Busy. There's a steady stream of fishermen putting old Isaac Walton's book, *The Compleat Angler,* to the test. Most 'angling' for a break from the war, and none 'compleat' without their bellies warmed by medicinal whiskey and food."

Lawrence chuckled. Harry and Dennis could be stand-up comedians with their throwaway lines. "How is Helen ... and the baby?"

"Fine, they're both just fine," Harry said, a shade hesitant, "but it's not good you haven't seen Kelsey yet. With luck, your arrival will give Helen a well-deserved break. I kept mum about that clandestine visit of yours by the way." Suddenly, he sprang to his feet. "Must make a phone call. I'll be back in a tick."

Lawrence did not miss the well-thumbed racing form protruding from Harry's jacket pocket, nor the reproach in his voice. Harry was right. How did a husband gloss over seven months of neglect? He couldn't *keep* trotting out the war as an excuse. And if Helen felt overlooked, did Alex and Margaret? Would he ever arrive home without handling marital strife? He was glad when Harry reappeared with a smile and a jaunty spring to his step.

Over coffee, they avoided further family talk, and instead discussed the defeat of Tunisia and the surrender of Field Marshal Rommel's Afrika Korps.

"Since Irish war news is minimal, Harry, how do you know so much?"

"I've got my sources. There's my newscaster chum, Richard, and don't forget Kenneth. I see you've got his book. Any good?

"I fell asleep over it."

Harry made a slow reach for his wallet. "Right, well ... let's go. Drinks on me?"

Lawrence grinned. He wasn't going to fall for *that* ploy. "Of course," he said.

While he familiarized himself with the car—its sweeping fenders, outrageously long hood, and massive headlights, Harry stowed the luggage.

"Catch!" Harry said, tossing the car keys. "You drive. We're collecting Alex for the weekend. I'll be the navigator."

Forty-minutes later, they pulled up at the school on the outskirts of Athlone—an historic town because it had possessed the sole bridge over the River Shannon when county wars had plagued Ireland.

"Alex said to look for him in the bleachers."

Lawrence spotted him cheering on a football team from the sidelines. His son had sprouted in his absence. "Hello, Alex, how is your team doing?"

"Dad! I almost didn't recognize you. We're up three-nil. I hope to join the squad as a midfielder next year."

"Great. Harry says you make good passes and dribble the ball well. I trust you're packed? We should go."

"Can't we watch ten more minutes?"

Lawrence tapped his watch. "No, the other side won't win now."

At the car, Harry claimed the back seat. "You two catch up; I need a nap."

Alex climbed in, and as they journeyed, Lawrence endured sullen answers to his questions about school life, friends, and favourite subjects. It made him examine his own reticence when Helen plied *him* with questions. No wonder she bristled. At Castlebar, he detoured to the golf course. "Need to stretch my legs. Alex, you come with me. Harry, we'll meet you in the clubhouse."

With his son in tow, Lawrence took a side path alongside a fairway. A twosome trudged past, golf bags slung over their shoulders. From somewhere, an errant ball zinged overhead and rattled among the trees. "What's got your goat, Alex? We can't solve things between us unless you stop sulking. I noticed that dig of yours about not recognizing me."

Alex kicked at a broken tee. "So what? You're a stranger. Dads come home; you don't. When you do, you lecture us. No fishing or playing golf with you. Nothing.

You don't know me or Margaret. You told me to look after Mum, and I've tried. All you've done is send a bunch of flowers. You're always telling us you're too busy fighting the war, but you're not a soldier; you're a civilian. You don't wear a uniform." Red-faced, he halted as fast as he had started.

Lawrence stifled a laugh. His son looked and sounded the same as Harry had at that age. "Well done, lad! Now listen to me. Even if I'm not in combat uniform, I *am* fighting, but with my brain, not my body. I don't stay away from home because I *want* to. I have no choice. Many fathers will *never* come home. How would you like being an evacuee in a stranger's house, or hiding under your school desk every time a siren blared? You play football and don't get strafed by Messerschmitt fighter-bombers; neither do you wear a gas mask nor spend hours in an Anderson shelter. Be thankful your mother and sister are alive, that you are safe, and Uncle Harry is here. War is not a game. Shape up, Alex, or it will be military academy for you. Every school report claims you could do better. When we continue on with this trip, I suggest you exercise your brain and think about what I've said."

They were silent as they walked back to the clubhouse. Alex picked up a stick and swung it back and forth like a putter. "Do they teach shooting and have target practice at military academies?"

"Of course."

Alex smiled and knocked the head off a daisy.

CHAPTER 23

AUGUST 1943

HELEN SMOOTHED HER new dress over her hips, hoping Lawrence would appreciate the russet colour—a colour she had favoured over the obligatory white at their wedding in Dunblane Cathedral—and not notice the extra pounds she still carried from Kelsey.

Someone clearing their throat made her look towards the bar's entrance. "Lawrence? Goodness! How long have you been standing there?"

"Long enough to see having a baby agrees with you."

She bobbed a curtsy. "You're just being nice. How was Alex when you saw him?"

"Mutinous. To appease him, Harry and I are taking him trout fishing near Castlebar. Right now, I'm anxious to meet Miss Kelsey McKellan. Where is she?"

"Asleep in the nursery, I hope. Come on. Patrick can manage without me."

Kelsey was sucking the paw of Margaret's knitted rabbit when they arrived. Lawrence stroked her plump cheek and attempted to pick her up, but she opened her eyes and gave a loud screech. He started backwards. "Good heavens, she's got good lungs. What's that on the corners of her mouth?"

"Milk. She's teething, so she drools. Look, she's smiling now."

"She has lovely grey eyes. For now, let's allow her to drift back to sleep. Where is my other daughter?"

"At a friend's birthday party in Ballina. I told her you would understand. We'll collect her tomorrow after breakfast."

"I would like to pick her up on my own, if you don't mind. That way we can get reacquainted. Speaking of which, Mrs McKellan, have I got you to myself tonight?"

"You have. Settle in while I arrange for supper in our room and make a general check that all is well with the staff."

§

Lawrence waited until Helen's footsteps had receded down the stairs before entering their suite. It smelled of jasmine and roses—Helen's perfume. A breeze stirred the window's silken sheers. He walked over and listened to the estuary's restless ebb and flow, and felt inexplicably lonely, as if he belonged nowhere. He recalled Dennis saying, *absence makes the heart go yonder*, but surveying the room he felt *absence makes the husband ponder* more accurate.

Helen had redecorated the room. The walls were papered in soothing tones of lime-green and honeyed yellows, and Persian rugs softened the varnished floor. Against a wall, a rosewood bookcase carried novels by Virginia Wolfe, Hemingway, and Robert Graves—English, American, and Irish writers but not a single Scottish one. He frowned. Sir Walter Scott should have a place in that bookcase. Above the fireplace, photographs jostled for space on the mantelpiece: their wedding photo, Helen with Alex and Margaret at a beach, and a new one showing Helen with Kelsey asleep on her shoulder—Madonna and Child. He looked closer. He'd never seen such a soft expression in Helen's eyes. Had Harry snapped the picture? It should have been him. A fission of shame sent him to the liquor cabinet for a glass of scotch.

His suitcase—left by Alex no doubt—stood next to a new, three-panelled screen, which separated the L-shaped part of the suite. Curious, he stepped behind it and stood dumbfounded. Silk cushions lay in disarray on the quilt, and above the bed, a tapestry of iridescent material shimmered on the wall. The bedside lamps displayed cream shades fringed with tassels. What in hell had possessed Helen to make such changes? A Bedouin chief might delight in the colours and tassels, but a McKellan? At this rate, she would take up belly dancing next. He imagined her shimmying towards him, sweat oiling her skin, lips parted in a smile, breasts jouncing. Shaken by the erotic image, he strode into the bathroom and ran a hot bath. When it was full, he slid beneath the water's surface until reality brought him gasping to the surface.

§

On her return, Helen found Lawrence relaxing in lightweight clothing, and Kelsey cocooned on his lap. "The two of you make a perfect picture," she said. "I hope she didn't squeal this time."

"Not once. We're getting acquainted." He gestured towards the mantel. "Whoever took that photo has a good eye."

Helen stiffened and answered quickly, "Harry is quite adept with a camera." She tried to lift Kelsey, but Lawrence stopped her with a shake of his head.

"Let her stay until supper arrives. Come and sit beside us. Look what I bought in Dublin. A book of essays by Inglis. They're quite revealing, politically."

"I'm not surprised, although I've only read his newspaper articles."

"Is he still playing darts ... coming to your Friday night singsongs perchance?"

"No. He's more often away on assignments these days. Lord knows where." Idly, she picked up the book and thumbed through the pages. "I'm not mad on essays. Give me a good biography, or better still, a historical novel." She put Kenneth's book on the coffee table and launched into Harry's conversion of the boat-shed. For good measure, she included the contributions of Alex and Margaret to the project.

"Speaking of family endeavours," Lawrence said, freeing an arm from Kelsey and making an expansive gesture, "the new carpets and wallpaper are excellent, but the rest has me worrying I will wake up with sand in my bed, or behave like a sheikh calling for my hookah."

"Hooker?"

"A Bedouin water pipe—not a camp follower."

She clicked her tongue and fixed her eyes on Kelsey. "So, the gypsy influence doesn't appeal to you? I thought our room a delightful contrast to the staidness of Edinburgh bedrooms. Never mind, it's easily changed. But not the cushions. I like them. Are you enjoying your new work? Is it still hush-hush?"

"Same as ever. I'm trying to get longer leaves though—a week every three months."

"That would be miraculous, but I won't count on it."

A light tap on the door signalled Brigid. She entered with a tray bearing steamed trout, salad, and a fruit flan. Helen moved swiftly and lifted Kelsey into her arms. "Bedtime," she cooed. "I'll be back in a moment," and left Lawrence complimenting Brigid on her midwifery skills.

§

Hours later, unable to sleep, Lawrence watched the moon cast a pale finger of light across the floor. Try as they might, he and Helen had circled each other warily all evening, and it had not improved. He rolled over and reached out to her. "Are you awake?" Although she said nothing, her hand grazed his. He moved closer and kissed the corners of her mouth, and her eyes. They tasted salty. "We'll come through this, Helen. The war won't last forever." He stroked her back until she turned and moved into his embrace.

In the morning, he left her sleeping and startled Mary when he stepped into the corridor. Her quick step back with the baby in her arms made him wonder if she had been eavesdropping. "Good morning," he said, tickling Kelsey under her chin. "You must be Mary, the nanny. My wife tells me you are of great help to her, and that Kelsey adores you."

Mary blushed. "It's a pleasure working here, sir. The little one keeps me going. She has a mind of her own, for sure."

"I'm not surprised. She's her mother's daughter. Is Alex up?"

"He's having breakfast with Master Harry, sir."

"What are you doing with Kelsey?"

"It's bottle time, and that means a nice cuddle with her mama, sir."

"Is this the usual routine?" Mary nodded. "Then don't let me interrupt."

§

On the day of his departure, Lawrence stood outside admiring the rain-silvered lawn. His leave had gone reasonably well, especially when sexual activity returned to the marriage bed after the first night. Kelsey no long turned purple when he picked her up, and the fishing excursion with Alex had lessened the boy's resentment. He and Margaret had reconnected well too when he fetched her from Ballina. As for Harry, it seemed his efforts to avoid trouble were working. Certainly, the new cheese and butter enterprise with Murphy flourished.

Although he did not take Helen away for a break, he did end the leave with a shopping spree to Ballina with her and Kelsey. He bought soft toys, baby clothes, the latest BB gun for Alex—that had brought a smile—and a sewing machine for Margaret. Best for him personally was finding an illustrated copy of Peter Pan written by J. M. Barry, a Scottish author. He put the book in the middle shelf of the rosewood bookcase.

Satisfied with his assessment, he carried his suitcase to the car parked in its usual space next to the kitchen. Appetizing aromas wafted from the window and Flynn appeared, wagging a hopeful tail for scraps. "You've been swimming in the estuary, haven't you, old boy?" Lawrence said, crouching to scratch the dog's damp belly. Flynn thumped his tail.

From the kitchen, Mary's voice carried through the open window. "Is it the luck with them cards keeps our Harry's farm ticking along so well, Murphy? He's mixing with shady types, so I'm told." Lawrence stayed still as stone.

"Ach Mary, are you always for stirring up gossip? He's got friends everywhere, our Harry—rough types, farmers, tinkers, businessmen, you name them."

"And what gossip might I be stirring?"

"Nothing now, although long afore you came here, I'm on my way home from a late night with me pals and passed him on the headlands. Later, I heard tell he was laying wagers over in Ballinrobe, the money coming out his pocket thick as salmon. He wasn't the only farmer doing that, but no matter, that's history. He's doing grand now."

There was a pause broken by a tap running and the clatter of pans before Lawrence heard Mary's voice again. "I don't know about Master Harry, but Kelsey has me wondering—the red tint to her hair and those eyes of hers. Shouldn't we be seeing a likeness to the master?"

"Jaysus woman, if you don't hold your prattling tongue, I'll be putting you out the door. Quit thinking. It ain't good for you."

Lawrence crabbed away from the window and walked slowly to the car.

"Dammit, man, you look miles away," Harry said, rounding the corner. "Is London beckoning you that much with new challenges? For us, it will be routine as usual."

Lawrence grunted—there was nothing routine with Harry, and Mary's comments stirred odious speculations.

CHAPTER 24
SEPTEMBER 1943

Cooper looked up from the kitchen table and rolled his head to loosen his neck muscles. "I should quit reading these feckin' newspaper rags, Daecon. Now Kenneth is yapping about *Ireland maintaining its neutrality* and *more vigilance needed against those who nurture empathy for the enemy.* Empathy? He's a bleeding head case, our Kenneth. He needs straightening out." The two men were in Cooper's west-coast hideaway, planning ways to kick-start a new scheme without provoking IRA scrutiny.

"What you got in mind?"

"Plenty. But right now, ask Kathy to buy a rubber ducky and rouse Aaron. I've a small job for him in Killala Bay."

"At the hotel? Why don't you use me?"

"Don't be daft. We don't want us linked that much, do we? Aaron is the man for the job, and when he's done, he can hang about and watch my back."

§

The bar was at full throttle when Cooper saw Aaron saunter in the side entrance and join him at a table near the dartboard. "That errand didn't take you long. Any trouble?"

"None. Found the old biddy as easy as downing a pint."

Cooper grinned. "Speaking of pints, order us a couple. Tell the chest at the counter where we're sitting. I'm figuring my journalist chum won't be slow getting here, seeing as it's singsong night. When he shows his face, stay close." While he waited, Cooper scanned the crowd. No sign of Harry. Still lying low. *Dandy job the vet did so Deacon says—bet there's plenty vets done them jobs over the years.*

Cooper and Aaron were half-done with their drinks when Kenneth arrived. Cooper watched him scan the room, then advance towards them the way a boxer enters the ring. Aaron vacated his chair, and Cooper pushed it towards Kenneth with his foot.

"You and me needs to talk," he said.

"No, we don't. From what I know, you shouldn't be here."

"Sez who? You'd be smart to quit your holier than thou prattle."

"I think—"

Cooper thumped his fist on the table. "I don't fecking care what you think! What's happened to you? You rant on about smuggling, then this vigilance and empathy shite, and yet our boys still waste away in prisons. There hasn't been a bloody word from you since the bastards released Brendan, a wreck of a man. Buying a fecking cradle from him don't count. You're a slacker. You haven't continued to badger the government. Not a fecking word." For emphasis, he thumped the table again.

Seamus, doing his Friday-night duties, stormed over. "Hey you, quit the racket." Cooper gave him a murderous look, then shrugged and leaned back.

"Short of a prison break, what do you suggest?" Kenneth asked when Seamus left. "Have you not learned yet that the government turns a blind eye when it suits them? I hear your northern chums paid you a visit."

"So, you've fallen back on gossip, instead of facts, have you?" *Time to make this boyo sweat.* He jerked a thumb towards the bar. "A fancy piece, the missus. Be nice if she stays that way. You must have scared her. She ain't there now. How old is the new kitten in the litter? Wouldn't want her in harm's way, would we?"

"Quit playing the scare game, Cooper. I doubt your northern pals gave the nod to this visit. You're forgetting they need a public voice sympathetic to Ireland being united. That's me. The likes of you they can find under any stone."

Cooper covered his mouth with his hand and yawned. "You think so?" He sniffed the air. "That's a strong reek of ambition you're wearing, Kenneth, boyo. It could kill a man. Keep your snoz out of my business. Just to prove a point, you best go upstairs. There's a wee present in the nursery." The shock on Kenneth's face was worth the risk of breaking his word with Sweeney. He laughed at Kenneth's open-mouthed stare and beckoned to Aaron. "Let's go. I'm thinking we'll finish our drinking elsewhere."

§

Mindful of Kenneth's warning about Cooper, Helen left the bar when Kenneth moved to Cooper's table. Instinct took her to the nursery where she found Mary sitting beside Kelsey's crib clutching a rubber duck. A gift tag hung from its neck. "What are you doing, Mary? Where did you get that?"

Mary stood and handed Helen the duck, tag uppermost. "I've been keeping watch over Kelsey, Ma'am."

Helen read the tag. *A Gift from Uncle Cooper*. "My god, he was here? In the nursery? Stop wringing your hands, Mary. Sit! Tell me what happened."

Mary crumpled back into the chair. "I only met him the once, Ma'am. I worked a year in an orphanage until it closed. Doted on them poor strays. Fell to washing the hospital's floors and taking in mending and alterations. Met all sorts."

"Get to *Cooper*. How did you meet him?"

"A customer said she could find me work as a nanny. When me and Cooper met the once, he told me to wear a nurse's uniform, fancy it up with an apron, and he'd arrange references for me."

"Did you not suspect something, Mary? You put Kelsey in danger. Tell me about the duck."

Tears flooded Mary's eyes. "I'm not a bad woman, Ma'am. Please forgive me. I'll leave right now."

Helen waved the duck at her. "For the love of god, stop bleating and tell me about *this*."

Mary opened her mouth to reply when the door flew open. "Jaysus, Mary, what have you been doing?" Kenneth burst out, taking in the scene. "Explain yourself and stop your sniffling."

"Go easy, Kenneth," Helen said, seeing Mary cringe.

"I was making bread batter in the kitchen when a fellow I'd never seen calls me over to the doorway," Mary quavered. "Tells me I owe his boss a favour and to put the duck in Kelsey's crib. Seeing as it was only a toy, I said I would, but something didn't feel right, so I stayed and held the duck until her ma come."

Kenneth paced back and forth, then stopped and looked Mary in the eye. "Has Cooper wanted other favours in return for this job?"

"Just to tell him if anything odd happened. That was it until tonight."

"What if Cooper demands more? How can Mrs McKellan trust you?"

"I don't know, but I told the fellow I wasn't doing no more favours. I swear on all that's holy, I've never set eyes on Cooper since we first met. On my life, I wouldn't let harm touch the wee one or the family." Helen give Kenneth a pleading look.

"You're fortunate Mrs McKellan has a forgiving nature. No more running errands for strangers, and curb that tongue of yours. Not a word about the McKellans and their friends, understand? If you ever sense trouble, tell Mrs McKellan. Respect these instructions as you do the Holy Trinity. Have we your word?"

Mary stumbled to her feet. "You have, Mr Inglis. I promise. I'm ever so sorry, Ma'am."

"All right, Mary. Take the weekend off to think about this, and if you want to stay friends with Murphy, be careful. He has no time for Cooper. He would *never* forgive you if he knew what you did tonight."

When she left, Helen grinned at Kenneth's surprised look. "A little coercion never hurt. Now it's your turn. I suspect, you know the reasons behind this, don't you?"

"It's my editorials. Cooper wanted revenge and planned this to teach me a lesson."

"My God, Kenneth. He *knows* about us?"

"No, he gambled. He trades on blackmail and intimidation, but he won't push like this again. Trust me. Being a newspaper man has its powers. I'll get rid of the duck, so put this behind you. I see Kelsey is awake. May I hold her?"

Helen nodded. Seeing Kelsey in his arms made her wish they could spend more time together as a family. Unaccountably, he caught her thought.

"Without disturbing the status quo, can we do more of this?"

She laughed. "You mind reader. Yes, but only in Benevolence. Will that work?"

"Always."

CHAPTER 25
SPRING 1944

A BLUE SKY, STRETCHING as far as she could see from her office window, promised a rainless day. Pleased, Helen helped Kelsey wobble barefoot to her stroller, then wheeled her into the kitchen garden.

"Doggie," Kelsey said, flapping her hand at Flynn. He trotted over and pushed his wet nose into her hand.

"Mum," Alex called from Harry's car, parked at the front entrance, "we're ready to leave."

Mary, who had been planting peas and lettuce in the kitchen garden with Brigid, wiped her hands, and hurried across to help settle Kelsey into Harry's homemade bucket seat. "It's good weather, Ma'am. Has Kelsey got her rabbit?"

Helen smiled. "I wouldn't dare leave without it." Margaret's knitted rabbit was still the favourite, despite a teddy bear from Lawrence during his two-day Christmas visit—the possibility of longer breaks had never materialized. For some unfathomable reason, he had been curt with Mary, and had not taken his customary tour of the farm. She had been thankful when he left.

Today, Harry was taking the family to the races and Kenneth had hinted that he might come. To keep gossip at bay, he only dropped by the bar for the occasional Friday night singsong or a game of darts with Harry, but at Benevolence, they were a family. Last week, when she'd arrived with Kelsey for an afternoon together, she found a blue-painted high chair in the kitchen, and he had turned a corner of his study into a play space. A growing problem might develop when Kelsey could talk, but that was months away. Right now, the sun was out, Alex and Margaret were reading, Kelsey was clicking wooden beads and blocks around on a children's abacus, and Harry was in charge of the day.

§

Rather than take his eyes off the road, Harry nudged Helen in the passenger seat to retrieve a packet of Navy Light cigarettes from his jacket pocket, light one, and put it between his lips.

"Can't you quit?" she asked.

"I'm working on it." It was an old refrain. He blew a smoke trail out the window, his mind on Ballinrobe. The town was God's gift to County Mayo. The market allowed him to sell his produce *and* place bets, plus Biggins Pub on Bowgate Street sold Bushmills single-malt whiskey. Not that Biggins would be a feature today, or taking a tumble with the dark-haired waitress after closing hours. He shifted the car into a lower gear and winced. His shoulder still hurt. Although he and Deacon got together for a drink or met at farm auctions, he hadn't laid eyes on Cooper for months. A good thing too, although he missed the money.

"Almost there," he said, pointing ahead to the racetrack's entrance.

Alex lifted Kelsey from the safety seat and held her on his knee. "We're going to see racehorses," he said.

Margaret sniffed. "She's only a year old, she doesn't understand."

"She does; she's smiling."

"Don't be daft."

"I'm not."

Helen shook a finger at them. "Don't start you two."

Harry parked and killed the motor. A few yards off, the pedestrian walkway bustled with vendors hawking programs, drinks, ices, and souvenirs, all for bargain prices. Makeshift booths sold beer, cotton candy, and sausages on sticks. Harry eyed the roped-off tracks curving into the distance, thinking it the best sight in the world, and hoped Lady Luck would smile on him today.

As everyone clambered from the car, a familiar voice asked, "Need any help?" And there was Kenneth, planting a kiss on Helen's cheek before lifting Kelsey from Alex, so he could set up the stroller.

Harry grinned. *Kenneth and his daddy skills.* "Nice seeing *you* here. Never knew horse-racing interested you."

"Then you don't know Irishmen. We don't have to gamble to enjoy watching horses gallop."

"Where *are* the horses?" Alex shouted over the noise.

"In the parade ring, silly," Margaret said.

"Harry, how do you judge a good horse?" Helen asked as they walked over.

"You look for an eager eye, a healthy coat and good stride. You also have to understand their body language. Stay away from those that have their ears pinned, toss their heads, or swish their tails."

"Why? Is tail swishing bad, Uncle Harry?"

"No, Margaret. It's a way of communicating how they feel. Sometimes it means they've had a good dump, or the bit hurts, or there are too many flies around. But here in the ring, it's often a sign of frustration. See that bay over there? He's showing the whites of his eyes, which means he's fearful. And that one with the dancing fee? He's eager to get going."

More interested in ice cream and a young girl, Alex broke away with the shilling he'd won off Margaret in an I Spy game, and headed to where the girl stood by the ice-cream vendor. Harry winked at Kenneth and cocked a thumb at Alex's retreating back. "There's a healthy sign. Into his teens and feeling his oats."

Margaret leaned over the paddock's rail to admire a black horse walking towards her. "Oh, what a beauty," she said, and stretched a hand to stroke its silky muzzle before the jockey led it away.

Kenneth tapped her on the arm. "That one is *mine,*" and pointed to a gelding standing on three legs, with the fourth hoof drawn up slightly.

"That's Dancers' Tango," Harry interjected. "I wouldn't bet on him. That resting hoof of his hints he isn't raring to go. But the one you're looking at Helen, that's Murphy's Quickstep. Good cantering style. Sometimes breaks into the air instead of out at the starting bell, but he has an excellent jockey."

"Then that's my horse," Helen said. "Have you chosen yours?"

"I'll check with my favourite tout and decide after I've talked to him. Kenneth, would you save us a good spot at the rails? I'll catch up."

Kenneth raised his eyebrows. "While you get the inside story? Maybe I'll pick a dark horse while you're gone."

"If it wins, then I'll believe clouds can rain salmon," Harry laughed, before heading towards the stables.

Out of sight, he tilted his hip flask and let a stream of raw whiskey burn its way down the back of his throat. This was the life: the crowd's excitement, horses itching to get into their stride, and a wee spot of money burning a hole in his wallet. Pocketing the flask, he sauntered into the barn and breathed in the warm, sweet smell of hay and fresh horse droppings.

"Are you here, Mick?" he called, and advanced deeper into the stables, his boots making wet tracks on the hosed-down cement.

"He's not, but have you a tip for an old pal?"

Harry blinked and readjusted his eyes to the gloom. *Bloody hell. Him.* "O'Malley's Triumph. Ten to one odds, last time I looked."

"Right you are, then," Cooper drawled coming into view. "You look surprised. Did you think I'd gone to my maker? Or did you think we'd leave you alone for all time after rescuing you that night?"

"Thanks a bunch for reminding me," Harry said. "I've paid my debt to you. So, don't try roping me in on any of your other schemes.

Cooper flapped a dismissive hand. "Don't be giving me the guff, Harry. Beyond having a chat with your pal Inglis, we've kept well away from you." He tilted his head, and peered at him. "What's with the surprise on your face? Did your pal not tell you we met in the hotel bar? My, that Inglis is close." He spat on the floor. "To business. We need your potato cellar. The disused one. Daecon says it's perfect, since trees screen it from the road."

Harry chewed his bottom lip and imagined his fist connecting with Daecon's nose. "What do you want with my cellar, for chrissake?"

"To store black market stuff that will fetch a few quid when it's safe to sell."

"What *stuff?*"

"That ain't your concern."

Harry grimaced, but if Cooper wanted his cellar, then why not charge rent for it?

Cooper laughed. "You're an easy one to read, so you are. We'll keep the cellar padlocked—dirty the lock, so it won't look new. All you have to do is forget the cellar's there and get paid monthly."

Harry made an effort to banish a nagging image of Lawrence scowling at him. Letting Cooper rent his cellar for dead storage wasn't doing anything *active*. He wasn't breaking his word, not really. Besides, he could always claim ignorance of its use. *If I let the bastard wait a while, maybe I'll get a better price.* "I'll think on it," he said.

"You'll tell me now."

"No, I need time."

"Ah now, Harry, you wouldn't be snubbing me, would you? I've ways of persuading you."

Alarmed, Harry scanned the line of stalls on either side, but there were no thugs swinging bicycle chains or brandishing clubs.

"I said I'll think about it."

"Do you have fire insurance, boyo? Is the water in your paddock safe? I've heard tell bad things happen to farm stock around these parts. Think on that, and do it fast."

Before he could answer, a voice shouted from the stable's doorway. "Harry, are you there? They'll be closing the betting for the race, if you don't come now."

Kenneth's voice. "I'll be right with you," he called, and blocking Kenneth's view so Cooper could retreat into an empty stall, he strolled into the sunshine. "I found my tout, and you'll see the benefits of that when my nag crosses the line first."

"Maybe your winnings might not be worth the effort."

Was he being a smart arse? Had he spotted Cooper? You couldn't always tell with Kenneth. "It's always worth the effort," he said, and making a 'follow-me' gesture, hurried him away from the stable and towards the betting office.

The horses were already pawing the ground in the starting stalls when they caught up with Helen and the others. The loudspeaker blared, "They're off!" and the jockeys leaned low on their animals' necks and fought for position.

"Come on, Dancer!" Margaret shrieked.

"Look at that! My horse and its jockey are as smooth as dancing partners," Helen enthused.

Harry guffawed. "Yeah, they'll look great doing the foxtrot while the rest of the field quicksteps past them."

"Maybe female intuition guided her to choose a horse that will waltz home," Kenneth said, giving Helen her tickets for the next two races.

"Intuition?" Harry laughed. "I wouldn't gamble on that, but if a jockey knows his animal, he can pull on its head with the reins and make it take long, or faster strides." *Like me and Cooper, but he won't pull my reins this time.*

"Coming hard down the backstretch, head to head, is Fast Boy and Proud Dragon," the loudspeakers blared. "O'Malley's Triumph is bearing in, Noble Blazer is fading to Gentleman Dandy, and Murphy's Quickstep is running wide."

Harry swept the field with his binoculars until he sighted the red and white silks of his jockey, riding monkey-crouched over his horse's withers. Behind him, others were trying to catch up, some using their crops on the animals' flanks. *Here's hoping I won't be a non-runner or worse, because I stalled Cooper.*

"It's cruel to beat the horses, Uncle Harry," Margaret wailed.

"True, but it makes them run faster." *Damn Daecon and his big mouth.*

"What a softie," Alex scorned.

Margaret tugged Helen's sleeve. "I've just seen Moira and her parents. Can she and I go to the tea tent?"

"Yes, but no wandering around. We don't want to lose you."

"Into the clubhouse turn, it's O'Malley's Triumph, Proud Dragon, and Murphy's Quickstep!" the loudspeaker boomed.

A welter of hooves thundered past, gouging the turf into flying clods. Kelsey gave a high-pitched scream. Kenneth scooped her into his arms, just as the animals raced towards the three-eighths pole, the leaders less than three furlongs from the finishing line.

"Hooray!" Alex yelled, as O'Malley's Triumph nosed past Proud Dragon to win.

"Didn't I tell you that was the one?" Harry whooped. *That should please Cooper.*

"I should have listened to you. I fancied Fast Boy."

"That's your trouble, Kenneth; you play too cautious a game. You'll never make big money that way."

Kenneth waggled his finger. "But it makes for a less bumpy road, Harry."

"Philosophizing again, are you?" He winked at Helen, who had bet to place. "Well Ma'am, I see your horse came in third. If you're as lucky with the other races, you'll be in clover."

By the end of the fourth race, Kelsey was peevish and started whingeing. "It's time we went home you poor little thing," Helen said, "you've missed your nap. It's been fun, Harry. We've done well, but don't expect a bonus because of your tout."

"What, not even five percent?" he teased. "I'll get your winnings and meet you in the parking lot."

Heading towards him when he left the pay booth came Daecon and a burly West Country farmer he recognized from the smuggling runs. Their weathered faces broke into grins.

"You're not away so soon, are you?" Daecon asked.

"You bugger. I've got a bone to pick with you."

"Ran into my cousin then, did you?"

"I did, and I should knock your block off."

"Ach now, Harry, you don't want to swing at me and put that arm of yours in trouble again, do you? Me and Connor here will be in Nosens Pub tomorrow evening. Not everything has to be business."

Why fight the messenger? Besides, he and Deacon had good times together. Salving his pride, Harry nodded and hurried away. On rounding the corner to the car park, Alex came towards him through a mess of ticket stubs, cigarette butts, and sandwich papers. He held a packet of potato chips in his hand.

"Uncle Harry, a friend of yours bought these for us at the kiosk. I've just given Margaret hers."

"What friend?"

He pointed towards a grey car, parked a row to the left of Harry's. Cooper, with his head poked out the car window, waved goodbye as casual as you please. *The bastard.* Harry grabbed Alex's chips and stamped them into the ground. "Don't bloody accept things from people you don't know."

White-faced, Alex swore at him, but Kenneth's arrival changed the scene to one of angry silence. "Harry, if you're up for a game of darts, I'll drop by the hotel later," he said.

Harry pulled air into his lungs and muttered to Alex, "I'm sorry, but that *friend* is no friend of mine." To Kenneth, he said, "We'll do it tomorrow. I must drive this lot home, and I've the animals to feed."

"Then give yourself a break. I'll take the family home."

"I'd like that. I had an early start this morning."

"Can we stop off somewhere to eat, Uncle Kenneth?" Alex asked, casting Harry a cheeky look. "I can't get a thing to eat around here."

§

The sky had a threatening, greyish look when Harry pulled up at the farmhouse. The run-in with Cooper had made him apprehensive. He clenched his teeth on stepping from the car, but only familiar croaks eddied up from the pond. A crow screeched in the distance. Staring into the silent field, nothing stirred other than the shimmy of leaves and catkins in the alder copse.

Humming *You Are My Sunshine,* he walked towards the house. A metallic odour like a rusted bucket caught him before he reached the front door. He tracked the smell to the back of the house. On the fence, a gutted lamb hung from a hook, its throat slit, its entrails roping to the ground. From the pools of coagulated blood, he estimated the butchery was less than an hour old. He was no fool. There'd be more slaughters. Refusing his cellar wasn't worth it. No one should mess with Cooper.

CHAPTER 26

SEPTEMBER-OCTOBER 1944

LAWRENCE SURFACED FROM the South Kensington tube station and hastened to the Red Lion Pub on Old Brompton Road. Today was Molly's birthday, and undoubtedly she and Dennis were already into their second pints. He patted his pocket. Molly loved Cadbury's chocolate and Remy Martin cognac. Monty Phelps had supplied both from his trove of hard-to-find items.

Molly had invited Dennis and him for dinner at her flat. Dennis had insisted on supplying the main course—a rabbit snared at Bletchley Park. A miracle, since Bletchley's rabbit population had long disappeared into cooking pots.

He hadn't had seen much of Dennis. But for Molly and him, the next subterfuge after the Mincemeat deception involved hoodwinking the enemy into believing the Allies were landing at Calais, rather than the Normandy coast. No corpse this time, instead, rubber tanks, dummy aircraft, fabricated radio chatter, and false information fed to the enemy by double agents. The trickery had laid the groundwork for the D-day landing and liberation of France.

Walking briskly, he scanned the sky as he passed two boys racing paper boats across a water-filled crater. It had become habitual to look for doodle-bugs—V1 flying bombs, which rained down on London in unrelenting vengeance one week after D-day. They sounded similar to two-stroke motorcycles, until the engines cut out and the winged bombs landed and exploded on contact. But worse followed: V2 rockets, and they were silent devils.

Big Ben struck four o'clock as Lawrence pushed open the Red Lion's heavy oak door. He liked the cramped, friendly bar—its dark-timbered roof and frosted windows reminiscent of Elizabethan times. Union Jacks covered the ceiling, and solid oak tables crowded the floor. Dennis saw him first, and giving a cheery grin, raised a pewter tankard of beer. Molly waved and wiggled along the bench to make room for him.

"Here you are, matey," Dennis said, handing him the foam-capped mug. "Thank the gods our breweries are still producing."

Lawrence kissed Molly on her neck. "Happy birthday," he murmured. Dennis broke into a bawdy rendition of birthday lyrics, involving windmills and thrills. "Aiming to take in a nude show at the Windmill Theatre later tonight, are you?" Lawrence teased.

"What! With a lovely lady present? Not on your life," Dennis winked. "There's that good rabbit stew to enjoy at Molly's first," and pointed to a well-wrapped box hidden under the table.

"Oh, those poor Bletchley bunnies," Molly said in mock horror.

"Another drink?" Dennis countered, looking sheepish.

An hour later, they exited the pub and were across the road when Dennis stopped and slapped his forehead. "I've forgotten the haloed rabbit." He rushed back and reappeared in the doorway moments later. "The little bugger won't hop away from me again!" he shouted, and held the box aloft.

Lawrence caught the roguish grin, before a fist of pressure flung him into the railings of a basement flat. An ear-splitting *whomph* followed, and then silence. Dazed and disoriented, he struggled to a sitting position and banged his ears to bring sound back. Where was Molly? Dust particles clouded the air. Coughing, he wiped his eyes and saw her sprawled on the top step, leading to the basement flat. Her face had the pallor of cement. He crawled over and shook her shoulder. "Molly? Talk to me, Molly!" He brushed the hair away from her face and saw she had cuts on her forehead and a grazed cheekbone.

Slowly, she regained consciousness, her eyes darting from him to the stairs and then back. "What happened?"

"A V2 bomb. Can you move?" She bent her arms and legs, then nodded. His ankle looked swollen, and every breath hurt, but he could stand, so he helped her to her feet. "We need to find Dennis."

The dazed and injured were everywhere: a mother protecting her child from the dust with a scarf, a couple clasping each other as if they might never let go, an old man bleeding from his mouth, a woman vomiting into the gutter beside a shattered body. Lawrence cocked his head to the sound of sirens wailing in the distance.

To avoid live wires, he told Molly to stay well behind him. Picking his way over water spewing from a burst main, he arrived where the Red Lion had been. The entrance had vanished into a crater, the sides of the building leaned outward, and slabs of cement, tangled wire, and pockets of fire covered the ground. Molly caught up with him and clung to his arm. Neither spoke. They knew Dennis was gone. When the medics arrived, they pointed to others more in need. In the end, a driver in a delivery truck dropped them off at Dover Street.

Next morning, after a restless night at Molly's flat, Lawrence visited her doctor and had his fractured rib cage bound in elastic bandages and his ankle strapped. Molly escaped with a broken wrist and bruising. But losing Dennis devastated them both. When Lawrence checked in with MI5, they ordered him to take a week's recuperation—a suggestion Molly thought wise.

§

Harry met him at the airport armed with crutches. "Well, old chap, you scared the wits out of us. It's blankets and pillows for you."

"Got something stronger?"

"You have the temerity to ask me *that*?" Harry said, patting his hip pocket.

Three aspirin, followed by several swigs from the hip flask, and Lawrence didn't stir until the motion of the car ceased and Harry shook his arm. "Home is where the weary soldier rests. You were out before we left Dublin's outskirts." He tooted the car horn, and within seconds Helen appeared, with Alex.

"Don't turn me into an invalid," Lawrence growled, clambering out.

In the foyer, Helen took him into the reading room, where she explained that she and the children had rearranged the furniture to allow room for a bed. "This will save you using the stairs."

"Good thinking," he said, as Alex helped him onto the sofa.

Margaret arrived with a jug of water and poured him a glass. "Are you bandaged?"

"Ribs strapped and ankle immobile. No need to fuss. Have you come from volunteering at the nursing home?"

"Yes. Ernie collected me."

"Ernie?"

"Her boyfriend," Alex chipped in. "He's my driving teacher. I got fed-up steering Uncle Harry's tractors around in the fields. What happened, Dad?"

"I lost a colleague. I'll tell you later." A cough made him clutch his chest.

"Don't talk, Daddy; we'll look after you," Margaret said.

Lawrence smiled, then waved her and Alex away. Once the door closed, he said to Helen. "Maybe we should sleep here permanently."

"Not a good idea. The bar's side entrance is only feet away." She patted his arm. "Can you recall anything of what happened?"

"I remember little. Dennis worked in a different department from mine, but sometimes we met in our favourite pub. That night he was pie-eyed, so he waited in the pub while I got his car. That's it. I came to in an ambulance. An attendant told me a V2 landed and obliterated the pub. There were no survivors."

"It's terrible that your friend died, but I can't help being glad you fetched the car." She laid her head on his shoulder. "Rest now, and enjoy our pampering."

Lawrence shifted his weight to reach the water, took a drink, and sighed. "I'm sorry for my long absence. Thank you for not berating me. Will you fetch Kelsey? I promise not to let her clamber on me. She needs to know her daddy is alive and well."

CHAPTER 27

MAY 1945

On Monday, May 8, Helen and the children were having breakfast when Harry rushed in, scooped her out of the chair and waltzed her around the room. "The war is over me darlin'. Germany has surrendered. The BBC just announced it, plus a national holiday." Alex and Margaret whooped loudly.

When the staff and guests heard the news, their jubilation was overwhelming. Despite Ireland being neutral, the war had overshadowed everyone. Helen sat down with Harry to plan a celebration party. Once they had decided upon the date, she telephoned Lawrence.

What could possibly prevent him from coming home for a few days? We haven't seen him since his recuperation eight months ago. Even so, familiar with his lukewarm reactions she prepared herself for a skirmish.

He responded true to form. "Helen I can't drop things to rush home for a *party*. I'm surprised you and Harry have even considered it."

Inwardly comparing herself to the estuary seagulls, screeching and fighting for whatever slim pickings they could scrounge, she said, "But, Lawrence, it's a happy occasion. It should be for you too, despite the loss of your friend." Seeking comfort, she dropped her hand and patted Flynn's head.

"You haven't grasped that demobilization and re-assimilation of our forces back into civilian life will take months. Britain is short of food, housing, and clothing, and besides, the war hasn't ended. The Far East fight alongside the Americans is still ongoing."

"How awful. You sound as if you've become a clean-up man."

"I have. War-crime trials in Nuremberg will occupy many of our top brass, which leaves me and others minding the chickens."

"Well then, I will just have to do my best to explain the reason for your absence to our children." Choosing not to bicker, she turned to family news. Kelsey swam like a seal, and was learning to ride a tricycle. Harry's resident rat population had dwindled, thanks to Alex and his air gun, and Margaret was of an age to increase the human population. She had been for over a year, but it startled him, which showed how little he understood female urges.

"Good God. And Harry?"

"He's doing well. He and Murphy have expanded into a co-operative food venture. It's—" The phone went silent—likely because Lawrence had clamped his hand over the receiver. Was he with someone? She waited.

"Helen? I just checked my calendar. I can take a two-day break early July."

"Good. We'll look forward to that."

After he hung up she sat staring out the window until Kelsey said, "Mama, Walkies. Flynn."

"Those are the best words I've heard all morning. Let's go."

§

News of the party spread fast, and on the day, locals and guests filled the dining room to capacity. There were free canapes, plus sliced beef and buns, and two soup tureens brimming with Harry's potent punch.

Following a few long-winded toasts, Harry and Kenneth led a singsong. The exuberant voices made Helen wonder how long before Scottish voices rang in her ears.

The sight of Mary and Murphy holding hands, and Harry's stable boy, Mickey, clutching Brigid proved changes were coming. When the boy whispered something to Harry, Harry jumped onto a chair. "Three cheers for Mickey and Brigid! They're betrothed!"

And not a moment too soon, Helen thought, since Brigid clearly showed the fruits of Mickey's romancing. As to that, where was Alex? She saw Margaret flirting with a youth in his late teens, and crooked her finger. "A good thing Seamus is pretending not to notice sixteen year olds in the bar tonight. Please would you check on Kelsey. I should stay here."

"Why can't Mary do it?"

"Because it's her evening off."

"Pity Daddy isn't here."

"He's coming in July."

"About time. Uncle Kenneth needs to know he's not family. Have you seen how he dotes on Kelsey?"

"My dear girl, have you ever known an Irish person who doesn't dote on a child? If you and Alex herd the young guests together, you could have your own party in the table-tennis room. I'll have Patrick fill two jugs of homemade ginger-beer, and there's lots of food." Margaret's face lit up. "Don't forget Kelsey, and report back here first," Helen reminded her, relieved she had diverted Margaret's keen eyes and sharp tongue.

Much later, Helen grabbed a coat and joined Kenneth on an upturned rowboat to watch dawn break over the estuary. A wind had heaved collars of foam against the rocks, and above the high tide, a seagull wheeled in circles. Its mournful cries made her to hook her arm more firmly through Kenneth's.

"Everything will change now, won't it?" she asked.

"Not everything. Small changes here—more tourists perhaps, less rationing, that sort of thing, but elsewhere, yes. A worry is how Russia, America, and Britain will cooperate. Russia is not likely to forget being rebuffed by the Allies, who left them to fight alone for a year while they opened a second front."

Helen extricated her arm and scratched at the boat's peeling paint. Lawrence might well decide to sell and return them to Scotland.

"Forget politics, Kenneth. Where are *we* in the new landscape?"

He picked up a large beach stone by his feet and lobbed it into the water. It landed like a shell-burst. "We've both avoided the answer to that for a long time. I expect Lawrence will want Alex in a kilt, Margaret in Edinburgh, and you preparing haggis or cooking kippers on a Scottish stove."

"God save me. And Kelsey?"

"She's just a toddler. She won't miss me for long."

A strong current at the mouth of the estuary swirled sand and seaweed to the surface. *Muddying clear waters,* Helen thought, watching the disturbance. She felt a lump rise in her throat. "Why do you make it sound so cut-and-dried?"

"Because we have to face the truth. But calm yourself. We'll find ways to connect. Right now, let's cope with life's cards as they're dealt."

Helen shifted her seat on the boat's keel. "Do you know how much you sound like a jaded novelist?

"A novelist? That's an ambition of mine. I'll follow up on that one day."

Five years ago, she hadn't set eyes on him; now they were lovers and Kelsey very likely the proof of that. "Well then, all that remains for me is to stay the cool, calm, collected Mrs Lawrence McKellan, and to quote Vera Lynn, say, *we'll meet again; don't know where, don't know when.*" Resorting to drama, she dusted sand off her coat and stood up.

"Not so fast, milady," Kenneth said, grabbing her hand. "There's an art studio with a comfortable sofa nearby. As for the quote, do you know Marie Lloyd's, *a little bit of what you fancy does you good?*"

Helen stuck her tongue out. "That's if you can catch me," she said, and ran along the beach.

CHAPTER 28

DECEMBER 1945

CLIVE RICHARDSON, IRISH Sub-Section director for MI5, had memorized the *Book of Proverbs* in his teens. His quotes regularly made staffers mine their memories for pertinent information, in vain hopes of dodging his religious grenades. He was a nondescript man. The colour beige rose in Lawrence's mind whenever they met.

When Lawrence received his summons, he worried that Richardson had uncovered Harry's smuggling and his own complicity.

Access to the director's sanctum on Blenheim's third floor was gained privately via a well-worn back staircase. When he arrived, the director peered at him over granny-glasses and waved him to a cane-backed chair facing his desk. "*Watch the path of your feet,*" he quoted, and flashed a thin smile. "Won't be long. Just updating myself on the latest report from Ireland."

What path did he have to watch? Striving to appear unperturbed, Lawrence looked at a painting behind Richardson's desk. It portrayed the first Duke of Marlborough astride a white stallion, charging towards him brandishing a sabre. How many ways could a man's future be severed? Was the painting placed there on purpose? He looked away. Rows of gun-metal grey cabinets lined one wall. What god-awful secrets did they hold? Did MI5 court-marshal delinquent employees? Could they imprison Harry for treason?

He returned his gaze to Richardson in time to see him put aside the report, polish his glasses with a handkerchief, and plant them to his nose. "Tell me, McKellan, do you believe you helped the war effort?"

His weasel face induced visions of dismemberment by sharp teeth. "Only as a team player, sir."

"By the fruits of his labour, ye shall know him, McKellan. That Admiralty talk you gave—good work."

Lawrence relaxed his back, and breathed easy. He'd misjudged the reason for the meeting, although Dennis's maxim stayed with him. *Believe the Intelligence Service but distrust every word they say.*

"Since the Americans have flattened Hiroshima and Nagasaki with atom bombs, the war is finished. That means many of our best men must return to civilian life."

So, I'm being let go. "I doubt few of their old jobs are still available, sir."

Richardson gave a ghost of a smile. "Change is healthy, Lawrence. Montagu is now Judge Advocate of His Majesty's Fleet, Turing has joined the National Physical Laboratory and *whoever troubles his own household inherits the wind,* which explains the ousting of Churchill. MI5 and MI6 are altering their perspectives too, which brings me to you. We want you with us for the long term."

From annihilation to life in a matter of minutes, Lawrence thought. "In what capacity, sir?"

The Director promptly launched into his department's future. The need to check for spies in Ireland's south, the operational drawbacks related to transport, fuel, and electricity, and England being exposed to IRA agitators.

"You have ears to the ground, so to speak. Your wife manages a hotel. She hears gossip. Your brother might detect farmers in collusion with the IRA. No one, including reporters sympathetic to the IRA cause, will escape our scrutiny. Your architectural business will provide good cover."

Lawrence kept a poker face. To view Helen and Harry as assets made him uneasy. Just how extensive was Richardson's knowledge of his family? Did the reporter comment imply Inglis? "May I give you my decision tomorrow, sir?"

"You may. Same time, but, as the scriptures preach, *do not leave hastily to argue your case for what will you do in the end?"*

Lawrence suspected no offer from Richardson was painless, but the covert life had leeched into him. It seemed practical to discuss with Molly the implications of him staying in London.

He took her to Rules, London's oldest, most elite restaurant—she knew it only from the outside, when she walked past the entrance. While they sipped aperitifs, he told her of the private dining rooms upstairs: The Charles Dickens room, frequented by the author; the Edward VII room, where the King entertained one of his mistresses, and the room Graham Greene had featured in his novel, *The End of the Affair.*

Molly blew cigarette smoke towards the ceiling and eyed him with amusement. "Instead of writing a 'Dear John' letter, are you treating me to a 'Dear Jane' dinner?"

"Far from it. Let's enjoy our meal, and then we'll talk." Her smoking was a new habit, possibly started following the V2 disaster. He evaluated her face while she sipped her wine and took in their surroundings. There were those who might suggest Molly's mouth needed less width, her nose more length, her jaw less breadth, but to him, she was attractive. Her father—a professor at Coventry University—and her churchgoing mother had both died during that city's bombing in 1940. If Molly was on edge sometimes, no wonder. He refilled their glasses, and then cut into his roast grouse, which sat on a bed of mushrooms and barley. Food rationing was still on-going, but the landed gentry regarded Rules as their own, and kept it well-supplied with game.

He kept up a light conversation until their plates were empty, and they had reached the coffee stage. "I met with a department head today. They want me to stay on." Did her eyes brighten? Molly gave little away. "If I accept, I will have to delay a few plans. My marriage is not happy, but I can't see Helen or me divorcing."

"That's not my business, Lawrence. That's for you and Helen to decide."

He nodded. "What changes do you envision for yourself?"

"Not much. I will continue working for the government in Whitehall." She sweetened her coffee with another sugar lump and smiled. "I know you're fishing, Lawrence, so I'll make it easy. I enjoy our relationship, and will share with you as much or as little time as you can manage. Does that help?"

"Yes, it does. Please mark on your calendar March 30, 1946—Oxford vs Cambridge boat race. We'll go together to cheer on Oxford's win."

"Don't you wish. Bet you five pounds, the light blues win."

§

Prior to seeing Richardson again, Lawrence wrestled with the rights and wrongs of the offer. To use Helen and Harry as 'ears to the ground' smacked of deceit but the new position promised an increase to the family fortunes, which was important when Alex went to Sandhurst and Margaret pursued her nursing career. The other positive was that he could watch Harry and Inglis. If Inglis's nationalist ideas led to the IRA, what a coup to nail him.

"Thank you for your endorsement of me, sir," he said, shaking his new boss by the hand. "I had not looked forward to leaving the Service. The fact I can use my architectural work as a cover is a strong inducement, too."

Richardson gripped Lawrence's shoulder. *The rich rule over the poor, and the borrower becomes the lender's slave.* A word of caution though. You stay bound by the Official Secrets Act. Keep your Belfast activities under wraps, and report only to me."

"I will, sir."

The director wished him a happy Christmas and ended their meeting with a final quote. *"Be perfectly united in mind and thought, and be content."*

Lawrence left Blenheim with a proverb of his own. *Success realized is sweet to the soul.* He enjoyed the challenges, the intrigues, and of having a secret persona. Maybe the gambling streak in Harry had turned into something just as addictive within himself. At least, now, he could look forward to an Irish Christmas with the family and suffer no complaints from Helen.

CHAPTER 29

MARCH 1946

THREE MONTHS LATER, Lawrence stared in disbelief at the plane taxiing towards him. *A Westland Lysander.* This was his transport? A gull-wing prewar monoplane? When the plane came to a halt, the pilot pointed to the fixed ladder, and then to the bench seat behind him.

Lawrence clambered in and slid the canopy shut. Once the plane was airborne, he watched the land grow smaller through the side window. Flying to Ireland without the family knowing reminded him of his clandestine visit to Harry three years earlier.

Much had changed since then. Harry's co-op venture with Murphy was successful enough that he had expanded the dairy again, and now had a team of workers. He had even built a shooting range on the property, so Alex could practice with his air gun. Knowing Alex, it wouldn't be long before he graduated from a pellet gun to a .22 rifle, and from rats to deer. Helen's enthusiasm had seemed forced when he arrived, but Kelsey proved a saviour. When she toddled from behind her mother's skirts and decided he wasn't a stranger, she held her arms up to be lifted.

The plane arrived at Nutts Corner Airfield on time, but wind and rain hounded him as he ran towards a soldier waiting next to a land rover. The fellow gave a half-hearted salute. His resentment at having to wait for the plane's arrival in the blustery weather reminded Lawrence of Alex.

He did not look forward to meeting Sergeant Stockwell. Richardson had been less than helpful with information, but from others, he learned that the man had a short fuse, was a keen Protestant and had it in for the Catholics.

Gap-toothed blocks of houses came into view as they passed Belfast's crippled dockyards—a punishing testament of Germany's hostility to Northern Ireland's connection with England. And surely of no surprise, Lawrence thought.

"Headquarters, sir," the driver said, turning into a small yard.

The flat-roofed building, with narrow windows cut into its red-brick walls, gave no sign of its use. Inside, scuff marks smeared the linoleum floor, light bulbs hung from electric cords, and metal chairs leaned against the grey wall. Only a dog-eared calendar and a vase of drooping flowers gave token relief. Comparing the barracks to Blenheim Palace's opulence gave him a guilty twinge.

A dour corporal, his boots striking the floor hard as he marched, escorted Lawrence to Stockwell's office. They passed a secretary hunched over the typewriter—her fingers a blur of typing efficiency. He saw no other personnel. The sergeant snapped to attention when the corporal announced his arrival.

"Pleased to meet you, sir. Was the flight okay?"

Lawrence looked into implacable eyes, extricated his hand from the sergeant's and took a seat on a wooden armchair. "Just a few lurches on the runway. I'd like a glass of water, please."

Stockwell barked the order out the door. Seeing an ashtray, Lawrence played easy-going and lit a Player's cigarette. The sergeant's disposition reminded him of a belligerent boxer dog his father owned. An image of Harry struggling to hold the animal, suggested that the sergeant needed a strong leash. "Care for a cigarette, sergeant? You can sit. Tell me what you do here."

Stockwell took the smoke offered, lounged back in his chair, and dished out information in tedious, precise portions. He bragged of his network of watchtowers and road barriers, and the constant alertness for IRA booby traps in public buildings. He only stopped when the receptionist brought the water.

After she left, Lawrence asked to meet the rest of his personnel, but Stockwell yawned and tapped cigarette ash on the floor. "For security reasons, our boys—including our informants—don't come here. When they call, we meet at pre-arranged locations."

This chap makes a puppy of Yarrow. Time to rein him in. "You mean to say you *wait* for them to call? You don't *push* or *check* them in the field? Have they given you a *crumb* of information on stolen armaments, sergeant, or a *morsel* on the restructuring of the IRA under its new leadership?"

A muscle jiggled under Stockwell's left eye. "Our chief field man reports it's quiet as a cemetery."

"In that case, you're slipping, sergeant. The IRA never idles."

"You think I'm not doing my job? Let me tell you, *sir,* when the IRA goes to ground, it's harder to find them than pry a halo from a saint. To discover hidden caches from long-ago robberies would be bloody miraculous."

Lawrence raised an eyebrow. "We don't rely on miracles." He stubbed out his smoke and folded his hands in front of him. "You need a classification system that tracks names and locations of friends and enemies."

"Our men in the field do that, sir."

"No, they don't. I'm talking about thorough surveillance. That means knowing who and where suspects meet, and watching for suspicious behaviour. The work involves photographs, inventories, records, and a cross-reference filing system."

Anger bordering on rage suffused Stockwell's face. "What are we, bloody secretaries?"

"Sergeant, curb your tongue. You're talking to a superior officer. You've shown me nothing. A military unit without good intelligence-gathering is as inefficient as guns with no bullets. When I return to London, I'll set up information-retrieval methods pertinent to this detachment. We'll send you details, along with two experts to help train your staff."

Stockwell's bulldog stance collapsed. "They won't find mistakes. We're a conscientious bunch."

"That's debatable. The climate is ripe for old rivalries, sergeant. London recognizes that." He rose to his feet. "Next visit, have your personnel on hand."

The sergeant remained close-mouthed until they arrived at the exit. "Sir, your comment as to armaments makes me think we should put an undercover man in County Mayo. Apparently, there's a troublemaker there called Cooper who recruits men for bank robberies, smuggling, black marketing, and such. Maybe he's IRA. Don't you own a hotel thereabouts? You never know, he may even have been in your bar."

Alarm coiled low in Lawrence's stomach. *So, the bastard has done some homework.* He forced a tight smile. "You think the government can finance undercover agents wherever you *suspect* IRA tentacles, sergeant? Stay focused. The first step here is to get your filing techniques updated and running. I'm sure the director has informed you that my movements in Belfast are confidential." A slight flicker in the Stockwell's eyes made him wonder what else Richardson might have divulged?

Rain still shrouded the day when he emerged from the building. On the ground, gulls squabbled over a morsel of discarded bread until one rose in the air with its prize. Seeing them, Lawrence wasn't sure who had won the contest between him and bulldog Stockwell. He avoided another bone-crunching handshake, by giving the sergeant a curt nod and leaving.

During the return flight to London, he shuddered at the prospect of further Belfast meetings, let alone reporting to the Blenheim weasel. For the first time, he wondered if he had made a wrong turn and his ambitions would dispatch him to hell.

CHAPTER 30

MAY 1946

THEY MET AT Dublin's Shannon airport—Helen arriving by car and Lawrence by air. She spotted him first, coming through customs, a raincoat slung over his arm and carrying his familiar overnight suitcase. A woman and a little girl clutching a teddy bear stood next to her. The child reminded her of Kelsey. "Look, Mama, there's Daddy!" They waved and looked so happy. Envious of them, Helen sighed, but mustered a smile as Lawrence approached.

"Spring in Dublin and a welcome smile from you," he said, embracing her.

She kissed his cheek and threaded her fingers between his, as though they were a happily married couple. At the car, he took the keys from her and drove the River Liffey route towards the Shelbourne Hotel. He had booked them a room for the night.

Feigning tiredness from her drive, Helen closed her eyes, but her mind was restless. Had Lawrence found a buyer? A house lined up for her to view in Edinburgh? What about Margaret and Alex? Could Harry afford to buy the farm? So many questions. She did not open her eyes until they arrived.

Their suite with its treed view overlooking St. Stephen's Green, was pleasing, so too the vase with its profusion of flowers on a central table, but the room, with its brocaded chairs and voluminous sofa, reminded her of a stage set. All it needed was for her and Lawrence to play their scripted parts.

"Would you care to join me in a glass of wine?" he asked.

It was such a perfect opening line, she almost laughed. The silver tray with its unopened bottle and two glasses, the flowers, and an expensive suite made her wonder what Lawrence was after. It was too staged. "Let's keep the wine for later," she said. "Right now, that marble bathtub looks very inviting." With a wave of her hand, she indicated it through a doorway. "I'll meet you downstairs ... unless you would like to enjoy a bath for two?"

"No, I'll ... I'll change and leave you to unwind. You'll find me in the lounge."

"Right, I won't take long." In the early days, he would have jumped at the chance, and she would have been more flirtatious, she thought. They were no longer the same people.

§

When she joined him a half hour later, he took her hand and gave her an admiring look. "You look relaxed, and eye-catching. I hope you're hungry."

The head waiter escorted them to a table beneath a chandelier which to Helen's mind shimmered like the Pleiades. But, taking her seat, she felt more earthbound than a twinkly goddess. Across from their table, a four-piece band played a selection of show tunes.

"No Irish jigs here," Lawrence murmured.

"No, and no Scottish reels either, with their kilted manoeuvres," she replied.

Lawrence took on a Scottish brogue. "Ach lassie, Scottish I am and forever will be. There are many ways to dance."

Touché, she thought, as he signalled the waiter over and ordered roast lamb for two and a bottle of Chablis. When the waiter left, he cleared his throat. "Do you know the Nuremberg war trials won't end for at least another six months? First the major criminals, then the doctors and camp guards."

"Lawrence, don't tell me we're going to sit here talking war. Yes, Kenneth told us. He's already attended a trial."

"That's surprising. Surely there's enough news of interest in County Mayo for a small-time journalist? Anyway, I have to run something past you, and I need your cooperation."

She tilted her head at him but had to wait because their waiter appeared with their order. "The lamb is lightly rubbed with garlic and basted with butter and white wine," he said, leaning in to place mint sauce on the table. The wine steward arrived next and poured a sample of Chablis. Lawrence swished a mouthful and nodded his approval.

"My goodness, what a performance," she said, tapping her foot impatiently. "Let's hope they stay away long enough for you to tell me more."

"I need you to run the hotel for another two years—until Alex is eighteen. I've registered him at Sandhurst."

To buy time, she cut a bite-sized morsel of lamb and skewered it with her fork. To stay in Ireland longer was an unexpected gift, but why tie that to Alex and Sandhurst? Something was off. "Lawrence, your son keeps telling you he doesn't want a commission. That's what Sandhurst does isn't it, train young men to be officers? Alex is a loner, not a leader."

"He can learn. He's a McKellan, not a Smith or a Jones. I won't have him being an ordinary private. His overall school reports are disappointing, and he's expressed no wish for university. I warned him I'd send him to military college if his schoolwork didn't improve."

"You're not being fair. Alex may not excel at history and literature, but he's a whiz at math and science, and Harry says he can repair or take apart farm equipment after only being shown once."

"So, you think our son should be a mechanic?"

"Stop it; you're showing that Oxford snobbery of yours. You haven't mentioned Margaret."

"She's no problem. Dublin's University College offers a nursing programme, and she can switch to Edinburgh Infirmary later. Kelsey needs no planning; she's too young. We'll get a governess."

Twenty years of being Lawrence's wife was long enough to know he was following a hidden agenda. But what? And he hadn't mentioned Harry. She looked up to find him watching her. "You're hiding something."

"That's ridiculous. I—"

"Then why disrupt us at all? Your architectural firm could expand and branch out in Dublin just as well."

"That won't work."

"Why? I don't understand." Above the chatter of diners, she heard the quartet play a familiar Cole Porter song, *Let's Call the Whole Thing Off,* and wondered if that wasn't such a bad idea.

Lawrence wiped his mouth and put the napkin on the table. "Because my partner, George, is a smart businessman. He has recommended opening a London office. The city got it in the neck during the Blitz and building contracts are pouring in. We are going forward with that plan. Our children's heritage is *Scottish,* Helen. I have no intention of our staying in Ireland indefinitely."

The way he now sat back—eyes too intent, voice too controlled—reminded her of something Harry had said. *To win at cards, sometimes you play the bluffer's game to unsettle those who expect victory.* "Bravo, Lawrence. I feel like clapping, but I'm not fooled. You're only telling me half a story."

"So, you want me to dot the i's and cross the t's? Very well. Since I will be in London on architectural business, I will also be doing work for the Service."

"Don't you mean the other way around. I read a quotation in the knitting section of the Women's Weekly. *The last shall be first, and the first shall be last.* Don't laugh; it's applicable. What did your bosses do? Snap their fingers, and you stood to attention?"

"Be nice, Helen. It's a good offer. You should be happy. You get two extra years in your beloved Ireland, and from what you tell me, Inglis will be abroad more than at home, so our children won't have to suffer his rabid ideas."

Why in the world is he mentioning Kenneth? Has Lawrence overheard gossip? As for being happy? I am, but Margaret yearns for Scotland, and Alex has his mind set elsewhere. "You haven't mentioned Harry. Where does he figure in your plans?"

"The farm is thriving, and with his dairy and co-op venture going well with Murphy, perhaps he will manage to pay off the lease in two years. If not, then I'll find someone else to take it on."

She couldn't argue. As always, Lawrence reined in the family. She would comply. Margaret and Alex would continue without their father, and Harry would continue working the lease. She heaved a sigh. "All right, onward we go. One final point: Harry and Kenneth are hatching a horse enterprise, so stop sniping at Kenneth every chance you get. It doesn't matter what his politics are, he's become a good friend to us."

The prompt arrival of the dessert trolley forestalled further talk. Helen took a fruit flan and suggested a lemon tart for Lawrence. The band broke into a foxtrot and Lawrence held out his hand and led her onto the dance floor.

If anyone can make foxy moves, it's my husband, Helen thought, moving into his arms.

CHAPTER 31

MAY 1946

Kelsey stood with Mary at the hotel's entrance, clutching a card, when Helen and Lawrence arrived. On her feet, which were usually bare, she wore shiny, black shoes, and her hair was the colour of burnished copper.

Helen kissed the top of her head. It smelled of Mary's lemon and mint shampoo. "Kelsey, look! Here's Daddy," she said, pointing to Lawrence. Kelsey held up her card.

"For me?" Kelsey nodded. "My goodness, you've made a map of Scotland! What a clever girl. What's this red dot?"

"Edbra," she said.

Lawrence chuckled. "Ed-*in*-burgh."

Kelsey corkscrewed a tendril of hair around her finger, then held her arms above her head. "Up! I want up."

Lawrence gave the card to Helen and hoisted Kelsey onto his shoulders. "You're getting too big for these uppies of yours."

"Uncle Kenneth lifts me."

"He does, does he?"

"Yes," Kelsey said, and traced his hairline with her finger. "Where's hair gone?"

"A giraffe nibbled it at the zoo. Now down you get; the doorway isn't high enough." He lifted her off his shoulders and passed her to Mary.

As they trooped into the foyer, Margaret hurried out from the kitchen, dressed in a green sweater and kilt. Lawrence slipped an arm around her waist, and twirled her until the kilt flared. "What a fine Scottish lass, and you're wearing a tartan. How did you manage that?"

"From a shop in Dublin. I've been learning to make dumplings. Are we returning to Scotland now?"

"Not yet."

"But we've won the war. You promised."

"I know. I'll explain later."

"Hi, Dad," Alex said, entering the foyer with the suitcases.

"We're not going back to Scotland," Margaret said.

"Great. Fine by me." He grinned and took the luggage upstairs.

"Dinner in thirty minutes, everyone," Helen said, which was another way of saying 'time out'. Left alone, she took Lawrence's arm. "Margaret is not a happy girl with the news. Let's fortify ourselves and wait in the family dining room. By the way, in your honour, Murphy has prepared braised rabbit in Guinness, and bacon dumplings."

"Rabbit? I ... I haven't eaten rabbit for a long time. Where is Harry *this* time? He's never around when I arrive."

"I've no idea, but he'll be here tomorrow afternoon."

At dinner, Margaret sulked until Lawrence explained that attending Dublin's Nursing College would help her gain entry to Edinburgh's Royal Infirmary.

Unaware of his father's long-term plans for him, Alex enthused over Harry's improved shooting range. "He's even made pop-up targets. Come and target practice with me tomorrow, Dad."

"Not my idea of fun. I'm surprised the cows haven't stampeded."

"The range isn't that close to the barn. Besides, the cows are used to the bangs."

More interested in making castles out of her mashed potatoes, Kelsey studded them with peas. "One, two, three, four, um ... ten," she said, pressing five peas into the mash. Beside her, Lawrence mixed gravy into his potatoes but left the rabbit.

The following day, while Helen and Patrick readied the bar for the afternoon trade, Lawrence came in with a newspaper under his arm and settled at a table. "I thought I'd keep you company. Harry will be here soon, right?"

Fifteen minutes later, Harry strolled in with Kenneth. Helen indicated Lawrence with a tilt of her head but stayed behind the counter. She had anticipated Lawrence and Kenneth coming face to face again, but it didn't stop a flurry of nerves.

"Good to see you haven't forgotten us, brother. Kenneth and I have just come from buying two horses at the tinker's camp on his property. I swear the horses understand gypsy talk, they're so well-trained."

Lawrence crossed a leg and bounced his foot, which suggested to Helen that Harry and Kenneth buying horses together was not good news.

Kenneth pulled up a chair. "Hello again, Lawrence; four years since we last met. The three-year-old geldings we've bought are fine specimens, and Harry is a rare judge of horseflesh."

"At least that's something. I understand you were in Nuremberg? You must have pulled plenty of strings."

"Not much. The newspaper world does carry weight you know."

They're already squaring off, Helen thought, looking at them from her vantage point. Each one reminded her of Flynn. Lawrence viewing Kenneth in the way Flynn circled intruders. Harry, wagging his tail and trying to please. And Kenneth on point but looking wary. Amused with her observations, she brought them pints of Guinness, as well as a full jug, and then returned to her station.

Harry downed a half pint within seconds. "I needed that. Why lose sleep over Nuremberg when we've got our own trials? Just now, I caught Brigid pushing her son in a pram, and there's another baby on the way. Ireland would be a grand place to start a roaring trade in latex—known for its expanding qualities." Not raising a laugh, he added, "Joking aside, there are too many pregnancies and too many mouths to feed on this fair isle. Is it any wonder there's poverty?"

"You and your pronouncements, Harry. The problems of Ireland are far more complex."

"So, what's your take on your country's problems, Kenneth?"

From where she stood, Helen beseeched Harry with her eyes to stop Lawrence from baiting their friend, but instead, Harry held his hands up in defence and said, "Man the barricades! War is coming!"

Ignoring him, Kenneth finished his pint in three gulps, refilled his glass, and shook his head. "You're an educated man, Lawrence; you know how Britain has messed with us for centuries. Ireland overrun with marauding Scotsmen, and greedy Englishmen using money and exploitative tactics to evict our people, take our land and our women. Result? The land swamped with Anglo-Irish families, our language stifled, and Catholicism viewed as a plague."

"You remind me of malcontents who whine over events centuries old, and lack the will to move ahead," Lawrence said, also refilling his glass. "Irishmen are indecisive, and just as prone to taking women not of their country."

"So, you're worried about your women. That's a new one. You're missing the point. This is the twentieth century, and you British—sorry, Harry—still occupy our country. You're naive if you don't recognize that this is at the root of our rebellions and riots. Those in power the world over wear blinkers when it suits them."

"And so do you. If it wasn't for the British today, your precious Ireland would be under a German boot, so don't spout rubbish."

Kenneth sprang to his feet and thrust his finger into Lawrence's face. "We've had a bellyful of you and your kind forever telling us how to run our country. I would sink your colonial attitudes into the Irish Sea, if it could be done without bloodshed."

"Don't jab your radical finger at me."

"Radical? You don't know the meaning of the word. That's because you're a Scotsman and Scotsmen hang on to the coattails of the English."

Shouting a curse, Lawrence sprang to his feet and hit Kenneth square on the jaw, hard enough that Kenneth staggered backwards. Harry caught and held him in a bear-hold. "Don't mess with my brother. He's an accomplished boxer from his Oxford days."

The unexpected sound of Helen's hand slamming the table in front of them silenced all three men. "Stop it! You're worse than rabid dogs. Kenneth, be quiet. Lawrence, sit down."

Harry pulled Kenneth onto a chair and called Patrick over to mop the table of spilt Guinness. Helen stood with arms crossed. "Kenneth, get that chip off your shoulder. You've had your say, rudely I might add. Lawrence, your overbearing views are enough to make anyone throw up. I've told you, I won't have you insulting my Irish friends. And, Harry, don't look so innocent. Your behaviour is every bit that of a boxing fan at ringside."

A bubble of laughter rose to her lips. The disbelief on their faces was almost worth the fight. Now to release her bombshell. "To those of you who don't know, Lawrence has decided that we're staying here for at least a further two years. That means this hotel remains *my* home. I'm the manager, and I'll have no political bickering from *any* of you. We open in five minutes. Behave like gentlemen and shake hands, or get out of my bar. I'm sick of watching schoolboys play King of the Castle."

Contrite, Harry flapped a napkin in surrender while Lawrence and Kenneth muttered apologies, but there were no handshakes.

CHAPTER 32

JULY 1946

"Excuse me, ma'am, there's a surprise visitor for you at the front desk." Deidre said, sounding excited on the house phone. *Surprise visitor?* Helen hurried from her office, patting her hair in place. In the foyer, a woman stood facing her with a big smile on her face.

Helen gasped and threw her arms out in welcome. "Jill! I thought you weren't coming until next month. It's been so long."

"I couldn't wait any longer, and August is a busy month for both of us in this business. Deidre and I hatched the surprise together. Sneaky phone calls to make sure you were here. She won't be in trouble, will she?"

"Good heavens, no. I might even give her a bonus."

"I believe I saw Alex playing croquet when I arrived. He's become a young man since I saw him. An expert croquet player too. The ball just whizzed through the hoops. He would demolish me if we played billiards. I was pleased that he remembered me shooing the donkey out of the dining room six years ago."

Helen laughed. "That incident grows funnier with every telling. I'll let him know you admired his aim. He wants to train as a sniper. Lawrence wants him at Sandhurst. They're at loggerheads about it."

"Hmm, I might be helpful. Would you mind if I strolled out and joined Alex in a game? He's more likely to open up in an informal setting."

"Go ahead. We have loads of time to catch up on our news. I'll have your luggage taken to your room."

The family gathered in the private dining room to welcome Jill. Harry strolled in wearing a white shirt and trousers pressed to a razor-edge which made Helen wonder if her dear brother-in-law had designs on her friend. Kelsey, in a yellow dress honey-combed with smocking, sat in a booster chair between her brother and sister.

Conversation ripped along until Margaret and Alex finished their apple pie and left to meet friends in the village. After Mary whisked Kelsey off to bed, Helen suggested an evening stroll to Jill and Harry.

The sky was softening to shades of pink and turquoise when they reached the studio. To watch the rising moon, Helen proposed drinks on the deck. Through the open door, she heard Harry filling Jill in on the farm and his new horse venture.

She joined them with a Murphy concoction of Irish whiskey blended with honey. "To sip, not gulp, Harry," she teased.

"I love this place. The silence is blissful after London's roar," Jill said, cocking her head to a lapwing's plaintive 'pee-wit' call.

Harry lounged back with a cigarette and gave her a sympathetic look. "It must have been rough in London. Did your hotel suffer much damage?"

"Other than a few broken windows and falling plaster, it escaped, and yet two buildings opposite me collapsed in ruins. It will take time and money to fix the damage. Meanwhile, we cope with a lack of housing, rationing, and hundreds of men looking for work. It's causing huge social upheaval."

"I'm sure it is, but I expect the women are delighted to have their men home," Harry said, blowing smoke into the air.

"They are and they're not. For six years, they kept the farms, factories, transportation, and other services running. Now they are back to being domestics. It's a breeding ground for resentment."

"Maybe I should fly over and help make them happy."

Helen looked at him over the rim of her glass. "Harry! You're lucky Kenneth isn't here. He would box your ears for saying that."

Jill laughed. "Am I going to meet him?"

"You are. He's invited you, me, and Kelsey to a picnic lunch tomorrow at the gypsy camp. There's a young girl called Sorcha, four years older than Kelsey, who treats her as her little sister. Sometimes Harry and I join Kenneth for evenings around the gypsies' campfire."

"Lovely. Harry, what's your opinion on Alex and Sandhurst?"

"No one should force another into a career they don't want. Believe me, I know all about that thanks to my father when I was a lad. With proper training, Alex could shoot a fly if it moved. The problem for him lies in convincing his father."

Helen sighed. "Sometimes I think I'm wrong to support him. I know I'm being unrealistic, but I wish Alex had chosen a less lethal occupation."

Jill reached out and took Helen's hand in hers. "Helen, a sniper's primary mission is to reconnoiter and protect his comrades. Protect is the keyword, so remember that. Since you and Harry both want Alex to succeed, gather information about him. Keep his school records, note his athletic abilities, his work ethics, what he wins in shooting competitions, the farm machinery he fixes, and whatever else comes to mind. I know a colonel who, if he sees promise, will help him."

"Who is this colonel of yours?"

"My brother. He owes me one."

"Aha. As the saying goes, it's not what you know, it's who you know—or so *I've* found."

Helen laughed. "Touts are not colonels, Harry."

§

Overnight, rain saturated the ground. Helen heard it drumming on the roof, but by morning, the sun was out and the lawns and trees sparkled with diamonds. Jill took Alex on in a game of tennis before breakfast, and from his cheerful expression, Helen knew Jill had instilled new confidence. He showed it by offering Margaret driving lessons. "We can use Harry's old car and practice in the backfield," he told her. "You can't continue relying on boyfriends to drive you."

"I suppose not, but it's more fun," she said, and poked him in the arm.

Helen drove them to the farm before lunch, and then continued on to Kenneth's with Jill beside her and Kelsey secured in the back. On the way, Jill pointed to a field where straw-hatted men were cutting hay into swaths for the first stage of drying. "Are they gypsies?"

"Yes, most of them. When their wagons come trundling along our roads, it's a sure sign winter is behind us. A lot of the gypsies work the fields. The Travellers—that's their real name—go back centuries. Rummage through my handbag. You'll find an article Kenneth wrote on them."

Jill put on her glasses. After Kenneth explained their history and how their numbers increased through evicted tenant farmers, he praised their talents in bead-work, weaving, and painting, and ended by saying, *The Travellers are part of our Heritage and have a right to legal settlement.*

"It's a shame people misunderstand them. The same goes for gypsies in England. I believe their nomadic life threatens people, because it's so different and they are free of all the rules and regulations we follow. Not that they don't have their own laws and customs," Jill said, as she returned the clipping to the handbag. "Helen, are you having an affair with Kenneth?"

"What gives you that idea?"

"Because you're more confident. Outgoing. And, you have an inner-happiness. But I see the cautionary glances Harry gives you whenever Kenneth's name crops up. And Kelsey—she's different from the other two. Is she Kenneth's?"

In her heart, Helen knew Jill's loyalty towards her was unshakable. She gave a quick smile. "Our little passenger's paternity is questionable, Jill, but in my bones, I believe she's Kenneth's. Even before we moved to Ireland, Lawrence and I had differences. I expect separation makes for different bedfellows more than we admit. Since we're being candid, why did you mention, in a letter long ago, that you'd seen Lawrence in mixed company?"

"That was a mistake. One I should never have made. The thing is, I loathe inequality between the sexes. But the woman with Lawrence was different. Very sure of herself. Tall, just a few inches short of him. Behaved like an equal, and I thought her a threat to you. She didn't strike me as a warm person. She'd be at home in a library."

Helen sighed. *An academic. Yes, Lawrence would definitely find that appealing.* "It's good we've been candid. I won't have to pretend around Kenneth when I'm with you, but let's not visit this subject again; agreed?"

"Not another word."

"Look, smoke," Kelsey chirped, as they turned into the lane leading to Benevolence. Blue tendrils curled above the trees from the gypsy camp.

Carrying a pork pie and strawberries, Helen pushed open Kenneth's wrought-iron gate. Jill stooped to admire its leafy design. "This is a work of art."

"After Kenneth's article appeared, he woke up one morning to find his old, battered gate replaced and this one swinging on its hinges," Helen said.

"Uncle Kenneth!" Kelsey called, running towards him.

"Hello, pixie. Who have you brought to see me?"

"Mummy and Auntie Jill," she said, and scampered into the kitchen.

Kenneth shook Jill's hand. "So, you're the friend that brings happy smiles."

"It's mutual. What a lovely cottage. No wonder you call it Benevolence."

They found Kelsey sitting on the kitchen floor, stroking a tabby cat that had wandered in from the gypsy camp. Kenneth apologized for his scruffy appearance as he swiped his trousers free of sawdust. "I've just finished building a tree house in the lower branches of an old Yew tree. It gives a grand view of the river."

Kelsey squealed. "A *tree house*?"

"Yes, and one you're about to see." Holding the picnic hamper in one hand and Kelsey by the other, he led the way to where the trail ended at the river.

Sorcha was already there, her legs hanging over the tree-house platform. She clapped her hands on seeing them. "Sorcha is a fairy," Kelsey whispered to Jill. "She makes daisy chains and talks to birds."

Kenneth swung Kelsey up onto the house platform, while Helen opened the hamper and Jill spread the blanket. A rope dangled from the tree and Kenneth attached a basket. Into it, he put ginger snaps, pie, and strawberries.

"This is your delivery basket," he said, looking up at the children's eager faces. "Hold the rope and pull."

Giggling, the girls leaned over and hoisted the basket aloft, but a small object fell to the ground from Kelsey's pocket. Jill picked it up, stared at it in amazement, and showed it to Helen.

"It's for Sorcha!" Kelsey shouted, peering down.

"Where did you find it, darling?"

"Uncle Harry's field, Mummy. It's mine."

"Helen, look. It's live ammunition. A .303 calibre bullet, used in British Lee Enfield rifles."

"How do you know that, Jill? I thought you just supplied firemen with tea and biscuits during the war."

"My brother's gun cabinet holds rifles and has an ammunition drawer."

"Kenneth, tell me Harry and Alex don't target practise with these?"

He plucked the bullet from Jill's hand and dropped it into his pocket. "No, Helen, they don't own rifles that use ammo like this. Don't worry; I'll sort out the mystery."

"It's mine," Kelsey wailed again.

Kenneth shook his head. "I've something shinier. Lower the basket." When it arrived, he produced a shilling from his pocket and held it up. "See, Sorcha will like this; I promise." He wrapped the coin in tin foil and Kelsey, happy again, pulled the basket up onto the platform.

After that, the picnic proceeded without incident, although Helen sensed from Kenneth's face that Harry was in serious trouble.

CHAPTER 33

JULY - DECEMBER 1946

HARRY BOLTED UPRIGHT from a deep sleep to someone hammering on the front door. He shouldered awkwardly into his dressing gown and stumbled downstairs, half expecting to see Lawrence again. But it wasn't; it was Kenneth. "What in hell brings you here at this hour?"

Kenneth pushed past him and took a seat on a kitchen chair. He looked ready to explode. Harry grabbed the scotch and two glasses from a cupboard and poured an ounce for Kenneth and two for himself.

Glaring at him, Kenneth planted a bullet on the table. "Are you and Alex using these fuckers on your firing range?"

"How could we? That's military ammo. Where did you find it?"

"Kelsey found it in your front field. On the path leading to the road for chrissake. Can you give me a good reason for that?"

"Poachers?"

"We're not in Africa. There's no big game here. Do you have a cellar in the front field?"

Harry chewed his lip. Goddamn Cooper! After finding the gutted-sheep hanging on his fence, he'd closed his ears and eyes to the bastard's antics. But now, here was his best friend ready to throttle him. "Can't this wait until morning?"

Kenneth tossed his drink back and wiped his mouth. "No, it can't. We need the cover of darkness. Odds on Cooper's men have crammed your cellar with contraband, and God knows what else. You don't have to tell me. Your face is a dead giveaway. You're one of those blundering smugglers, aren't you?"

Under Kenneth's unflinching stare, Harry cracked. "Yes," he mumbled, but when Kenneth leaned forward with a hand cupped to his ear, he shouted louder. "Yes!"

Aware Kenneth would dig the truth out of him, he omitted the Belfast bookie part and Lawrence descending on him, but confessed to the smuggling, how his shoulder got banged up, Cooper cornering him at the Ballinrobe racetrack, and how he'd found a lamb bleeding its guts out at the back of his house. "That did it, Kenneth. I feared, if I didn't let Cooper use the cellar, he'd harm the family." He drained the last of his scotch and waited.

"That admission couldn't have been easy, Harry. I've had my run-ins with Cooper. I know how he operates. Much of what you've said doesn't surprise me." He stood up. "Okay, grab a flashlight; let's investigate that cellar of yours."

"It's padlocked. I don't have the key."

"Get the damned flashlight."

In his bedroom, Harry pulled on a pair of work pants, a thick sweater, and seized the flashlight from the bedside table. Feeling like a truant schoolboy, he joined Kenneth at the door.

Rain pelted the ground. They trudged across the field, their feet squelching tufts of grass into the mud. An insomniac cow mooed in the barn. Harry led the way, the flashlight beam sweeping the ground. He halted at a mound of twigs and stones that camouflaged the cellar's doors. They were the ground-level kind that opened upwards and outwards. Bending, they put aside the debris, and Harry pointed to a heavy chain which threaded through bracket handles and held a formidable grease-smothered padlock. Kenneth took the flashlight and swept the ground on either side of the doors in widening circles. They found three bullets.

"Well, Harry, these prove your cellar holds ammo. They must have dropped the loose bullets on the way in, or on the way out."

"The chain and padlock aren't mine. If we break it that will be the end of me."

"Leave it. We'll replace everything and go indoors. I've got a plan."

§

After Kenneth left, Harry tipped another two inches of scotch into his glass and went over Kenneth's plan again. "Meet Daecon today. Tell him your baby niece found live bullets near the cellar, that her mother has raised questions, and that Cooper should empty the cellar fast. If Deacon objects, warn him it's possible Helen will tell me, and being the investigative fellow I am, he and Cooper could end up drowning in cow shit."

Bleary from lack of sleep, Harry dozed in his armchair until sunlight tapped on the window. Rubbing his eyes, he staggered to his feet. The cat slid to the floor and meowed. He spooned food into its dish, and then hurried out to the barn. His cows needed milking, and his help would arrive soon.

§

Nosens Pub was jam-packed when Harry arrived. He wrinkled his nose. He'd never developed a liking for the funk of sweat, pigs, and cow shit—nothing like the sweet aroma of horse manure. He found his quarry at the pool table, aiming the last ball into the end pocket. After it disappeared with a loud thwack, Daecon threw a cocky grin at his humbled opponent and strolled over.

"How're you doing, me old cocker? You look worse than an empty beer keg and that's unhealthy. Come and have a pint." He led the way to a table occupied by two farmers and stacked with mugs and two full pitchers. "Help yourself."

When Daecon's reddened nose resurfaced from his pint, he clicked his glass against Harry's full one and launched into a story about an escaped pig. "The poor devil headed into the convent gardens. Chased by two nuns with brooms, it blundered through a pair of bloomers. Half-blind from its saucy headgear, it then ran amok in the village, scaring everybody witless."

Letting go his impatience, Harry laughed along with Daecon's cronies. The conversation soon turned to Ballinrobe's horses, which one was running and what a shame their favourite jockey was a-bed with a broken collarbone. After Deacon's friends left, Harry pursued his goal.

"I went by your place earlier, Daecon. You've been ploughing new pastures."

"Aye, expanding my barley and oat crops. Hired tinkers to remove them stones."

"Stones, is it? In my fields, they'd be picking up live bullets."

"Mercy me! From that target range of yours?"

Harry ground his cigarette butt in the overflowing ashtray, and repeated what Kenneth had told him but in his own words. "Don't mess with me, Daecon. My baby niece found live bullets near the cellar. I had to dodge a heap of questions. You bugger. Storing black market stuff in my cellar, my arse. I want everything gone in forty-eight hours. Who knows what my sister-in-law will say to my brother? Or what the little one might say. The last thing I want is the local constabulary bloody nosing around my place."

"Easy, Harry, no need to panic. Is Kenneth in the know?"

"No, not yet, unless Kelsey's mother tells him."

Daecon rolled his eyes. "Well, Cooper has been unloading the cellar since early July. Them bullets likely fell from an open carton. There's nothing left in your cellar now except household stuff and ladies' items. Black market goods ain't bringing in the money right now, but it's smart to keep it on hand. We've also got a few crates of scotch left too, Harry. You ain't having the key, but we'll see you get a nice bottle now and then."

Either Daecon is a glib liar or else he's telling the truth; either way, Kenneth told me to keep in with him. "That's better. It's good to keep your landlord happy." Grinning, he brought out his cigarettes, offered one to Daecon, and ordered two whiskies.

§

Two days later, Harry got the nod of approval from Kenneth. "Well done. I'm glad you kept me out of it."

"Do you think Daecon spun me a yarn?"

"He'd be a fool if he did. You can always threaten to break the lock and see for yourself, but I wouldn't recommend it."

"Right ho. If I'm given a bottle of scotch, we'll share it, okay?"

§

Weeks later, Cooper was wakened from a deep sleep by the shrill of the telephone in his Dublin house. He swore into the receiver. "Fecking hell, this better be good. There ain't a rooster up and crowing yet."

"Quit with the whining. This is the love of your life, Kenneth Inglis. If you've read the newspapers, you'll know the Emergency Powers Act has lapsed."

"So, you woke me for that? Why cheer? That fecking Act put good men of ours behind bars."

"That's why the call. I was at the Collins Bridge gun salute and—"

"Are you wanting me to shake your hand and say you're a marvel?"

"For chrissake, let me talk. An Irish Times editor wants me to submit a piece on the Act. So, I'm appealing to de Valera to release the men incarcerated when the Act expanded police powers. It's what you've been after, right?"

He's full of shite, but if he pulls it off, he'll be a grand asset. "It is, but I ain't holding high hopes. Now get off the fecking phone. It's bloody freezing standing here naked."

§

In mid-December, Cooper strolled into his da's Belfast pub to meet Eamon, and saw the crowd on their feet, thrusting fists in the air and singing a revolutionary song.

"Eamon, what's going on."

"You haven't heard? Twenty-four of our men walked out of prison yesterday, thanks to an Irish Times article."

"Is that a fact?"

Before drifting off to sleep in Eamon's attic, Cooper decided a bottle of single malt scotch from the stash in Harry's cellar was just the peace offering to give to his old adversary and new pal, Kenneth Inglis.

CHAPTER 34

JULY - AUGUST 1947

IT TOOK MONTHS to create an efficient surveillance department in Belfast, and get Stockwell's agents trained to the new system. After meeting the sergeant for the first time more than a year earlier, Lawrence made a point of seeing him every five months to keep updated, and to test the new system. To say the sergeant was resistant to the changes was a flagrant understatement.

To Lawrence, Stockwell's reports resembled Helen's bullet-point shopping lists. The sentences were one-liners, but there were pages of them, and the reports made for tiresome reading. No connection between Inglis and the IRA had surfaced, and Cooper appeared to have fallen into obscurity. Lawrence saw this as a plus, since it stopped Stockwell nagging for an agent in County Mayo. A second advantage was that it kept the man's terrier nose out of Harry's activities. But on the negative side, Cooper's low profile lessened the chance of connecting the dots from him to Kenneth, and thus to the IRA.

Irritated at wading through another padded report, Lawrence stuffed it into his briefcase next to Molly's bagged lunch. At noon, he walked to a rose-covered pergola, which overlooked Blenheim Palace's Great Lake. He liked the lake's placid surface. It lifted him from the tangles of his life so he seldom viewed the tumbling, surging, cascades at the lake's western end.

After finishing Molly's egg sandwich, he crunched into an apple and turned to the report. Under Miscellaneous, a small item caught his eye. Northern Ireland's new railway service—the Enterprise Express which ran between Belfast and Dublin—had doubled its daily cross-border service and advance bookings were now available. Energized, he tossed the apple core into the water and hurried back to his office to place a call to Belfast.

"Sergeant, I read your report. Border crossings on the Enterprise Express need custom checks. Make a list of bookings since the new service began." He let Stockwell's gust of annoyance pass.

"Who are we looking for, sir?"

"Kenneth Inglis, a journalist with the *Mayo Daily Leader*. He's an IRA sympathizer, and a possible spokesman."

"Anyone else?"

"Cooper. You already know the name."

"Is that his first name, sir?"

"Yes, but I don't have his family name."

"Bit like looking for a sober man in an Irish pub, sir."

He chuckled. Sometimes the man showed glimmers of humour. "Too true, sergeant. I'll be in Belfast next week."

§

The usual driver met him and drove to the compound as if he were a Grand Prix driver. Lawrence knew the soldier deserved a reprimand, but the white-knuckle drive made a dull day better. Nothing had changed, other than barbed wire strung on top of the perimeter fencing, and a new Quonset hut. "For storing arms and ammunition, and two military jeeps," the driver said, pointing to them.

Stockwell brimmed with self-satisfaction, as he ushered Lawrence into a small office with a narrow window that offered little light. Lawrence crossed to a wall-mounted corkboard, and surveyed thumb-tacked articles carrying Kenneth's byline. Several of the clippings had creases and yellowed edges. "What did you do, sergeant? Rob the library's archives? You've put in a lot of work here. Have you found a biased pattern to his writing?"

"An increase in political rant, which resulted in a handful of prisoners being released after the Emergency Powers Act expired September of last year, but I didn't find patterns, sir."

Lawrence pulled up a chair, took a sip of cat-piss tea, and glanced at the voluminous list of information the sergeant handed him. Each page was headed with columns reading Occupation, Nationality, Domicile, Religion, and Police Records. "Is there information on Cooper on one of these pages?"

"Yes, sir. Section three. Full name, Cooper O'Neil. Family history. Education. Criminal record. Known Belfast and Dublin addresses. Friends. Acquaintances.

Suspected of a raid on the Magazine Fort in Phoenix Park, Dublin. No record of activities during the war years, but suspected of smuggling operations along the coast. I understand you helped put a stop to that, sir?"

Lawrence shrugged. "R.A.F. Coastal Command did the real work. What have you got on Inglis?"

"Relevant articles are on the corkboard, sir. O'Neil and Inglis go back to when Inglis was a cub reporter. His criticisms of government treatment of IRA men are in the file too, sir."

"Good. There may be other links." Left alone, Lawrence massaged the back of his neck. The Cooper-Kenneth association ran deep. Then there was Kenneth's friendship with Harry and Helen, and his Friday nights at the bar. *Can't imagine Stockwell being unaware of that, or does he think it too delicate to raise? If it is; at least it hinders him digging into Harry's activities.*

He stood in front of the corkboard and compared Kenneth's earlier articles to his newer ones. There *was* a pattern. His writing had become more political. What persuasion had Cooper used to strengthen Kenneth's radical perspective? Could it be a three-way tit-for-tat? The IRA gets a respected media voice, Cooper uses Inglis to further his own ambitions, and Kenneth promotes himself with exclusives? The similarities to his own behaviour with MI 5 vexed him.

Disliking the insight, he resigned himself to more scanning of the lists, until he saw *H. Sullivan*, Helen's maiden name. What was she doing travelling to Belfast? Further on, he discovered it was Herbert Sullivan. He pushed away from the desk, and peered through the grimy window to a world of tenements and dark alleys. He was chasing shadows.

A draft at the door announced the return of Stockwell. "Excuse me, sir, London on the phone."

He took the call in the sergeant's office, aware of him hovering by the door. "There's a family emergency at the hotel, sergeant. Is there a regional airport within distance?"

"Yes, sir, outside Ballina. You can land within the hour. It's a short drive from there."

No flies on the sergeant. Wouldn't put it past him to have visited the bar. "Excellent. Please have a car fuelled and ready for my arrival. Your lists are thorough, sergeant, but they call for further scrutiny, so I'm taking them with me. I will see you're informed if we find something of interest."

§

Helen was not having a good day. Two of her staff were sick, Brigid's baby had croup, and Mary was attending a friend's wedding in Cork. After spending part of the morning with Deidre, stripping and making beds and then setting tables, she joined Deidre for a tea break behind the reception desk. They were discussing the Abbey Theatre's latest show when Alex burst into the foyer. His face and hands mud-streaked, and his trousers torn.

"Mum, I've lost Kelsey! It was her turn to hide. I've searched everywhere! Is she here? Have you seen her?"

"Alex! Slow down. She's not here. When did she go missing?"

"I'm not sure. Maybe an hour ago."

An hour? Oh my God that's a lifetime. What to do? Mustn't panic. "Let's start a search. You and Deidre get Murphy; we're between meals, and rouse Patrick. He's in the bar doing an inventory. The four of you spread out. Search the kitchen garden, hedges, and ditches, and don't forget to check Flynn's kennel. If she's not there, take Flynn with you; he's got a good nose. Keep calling her name. She won't have gone far. I'll search the main-floor rooms before alerting the police. Check back with me in twenty minutes."

Fighting panic, Helen went through each room, looking in cupboards, behind curtains, and under tables, and constantly called Kelsey's name. When no child-like voice responded, she gave up and ran to her office

"I'm sorry, Mrs McKellan, no one has contacted us about finding a little girl," Constable Malloy said. "Let's get a description of your daughter, her age, clothes she was wearing, last seen, and then we'll put out a 'Be On the Lookout' bulletin. We're a small community, Mrs McKellan. You and your family are well known. Someone will see her."

When Alex reappeared, she gave an involuntary start, hoping for good news, but he shook his head and slumped into the armchair. "Murphy and Deidre have gone back to work, Mum, but said you're not to worry about the guests, they'll look after them." His voice broke and he covered his face.

Helen hurried to him and lowered his hands into hers. "Look at me, Alex. It's no one's fault. Don't blame yourself. Even as we talk, the police have started their search. Constable Malloy has promised to call when he has news. I'll wait an hour, then phone your father. You change and get something to eat."

After he left, Helen sat at her desk in a state of paralysis and stared at the phone. She wanted it to ring and not ring. Malloy's news could go either way. She was unaware that Deidre had tiptoed in until she saw a cup of sweetened tea steaming in front of her. Looking at her watch, she saw an hour had passed. It was time to call Lawrence.

His assistant, Monica, answered. "Mrs McKellan, I'm sorry, but your husband is away at present. Do you wish to leave a message? You sound anxious."

"I *am* anxious, Monica. Tell him his youngest daughter is missing, and a police search is underway. Call me back the instant you reach him. Thank you." How polite she sounded, how bitter she felt. In five years, she had only reached Lawrence directly on four occasions. She drank her tea and waited—each minute a torment. The phone rang ten minutes later.

"Mrs McKellan, your husband asked me to tell you that he's on his way."

Determined not to pester Malloy, but bent on keeping the phone within arm's reach, Helen tidied her desk, sharpened pencils, gathered rubber bands, and collected paperclips into an envelope. Deidre came with an offering of soup and stayed until the bowl was empty. When she left, Helen turned to arranging her bookshelf, until through the open window she heard the high-pitched squeal of car tires racing down the hill and braking to a halt at the front door. She ran into the foyer in time to meet Lawrence striding through the entrance.

"Thank God you're here. I can't leave the phone. Come." She grabbed his hand and rushed him to her office. Once there, words tumbled out as she related the events. "The police said they'll call once they have a lead."

"Where's Harry?"

"In Dublin. How did you get here so fast?"

He didn't answer. "Have you eaten?" She nodded. "Then I'll get some tea," but stopped halfway to the door when the phone rang. Helen answered.

"Mrs McKellan? Constable Malloy here. We have your daughter. At this moment, she is playing with the station's cat."

"Playing with a cat? Lawrence, they've found her."

Lawrence grabbed the phone. "This is her father. Where did you find her?" Helen leaned in to listen.

"We didn't, sir. Sweeney McCourt, a farmer, brought her in. He'd been at the hotel in his hay cart to drop off a wheelbarrow. We gathered from your daughter that she hid from her brother in McCourt's cart under a tarpaulin, and fell asleep.

McCourt returned to his farm, unaware he had a passenger. She said her nanny told her not to talk to strangers, so she stayed put until the cart stopped, then after a time, climbed out, but got lost. Must have walked in circles because she recognized the cart and climbed in again. That's where McCourt found her."

"No harm to her?"

"None, sir, she's fine. Officer O'Hara has just left. Your daughter will be with you faster than if you came to fetch her."

Helen saw no joy on Lawrence's face when he hung up and turned to her. "What possessed you to put Kelsey in Alex's care? Don't we have a nanny? I can't afford this, Helen. Panicked phone calls and racing from work because of your negligence. I'm not going to wait. I'm putting the hotel on the market. Tomorrow. Try to keep everything together until we move. The answer for Kelsey is a Scottish governess as soon as possible."

Helen felt sick. Clenching her hands against her stomach, she sat down where Alex had been. "Instead of attacking me, you should be relieved and happy Kelsey is safe. And where's your concern for your son? Alex is out of his mind from worry. Don't throw negligence at *me.* What have you contributed to the children and me over the past six years? Paltry letters. Hurried phone calls. Unexplained absences. Since our stay in Dublin, do you realize you've only been home three times? What I see beneath your veneer of love is selfishness. There's no warmth, no intimacy, and looking at you, I see no delight in your family."

"Stop this. We're both tired. Once I'm sure Kelsey is fine, I'll eat a decent meal, sleep, and leave in the morning before anyone is up."

"Go to hell," she said, and left to tell everyone Kelsey was safe.

When the police car arrived, she rushed out and gathered Kelsey onto her lap, then kissed her and wrapped her arms tight around her. "You must not give us frights like that again but what an adventure you had!"

Alex came and knelt beside them. "So, you slept in a hay cart and the farmer's horse never said a word. What a naughty horse. No wonder I couldn't find you. No more hide and seek for us though. Instead, I'll teach you how to draw and paint."

"That was not good of you to climb into a stranger's cart, Kelsey; don't do that again," Lawrence's scolded, but he rested his hand on her shoulder for a moment before thanking the officer.

Helen touched Alex's arm. "Alex, come inside. The staff are waiting for us."

When they entered, Murphy and Patrick beamed, and Deidre snuffled into a hanky, then all three kissed and petted Kelsey, before Helen carried her upstairs. After giving her a bath and a cup of cocoa, she tucked Kelsey into bed, and left Alex reading *The Tale of Peter Rabbit* to her.

Murphy was preparing the evening meal when she entered the kitchen. He looked up and poured her an ounce of brandy sweetened with honey. "This will help, Ma'am. You've had a nasty shock. Me and the staff are right glad the wee one is home and safe. Mary will be here for you tomorrow. Is the master staying for a while?"

"No, he's leaving early. A plate of cold cuts, ham, beef ... whatever you've got will do him for supper." To avoid Murphy's perceptive eye, she retreated to her office.

She needed to think. *Damn the war.* It had engulfed all of them—picked them up, shaken them in its fist, then scattered them onto a playing board where their weaknesses defeated them. She wanted to run, to hide with Kelsey, go to Benevolence. What if she refused to leave? But how could she? She was the glue that held the family together. It wasn't the right time. Was there ever a right time? Maybe Lawrence had a point. Sometimes managing the hotel *was* stressful. It *did* eat at her time. Maybe returning to Scotland *would* mend the marriage. She returned to the kitchen, and emerged carrying a tray of cold ham and slices of pie for two.

CHAPTER 35

NOVEMBER 1947

The grandfather clock chimed five in the predawn, as Helen tiptoed down the stairs. She had done this many times: left the hotel and driven to Kenneth before staff and guests were about.

Outside, she pulled her coat closer against the damp air and got into the car. Tentacles of mist rose from the estuary, and her studio had become a ghostly mirage. Her car pushed slowly through the fog, but a half-hour later, she stood in Benevolence's kitchen, her coat slung over a chair. The kettle still felt warm, which meant Kenneth was having tea in bed. She reheated the water and made herself a cup too.

"Good morning," she said, coming into the bedroom and kissing him.

He turned back the covers. "You need warming up; it looks chilly out there."

"It is." She stepped out of her skirt and climbed in beside him. "Lawrence has sold the hotel. The buyers signed the papers yesterday. They're the middle-aged couple I mentioned, who toured the place last month."

"What's the possession date?"

"March. Just after Kelsey's fifth birthday. He's already made a list of Edinburgh houses for me to see. Since Kelsey's misadventure in the hay cart, he's been different—less inclined to sit her on his knee or talk to her. I don't remember him being the same with the others at that age. Sometimes I wonder if he suspects us."

"I'd be swinging from the end of a rope if he did. Don't worry. Is Harry staying?"

"After the bar closed, we enjoyed a nightcap and had a long discussion. Another year, and he could have bought Lawrence out. I know Lawrence won't extend the lease—he told me that—so I'm gifting Harry the balance from my mother's estate. I'm glad to help him. He's been a source of support to me and the children for years. He says I'm to bring Kelsey—and the other two when they're free—to visit him whenever we want."

Kenneth rolled over and kissed her. "You will always have an Irish home."

After they dressed, they went into the kitchen where Helen made a breakfast of scrambled eggs and bacon.

"I used to dream of stalling the inevitable," she said, swiping butter onto the toast, as if leaving was the toast's fault. To sweeten her mood, she dropped two sugar lumps into her tea. "I wish someone special would pop into Harry's life. Please look out for him. He'll need your advice now and then."

"He already has that. I've roused him in the middle of the night more than once to give him hell. He's the brother I never had."

"Hmm, so you share secrets, do you?"

"You could say that. Speaking of Irish homes, I've been thinking, with Alex and Margaret close to leaving the nest, don't you think it's time you and Kelsey came to live with me?"

Caught by his words, she looked beyond the window to where a flock of coal tits had landed on Kenneth's denuded beech tree and pecked the suet he had hung from the branches. Just as he nourished the birds, he sustained her too, and she knew there was no happier place for her and Kelsey than beside him, and yet ...

"Stop arguing with yourself, Helen. Stay with me. You could pursue your art, even teach piano if you wished. And Kelsey? Wouldn't it be grand for us to watch her grow into a young woman?"

"It would but I can't Kenneth, I can't throw away nineteen years." Attentive to his gaze, she told him of her impulse to take Kelsey and leave Lawrence after he'd accused her of negligence. What stopped her, she explained, was her need to hold the family together. Now she must give the marriage the same chance. "Don't you see? Without the war and hotel responsibilities pulling at Lawrence and me, our marriage might work again, as it did in those weeks before the hotel opened. If I came to you now, without trying, I would always wonder."

Kenneth shook his head and pressed his hands together. "There are times I wish to hell you didn't have that infernal fairness of yours."

Sadness tinged his eyes. She reached across and touched his hand. Although her decision hurt, she knew it was right. She must propel herself forward, whatever the cost. "When we're settled, I'll find a way for you to keep in touch with Kelsey. This is wretched. What lies ahead for you?"

He pushed his plate aside and gestured towards his study. "There's a letter in there from our chief editor in Dublin. The paper is growing, and we're hoping to merge with the *Irish Times*. They want me to work as their special overseas correspondent. It's a plum position, but I delayed accepting until I knew where we stood. I'll take it now. It starts the end of March. The work will bring me to London; so, you won't be seeing the last of me."

"You mustn't count on that," she said, clearing the table.

After Kenneth had set the dishes to dry, he led her into his study. Every flat surface spilled over with books and titles she couldn't see, plus a tangle of notepads and articles. Next to photographs of herself and Kelsey, a blank sheet of paper languished in his typewriter. He withdrew a storybook from the desk's top drawer. "This is for Kelsey," he said. He had written a children's short-story collection based on Irish legends and dedicated the book to *Kelsey McKellan*.

Helen blinked. *Don't cry. Not now*. "Where did you find the time?"

"I wrote at odd intervals, whenever I was away on assignment. It brought me closer to the two of you. I shall continue on now with volume two."

§

Two weeks later, Margaret, who was enjoying a break from the Dublin College of Nursing, gave a whoop of delight on learning the hotel had sold. Alex, also home, showed his displeasure by slamming out of the family dining room in search of Harry. Alarmed, Kelsey curled herself into Flynn on the floor and sucked her thumb. Worried for her, Helen took her upstairs. In her suite she cuddled Kelsey on the sofa and read one of Kenneth's stories.

Later, in the afternoon, while shortening the hem of a dress, Helen heard cries erupting from Margaret's bedroom. She dashed along the corridor and opened the door, then stood appalled at the scene. Margaret had Kelsey across her lap and held a hairbrush in her hand. Kelsey's bottom resembled a pincushion.

"Margaret! Stop that!"

"She deserved it. Look!" Remnants of pink and white lace cluttered the floor. "She tried to make a doll's hammock out of two of my best bras."

Kelsey struggled free, pulled up her knickers, and ran to Helen. "Oh, your poor little bottom," Helen said, "we'll put calamine lotion on that. But, you were naughty. You must not come into Margaret's room and play with her things. And Margaret, don't lay a hand on your sister again, ever."

"Sister? Really?"

Helen grabbed Kelsey's hand and shepherded her through the doorway. "Come on, darling, let's use the magic lotion, and then Mary will take you and Flynn for a walk. Margaret, wait in my suite."

She found Margaret sitting resentful and glum on the sofa, leafing through a magazine, when she arrived. "Margaret, you are *fourteen* years older than Kelsey, and training to be a nurse. Instead of punishing her, you could have explained why she was wrong. What made you behave that way? It's worrying. I don't understand your bitterness."

"I don't care. It's true what I said."

"Don't you love your sister?"

"How much *is* Kelsey my sister? Look at her hair and eyes. Where's the family resemblance?"

"Oh, for heaven's sake! With that logic, I suppose you could accuse Alex of not being your brother. Last time I looked, he had freckles and the fuzzy beginnings of a red beard.

"You're just trying to be clever. I know what I see and hear. In the village, tongues wag about you and Kenneth."

"I'm not surprised. I manage a hotel and bar where the locals often drink too much, and Kenneth writes articles that get people rattled."

"But why do they hint at things?"

"Because your father is seldom here, and I'm alone. I'm a perfect target. Haven't you learned that gossip here is as popular a pastime as tea?"

But her reasoning didn't dent Margaret's rancour. "You're always playing centre stage, Mother, smiling here, laughing or talking there. You're a flirt. If Dad—"

"Does it escape you that I must be friendly with the customers?" Exasperated, she caught Margaret's hand as she attempted to stand, and tugged her down. "Margaret, we can't have this between us. Kelsey *is* your sister, every bit as much as Alex is your brother. I know it's not always easy being the eldest. I've been stricter with you, but that's the penalty of being the firstborn. You're expected to set a good example."

"That's outdated."

"Your father would disagree. Whatever you think, try to practice kindness and compassion. And, if you get pulled into gossip, defend the family—that's what Alex would do."

"You've never loved me."

Helen sighed. "I do love you, but love is like a flowering plant. It needs tending. The hotel and the war demanded so much from your dad and me. It sapped our energy and diminished our attention to you and Alex. That will change now. A new chapter begins in our lives. Am I making sense?"

Margaret's eyes glistened. "I suppose so. May I leave now?"

"On one condition. Never treat Kelsey the way you did today. The move will be stressful. Behave like a big sister, and help her."

Margaret's voice quavered. "I'm sorry. I'll try."

After she left, Helen steadied herself and, determined not to look backwards, joined Patrick in the bar.

CHAPTER 36

MARCH 1948

BLUE CLOUDS OF pipe tobacco and cigarette smoke drifted through the open door of The Brown Cow—Harry's and Kenneth's new watering hole located five miles from the hotel.

Harry drank from his tankard of Guinness and surveyed the room. You'd know something was afoot. Half the locals from the village were there, and a goodly number in from Ballina. Helen had certainly made her mark. *They'll be here soon. Lawrence, with his Master-of-the-Manor air, Helen pretending her new life will be bloody wonderful, and the staff wondering what lies ahead without her.*

Good thing this wasn't last year's big snow. Springs frozen nine-feet deep. Drifts high as telegraph poles, and him and Alex using old barn doors as sleighs so the horses could ferry dairy supplies to the hotel.

A spanking new lock had appeared on his cellar doors. *Cooper no doubt thinking the cellar safe to use again.* Twice, Old Flynn, now living with him, had awakened him with warning growls. Daecon even had the cockiness to tell him to quit investigating every bark and fecking sound he heard in the middle of the night.

Glad to see Kenneth approach, Harry bought him a pint. His chum's cheerful expression didn't fool him though. *Poor bloke.* Good thing he was heading overseas for a spell.

"Thanks for the pint. What a turn-out. They're getting a good send-off."

Harry agreed. The locals were everywhere: quaffing ale, perched on stools, sitting around tables, playing darts, and helping themselves to food in the parlour. At the other end of the counter, Murphy shouted drink orders, while Brigid—cheerfully building up Father Gareth's congregation—bedazzled her girlfriends with a lively jig step.

"Seven o'clock. They should be here."

"Ten minutes yet, Kenneth," Harry said, giving a friendly nod to four tourists trying their best not to stare. "They're likely wondering what kind of a wake this is—nary a wet eye, and yet half the people are wearing traditional black for the dearly departed."

"They'll know soon enough they're witnessing a 'British' wake, because instead of a flood of Irish migrants sailing towards the Statue of Liberty, it's a Scottish family setting sail for Edinburgh."

And with that said, Lawrence and Helen arrived—he resplendent in a tuxedo, and she a jewel in the crowd, wearing a silky, dark-blue dress.

"I think I'll just stand here and admire her forever," Kenneth murmured.

Harry nodded, himself still not quite believing Helen was leaving, although Kenneth appeared to have accepted the situation. They must have reached an understanding. Perhaps that explained her composure now; then again, she was one hell of an actress. "Quit gawking, Kenneth, let's plough through the throng." Together they elbowed forward.

"You look regal," Kenneth said, bowing low. "An Irish queen in St. Patrick blue."

"Thank you. Brigid suggested the colour, and Margaret and Alex gave their approval before going off to their own party tonight."

Harry noticed Lawrence stiffen and accept Kenneth's handshake with reluctance. His brother needed straightening out. "Lawrence, tonight you and Helen are our guests, mine and Kenneth's, so there'll be no reaching into your pockets this evening." That did it. Lawrence relaxed his manner.

"Thank you, Kenneth. Generous of you," he said, and flicked his eyes towards a trio of musicians setting up on a makeshift stage at the side the room. "I see some inevitable Irish ballads are on the way."

"Jigs, with this crowd," Harry said, throwing Kenneth a warning look.

On stage, a girl wearing a green plaid dress uncovered her harp and placed it front and centre. Beside her, a shirt-sleeved fellow fine-tuned his fiddle. Another man, with wide shoulders and thick forearms—*more likely used to lifting loads of turf,* Harry thought—adjusted the tension of his drums and twirled his sticks.

Brigid and friends crowded at the raised stage, with requests for their favourite dances. The fiddler smiled, tucked his violin under his chin, tapped his foot, and soon couples were stamping and whirling on the dance floor to the infectious rhythm of the music.

After a while, a fine tenor from Ballina jumped on stage and led the crowd with a singsong. Many added their lusty voices until the tenor soloed into *Danny Boy.* A respectful silence blanketed the room until the last note died away.

Harry noticed several of the hotel staff dabbing their eyes, and Helen biting her lip. It took the fiddler down-bowing into a boisterous jig again to break the spell. Helen moved into the throng of people, and Harry saw her smiling and chatting as if performing a starring role at the Abbey Theatre. She must have told Lawrence to circulate. He was off at the other end of the room, cornered by a town councillor well known for talking the hind leg off a donkey. Just then, a startling redhead hove into view.

Harry nudged Kenneth with his elbow and inclined his head in the girl's direction. "Look at that, will you? She's for me. As for you, why don't you ask Helen for a dance? Lawrence won't be escaping the council member for a while yet."

§

Helen saw Kenneth coming, and blocking a minefield of memories, awaited his arrival with a smile. "Pardon me, fair lady, may I have this dance?"

She curtsied and allowed him to lead her onto the floor. Once intermingled with the other dancers, she touched a jade shamrock, hanging from a gold chain on her wrist. "I don't know how this got into my bag, but I love it."

"We Irish are clever lads." Placing his hand on her back, he navigated her into the middle of the floor. "This way I get to hold you close and not raise eyebrows."

"So you say," she murmured, feeling the warmth of his hand, "but half the village is following our every move. This farewell is breaking my heart. Look at the staff. They've become like family."

"Careful, love. Those big, brown eyes of yours are threatening to drown us. Throw your head back, laugh. That's it," he said, and twirled her until her dress fanned around her ankles.

When she stopped spinning, she said, breathless, "Jill has offered me a refuge in her London hotel, if things become intolerable."

"Good and remember I'm just a phone call away."

Pretending cheerfulness, Helen called to a couple twirling past who owned the village bakery. "Kelsey and I will miss those iced buns of yours," she said and then murmured to Kenneth. "Thank you for Kelsey's wonderful book. She loves it. It will keep alive her lovely memories, and her Irish roots." She wished they could go on dancing, but the music stopped, and squeezing her hand, Kenneth guided her from the floor to where Lawrence stood watching.

§

Harry, aware Kenneth and Lawrence were now talking, with a nervous Helen beside them, looked at Rhoda, the captivating redhead. She wore a simple black dress, with a bright red sash emphasizing her small waist, but it was her green eyes that captured him. She came from Louisburgh, but after her husband's fishing boat pulled him under in a sudden storm, she had moved inland with her son, Liam. "I have a nursery garden near Ballina now."

Her lips parted in a shy smile, and Harry, inhaling the wind-blown scent of her hair, decided, *I'm keeping this one,* but he couldn't help but hear the gossip that threaded the hum of talk nearby.

"It's a terrible loss to have Mrs McKellan leave. County Mayo will be the poorer without her, don't you think, Father Gareth?" asked Andy McConnico, the local bank manager.

"I do. She's not of the faith, but generous to a fault."

"It's a painful loss for a certain journalist too," the banker's wife added slyly.

"Colleen McConnico, you're a wicked, downright gossiper," Murphy's Mary sniped.

"And you're not, I suppose."

Harry drew Rhoda away from the battlefield and steered her towards Lawrence, now entering the parlour with Kenneth behind him. "Let me introduce you to Rhoda," he said, "We've only just met, but I'm her happy captive."

Rhoda smiled and extended her hand. "Everyone will be sad to see your hotel under new management, Mr McKellan. I wish you and your wife the best." She turned to Kenneth. "I never miss your articles, Mr Inglis. The country needs writers like you."

Kenneth darted a look at Lawrence. "There are those who think not."

"He's a flea in the hide of the British Government; that's what he is," Lawrence responded. "Mr Inglis here wants one Ireland—the North and the South united. He should leave well enough alone."

"A Scotsman thinks I should *leave well enough alone*? Did you say that to the English when they strolled into your country?"

Harry threw up his hands. "Jaysus, you two! Are you forgetting this is a farewell party?" He shifted his gaze past Kenneth, and pointed over Lawrence's shoulder. "Helen's at the doorway looking for you." With a courteous nod to Rhoda, Lawrence walked away.

Harry put his arm about Rhoda's waist. "Kenneth and Lawrence will spar until rivers dry and fish fly. We should join the crowd in the other room; Murphy is getting ready to make a toast."

"Harry's right; Lawrence and I do scrap," Kenneth said, patting Rhoda's arm. "It's become a habit. Away you go. Right now, I've my eye on a slice of blackberry pie."

Holding Rhoda's hand, Harry entered the main room, just as Murphy raised his glass.

"Ladies and gentlemen, a toast to Mr and Mrs McKellan. We wish you both well. Scotland will be the richer for having you, and we the poorer." With calls of, 'here, here,' he added, "May good luck be with you each morning and night, and if you send me a recipe for haggis, I'll even eat it. To the McKellans!"

Someone started to sing *When Irish Eyes Are Smiling*, and Harry saw Helen's lips tremble as she bent her head, but when she looked up again, a sudden smile flowered across her face. Harry followed her gaze, and there, at the back of the crowd was Kenneth, raising his glass to her.

PART TWO

CHAPTER 37

JULY 1948

HELEN PICKED A drooping rose from the park's laden bush, inhaled its perfume, and looked across the street to her new home: a spacious, two-storey maisonette in a Victorian crescent. The private park had been the clincher—seven acres of walkways, wooded areas, lawns, and a children's play space complete with a roundabout, swings, and a slide.

"Where's Mary? Where's Brigid?" a bewildered Kelsey had asked on entering her new home, but the double-decker buses, Princes Street's floral clock, and the residential park soon distracted her.

"Time for lunch, Kelsey," Helen said, standing at the base of the children's slide to catch her as she careened into her arms.

"Is Alex coming?"

"No, darling, Alex and Margaret will be home next month. Today you meet your new governess, Mrs Stringer."

At the interview, the governess had reminded Helen of a wren—jaunty and small-boned, although her keen eyes suggested she was no pushover.

"I hope Kelsey being left-handed isn't a problem," Helen said. "I had to stop her Irish nanny from trying to switch Kelsey's crayons to her right hand."

Mrs Springer nodded. "It's cultural. Western religions perceive left-handedness as a separation from God's right hand. Tantra Buddhism see it as a sign of wisdom, and the Chinese as a sign of creativity. What matters is that Kelsey grasps reading, writing, and arithmetic, and develops an inquiring mind."

Those sentiments spurred Helen to hire her on the spot.

As expected, she was punctual, and brought teaching aids.

"I like that," Kelsey said, pointing to the colourful abacus.

"The abacus is a fun way to learn arithmetic, and the spelling board will teach you how to read," Mrs Stringer said, following Helen into the study where a card table stood waiting.

"Will a tea break in an hour and a half work?" Helen asked. Taking the governess's smile for a 'yes', she closed the door.

The postman had delivered a letter from Alex. She read it in the drawing room. Lawrence had entered him at Perth's Strathearn School, where he would stay until he reached entry age to Sandhurst. The school was an hour's drive from Edinburgh. Although the new year did not start until September, Alex had joined the school's summer army cadet camp. The letter told about field trips, canoeing, making lean-to's, fire pits, and other survival techniques.

Since meeting Jill, Alex's progress at school had improved, and Helen believed that, with help from Jill's brother, the colonel, Alex could avoid Sandhurst if he wanted to follow that route. She left the opened letter on the hall table for Lawrence, who was once again in London.

"Waverly Station should name a cabin on their overnight train after you. Maybe we should move south," she had said, a shade nettled when he left. Again, he repeated why Edinburgh was preferable to London. Alex and Margaret were closer and Scotland was a good environment for Kelsey to improve her education.

In the kitchen, the telephone rang. It was Margaret.

"I'm in London, Mother."

"How did you manage that?"

"We got a surprise break, so Annie and I jumped at the chance to be tourists."

"Any chance of seeing Jill?"

"Not enough time. We leave tomorrow." *Long silence.* "Is Dad home?"

"No, he's in London too. At the Arts Club."

"That's near Dover Street, right? So … I *did* see him. Annie and I were on a bus tour."

"That's miraculous—spotting someone in a city of eight million or more—was he alone?"

"No. Walking with someone about his height. How's Kelsey?"

That's a quick change of subject. "She's having her first lesson with her new governess."

"I hope they are well-suited. I'll buy Kelsey a souvenir. Say hello to her. Must go. Bye."

Mid-afternoon, Helen—preoccupied with Margaret's curious phone call—wheeled the tea trolley towards the study. If Margaret had seen a man, she'd have said so. *Someone* implied a woman. She recalled Jill saying, *'Tall as Lawrence. Not a warm person'*. She opened the door and shoved the tea trolley in, making the cups chatter on their saucers.

CHAPTER 38

AUGUST 1948

HELEN EYED HER sponge cake with alarm. It wasn't soft and high like Murphy's. She would pretend it was a pound cake. She set it in the pantry to let the icing harden, believing these days that she made a better cleaning lady than a cook. Sometimes she wished she were a man.

"Margaret will be here soon," she called to Alex and Kelsey. According to Lawrence, Margaret had been reluctant to visit, claiming she needed more study time for a forthcoming test.

"I told her that her family had priority over a test," he'd said. Helen had smothered a laugh at that comment.

The front doorbell chimed just as she finished drying her hands. "Coming," she called, and opening the door saw Margaret sniffing the air.

"You've been cooking roast beef, Mum. It smells wonderful. When did you last cook one?"

"Too long ago to remember," she said, embracing her. "Kelsey inveigled Alex upstairs to look at her drawings. They'll be down in a minute." Over Margaret's shoulder, she noticed Lawrence exiting the study, and stepped aside.

"Good to see you, Margaret" he said. "I believe you're old enough for a glass of Harvey's Bristol Cream sherry now."

"Dad, I'm twenty, not eighteen."

The sound of Alex bounding down the stairs drowned out his response. "Hi, Margaret, long time, no see."

"I'm learning how to fatten stick people!" Kelsey shouted from behind him.

"Excellent because Alex is the expert. Let's follow Mum into the living room. How's your governess?"

"She's nice. I can say the alphabet and sound words too."

"You'll be reading soon," Margaret said, settling on the sofa beside Alex. "How was camp?"

"Great. Three of us won places on the inter-school rifle team."

"Who would have thought shooting rats with an air gun would bring such rewards? I suppose ideas of farming are long gone?"

Alex shot a look at his father approaching with Margaret's sherry. "No. Farming is still on the agenda."

"Left, right! Left, right! Moo, moo!" Kelsey said, jumping to her feet from a footstool, and marching round the room.

Lawrence frowned and pointed her back to the footstool, but Kelsey squeezed herself between her siblings. "Cadet weekends are fine, Alex, but prioritize and apply yourself to your school work," Lawrence observed. "You need top marks; otherwise Sandhurst's doors will slam shut. Keep in mind that good connections are found among officers, not army privates."

Alex rolled his eyes. "I doubt good connections will help me milk cows."

"Alex, stop goading your father," Helen warned.

"Look! Margaret's got presents in her handbag!" Kelsey squealed.

"Let's enjoy dinner first," Helen said. During the meal, she was glad that the saying, *children should be seen, not heard* had not cowed her children. Kelsey asking Lawrence where did the wind come from engaged his interest, as did Margaret's answers to Alex.

"Our housing is not so different from a boarding school. Lights out by 10:00 p.m. Up by 6:00 a.m. Beds checked for tight sheets and mitered corners. Rooms inspected for tidiness. Chores completed before breakfast and penalties for dust bunnies." Kelsey's eyes widened. "Not rabbits, silly," Margaret said.

"Sounds as if you're in the army."

"Except nurses help heal not injure people, Alex. Still, I suspect our matron is as intimidating as any sergeant-major."

The pound cake halted further discussion until the last crumb had gone. Back in the living room, Kelsey unwrapped her present first. "It's a clock!" she said, touching the raised wooden hours and twig-shaped hands on its flower-painted face. Then she pulled a face. "I can't tell the time."

"That's why you have a governess. Now hush, Mum is opening her gift."

Helen held it up. “What a lovely surprise. I needed some good linen napkins, but Harrods Emporium is a very expensive shop.”

“Harrods? When were you in London?”

“While you were there, Dad. Annie and I saw you from a London double-decker. You were walking along Dover Street with someone about your height. The Arts Club is close by, isn’t it?”

He gave a brief smile. “Yes, but I expect you saw someone resembling me. I’m seldom there until late in the evening.”

Margaret nodded and sat back in her chair, but in Helen’s opinion, she didn’t look convinced. “Lawrence, what did Margaret give you?” she asked, tactfully.

He showed her a book of Walter Scott’s poetry. “He’s one of my favourite writers, Margaret. I can quote many of his poems. *Whose heart hath ne’er within him burn’d, as home his footsteps he hath turn’d, from wandering on a foreign strand!* Stirring words. If you take future excursions into the Highlands, rather than south to London, they will stir you too.”

I could quote one myself, Helen thought. *‘Oh, what a tangled web we weave when first we practice to deceive.’*

“Your gift reminds me, Margaret, that I should introduce Scottish stories to Kelsey,” Lawrence continued.

“I like Uncle Kenneth’s ones,” Kelsey piped up.

“Wait ‘til you hear *The Legend of Nessie, the Loch Ness Monster* and *Old Shellycoat the Bogeyman*. I’ll look for—”

“Careful, Dad. I remember Alex and me, older than Kelsey is now, being scared of Pookas.”

“What are Pookas?”

“Phantom horses that gallop around at night, Kelsey. Speaking of which, I should get back to my studies.”

“May I drive you back?”

“The bus suits me fine, Dad.”

“Thanks for the Swiss Army knife, Margaret, it will come in handy” Alex told her in the hallway. “If we were in Ireland, I could drive you.”

“Next year you will be eighteen and can get a license. Meanwhile, my boyfriend, Robert, owns a Morris Minor, so we’ll come and free you from school one fine weekend.”

“Robert? Who is he? Tell us more.”

"We've only been dating a short time, Mum. He's twenty-three and studying law at Edinburgh University. He's from Aberdeen, Dad."

"A Highlander? Excellent," Lawrence said, holding out her lightweight coat. "I'm encouraged by your choice of career. The Service Industries are the right vocations for women."

Helen laughed. "That said from a husband who made his wife a hotel manager."

"That's a service industry, Helen."

Helen felt Margaret's arm link through hers. "The world is full of service industries, Dad. The army, navy, and air force being excellent examples."

To Helen's amusement, both men looked incredulous. "How about we women take Kelsey to the Chocolate Shop next week," she said, "and leave the men to their old-fashioned ideas?"

Margaret winked. "Love to."

§

Helen hummed while she filled the sink with sudsy water and washed the dishes. Margaret's warmth towards her and Kelsey was a lovely change. Maybe seeing her father with another woman had provided a fairer perspective on her parents.

"Nightcap?" Lawrence asked, waving a bottle of brandy at her from the kitchen door.

"A small one would be nice."

When she entered the living room, the quietude of the flat made her think she had moved into a retirement home. With Margaret immersed in her own life, Alex off to boarding school, and Kelsey going in a year, what use was she to anyone? Especially with Lawrence absent on frequent business trips. She had not counted on feeling so displaced returning to Edinburgh, and missing Kenneth was a chronic ache. She sighed.

"Are things that bad?" Lawrence asked, returning with the brandy.

"I'm just thinking that I'm not very useful or active these days."

"Would a holiday in the Highlands help?"

"It won't solve my problem but it would be nice. We could go after we drop Alex off at school. Kelsey can miss a week with Mrs Stringer."

"I hadn't meant going so soon. Let me have a talk with my good friend, John Duncan. He's Chairman of the Edinburgh Antique Society. It's attracted wide attention since he took the helm. It occurs to me that he would very much appreciate someone of your calibre on one of his committee. Not only would such an opportunity give you a new interest, you would meet some excellent people—in fact the cream of Edinburgh's society wives."

"Antiques? That *would* be interesting, and very thoughtful of you but forgive me, I'll skip the rest. I'm not interested in bridge clubs and gossip."

CHAPTER 39

NOVEMBER 1948

HARRY FORKED A final hay load into the cow stalls, best not to let the weather catch him—capricious as a woman who demurs for a day then drops her white petticoats overnight. But snow showed up unwanted footprints. Cooper must still be using the cellar, since Daecon slipped him five quid a month, though there'd been no midnight noises. He missed old Flynn. *Might be time to replace him with a border collie.* They were grand at rounding up four-legged strays or warning off two-legged intruders for that matter.

Smells of Rhoda's Dublin Coddle—onions mixed with sausages, bacon, and potatoes—enticed him towards the house. She was a grand cook, and as energetic and saucy a lover as he could ever want. He'd suggested she move in with him full time and sell her house, but she showed her independence by telling him that one day her house would be Liam's. Nice lad—worked in a boat-building yard and visited her twice a month from Cork. Still, Rhoda compromised by settling into the farm for regular three-day weekends. The arrangement worked well. Allowed time at the tracks, nights out with the boys, and evenings with Kenneth at The Brown Cow when he was home. Neither of them frequented the hotel bar now—colourless without Helen and her staff.

"Kenneth just phoned," Rhoda said, when he trudged through the door. She had set the table for three. "I've asked him over for lunch. He's just back from Belfast. I wish he had a lady friend."

"Not him. He prefers casual friends."

"That's a shame. Listen! I think I hear his car."

Harry opened the door. "Come in Kenneth. I have an excellent scotch just waiting to warm the cockles of your heart."

"Hullo, there," Rhoda called from the kitchen, as Kenneth took off his coat. "Come and sit at the table and tell us your news."

"There's a big gun salute celebrating the Republic of Ireland bill in Dublin during Easter weekend. Come with me. I'll get you press passes." He took a sip of his drink. "This is a fine scotch, Harry."

"Didn't I promise to share a bottle of Deacon's best, if I ever laid hands on one?"

"And where might Daecon store such nectar of the gods?"

"In the chamber of Hades, I'm guessing."

Amused with their private joke, both men tucked into their food and talked about the Irish Open, where a Welshman had the cheek to beat Ireland's Harry Bradshaw at Portmarnock Golf Club.

"I've turned the old rifle range into a pitch and putt," Harry said, taking more coddle. "Come spring, I plan to teach Liam some basics. Alex, too, if he ever gets over here. I miss him."

Kenneth stopped eating. "Is all well in Scotland?"

"I think so. I'm due a letter, so I'll let you know."

"You're away a lot these days, Kenneth. Do you go far afield?"

Kenneth relished his last mouthful before answering, "Well, Rhoda, apart from going to Belfast, I'm over in Europe most of the time."

"Europe? What takes you there?"

"The paper needs to know how our new Republic will merge with the United Nations. It's a long, complicated undertaking and involves trade agreements. In fact, Harry, I'm going to London in March." Smiling at Rhoda he produced a small package from his pocket. "This is for you."

London in March? Was that a hint to tell Helen? Harry wiped his plate clean with a crust of bread while Rhoda exclaimed over Kenneth's gift of Yardley's soap, then glanced at his watch. "Mary and Murphy need a dairy delivery today. It won't be long before their tea-house becomes a full-blown restaurant."

"Next time, we'll have lunch there—my treat. You're a grand cook, Rhoda; thanks for the meal."

"Remember now, Kenneth, you're with us for Christmas."

"I wouldn't miss it. I've circled the date in red. By the by, Harry, I'm home for the week, so get your dart arm working."

CHAPTER 40

MARCH 1949

"STAYING AT THE Hermitage is ideal for the antique show, and three days with Jill will be a treat," Helen said. "We haven't seen each other since Kelsey was three." She and Lawrence were dining at the Edinburgh Arts Club—a male institution that smelled of cigars and shoe polish.

Lawrence toyed with his wine. "It's a long way just to attend an antique show."

"Blame John; he came up with the idea when I mentioned London, and said I could purchase an item for the society while I was there."

"Have you made suitable arrangements for Kelsey?"

"Yes. Mrs Stringer and two teachers have an annual event that prepares children for boarding school. They live as students in a real one for five days. Margaret needs practicum work, so they've offered her the matron position.

"What happens if a client requires me in London?"

"Are you throwing up roadblocks? Go! Kelsey is in safe hands."

"I'm sure a lady from the society would have been delighted to accompany you."

"Perhaps, but that would not delight me or Jill. Am I permitted coffee in your club's sitting room with its leather-worn chairs, Lawrence, or are women still barricaded from there?"

§

The overnight journey four nights later, with its monotonous clatter of steel on steel, soon lulled Helen to sleep. Next morning, she ate a breakfast of eggs and steamed haddock in the restaurant car, hoping the meal would settle her since her mind whirled with questions but no answers.

In a phone chat, Harry had said Kenneth might be in London the same time as her. "I'm not seeking to meet him," she said, but what if she did? She called collect. "So could we meet? Nothing else," she warned.

"Didn't I say you hadn't seen the last of me," he chuckled. "Once I'm there, I'll have a hand-delivered note given in at Jill's front desk for you with my phone number on it."

But what if a newsworthy event stops him, she fussed later. In that event, she would send him the photos she'd taken: Kelsey on the garden's swing, standing with Mrs Stringer, playing monopoly with Margaret and Alex, and one of her and Kelsey at the zoo.

She had tried to dissuade Jill from meeting her at Euston Station, but before her feet hit the platform, Jill was there, hurrying towards her. "I can't believe you're here. Six in the morning and no dark circles under your eyes."

On the way to The Hermitage, she mentioned Fortnum Masons on Jermyn Street as excellent for lunch or tea. Helen recalled the street from her twenties. It was where her father and well-heeled friends bought luxury items, such as Havana cigars and gold-plated Dunhill lighters. No wonder Jill's hotel nearby did a brisk business.

The front-desk clerk welcomed her with a warm smile, then reached behind him and gave her the room key, but no envelope.

"Once you're unpacked, you'll find my office to the left of our antique elevator. We call it the birdcage," Jill said. "It clatters and clangs but works fine."

Helen's mood lifted on entering her room. A gas fire danced flames in the grate, and the bed was a cumulus cloud of white linen. *Have faith,* she scolded herself. *Kenneth won't break his word.*

Jill waved a catalogue at her when she arrived in her office, bathed and refreshed. "Our first stop is Sotheby's. Their book auction starts at ten thirty. Afterwards, we'll eat at Fortnum's, and then visit the silver vaults."

"You'd put a Thomas Cook tour agent to shame. Maybe I'll find a Georgian mustard pot to match my spice shakers." She had never seen the vaults with their thick four-foot walls lined with steel, but she knew they had been strong enough to survive a direct hit during the blitz.

"I see you've got a good pair of walking shoes."

Helen wiggled her brown and beige Oxford lace-ups. "My feet have a love affair with these. At Sotheby's, keep your eyes peeled for a book on Scottish art—something for the Society's front-hall table."

"There's also Christie's auction tomorrow morning. We'll lunch here afterwards, and then I'll leave you to your own devices for the rest of the day."

"Excellent. I want to buy Kelsey a present from Harrods' toy department." Now for a white lie. "In the evening, I hope to catch up with a girlfriend for dinner." Jill nodded, and relieved at not having to field questions, Helen spooned marmalade onto a toasted crumpet.

Kenneth's letter arrived while they were out—hand delivered and given discreetly to Helen by the desk clerk after Jill had gone. Burdened with a large illustrated book featuring Scottish antiques under her arm, plus her new mustard pot, she raced up stairs.

Once there, she kicked off her shoes, dumped the book on the bed, and tore open the envelope.

> *Helen, my love, welcome to the heart of the British Empire. I'm hoping tomorrow evening can be ours. I'm staying at a colleague's house. Here's his number. I was thinking you might enjoy a good Irish dinner—what else in enemy territory—at the Hibernian? Did you know the name is classical Greek and means the Island of Ireland?*

Helen's mouth broke into a smile—she missed his humour.

§

Next morning, she bid on two prints at the auction, one called *The Grassmarket*, the other *St. Andrews from the Pier.* Later, as Jill had promised, they had lunch in her private dining room, where they spoke of Harry and Rhoda, looked at Helen's photographs, but avoided talk of Lawrence and Kenneth.

Before walking to Harrods, Helen dropped by Jill's office, where she found her working on the accounts. "Jill, I haven't been straight with you."

"Don't fuss. I never bought your girlfriend-for-dinner story."

"I'm meeting Kenneth at the Hibernian for dinner."

"Helen, I'm glad for you. You don't owe me explanations."

"I do, Lawrence might arrive and stay at his Club, and look for me."

"Yes, I expect staying with independent me doesn't sit well. How can I help?"

Helen gave her the Hibernian's number. "Please phone should Lawrence call. Our reservation is under Inglis. Is that putting you on the spot?"

"Not one bit. Everything will be all right. Now, smile and stop looking so worried. You and I will catch up later."

§

Helen made her way to the restaurant with her purchases—a London double-decker money box for Kelsey, plus a pair of sleek leather gloves for Margaret. When she entered, Kenneth was beside her before she could look around. He kissed her on both cheeks and guided her to a private booth where they could sit together. "Don't talk," he said, touching her lips. "Just let me look at you." He rested his eyes on her as if he would devour her.

She wanted to meet his gaze, but overcome by emotion she delved into her handbag with unsteady hands and gave him the photographs.

"It's hard to believe Kelsey is six" he said, brushing her fingers. "Does she remember me?"

"She does, and she reads your stories for herself now."

While he lingered over the photographs, she tried to memorize every feature of his face. The way he frowned in concentration, the dimpled chin, his crooked smile—simple details to console her when she was alone.

After the waiter brought their Irish stew, made with lamb, and a basket of wheaten soda bread, she gave him the latest on Alex and Margaret—their aspirations and student life—and then filled him in on Kelsey. "Right now, she's in a mock boarding school preparing for the real thing."

"I've never approved of boarding schools for young children. Are you not worried she'll be lonely?"

"I am, but she's fearless like you and has a cheerful nature. I wanted a day school, but boarding schools are an upper-class symbol to Lawrence. Thanks to the war, Alex and Margaret escaped that fate in their early years. Now, please tell me, has much changed at home in a year?"

"So, Ireland remains home to you?" She nodded. "I'm glad of that. Since the South has finally thrown off the monarchy, there's grand celebrations planned in Dublin, and Harry and Rhoda are meeting me. I'm still covering home events, but the Republic's wish to join the UN also has me in Europe."

"Is that Cooper man still around?"

"Gone to ground, but I expect he and his IRA chums will attend the celebrations. I might even shake his hand."

"Kenneth, stop fooling. You haven't joined the movement, have you?"

"Not a chance, but I share his wish for a united country."

"Yes, you infuriated Lawrence on that score," she chuckled, recalling their bar scuffle. She savoured a mouthful of stew, then drank some Guinness. "I haven't had this since I left. Do you ever drop in on the hotel bar?"

"Most of the regulars you'd remember frequent The Brown Cow now, like Harry and me. We inveigled the owners to make space for a dart board," he said. His expression changed to bafflement as he looked at her. "Why no letters from you, my love?"

"I tried to write, but each attempt weakened me with longings and wishful thinking and I couldn't afford that."

"God knows the times I've wanted to call. We share the same feelings."

"I know we do, Kenneth, but that's where the similarity stops. You have no family ties, with their obligations and responsibilities, but I ... I explained this to you in Benevolence. Never seeing you is a torment but I expected that." His grip tightened. She loosened it. "Please, Kenneth, you must release me and find someone with whom you can build a real relationship—not the silent purgatory we suffer." Her eyes brimmed.

"Jaysus, is it that bad?"

"Yes, because there's no fulfillment." Over his shoulder, she saw their waiter approaching.

"Mr Inglis, you have a phone call. A Mrs Armitage."

"That's for me," Helen said. "Ask her to wait a moment, please." Once he left, she explained the reason for Jill's call then stood and put a restraining hand on Kenneth's shoulder. "You are the love of my life, but you must let go."

"What about Kelsey?"

"Boarding school starts in September. I'll send you her school address. Write to her. Get to know her again."

§

Twenty minutes later, she entered the hotel to find Jill waiting. "You certainly know your husband, my sweet. Tell him you're just back from eating at Lyons Corner House. Invite him for a drink, if that helps."

"Sorry I missed you," she said, ready with Jill's excuses, when Lawrence answered. "What brings you to London?"

"A contract promising excellent returns, I hope."

"Would you like to meet me here in the bar?"

"Have you eaten?"

"As I mentioned, I ate at Lyons."

"So you did. What did you buy at the auctions?"

She rattled off the auction items, and included the gifts for Kelsey and Margaret. Another long pause. "A present for you too. A print. I hope it pleases you." Thank God she'd bought one.

"Well, since you've dined, I'll eat here and pass on the bar. It's been a busy day. Tell me your agenda until you catch the night train home tomorrow."

"A walk in Hyde Park, and then Jill and I are going to the Tate Gallery. Join us."

"Not sure I can. Get some rest. I'll check my schedule and call you later."

§

Once he'd hung up, Lawrence mulled over the conversation. Helen's explanation dovetailed well with Jill's—almost too well, which was one of the three reasons he had come to London—to check on Helen, meet his bank clients, and see Richardson.

Richardson had come first. They met in the director's sanctum within an hour of him arriving at Euston station that morning.

Richardson stirred his habitual cup of tea. "In using your business as a cover, Lawrence, I trust you are being discreet."

"Absolutely, sir. Is there news on the Dublin celebrations? Stockwell's reports are minimal these days. Understandable, I suppose, since IRA membership declined through the war years. But, under its new chief of staff appointed seven months ago, I expect there's a slow resurgence now."

"Indeed, which is why I called this meeting. There are rumours of a border campaign being planned."

"They'll need arms for that."

"Precisely, and since IRA ambitions are being thwarted through increased surveillance, it occurs to me that they will mount raids on military installations over here." He drummed his fingers on the desk, then stopped and pressed his palms together. "I want you to review security in our military barracks around

Britain. Your work has made Stockwell's surveillance system efficient, so I see no advantage to further Belfast visits from you. One question, however: I notice that you stopped pursuing that journalist, Kenneth Inglis, and his possible IRA connections. Why the change?"

Lawrence fixed Richardson with a steady stare, realizing that, to keep the spotlight off Harry, he must divert with boring facts. "Eighteen months ago, I asked Sergeant Stockwell to gather Inglis's articles into a file. I acted on a hunch, because through his articles, Inglis succeeded in obtaining the release of IRA internees. Stockwell was thorough. I also had him assemble lists of passengers who used the Enterprise Express. I brought that material back to London, but neither Inglis's name nor Cooper's surfaced. Furthermore, I found no inflammatory articles, and no evidence of IRA and Inglis collusion. The Republic's integration with the United Nations now takes him to Europe."

"Well, thank you, Lawrence. *Truthful lips endure forever.*"

But, later in his room, three of Richardson's comments during their meeting bothered him: one, in the director's quote from Proverbs, he'd left off the second part—*a lying tongue lasts only a moment;* two, being closed out of Belfast; and three, Richardson's query at the end.

Had Stockwell found a connection between Kenneth, Cooper, and the IRA and opened up that damned smuggling fiasco again without him knowing? Had Richardson removed him from Belfast because Kenneth's friendship with the family raised serious doubts about him? On the positive side, his new assignment made sense, and moving the family to Edinburgh surely emphasized his *supposed* disinterest in Kenneth. Was he here now? Was Helen really at Jill's? Worth checking.

Her sleepy voice answering on the fourth ring settled that question. "Sorry to interrupt your beauty sleep," he said, "I can't make the Tate tomorrow, but I'll meet you at the station, and we'll travel home together."

CHAPTER 41

APRIL 1949

CLIVE RICHARDSON SETTLED back in his chair full of expectations. In his hand, he held Stockwell's report, based on his latest task. The assignment had proceeded from Lawrence's reasons for dropping Inglis. His reasons had sounded valid enough, but they were long-winded and reminded him of the famous line in Hamlet: *The lady doth protest too much.* It had led him to act on a hunch of his own.

Eager to see the results, he adjusted his glasses.

Report by Sergeant Stockwell, Belfast: Started surveillance of Cooper O'Neil and Kenneth Inglis on April 4, 1949. Subjects attended official Dublin celebrations on April 18, 1949 to recognize Republic of Ireland. Surveillance was carried out by Sergeant Stockwell, Agent Johnson, Agent Richmond, and Corporal Peters.

Richardson smiled. He and Corporal Peters both shared a talent for lip reading. He read on. The report covered the weather, the military parade of the Republican Army, the soldiers lining O'Connell Street, and the crowd control. He could understand Lawrence's frustration at the sergeant's padded reports. He skipped to the key part.

No contact between subjects, Cooper O'Neil and Kenneth Inglis. Inglis joined Harry McKellan and girlfriend on press balcony of Gresham hotel.
Corporal Peters continued surveillance when event ended. Observed Cooper O'Neil, Eamon O'Neil and IRA man meet at Conway's Pub, Parnell St.16:00 hours. Conversation included unification of Ireland and that arms and ammunition were needed. Cooper O'Neil claimed a hidden supply of both

items. Once IRA man left, Cooper O'Neil told his brother he used a cellar on Harry McKellan's property. Meeting ended 16:25 hours.

Richardson ignored the sergeant's proposal that followed. The revelation about Harry McKellan shocked him, but it certainly explained the diffidence in Lawrence when they met. *He who conceals a transgression seeks love, but he who repeats the matter separates friends.* He felt some sympathy for the man. Sighing, he picked up the phone and contacted Belfast.

"Sergeant? I've read your report. Rather than follow through on your proposal, here's what I want you to do ... "

He ended the call with a caution. "Remember, we have ways of dealing with any breach of confidentiality. Call me direct, after completion of the mission, and be sure you type the report. Keep it concise and no copies."

The second report arrived on Richardson's desk through military channels.

Operation Crypt completed Tuesday, April 26,1949. Team: Sergeant Stockwell, Corporal Richard Avery, Private John Brent, Private Peter Wilson. Nighttime operation. Target: Rogue 1- Killala Bay, County Mayo. Objective: To ascertain use of cellar and contents on farm property.

Detail: Team dressed in black. Rain obscured moonlight. No dog on premises. Cellar located front side of property. Entrance covered by debris. Secured with chain and padlock. Private Wilson shimmed lock. Wooden steps led to gouged earthen floor.

30 crates found. Military stencils identified 25 crates as properties of Belfast and Derry Barracks. 5 from Skoda munition works, Czech Republic. 4 broken open. N.B. A military lorry carrying small arms ammunition was ambushed in 1943 in Belfast. Second raid occurred in Derry same year.

Also found two live bullets at base of steps. Corporal Avery, with 16 mm still camera and flash attachment, took photographs of crates and shelves, including black-market items. Sergeant Stockwell stood beside crates with Irish Times as proof of time and cellar's contents.

Humming the hymn, *We Shall Overcome,* Richardson locked the report in his safe and then ordered round-the-clock surveillance of Cooper O'Neil and the cellar. There were limitless ways to use information.

CHAPTER 42

JULY 1949

AT TWELVE NOON, Lawrence entered the Black Swan Pub—a favourite of personnel from the Aldershot military garrison. He saw Alex waiting for him at a table by himself and glancing nervously at the door. *And no wonder,* Lawrence thought.

"I'm going camping with two friends after school graduation," Alex had announced at the start of the summer holiday but he'd lied. The camping trip resulted in him and two boys hiking south to enlist as army regulars.

Lawrence noticed two youths at a table across from Alex, eating door-stopper sandwiches. When one of them jerked his head at his entrance, he knew they were the other culprits.

"Dad, can I get you a drink?" Alex asked, jumping to his feet when he stopped at the table.

"Yes. A scotch and water." Alex gave the order to a passing waiter.

"I wasn't sure you'd come, Dad."

"From your voice on the phone, I suspect that's what you hoped. I'm disappointed in you, Alex. Why have you stabled yourself with drays when you're a thoroughbred?"

"Because they aren't puffed up with self-importance. But seriously, I'm here because Sandhurst doesn't do in-depth sniper training. Colonel Armitage approved my marks in math, and commended my efforts in Scotland's inter-schools rifle competitions. I'm very grateful to Jill for her help."

"Help? I see it as connivance. Worse still was the complicity of your mother and uncle."

"Dad, all they did was keep track of my marks and urge me to work hard."

"I trust you realize being a sniper puts you on the front line and makes you a target?"

"That's what happens to soldiers, Dad."

"Yes, but snipers top the pyramid."

"The bomb-disposal chaps might disagree with that."

Lawrence laughed. "You should have considered being a lawyer. You certainly know how to argue, but let's stop this. There's no point. Are you impressed with the camp?"

Alex swallowed a mouthful of cider and launched into an enthusiastic description of the garrison's size. "It's divided into two camps. The north has six barracks and includes offices, a library, and infirmary. The south is bigger. At one time, the barracks were long wooden huts, but they're red brick now. It's a huge complex. There are seven-thousand acres of open training ground behind the garrison, so I'm looking forward to the long-range precision shooting."

Lawrence nodded. He knew. On his list of military garrisons requiring security checks, Aldershot had been first. Alex will have a rude awakening once they issue him with boots, a billycan, utensils, and a kit bag, and then assign him to his barracks, he thought.

Before he ever sets foot on a rifle range, he will have endless drills on the parade square, arduous physical training, ten-mile runs, and enforced marches. He will learn that sergeants do the hands-on work, but officers understand the larger view of the battlefield. That will always be denied him. "Well, Alex, you've made your choice; I hope it works out for you. On your explorations here, take a look at the bronze statue of the Duke of Wellington astride his horse, and wonder why it's not a private sitting there. You'll find him on Round Hill behind the Royal Garrison Church."

Alex's eyes widened in surprise. "Have you been here before?"

Lawrence gave a half-smile, and suggested they eat since he had a train to catch. When they left, he looked across to the two youths and said, "Tell your fellow miscreants over there, Alex, that you are walking me to the station."

§

Harry received the first of Alex's letters in August.

Uncle Harry, please send horse liniment. I've blisters on my feet. You and Uncle Kenneth wouldn't find me in your front field even if you looked now. Beware the sniper in the bush. I've done night exercises, battlefield first aid, radio procedures, and guard duty, and now use a.303 Lee Enfield rifle for long-range shooting at camouflaged targets. I'm being transferred to Bovington Camp in Dorset. There's a legendary war sniper willing to train me. My unit has gone to Germany, but not me or my new friend Mike. He's a jazz musician from London, and while I and other snipers crawl around in the mud, he tours England with our garrison's dance band! I got socked in the ribs for asking how bandsmen could defend our country with clarinets and tubas. Up early, so goodnight. Alex.

Another letter came in September.

Hi, I'm in Bovington! The camp is only six miles from the historic town of Wareham. I get little off-duty time, but Mike and I hooked up with two girls, a blonde and a brunette—mine's the blonde. We've been canoeing on the river Ware. You would like this place. It has a great pub and good fishing though I haven't had time for that yet.

I've finished my basic sniper programme. Now, I'm into advanced training. Here's a photo of me carrying a modified Lee Enfield no.4 Mk 1. It calibrates longer distances. So, you've changed our range to a small golf course. I'll look forward to swinging golf clubs with you and Liam. He sounds a good chap. Don't tell Mum about my training. She probably thinks life is just one big holiday for me. Can't blame her, because I write about pubs, new friends—not all of them, ha-ha—and Dorset's sandy beaches and fantastic seafood. My instructor says my progress will propel me into service faster than normal. That should please Dad. Must go. Hi to Rhoda. Night patrol tonight. Alex.

CHAPTER 43

SEPTEMBER 1949

St. Catherine's private School for Girls, set on twenty-five acres, boasted two playing fields, twelve tennis courts, a clock tower on the main building, and ten boarding houses. Another house, a mile from the others, overlooked the North Sea. This was the one Helen chose for Kelsey.

"I don't like wearing ties," Kelsey said from the backseat of the family car, as it sped across the Firth of Forth Bridge in driving rain.

"Alex and Daddy wear ties."

"They're boys, Mummy."

The short exchange brought back the shopping spree for Kelsey's uniform with Margaret. Lace-ups the colour of cow pats, a green tunic, matching knee-highs, white blouses, and a purple cloak with a hood.

§

"St. Catherine's won't be the same as Mrs Stringer's school camp," Margaret said, in answer to Kelsey's spate of questions after they stopped in at the Chocolate Shop, laden with parcels.

"Will the dormitories be bigger?"

"Yes, but colder. Scotland's east coast is not Killala Bay. Lots of rules too. At mealtimes, we weren't allowed to ask people to pass things."

"What if I need more marmalade?"

"Stare at it and hope someone notices."

"What else?"

"Sunday walks, even if it rains. Pretend you're Alex. He goes on marches, whether it rains, or snows." Kelsey listened, mouth agape.

"But, you will also go to concerts, learn to dance, play tennis, and how to write letters," Helen countered, on a positive note. "Your uncles will love getting letters from you. And the school library has its own building."

Relieved, Kelsey closed her mouth and tried to peer inside Margaret's handbag. "No, you don't," Margaret said. "Finish your chocolate first."

Kelsey took one gulp and turned her mug upside down. Margaret laughed and reached into her carryall. Her hands emerged holding a bright-red alarm clock. The clock's numbers and hands were a luminous green. At her urging, Kelsey plunged the clock back into the bag, buried her face inside, then jumped up and hugged her. "It's magic. It shines in the dark."

Margaret scooped her onto her knee. "You can be a little toad, sometimes, but I love you. Promise to treat people's belongings at school with respect." Kelsey hung her head. She remembered.

§

"Look! There's the school library," Lawrence said, cracking open the car window. "Three hundred years ago, the Queen of England had Mary Queen of Scots imprisoned here before going to London to have her head chopped off."

"It's a very old story," Helen said, seeing Kelsey's dismay.

"She lost her *head,* Daddy?"

"She did, because she plotted to have Queen Elizabeth assassinated. She was imprisoned for eighteen years before the English did the dastardly deed. Here you will learn all about her because your new school teaches Scottish history ahead of English."

Helen couldn't restrain herself. "Such a pity Irish schools weren't allowed the same privilege." He rewarded her with a frosty look.

Although the rain had ceased, rivulets still streamed down the house windows when they arrived. Uniformed students milled about, waving and calling to each other, but the new ones hung back. While Lawrence hauled Kelsey's trunk from the car, Helen squeezed Kelsey's arm. "There are lots of new girls here like you. You'll soon make friends. Maybe you'll find someone like Sorcha."

"Sorcha didn't go to school."

"Then you must learn letter-writing so Uncle Kenneth can share your news."

A senior girl approached with a clipboard and smiled. "Hullo. May I have your name please?" Kelsey mumbled, but the girl heard and carefully crossed off her name. "Welcome to St. Catherine's, Kelsey. I'm Letitia Brownlow, your House Prefect. Please say goodbye to our parents and then follow me to where the other new girls are waiting."

Kelsey scuffed the ground with her new shoes. Her lips trembled, but she didn't cry. Helen felt her stomach tighten. *Thank God Kenneth isn't here to see this.* "I'll write every week; I promise," she whispered. "Next month there's a three-day outing. What a lot we'll have to share. Now give me a kiss. The time will rush by; you'll see."

Lawrence stepped close and patted Kelsey on the shoulder. "Run along now. Don't get into trouble. Remember, you're a McKellan."

CHAPTER 44

OCTOBER 1949

NORA 1 WAS Cooper's symbol of success. She was a small cabin cruiser possessing twin engines, a cabin fore and aft, an amidships salon, chart table, and a fold-down upholstered bench. Boats were for the well-heeled. A judge had bought Cooper' silence with it to save himself and his family from ruination. Cooper considered it his most successful shakedown.

He kept the boat moored at a jetty in Dundalk since the harbour was halfway between Belfast and Dublin. He couldn't recall all the people *Nora 1* had hosted. Corrupt politicians, judges, IRA lads, and now this one.

Standing at the rear of the boat, he scanned the dock and saw two men picking their way over ropes and nets. His lips twitched, his lackey and the scribe—Daecon and Inglis. Baiting Kenneth was the same as playing a fish. Give the bugger slack, let him run, then wind him into the net. For all that, he acknowledged he was as much of a friend as he'd ever had. He wasn't feared to speak his mind, nor too cocksure to agree with him sometimes. The trick these days was to snare him, so he'd use his writing and talking know-how.

"Are you a stranger to boats, Kenneth?" he asked, extending a hand to help him aboard as the water smacked against the hull.

"No, but we're not heading into the chop, are we?"

"Get away with you. What decent Irishman would refuse a wee sail on the Irish Sea? Fill your lungs with the sea air, me boyo. Daecon, the tide is on the turn. Get us out afore we're bottomed."

"Aye, aye, Captain."

After the bilge blowers had finished running, Cooper tossed a coin to a lad to slip the mooring lines, and Daecon eased the throttles forward. *Nora 1* politely chugged her way past a moored yacht and an incoming fishing boat. Once clear of the harbour, Deacon gave her full throttle.

A playful breeze grabbed at Cooper's hair. It felt grand: the sun on his face, a blue sky, and in command of his boat. He tossed a bottle to Kenneth. "Drink! Guinness settles the heaves. We'll trawl as we talk. We're heading for a rocky promontory which has drops and ledges sloping towards shore. The bass feed near the bottom, so it's a short, stiff rod you'll need. There's a longer one for the ladies, but I expect you know that." He grinned and added, "Deacon will fix your rod up, and if our lines screech, we'll haul in and see what we've caught."

Kenneth took a pull from the bottle and cast a distracted look at the prancing white caps. "I'm not here for my health, am I?"

"You are. The sea air will help your noggin think better. You've been a bad boy again. The South becoming a republic has blinded you to the bigger picture. Are you not keen to see the country united?"

"Cooper, you need a mountain of patience to gain reunification and representation in Westminster. It won't happen if there's violence. I've heard the rumours: border campaigns. That's not the way to go."

"We'll see. I'm glad me own plans ain't being screwed by busy-bodies."

"Do you mean the odd bank robbery to fund your northern chums, or maybe flogging black-market goods? Or, are you dabbling in armaments from your smuggling operations?"

"That newspaper ink is warping your brain, Kenneth," Cooper scoffed.

"I'm thinking you've stashed your ill-gotten gains around the countryside."

So, Harry hasn't yapped about his cellar—he's earned his monthly payment. "Daecon, will you listen to him? He thinks my operation covers the whole bloody country." He took a swig of Guinness and wiped his mouth with the back of his hand. "Let's get to business. The Brotherhood wants a stronger presence in Westminster. Don't be looking dumbstruck; I'm back in their good books, and they know we're buddies. They've read your essays and articles. You're a prize, because you ain't on bended knee to the British press. If you went to London on a wee tour and educated the Westminster snoots on our history, and Ireland's *democratic right to full Independence*—them's our boyos words—they'll grant you the inside track." He didn't know if that pleased or outraged Kenneth, the way he scowled at the water and then upended the bottle.

"I don't know, Cooper; strife and division divides the IRA ranks. I want Ireland united too, but without violence. How often must I tell you? You're not forgetting Bloody Sunday are you, when the IRA killed a dozen British agents, and the constabulary went to a football game, shot into the crowd and killed and wounded over sixty people? It's a tit-for-tat contest, and when we're drawn into peace negotiations, Westminster stacks the brokering in its favour. We're three decades on from Dublin's Bloody Sunday, but hatred still simmers. There's nothing I say will turn the tide. Besides, some say the IRA is a spent force."

"Spent? We're rebuilding. Those English sods in their jodhpurs and shiny leather boots years back stole our land, killed off many of our lads—wild deer besides—and I don't know how many Irishmen died in this last war, but I swear not a one of them Brits will honour their sacrifice. Them who bow to their British masters should take account of that. It's a crying shame. And why do we have to go to County Galway or the Aran Islands to hear our own language?"

The promontory up ahead halted his rant, which was good, Cooper decided. The boyo needed time to think, plus a flooding tide and an easterly wind pushing up the surf was grand for catching bass. Daecon slowed *Nora 1* to trawling speed, and shouted, "Check your lures!"

Kenneth paid out his line, then leaned over the railing as if the depths might harbour an answer. At last, he straightened. "You belong to the old guard, Cooper, judging everything by how your family suffered and what you saw. You want a united republican Ireland, by force if necessary. Those coming up now haven't lived through your times. They think the conflict is about religion, rather than a drive for territory and national identity. Respect rather than force will win them to the cause."

"There you go, Kenneth, a grand speech opener—just what the political branch of the IRA are looking for. Stir up sympathy for the past. Sew guilt in them Brits' rotten hearts and yet win the respect of the young. For a man against violence, this is your chance. Get out there with your fine words and change their minds. I'm telling you straight, if Ireland doesn't gain a political voice, sooner or later, London will see violence on its streets."

Leaving Kenneth to chew on that, he turned aside, but as he did so, a muscular band of silver broke the surface of Kenneth's line. Slapping Kenneth on the back, he said, "There's your answer, me old pal. A big fish just waiting for you. Like them speeches of yours, it just needs your honeyed touch."

CHAPTER 45

APRIL 1950

HELEN FILLED IN the anagram for SOOTED—D-E-S-O-T-O, a Spanish explorer—then folded the crossword and started a letter to Harry.

Good morning! I'm at the laundromat—surrounded by pin-curled housewives! My washing machine died. Before leaving for London, Lawrence insisted I bundle our dirty laundry into the car's trunk late at night to dodge matronly frowns from our neighbours! Speaking of matrons, Margaret has abandoned nursing and is now Assistant Matron at Elgin's private school for boys. Robert joined Elgin's largest law firm and wanted her close. I sense an engagement next. They are coming for Easter and collecting Kelsey on their way. I've planned a family outing to the zoo.

Has Kelsey written? She says farms need dogs for herding sheep, cats for catching mice, and another Flynn for Uncle Harry! I'm sure Alex has written to you. He censors his letters—scenic descriptions and food—but Jill clues me in on the military life, and being your nephew, I'm sure he cuts a swath among the local girls. He and Lawrence are at it again—this time about his post-military career. Alex hasn't budged from wanting to work the land.

The washing is done. Remember me to Rhoda—is Liam out-driving you on the golf course yet? Love, Helen.

§

To Lawrence's mind, the family outing was a success. The weather performed in their favour, and Helen and Margaret took the cue to take Kelsey outside to see a hippo being fed when Robert asked to speak with him after the meal. He smiled when Robert spoke up. "You're being old-fashioned, Robert, but I appreciate your curtesy. Of course, you have my permission to marry Margaret. I hope your good sense and maturity will rub off on my headstrong son when you meet. I'll enjoy having a lawyer as a son-in-law."

Later in his study, he poured himself a generous scotch and decided the last two weeks had gone well. He had left Molly in good spirits because Cambridge had won the boat race, Margaret was now engaged, Alex no longer felt like a bur under his skin, and he still had time to check final renovations to Lord Stirling's mansion. The celebratory opening was planned for the end of the month. The only cloud had been Kelsey toting around a new Inglis storybook, before Helen returned her to school.

"Uncle Harry sent it in a big parcel for my birthday," she said, but when he asked if she got letters from Uncle Kenneth too, she shook her head. "Daddy, you told me letters were private, so I can't tell you."

§

Helen took particular care dressing for the Stirling's party. Once she decided she was ready, she pivoted in front of Lawrence so he could appreciate the swish of the velvet gown, the long sleeves, braided neckline, and cut-away back. After she stopped, she realized she had deliberately chosen her outfit to stir Lawrence from his conventional perch.

"More worthy of Paris than a well-behaved Edinburgh affair," he said, eyeing her. "I suggest you keep your back to the walls." The drop in chatter when they entered their host's imposing drawing room proved the truth of his words.

Determined to breeze ahead, Helen greeted her host and hostess with poise and stayed dutifully by Lawrence's side. He knew several people and led her towards a trio of men. Bored by their talk about the vagaries of the weather and stock market, she scanned the room and saw Lillian Robertson, a shrew of a woman from the Antique Society, conversing with two friends. Instead of mixing, most of the ladies were clustered in small groups and talked amongst themselves. Pondering the wisdom of joining them, the pressure of Lawrence's hand on her elbow provided the answer.

"I need to talk business with the Lord Provost. See those three ladies near the Steinway. Join them, but don't tinkle the keys."

Helen recognized one of the women as the wife of Lawrence's business partner. After an exchange of greetings, she sat on the piano bench with her back to the keys and entered into a spirited discussion on the merits of the concert hall's new seating. Lillian loomed in front of them as the conversation turned to the planned performance of military bands on the castle esplanade.

"Well, Mrs McKellan, these surrounds are a far cry from your Irish pub, I imagine," she said attracting attention with her loud voice. "I hear you play the piano. Why don't you play a tune for us?"

Play a tune, as if she was a performing seal balancing a ball on her nose? Had Lawrence heard the request? "If you wish," she said, and swivelled around to face the keyboard. Above the heads of the guests, she saw Lawrence watching. *Too late to worry now*. She flexed her fingers and began with Liszt's Liebestraum, and ended with Chopin's Revolutionary Study. Someone called for an encore but Helen shook her head.

"Well, my goodness me, Mrs McKellan, I was hoping for a light jig, not fireworks," Mrs Robertson simpered. "Your husband looks *very* disappointed. Such a dashing man. I hear he's quite a target for London's West-End socialites."

"How trying for him," Helen said, visualizing her hands ringing Lillian's chicken-skin neck, "he finds empty-headed people so boring. Speaking of which, Lillian, I'm *amazed* you recognize the difference between a jig and a study."

A muffled laugh made her look over her shoulder to see her host. With a perfunctory glance at Mrs Robertson, he took Helen's arm and guided her into dinner. Once seated, he asked why she had not pursued a concert career. "Marriage and running a hotel took me on a different route," she said.

Her admission led to talk about Ireland, and his interest in Celtic culture. During a lull, she observed Lawrence with Lady Stirling at the other end of the table. *Interesting to watch his attentiveness towards her. Laughter, nods of agreement—the Lawrence of old*. Dropping her gaze, she accepted a second glass of wine from her host, while inwardly resolving a question in her mind.

Next morning, she entered Lawrence's study, where he was mounting prized stamps in an album. "I need to discuss something with you. Let's go for a walk. It's a cloudless day." Lawrence pushed aside his project, but made a point of glancing at his watch.

Once through the park's gates, she manoeuvred them towards the rock garden and came to the point. "Lawrence, it's time we made changes. We've become chronic bickerers, and unhappiness shadows us wherever we go and whatever we do. Last night was too much."

"How so? The surroundings and dinner were superb, and you enjoyed the piano, despite my asking you *not* to play."

"You dictated, and we scarcely spoke to each other all evening."

"Beyond my social behaviour, have you any other complaints?"

"I have. The war is long gone, but during our three years here, you spend more time in London than at home, and you've never once thought of inviting me to join you. I can't recall the last time we went out for an evening where it wasn't work-related." She let out a long sigh. "Is it a woman that makes you so neglectful and secretive, Lawrence?"

"A woman? You're being absurd. What gives you that idea?"

"Unpleasant remarks here and there."

"You're not giving credence to Margaret's sighting from a *bus,* are you?"

"I'm giving credence to more than that. Can't you see that our marriage has become an endurance test?"

"Sit down," he said, pointing to a bench. "The woman is a co-worker. Her name is Molly."

"And I suspect has worked with you for years. Molly and The Service. No wonder your family plays a poor third in your affections."

He gave a thin smile, and spoke in clipped sentences about his work—the secrecy, the long hours, and his slow detachment from the family. But listening to him, she knew from his many pauses, that he was censoring everything.

"You speak in half-truths, Lawrence. And I sound like a broken-down gramophone. Your indifference continues, as do your prolonged absences. Our marriage is nothing more than a convenience to you. Keeping us in Ireland was never about waiting until Alex was older, but about suiting your personal agenda."

"And during that time, you were faultless?" His voice grew cold. "I've only to look at Kelsey to suspect Inglis kept you warm in bed for bloody years."

"That warmth resulted from your negligence, Lawrence. I'm sure there were many occasions when you could have been with the children and me, but you found excuses." His eyes gave him away. "Maybe Kelsey *is* Kenneth's daughter, but maybe not. What I *can* tell you is that I ended my relationship with Kenneth the day I knew we were moving. I was fool enough to hope that being here would bring you and me closer, but it hasn't. You haven't changed, or sacrificed a thing." She stood up. "I'm going to London to work for Jill. All I do here is displace air."

"What about the family?"

"Don't hoist that flag. Margaret and Alex are adults now, and Kelsey won't suffer disruption thanks to boarding school. Her next holiday runs from mid-July to the end of August. Bring her south on one of your London trips, or I'll fetch her."

His face showed no emotion, and she wondered if he had half-expected this severance. She looked at him for a paralyzing moment, then left the park, closing the gate behind her.

CHAPTER 46

JULY 1950

At six-thirty in the morning, The Hermitage's foyer was empty except for Helen pacing from one end to the other. When the taxi bearing Kelsey stopped at the entrance, she rushed outside.

"Look, Mummy, Daddy bought me a new Dinky train engine!" Kelsey warbled and leapt into her arms.

"What fun. We'll buy some colourful passenger carriages for it at Harrods later," she said, catching her and holding her close before leading her inside. Lawrence followed with the suitcase.

"Does that work?" he asked, throwing a surprised look at the elevator.

"It's a dinosaur that flies," Jill said, arriving from her office. "Hullo, Kelsey, I'm your Auntie Jill. You've grown up since we met. Lawrence, will you join us for coffee?"

"No, thank you, the taxi awaits, and I'm late for a business meeting."

"I hope when you collect Kelsey in a month, you'll find time then. Helen, when you and Kelsey are ready, come and have a light breakfast with me."

Helen felt her face flush as Jill left. A business meeting? It wasn't even seven in the morning. "Jill has loaned us her Brighton cottage for three weeks," she said. "And Alex is joining us for a week."

"Hooray! He can take us sailing."

"How do you know Brighton is a seaside town?"

"I wanted to see where London was, Mummy, and Alex's camp. My geography teacher said I'd find them if I traced the map of England."

"Speaking of Alex, remind him he has a father, Helen—he never writes. Now, I must go. See you in a month, Kelsey. Margaret and Robert will be taking you back to school."

Relieved he'd gone, Helen dropped Kelsey's case behind the front desk and led the way to Jill's office. "We'll ride the birdcage to my floor afterwards. I'm on the top floor."

"Will you show me the underground? Are there really trains underneath my feet? And, can we see Buckingham Palace?"

Helen chuckled. "We'll do all that and more."

§

It wasn't hard to imagine a gowned and coiffed woman stepping out of Jill's Tudor-style cottage. It had a gabled roof, arched doorway, and a tall brick chimney. Inside, wooden beams crisscrossed white walls, and sunlight streaming through the latticed windows reflected off the hardwood floors.

Kelsey claimed the attic bedroom. Helen's overlooked the walled garden and a stone patio. Once unpacked, they walked the short distance to the seafront and West Pier. It became their favourite playground since it offered a paddle-boat trip to the Isle of Wight, and had an amusement arcade. One of Kelsey's regular pastimes was riding the small electric train, with its two open cars, between the boulevard and shingled beach. When Alex arrived, she showed him her collection of beach stones. "I like the whooshing sound they make when the waves roll them over them. I'm going to send some to Sorcha."

"That would make a very heavy parcel," Helen said, wondering how long before Kenneth learned about her separation from Lawrence.

On Alex's third day, the owner of the arcade's shooting gallery banned him, since he walked away with a panda, a tiger, and a black, woolly bird for Helen to remind her of the hotel's jackdaws.

"Why is Alex giggling?" Kelsey said, pointing to the postcard stand.

"He's looking at naughty pictures. Let's go and inspect the fish catch."

That evening, after a meal of mackerel baked in butter and lemon slices, Alex and Kelsey dragged chairs onto the patio while Helen aired the cottage and then brought out mugs of hot chocolate.

"Why can't Daddy be with us? Why don't you live together anymore?" Kelsey asked, holding the panda on her knees.

Helen met Alex's eyes for a second, before he looked away. She had let Harry and Alex know by mail that she and Lawrence had split up, and Margaret by phone, but how to explain parental separation to the young? Lawrence had told her to wait until Kelsey was with her. The moment had arrived.

"Sometimes, Kelsey, after many years of living together, people find it easier to stay friends by living apart—the way you and Margaret do now. That doesn't mean Daddy and I don't talk to each other. This Christmas, I'm hoping we can celebrate a family gathering at Jill's hotel. Will you be free, Alex?"

He grinned and gave her the thumbs up. "I will, and Kelsey, if it's icy, we'll skate on Hyde Park's Serpentine River. You'll enjoy that."

"But I don't have skates."

"What did you say? Kelsey without skates? That can't be allowed. We must ask Santa to fix that." Inside the cottage, the grandfather clock chimed ten times, and Kelsey's eyes drooped. "Come on, sleepyhead, get ready for bed," he said, "and I'll read you a story."

Left alone, Helen linked her fingers behind her head. It was good having Alex to herself—a chance to talk of many things, including the ongoing battle between him and Lawrence. On his return she switched their drinks to beer. "Alex, your father complains he doesn't hear from you."

"It's difficult, Mum. He keeps trying to steer me in directions I don't want."

"I know, but can't you try to foster a friendship? He might be more approachable now that he and I are separated. Please try."

After he promised, they talked of Alex's army life. The routine, the discipline, and friends—not scenery or food this time—and Helen's work in Jill's bar.

"It's different from our one," she said. "Better-dressed clientele, but less camaraderie and not a turf-cutter or farmer in sight. And no singsongs."

"Mum, does Uncle Kenneth know about you and dad?"

"No, it's best he doesn't. Are you in touch with him?"

"Sometimes. I sent him one of those ribald arcade cards today. I said I was here with you and Kelsey, and that you were managing Jill's bar. I'm sorry, Mum, I hope I haven't interfered."

"Don't worry, separations don't stay secret for long. We must go to bed. After dropping you off to catch your bus to Bovington tomorrow, I'm taking Kelsey to Somerset to see Cheddar Gorge."

"What's a gorge?" Kelsey asked in the car next day.

"It's a narrow valley with steep hills and a river. Cheddar Gorge's underground river has carved out huge vaulted chambers."

Two hours later, they entered a cavernous world lit by lights that cast an orange glow. On a raised walkway, they crossed pools of water and saw limestone columns hanging from the ceiling or growing upwards from the ground.

"They're giant teeth," Kelsey exclaimed.

Helen traced the domed interior with her eyes and felt as if she stood in a hallowed place. "The lower teeth are stalagmites and the upper ones are stalactites," she explained. "If you want to know which are which, just remember stalag*mites* *might* reach the stalactites, which hang *tightly* from the ceiling. They take thousands of years to form." In a way, she thought wryly, they symbolized her life. Her old life clinging, her new one developing.

After a tea of scones, jam and clotted cream in a nearby café, Helen found a bed-and-breakfast for the night. The next day, they returned to Brighton, closed the cottage, and caught the train to London.

A week later, having treated Kelsey to many sightseeing tours of London, she waited for Lawrence's arrival. This time, he consented to Jill's invitation to join them for tea. Luckily Kelsey's enthusiasm at all she had seen and done left no room for awkward silences. But when she left, Helen suffered sharp pangs of loneliness. Although work helped, there were moments when she felt as if she were treading water.

CHAPTER 47

NOVEMBER 1950

TO HELEN, THE Frogs and Moss Bistro on Old Brompton Road invoked choruses of amphibian croaking in Kenneth's fields, and memories of the soft matting around the paving stones leading to Benevolence's front door. When she stepped inside, she felt she was in a giant, barrel-top caravan.

She and Jill chose a windowed alcove, both relieved to rest after prowling the antique stalls on Portobello Road. Helen toed off her high-heels. "I wish I'd known about this place while Kelsey was here. Just smell the cooking aromas. Makes me ravenous."

"The most ravenous item is the waiter," Jill said, flicking eyes his way. The way he moved reminded Helen of Sorcha's father around the camp fire—all muscled elegance and the dancing feet of a matador.

"Good afternoon, Senoras," he said, "may I tease your taste buds with a sampling of our fine cheese dip and blarney puff balls?" With a sleight of hand, he produced a small plate, then spun away to fetch their order of Irish coffee.

"Be careful, Jill, the way you're fluttering your eyelashes, you may find yourself sampling more than potato puff balls."

Jill clasped her hands in prayer. "I live in high expectation."

"Beats me how you've avoided getting married again."

"I enjoy my selfish life too much. I notice you've been living a cloistered one since you separated. Don't you miss Kenneth?"

Helen averted her eyes. "Last time we met, telling him to find someone else nearly killed me, but how else to set him free?"

"So, that's why stayed in your room after you returned from the Hibernian. Did you tell Harry?"

"Yes, some of it, and he promised to try and avoid mentioning me. The thing is, Alex sent Kenneth a postcard from Brighton, so he knows about the separation. I'm hoping that it doesn't mess him up." The hard grip of her hands made her wedding ring dig into her skin. She hadn't counted on feeling so vulnerable. Excusing herself, she retreated to the restroom.

There were days when thoughts of Kenneth remained in the background, other days they drove her mad. She looked at the gold band on her finger, then pulled it off and dropped it in her handbag. A small rebellion, but it felt good. After a drink of water, she reapplied her lipstick, then made her way back to Jill. Beyond the window, a sudden deluge of rain pounded car roofs and bounced off the pavement. People ducked into doorways or scurried along, heads bent against the onslaught. Helen sighed. It was no fable that rain fell more softly in Ireland.

Jill looked uncomfortable and shook her head. "I'm sorry I upset you with my questions, Helen, but I had my reasons. Kenneth called this morning, and caught me by surprise. He told me he's giving a talk at the Dorchester Hotel tonight, and has put a ticket aside for you in case you come. I have his phone number. Please call him. There's nothing to lose by doing that, is there?"

"I would have liked it better if he had asked for me direct. It wasn't right to make you the intermediary."

"I told him that's what you'd think, but he said he didn't want to put you on the spot. Let's relax and finish our coffee. You'll have plenty of time to mull things over at home. But please don't let that cursed pride of yours defeat you. Tuck this into your handbag. It's his phone number."

§

The floor of the Dorchester ballroom had vanished beneath a sea of chairs when Helen arrived. She took an aisle seat at the back. She hadn't called Kenneth—wanting to gauge her reaction at seeing him again and discover for herself the side of him others regarded as an authority on IRA objectives.

The emcee introduced him as a respected journalist and author, known for his editorials and essays. He also commended his knowledge of Ireland's history. He ended by saying, "To challenge established beliefs is no easy task, but our speaker will question some of those convictions this evening. Ladies and gentlemen, please welcome Kenneth Inglis."

Gone was Kenneth's laid-back manner as he walked on stage. This man had an air of purpose. At his first words, Helen caught her breath. She loved his voice. Aware that his overseas work involved the Republic's efforts to join the UN, she wondered if he was also preparing the ground for IRA interests. It wouldn't surprise her. A united Ireland would be more attractive to the UN.

"If an alien from a distant planet arrived here tonight, on a first look, I expect he would find little difference between us here and those earthlings on the green isle to the west. That is until he discovered the green isle people have cultural and political differences constrained by religious beliefs, as well as conflicting ideas of freedom."

Helen tried to judge the audience's reaction, when a slight movement caught her eye. Across the aisle, a drab looking man with sandy hair bent to retrieve a notebook. When he straightened, he squinted at her through gold-rimmed glasses. He had the look of a government lackey paid to listen.

"One can point to many countries that battle for independence," Kenneth said. "Unlike Scotland and Wales, Ireland is a separate landmass. That creates a different frame of reference. Although two-thirds of Ireland became a republic, one third still pays homage to Britain. Does it not seem reasonable for the country to be united and Catholics and Protestants to coexist in mutual tolerance despite their different ideologies?"

Helen felt unease permeate the room. The man across from her now had his chin cupped in his hand and was leaning forward. At least someone was interested. As were three people sitting alongside her. Maybe they were Irish.

"A poet said Ireland could be divided into four groups," Kenneth continued, "the publicans, the priests, the peasants, and the politicians. He should have added a fifth group. The Irish Republican Army. To understand Britain's opponent better, let's go back to 1916, the year of the Easter Uprising."

While he punctuated his speech with pithy facts and opinions, Helen imagined Harry saying, 'There he goes, our Kenneth giving a history lesson.' She missed Harry and his devil-may-care behaviour, but Rhoda's charm and good sense seemed to have anchored him, possibly even rescued him.

Someone booed in the audience. Helen sighed. Kenneth wasn't one to sugar-coat the truth, but no one had walked out. After a time, a change in tone showed he was nearing the end of his talk. "If those in power in Westminster do not take positive steps to open dialogue for a united Ireland, offer fair trade, and give access to education for the needy, I fear violence will re-emerge. If *both* sides come together with open minds, better times can be a reality. I thank you for your attention."

The audience dispersed in silence, but the three to the right of Helen stood and shouted, "well done!" Across the aisle, the stranger showed no emotion. Helen stayed in her seat until the room emptied, knowing Kenneth would watch the door and scan the rows but make no move to leave until he was sure she wasn't there. When his eyes finally reached her row, she stood and hurried towards him. They met in the middle of the aisle.

"I've missed you," he said, holding her close. "It's been a bloody lifetime,"

"For me too," she said.

"It's thirsty work talking to an un-receptive audience. Shall we go to the lounge for a nightcap?" She nodded. Holding her hand, he guided her from the ballroom.

He chose a booth so they could be closer. Dropping her jacket on the bench before sitting down, she noticed the stranger from the audience sit at a table across from them. Although he was out of earshot, his presence caused discomfort until he became engrossed in a beverage menu.

A waiter shambled towards them to take their orders. After he left, Kenneth pulled a face. "I hope you weren't bored. I'm sure you saw that my plea for an open-mind fell on deaf ears."

"Not all ears. Some found you persuasive. Give it time. As the saying goes, *from acorns, mighty oaks will grow.*"

Kenneth moved closer and put an arm around her waist. "In a perfect world, we'd own a pub. I'd write novels, you'd pursue your music and art, Kelsey would become a young woman, and Alex would have his farm."

"But?" Helen prompted.

"But the world isn't perfect."

"Nothing stays static, Kenneth."

The waiter reappeared bearing their drinks, but left in a more agile manner after pocketing Kenneth's generous tip. "You've made a sainted farmer out of Harry," she said. "He was never that."

"Are you harbouring secrets?"

"I did." She lowered her voice. "I've never forgotten your warnings about Cooper."

He looked puzzled. "Where are you leading with him and Harry?"

"Harry and I had a pact. What Harry called a Mexican standoff, but it doesn't hold water now. He owns the farm, and I'm separated." She tilted her glass and had a long drink, then told him how the pact had arisen. "The thing is, Kenneth, that smuggling article of yours convinced me that Harry eased his debt by joining those farmers."

"So, Madam Sleuth, why are you telling me now, eight years later?"

"Because, for us to move forward together, there can't be secrets. I've more. Before I left Lawrence, we had a blistering row. He admitted to a close relationship with a colleague that started early in the war. Also that he worked with Intelligence, and he still does. He refers to them as *The Service*. I shudder when I think of the times I've heard that. I realized then why Harry dodged being alone with him after the Dunegan Bay incident. I'm sure Lawrence came over on the sly to confront him."

"That's a big leap."

"Yes, but I'm sticking to it. I'm afraid that's not all. He also voiced his suspicions about Kelsey and us."

"What did you say to that?"

Instead of answering, she looked away, almost wishing she had kept silent. She worked to keep her voice calm, and repeated what she and Lawrence had said in the park. "It was a nasty scene, Kenneth. I'm so sorry." Her hand trembled as she picked up her glass. Across from her, she saw the stranger rise from his table, leave money for the waiter, and walk past without looking.

"Helen, look at me. We've all made mistakes. It doesn't matter if I'm Kelsey's father or not; I love her and I love you. You are right. Those three words matter. Are you free now to take Kelsey out of that damned boarding school, and for the two of you to make your home with me in Benevolence?"

This time she needed no time to think. "Yes, with all my heart, but can we wait until July? You see, everyone will be dispersing, so I've planned one last family gathering at Jill's for Christmas, and it's best if Kelsey finishes her school year. Can you handle that?"

Kenneth leaned in and kissed her neck. "I can. Now, will you come back to my colleague's flat tonight? He's away, but I know eggs and bacon are in the fridge for breakfast, and there's a bed big enough for two."

§

It never failed to amaze Clive Richardson how circumstances sometimes put him in the right place at the right time. He sat at his desk, in his new London quarters, jotting down all he had learned. Sheer curiosity had taken him to the Dorchester. Not much of Kenneth Inglis's talk had surprised him, but what *had* raised alarm bells was the woman across the aisle—Lawrence McKellan's wife in the flesh—curvaceous and sultry, with that generous mouth and full lips. What tangled lives the McKellans led. He made a notation to have his department's 1943 flight manifestos to Dublin checked, plus articles and movements by Inglis re-examined for the same year. He then picked up the phone and requested greater surveillance of Kenneth Inglis, and to add Helen McKellan.

CHAPTER 48

DECEMBER 1950

HELEN LOOKED AROUND Jill's private dining room, knowing this was the last Christmas all the family would be together. If there was a forced exuberance with Lawrence being there, she didn't sense it. Next year, Margaret and Robert would be in Scotland, Alex overseas, and Lawrence in Scotland, or maybe not. She and Kelsey would be in Ireland with Kenneth. No one knew except Jill.

Over the BBC's broadcast of the Nutcracker Suite, Kelsey piped up, "Are we skating at Hyde Park tomorrow, Alex? Auntie Jill says the lake is frozen."

He winked. "Provided this dinner doesn't have me sleeping in late."

"Well, don't have second helpings. I want to use my new skates. Uncle Harry, will you and Auntie Rhoda still be here?"

"Yes, we don't fly home until the evening."

Not interested in skating, Margaret pestered Alex about his training, but he was non-committal. "I'm finished and expect deployment in the new year."

Aware of Lawrence's grouchy look, Helen deflected his focus. "Robert, I hope you and Margaret will come skating too."

"They won't be doing that. I've invited them to the club for lunch," Lawrence said.

"Wow, what an honour, Margaret," Harry joked. "Women in those hallowed halls is a rarity."

"Rubbish, Harry, women are always welcome on special occasions."

"Such strongholds will crumble one day," Jill teased.

When the phone in the office rang, Helen jumped up thinking it might be Kenneth. "I'll get it," she said.

"Good evening. To whom am I speaking?" a male voice asked.

It wasn't Kenneth. "The assistant manager."

"Mrs McKellan? The compliments of the season to you. A word with your husband, if you please."

How does he know my name? "May I have your number? I'll have him call you back."

"No, now Mrs McKellan. Tell him it's Mr Richardson."

"But he's having Christmas dinner with the family."

"Madam, please do as I ask; otherwise I will have to divulge your rendezvous with a certain journalist at the Dorchester."

Helen froze. No one other than Jill knew that—then she recalled the stranger. She left the receiver dangling and retreated to the dining room.

"A Mr Richardson demands a word with you," she whispered in Lawrence's ear. "He won't take no for an answer."

Kelsey saved her from dealing with the curious looks at the table by singing *Jingle Bells*. Harry jumped in with a percussive spoon accompaniment.

§

"Lawrence, I want you in Belfast tomorrow."

"What's happened? You can speak. I'm on a private line."

"An IRA man killed one of our agents last night and fled to a house in Derry. We trapped him, but in the scuffle, a gun discharged twice, killing the fugitive."

"That's not uncommon over there."

"True, but the fugitive was Cooper O'Neil's brother, Eamon. Their sister, Sophie, owns the house. She's in a coma under guard at the City Hospital. The second shot ricocheted and struck her. I want you over there to exert a calming influence on the authorities and prevent leaks to the press. It's precisely the situation Kenneth Inglis would expose. Exert pressure to block cross-border infiltration by his paper until we have control. Christmas gives us a small window. Confuse with false facts if necessary."

"Everything all right, old chap?" Harry asked, when he returned.

Lawrence scowled and rested a hand on Margaret's shoulder. "I'm sorry, dear, I'm afraid I must cancel our lunch at the club tomorrow."

"Gracious! Has a McKellan-designed building collapsed?" Harry asked.

"No, but we're in danger of losing a contract."

"Cheer up, Margaret," Alex said, flashing her a look, "since when has Dad been around for a whole Christmas?"

The mood in the room shifted, but Harry rose to the occasion. He sniffed loudly and wrinkled his nose. "Do I smell Christmas pudding on the way, Jill?"

"You do, and inside hide shiny sixpences wrapped in wax paper."

"A pair of leg-irons and chains in there would be good too," Helen said.

§

The evening after everyone had left, Kenneth called. "Is it possible to explore London with you and Kelsey tomorrow? Harry phoned from the airport to say you're both on your own."

He arrived in the afternoon and took them to feed the ducks at Hyde Park, then supper at the Hibernian, followed by the pantomime. "Tickets courtesy of the Press Club," he said. "Someone liked my Dorchester speech."

Abuzz with excitement, Kelsey sat between them, and during the performance suddenly slipped her hand into Kenneth's and said in a loud whisper, "I wish I could fly like Peter Pan."

"You can. Just close your eyes, pick your destination, and away you go. I've walked beaches with you, read bedtime stories to you—even seen you wrinkling your nose at bowls of porridge. Tonight, after I've told you a gypsy story, you can fly to your tree house and see Sorcha."

"What will you and Mummy do?"

"I'm sure we'll find something to occupy us. Right, Helen?"

Next morning, after breakfast with Jill, Helen suggested a ride on a ferry boat that plied the Thames. "What a funny name for a clock," Kelsey said, as the boat chugged past Westminster Palace, and Big Ben.

"That's the name for the giant bell inside the tower. Some say it's named after a famous boxer, others after the man who built it," Kenneth told her.

For a man who had no love of the English, Helen found it amusing that Kenneth knew so many anecdotes about London's landmarks. At noon, she took them to The Frogs and Moss.

When Kelsey saw the interior, she demanded updates on Sorcha and the tree house. Kenneth gave her news while they tucked into a baked fish casserole, and potato bread. Sitting there, all of them together, Helen wished they could return with him to Ireland that very day. In the evening they dined with Jill at the hotel, but after dessert, when Kenneth reappeared from a routine call to Ryan, his Dublin colleague, Helen sensed a change.

"Not good news, I'm afraid. I must leave early in the morning. A breaking story demands my attention. Kelsey, will you help me out? Since I can't take you to the zoo tomorrow, I want you and Auntie Jill to take Mummy for me. Will you do that, and say hullo to the elephants?"

She nodded but tears flooded her eyes. "I don't want you to go. When will I see you again?"

"Well now, in March, you'll be eight years old. That's a grand age to come to Ireland. Early summer, don't you think so, Helen?" he asked, and winked at her and Jill.

Kelsey clapped her hands, but Helen worried that his sudden departure and Lawrence's were somehow related.

CHAPTER 49

JANUARY 1951

WHEN THE OPERATOR of Belfast's Cairnstone Hotel asked who was calling, Cooper used the fictitious name Kenneth had given him. "Anthony McCourt," he said.

"Any news?" he asked, when Kenneth came on the line.

"None yet. Where are you?"

"You'll know soon enough. Look for Daecon. You'll find him parked at the side entrance at four thirty."

To while away the time while he waited, Cooper fed peat into the fire, put a kettle to boil, then lounged on a couch. Still nothing in the papers—no editorial, no inquiry, nothing—as if some bastard had slammed the lid down. *They can stay silent all they fecking like,* he thought, *Kenneth will ferret out the truth.*

He must have dozed off, for the next thing he knew Daecon was banging on the door fit to wake the dead. "I'm not deaf!" he yelled. He opened the door and pulled Kenneth inside by the coat sleeve.

"Take the damned blindfold off," Kenneth said. He rubbed his eyes and squinted at Cooper. "You look like hell. Have you had any sleep?"

"Not worth a snore. Getting into Belfast without them Ulster bastards catching me nearly had me shatting my britches." He flapped a hand towards the range. "Help yourself to a cuppa. The brew's strong enough to rust a spoon."

"The British are getting too slap-happy entering houses," Kenneth said, taking a seat and braving the tea. "It's a miracle Eamon lived this long. He knew the dangers. But going to Sophie's was irresponsible, and her getting shot bloody criminal. There will probably be a whitewashed inquiry."

"Meanwhile, Eamon is dead, Sophie lies in a coma, and we can't get near her. Could you go see her, Kenneth?"

"I can, but forget payback ideas. The authorities don't want her dying any more than you. You're all Sophie has now, Cooper, so stay safe. She's long moved on from the beating those Protestant schoolgirls doled out years ago."

Cooper stopped mid-way rolling a cigarette. "Did she confess that them scrubbers put paid to her having kids? Nah, I didn't think so. Ma and me begged her and Brendan to come south. Now see what's happened." He couldn't stop his voice from cracking.

Kenneth returned his half-empty cup to the table. "Hold strong, Cooper. Coming out of a coma takes time. I'll check on Sophie regularly. If there's a change, where can I reach you?"

"I'll get to that. You did a kindness buying that cradle from Brendan. My sister said you're a good man. I'm thinking she's right."

"Don't be going soft on me. I must get going. I'm dining with some nosy fellows at the Grand Central Hotel. Best you get the hell out of here and lie low."

"I'm leaving tonight. Here's Deacon's number. He knows where to find me. I owe you for this, Kenneth. By the by, you gave a grand speech in London—loving things up too it's rumoured. Have a care, my friend. A husband shamed is a dangerous man."

Kenneth shrugged on his coat. "Rumours are just rumours, Cooper. Keep the faith." Deacon blindfolded him again, before marching him back to the car.

§

Cooper crossed the border without incident and hid out on *Nora 1*. While he waited, he deluded himself into believing Sophie was only sleeping. In a week—maybe two—she would be her startling self again, her wide eyes flashing blue, her mouth breaking into laughter at a joke, or demanding he 'promise' this, or 'swear' to that, like she had done ever since he was a nipper.

In mid-February, a month from meeting Kenneth, Deacon slipped on board and Cooper sensed from the look on his face that Sophie had died—gone forever. Nothing prepared him for her loss. He had survived his father being beaten to death, his mother taken too soon from a heart attack, Brendan demented while imprisoned, and Eamon dead at the hands of the Brits. But Sophie? Sophie killed by a bullet never meant for her? He shrank into himself like an old man seeking warmth in a garret. When Deacon left, he fell into his bunk still dressed. He woke to cold sweats and nightmare sounds of bullets smacking into flesh and bone, hard-knobbed boots splintering doors, and Sophie screaming for him. Tears salted his face and crawled down his neck, and when night fell, it gathered into a darkness worse than hell.

The next day, Deacon arrived again, this time with food and a sealed envelope. Cooper recognized the writing as Kenneth's. He read the letter twice, blew his nose, and wiped his swollen eyes. "The boyo has been making waves. I'm going to the funeral. Listen to this.

Cooper, take comfort knowing that Sophie received her last rites from a priest in her parish. Her body is being released quietly and the authorities have arranged transportation to St. Aidan's church.

I've learned that a small honour guard of 'Brothers' will attend in respect of you and your family at the grave-site. I'm sure there will be a large gathering. Although the authorities blocked the Belfast press from printing opinions or articles—inciting unrest, they said—my story got through and has the authorities as nervous as hens running from a randy rooster.

Stay calm. There's not an Ulster Constabulary or British soldier will lay a finger on you that day. I'll see you there as a friend, not as a journalist. I'm sorry for your loss, Cooper. Sophie was a courageous woman."

"Kenneth has become a good friend to you, for sure," Deacon said. "We'll travel to my place first, Cooper. Kathy wants to come, so we'll rest and motor north to Derry from there tomorrow morning."

"Sounds good. I've had my fill of being isolated on board *Nora 1*. It's time I got used to company again. Speaking of that, if the Grim Reaper comes my way, Deacon, will you see I'm buried near Sophie?"

"I will, but let's dodge the bony creature and his scythe for a time yet."

Next day, when they arrived at the church, Cooper reckoned there were upwards of two hundred people crammed inside. There were friends from his old neighbourhood, pals of Da's, and blokes from the pub. To steady himself, he sucked in his breath, and with Deacon and Kathy beside him, walked to the front. Mid-way, he passed Kenneth and gave a quick nod. He would heed his words—no outward shows of anger, at least not here. But how to get from the grave-site to Deacon's car and then to the border without a tap on the shoulder from the constabulary? Daft to think there wouldn't be eyes watching.

To his relief, the small honour guard formed outside the church entrance—not at the grave-site. His hand ached from all the clasping and shaking. "Deacon, stay close." he whispered, "Kenneth can think I'm safe, but I smell proddies. I'm on to them." Turning aside to a group of Da's friends, he shook their hands. "I'm thinking it would be a grand honour if you joined us at the grave-site, and then walked me, Deacon, and Kathy to the car."

"We'll do more than that, Cooper; we'll get you to the border."

§

A month later, he met Kenneth in Nosens Pub and gave him a bottle of scotch from Harry's cellar. They'd left the cellar alone for months because a friend told him they'd seen someone spying. After keeping track of the fellow's routine, Daecon and two others emptied the cellar late at night, and told Harry he could have his cellar back.

"Want to thank you for all you did," Cooper said, shaking Kenneth's hand. "Did you get any trouble from your press friends or the constabulary after Da's friends got me away safe?"

"No, it pissed them off, but they left it alone, especially after my article."

"What did it say?"

"Accused the British and the constabulary of negligence for turning a simple theft into a full-scale hunt with guns at the ready. Eamon had only filched some booze. Got caught, resisted arrest, panicked and fled to Sophie's."

"Them rats get away with murder. Did you find who blocked the news?"

"I suspected someone, but could never prove it, so let it be."

"I'm not happy with letting things *be*. Would you be knowing if any big wigs are coming over to Ireland—some high-ranking politician or even royalty?"

"Do you take me for a fool?"

Cooper laughed. Curiosity to a journalist was like whiskey to a drunk. He looked past him to a bar chippie sashaying towards them, and called her over. "Two pints of the black stuff, me love," he said, and patted her on the bum before turning back to Kenneth. "No violence; don't want the constabulary after me. I'm thinking I'd like to embarrass the shite out of them, that's all. Get my boyos to throw eggs or dent their nice shiny cars with a few bricks. Slow them up, so they can hear some good Republican songs. Maybe stick a placard in their faces about innocents murdered because of their tactics. It would make grand radio and newspaper coverage; don't you think?"

"This *plan* of yours isn't exactly your style."

"That's what makes it perfect. Haven't you told me it's the written word wins the attention? Would be a grand opportunity for you to get the scoop too, I'm thinking."

"Jayus, Cooper, you'll be running for governor next."

Cooper grinned, paid for their drinks, and slipped his phone number to the waitress. "So, will you do it, Kenneth? Let me know if a bigwig comes over?"

"I'll think on it," Kenneth said.

CHAPTER 50

MARCH 1951

RICHARDSON REREAD THE confidential letter—his mind alive with possibilities. The Earl's wish to inspect military installations could play into his hands. Time to call the props boys, and see—if amongst their gadgets guaranteed to immobilize a man—they could construct what he wanted.

Minutes later, satisfied with their answer, he ran a finger down his appointments, then pressed the intercom. "Gloria, move the three o'clock to tomorrow and phone McKellan. He's in town. Then bring me the O'Neil file."

While he waited, he swivelled in his chair and contemplated Sloane Square beyond the window. It was a blustery day. Remnants of blown leaves made patterns on the park's railings, and pigeons huddled on stone mantels beneath slate roofs. What dangers did they face? The thought provoked a phone call to Major Andrews in Derry.

"Major, I'm sending you highly confidential orders. They should arrive on your desk tomorrow. If you don't have a well-trained marksman in the ranks, recruit one from Major Turnwell at Bovington."

"Understood, sir."

Humming the gospel song, *We Shall Overcome*, Richardson left his office for the upstairs boardroom. It would be pleasant to enjoy a lunch of smoked salmon on slivers of rye bread, and read more of his favourite spy novel before he collected what he wanted from props.

§

Lawrence arrived at Gloria Sureness's desk five minutes early. "Good afternoon, Gloria. You're looking well. Is he in?"

She gave him a warm smile as she tucked her white blouse tighter into her waistband—a move that emphasized her figure and caught Lawrence's appreciative eye. "No, but he told me to give you this," and handed him a sealed envelope.

Attractive woman—surprising she had never married, but then neither had Richardson. *Does she experience biblical love quotes whispered in her ear?* Amused at the thought, he opened the envelope and read, *Park. 2:15 p.m. usual place—R.* Taking a slim, gift-wrapped package from his pocket—a silver letter-opener—he said, "I understand that you have earned another promotion, Gloria. Congratulations. You'll be sitting in Richardson's chair before long." They exchanged smiles before she answered her telephone, and he departed for his rendezvous.

He took a shortcut that led him past bare-branched cherry trees creaking in the wind. The air threatened rain. His Belfast assignment to obfuscate the truth had not been a complete success. He had achieved delays but Inglis's article had skewered the cover-up. Were the police supposed to have knocked on the door first and said, 'Please sir, can we place you under arrest?' The thought reminded him of Dennis's frustration with protocol.

Richardson was waiting on a park bench. He rose, gloved hand outstretched, as if they were the best of friends. "Good to see you, Lawrence. Thought we'd take a few brisk turns around the park, despite the inclement weather."

"I've no problem with the weather, sir, but these 'turns around the park' often presage a covert assignment."

"Don't worry, just a need to share fresh air and review a few things."

The smoothness in his voice was not reassuring. *What 'things'? And why the briefcase?* On passing a troupe of bundled-up children, watched over by three nuns as black-draped as the witches in *Macbeth,* he imagined Richardson as the macabre snake in disguise.

Richardson cleared his throat. "A dickey-bird has chirped that Kenneth Inglis spent a lovely time with your wife two days after your Christmas dinner, Lawrence. Know anything about that?"

"We're separated. What she does is her business."

Richardson oozed concern. "So you say, but we always look out for our own. I'm impelled to quote, *a false witness will not go unpunished, and he who breathes out lies will not escape.* Does your estranged wife know that you still work for Intelligence?"

Lawrence watched a duck land on the small man-made lake. Its splash-landing caused a ripple effect, which stirred the brittle sedge grasses. *In-house blackmail is one of Intelligence's finer talents,* Molly had warned. An aquatic mole slipped into the water.

"Only the bare minimum," he muttered.

"Unavoidable was it, Lawrence?"

As they rounded the park for the second time, the swings hung silent. It had grown colder. Lawrence turned up his coat collar.

"You should know we've protected your family for years. In fact, since that smuggling incident at Dunegan Bay. We have a healthy dossier on your brother. Seems he's been a Cooper man for years. Our file on you grows too. Apart from fraternizing with a departmental employee—which we tried to discourage by seconding her to another department—and using your work with Stockwell for your own ends, we know you chartered an unauthorized plane and visited your brother. Since then you've played cover-up. Foolish man."

Lawrence sucked in biting air. "Why did you wait until now to confront me?"

"Some things must germinate—*the fruit being better than the flower.*"

"Two rounds of the park in foul weather for you to reach this point? It must be very personal."

"It is. Cooper is a loose cannon—he'll be nursing revenge after that unfortunate affair in Derry. To snare him, we need your wife."

"My wife? You can't be serious?"

"Perfectly serious. We've been watching Cooper for some time. He fell off the radar when his sister ended up in a coma, but when he resurfaced at her funeral, we put a man on his tail. As a consequence, we know his favourite haunts, whom he meets, and what he plans. The time is ripe to trap him, but it needs skillful planning, and you have your part to play."

So far, nothing Richardson had said hinted at Helen's role. And when he yapped on about the mutual aspirations of Kenneth and Cooper for a united Ireland, his patience snapped. "Why in hell are you telling me things I already know? Whatever use you have in mind for my wife, I won't allow it."

Richardson stopped to tie his shoelace, alongside a bench. "Oh, but you will, Lawrence. It's time you realized that the actions of your brother, and your cover-up, make both of you guilty of treason. Your son could suffer the same fate—apart from odd jobs around the farm, he used the shooting range. One has to wonder where he got the ammunition."

"That's absurd. You're bluffing. You have no case."

"Allow me to show you," he said, and sighing, withdrew a manila envelope from his coat pocket.

Lawrence looked at the contents in silence. *Harry's potato cellar? What the hell?* He studied each incriminating photograph, including one of Stockwell holding a dated newspaper. *Consequences be damned.* He tossed the envelope aside.

"You're seeing what you want to believe. You can accuse Harry of being a gambler, of being in serious debt, and being bought by a man like Cooper, but that's it. My covert visit was to interrogate Harry. He only discovered his wrongdoing when he grew nosy and got injured for his pains. Cooper, however, is a callous criminal. I'm sure he used violent tactics to coerce Harry into giving him the cellar. To claim my brother *and* my son are IRA-implicated is bloody rubbish."

"We have ways to prove otherwise."

"So, now it's blackmail—use my wife or else."

"Blackmail? No, more like *words spoken in right circumstances are apples of gold.*"

Lawrence threw up his hands and lurched to his feet. "You and your damned quotes. You're off your rocker."

"Be careful what you say, Lawrence. You will regret it. Inglis is an IRA mouthpiece. His trips to Belfast coincide too often with IRA activities. His speeches border on sedition."

"That doesn't make him an IRA member." *Now I'm defending the bastard.*

"No, but Cooper bates him with exclusives."

"So? Go talk to Inglis."

"He won't betray one of his own. Must gall you to suspect he could be Kelsey's father."

Lawrence's right hand balled into a fist, then he dropped it to his side. Richardson glanced at his watch, then shook his head. "Calm down, Lawrence. We only need Helen to do one simple thing. Once I've explained what it is we want, we'll drop in on the Hind's Head for that drink. You look ill."

"Stop patronizing me."

"Stop wearing blinkers. Harry faces jail, Alex dismissal, and your wife humiliating exposure. What a way to besmirch the McKellan name. Furthermore, we can have you retired on a private's pension."

"So, now you're threatening me? You're no better than Cooper."

"Do what we want, and we'll concede that Harry was an unwitting pawn and that you were merely trying to prevent further trouble. I'll also guarantee no one links

Helen to my plan. Whatever the outcome, however, you *will* take early retirement, but at your present level. Time for you to rectify an awkward situation, yes?"

"The listener must hold his counsel, for one man's plan may be another man's winding road to perdition," Lawrence muttered, looking at the sky.

"Hmm, from what book is that?"

"The Book of Lawrence, last chapter, verse one." For a moment, Lawrence thought Richardson would explode. His face flushed, and then to Lawrence's amazement, he chuckled.

"You nearly had me on that one. All right, Lawrence, sit down while I outline the plan. Incidentally, you will need this." He handed over the briefcase.

Lawrence's world grew dark, as he listened. There was no way out; the machinations of Richardson and MI5 held him in a merciless grip.

CHAPTER 51

APRIL 1951

THE ART'S CLUB's porter tapped his cap in welcome. "Nice to have you with us again, Mr McKellan. We had a touch of frost last night."

"That's spring for you, Carlisle, always changeable."

As are many things, Lawrence thought following the porter upstairs. Carlisle placed the luggage on a stand, and Lawrence placed the briefcase on the bed.

"Will you be requiring room service this evening, sir?"

"No thank you, I've eaten." Closing the door, Carlisle retreated downstairs.

Lawrence sat on a chair, and relived Richardson's instructions while staring at the briefcase. "Call Helen. Invite her to dinner. Her birthday is on the horizon. If she demurs, concoct a family matter. Arrive early. Explain you've come straight from work; your briefcase is a nuisance. Activate it, and leave it standing upright in her suite. It will fall open when lifted. After dinner, take a taxi and drop her back at the hotel. Remember the briefcase at the last moment and ask her to leave it at the front desk. You will collect it in the morning. That's it. The rest relies on the inescapable fact that women are inordinately curious."

"So, the briefcase falls open. A memo marked *Confidential* that refers to *Mountbatten* and *Classiebawn* tumbles out. Helen reads it ... You believe this harebrained scheme will work?"

"Yes, our resident psychologist, Dr Ogilvy, estimates there's a ninety percent probability of success. We will know if he's correct when the case is safely back in our hands—miraculous what treated paper can tell us these days. Helen *will* read the memo. When she replaces it, the lock will work and the case won't open again until it's back in our hands.

"Where does Inglis fit in this convoluted plan?"

"He arrives in London next week. He will obviously connect with your wife, and she, at some point, will tell him about the memo. We know they spend their nights at her suite or at his colleague's house. Once Inglis takes the bait, the rest is in our bailiwick. Our continued surveillance of Cooper will decide the outcome of our plan."

Far-fetched, Lawrence thought again, as he put the offensive briefcase to one side and stretched out on the bed. Helen was *not* predictable whatever a psychologist thought. Goddamn Richardson and his associates—himself included. If Richardson's plan worked, his life would become one of self-loathing. He'd pandered to the snake in *his* garden all his life—a snake fattened with deceit and ambition.

He picked up the phone and dialed.

"Hullo. Helen McKellan speaking."

§

A week after Lawrence's unexpected call, Kenneth surprised Helen with his invitation. "Benevolence is not close enough to spirit you away for your birthday weekend so I'm taking you to the Lake District—a slice of Ireland that got mislaid. Jill says you've earned a good break, so relax."

The Lake District did indeed remind Helen of Ireland. Peat smoke curled from village chimneys. The cobbled streets and whitewashed exteriors of shops and houses were as familiar to her as the village of Enniscrone. Even the mountains reminded her of County Mayo's Nephin Beg Range.

"I've rented us a cottage in Hawkshead—great hiking trails and lakes teeming with trout. A Dublin chum told me it's a favourite haunt of his," Kenneth said.

To have time to themselves, they bought supplies from a local farmer. For their first meal, a fisherman gave them two fat trout. The local bakery and greengrocer supplied whatever else they needed. That evening, being chilly, they lit blocks of peat in the cottage grate and fell to talking.

"A new school has started up in Ballina, and I've reserved Kelsey's place for the new school year, if it suits you," Kenneth said. "I've also designed an addition to the back of the cottage for Kelsey's bedroom and a music studio for you. When he's ready, Alex can cut his teeth farming the sixty acres of arable land I own just behind Benevolence."

"You're full of wonderful surprises. Alex will be pleased with that, and how blissful to have Kelsey coming home at the end of her school day."

"Yes, she'll be happy, and so will we."

On the second night, Helen made a typical Irish meal of sausages and a creamy Colcallon mash, plus a gooseberry tart from the baker.

"Keep this up and I'll be waddling," Kenneth said. "Maybe music can ease my overfilled belly," and proceeded to serenade her with Irish love songs.

She stopped his third song with a kiss, and told him his voice was not dissimilar to John McCormack, the legendary Irish tenor.

"That's a fine compliment, madam, although I could never sing sixty-four notes without drawing a breath like him. Did you know he and James Joyce were friends?"

"I didn't, but I do know Winston Churchill admired him."

"Churchill?" Using a leftover sausage, he chomped on his 'cigar' and growled, "We shall fight them on the beaches, we shall fight them in the hills ..."

Helen cheered loudly, but when he did the Mountbatten standing-at-attention act, he jogged her memory and she told him the Earl would be visiting Classiebawn Castle the second weekend in May. "It's very low-key. Isn't Classiebawn close to the border region?"

"It is. How did you get that tidbit of news? I've seen no statements."

"By accident. A week ahead of you arriving in London, Lawrence and I had dinner to discuss the sale of our Edinburgh flat. He left his briefcase in my suite, and being late when he dropped me back, asked me to leave it at the front desk for pick-up in the morning. Unfortunately, it had a faulty lock and fell open. Pencils, gloves, and envelopes tumbled out, along with a memorandum with Classiebawn on it. I was nosy. Have you ever been there?"

"No. Years ago, the English confiscated the land and gave it to people who put down an Irish rebellion. In time, the Ashley family became the new owners. Edwina Ashley is Mountbatten's wife. Was there more in the memo?"

Helen wrinkled her brow and leaned towards the fire to warm her hands. His question troubled her. "Nothing more. You won't write about this, Kenneth, will you?"

He laughed. "Not unless the government announce Mountbatten's visit first. Don't you worry. Let's go for a walk and yowl to the ancient wolves of the moon. It's full tonight. We'd be daft to waste another precious moment on politics.

CHAPTER 52

MAY 1951

ALEX HAD NEVER imagined his first assignment would take him to Northern Ireland—not when so many of his fellow soldiers got deployed to the war in Korea. But, on his arrival at County Fermanagh barracks, he learned that his marksmanship had earned him the posting.

At zero-eight-hundred hours—the Friday morning of the spring bank holiday—Major Andrews briefed Alex's unit. "Tonight, Lord Mountbatten will arrive at St. Angelo Airport and from there we are escorting him to the border after the local pub closes. The road from the airport has one T-intersection on Belleek's outskirts, and straddles the border between Northern Ireland and County Sligo. We believe that is where the rebels will stage their interception."

From studying a diagram, Alex chose the most advantageous position—a rooftop that gave an unobstructed view of the intersection, the pub, and the road to the airport.

Once in position, he took a bead through his Lee Enfield No.4 Mk1 service rifle, and saw the dark bulk of Sergeant Jones melt into the shadows near the pub. The team wore black fatigues, making it difficult to spot each soldier, and a quarter moon didn't help, but he knew there were two men with the sergeant, three behind the roadside hedge, three behind a dilapidated tractor, and to his right, three near a deserted barn offset from the main road. A camouflaged van with medical supplies hid inside the barn.

Across the intersection to his left, Alex watched the roadside pub discharge the last stragglers. From earlier reconnaissance, he knew only the publican and his wife lived there. The ground floor darkened within a half hour, followed by the upstairs lights going off twelve minutes later. The couple had gone to bed. Alex shifted position to ease his leg muscles and strained his ears toward the airport. Still no sound of a plane. The airport had been well-used during the war but had fallen into disuse until the army gave it new life. Corporal Davies had told him once he heard a plane, he would see action within the hour.

Although patience was a sniper's strength, the reality that he might take out a human target for the first time strained his nerves. Using the chimney stack for cover, Alex leaned his rifle against it, unbuttoned his fly, and let loose, thinking what a crazy place to spend his twentieth birthday. A low hum made him look skyward. He rearranged himself, checked his rifle, and fifteen minutes later, his walkie-talkie hissed.

"McKellan, do you read me? The bird has landed. Stand by. Over."

Alex pressed the talk button on his handset. "When the vehicles pass, tell me how many and calculate speed and distance apart."

Twenty minutes later, his walkie-talkie hissed again. "McKellan? Two sedans. Four-widths apart, travelling fifty-five miles per hour. Should cover the twelve miles to you in thirteen minutes. Picking up radio static. Maintain silence. Over and out."

Alex released his tension with deep breathing, and flipped up the rifle's ladder aperture sight. The forecast rain had held off, but the moon cast meagre light. The minutes dragged before headlights stabbed the darkness on the main road, and the first of the two sedans approached and passed below him. At the intersection, the driver made a stop-and-roll movement and continued forward. The second sedan, now lagging, made to follow, but an approaching delivery van from the secondary road, sped into the middle of the intersection and jerked to a stop.

Alex sighted on the van's side doors. Three armed men jumped out, and he picked off two as easy as tin cans on a stone wall. The other dropped into a crouch and aimed at the second sedan, but Sergeant Jones, flanked by soldiers, stormed from the shadows, shouting, "Drop your weapon! We have you covered!" There was a loud crack, and the sergeant lurched sideways and hit the ground.

Two more bursts of fire levelled the soldier to the sergeant's right and ruptured the sedan's radiator. Even as steam spewed upwards, Alex brought the van's driver into his sights and fired through the side window. The man's head mushroomed against the glass. Another shot rang out, and a solder limped for cover. Alex ranged his rifle over the pub, hunting for the rebel sniper, but without success. To visualize the trajectory of the enemy fire, he closed his eyes, then crabbed along the roof until the pub was directly across from him. At first, he saw nothing, then spotted the glint of a scope from the pub's upstairs window. He fired twice and waited. No return fire. Heart thumping, he ranged the road, the side of the pub, the ditch, the stone wall above it, but nothing moved. Patience ... watch ... wait ... fifteen seconds ... thirty. Then, from up the road, he spotted a vehicle coming to a stop. Was it a getaway car? Yes. The driver's door opened, and a man got out just as the fugitive broke cover from the ditch and ran toward him. Alex steadied and squeezed off two shots. The one from the ditch staggered towards the other. Both men fell. No one else exited the car. Where in hell was Corporal Davies? His walkie-talkie hissed.

"Hold your fire." It was the sergeant. Not dead, just wounded.

"Sir, I brought two targets down some three hundred yards out."

"All right. Get up there and investigate."

Alex raced along the flat of the roof and lowered himself into the attic. Cobwebs stuck to his face as he sprinted down the stairs, and darted across the road. At the intersection, a soldier held three men spread-eagled against the pub's brick wall, cursing at them to keep their arms up and not move. A few yards away, the publican and his wife huddled together in their pyjamas. More soldiers were sealing off the area. Both sedans had moved off the intersection and joined the van, now in full view. A medic was tending to the sergeant's leg.

Alex, his mouth thick with saliva and his chest heaving, held his rifle at high ready, and moving fast, checked the ditch, the shadows, and then scoped the field to his right. If a fugitive chose that route, two soldiers at the field's perimeter would nail him. At the site, he pointed the rifle's muzzle to the ground and moved towards the enemy sniper. He lay face down, arms flung out on either side as if in an expansive gesture towards the car's driver. Shreds of an ear trailed down the side of his neck. *My shot through the window,* Alex thought. Blood welled from a gaping hole where the bullet from his long-distance shot had exited his back.

Before Alex could check the second victim, Corporal Davies arrived in a military land rover. "I was ordered to the airport once the sedans had passed," he said.

From the intersection, one of the two sedans arrived. A ranking officer, bearing the crown and three-star insignia of a captain, got out from the driver's side. He pulled a photograph from his breast pocket, hurried over to Alex and Davies, and knelt to compare the photo to the body on the ground. He smiled when he got to his feet. "It's Cooper O'Neil, no mistake." He turned to Alex. "Good work, private. You and the corporal check his accomplice."

They moved away as the sedan's passenger, wearing the uniform of a royal navy officer also got out. Alex widened his eyes at the sight of him. *He isn't Mountbatten. He's a double.* The second casualty was bent over, head lolling onto his chest, arms slack by his sides.

"Is he dead? I recognize the car. It was at the airport. I should have checked it," Davies said, as he bent to help Alex ease the victim to a prone position. Blood trickled from the side of the mouth, and a dark stain had spread across the front of the chest. A camera and notebook lay strewn on the ground.

Alex scrambled closer, then cradled the body against his chest, and rocked him. "He isn't an accomplice. He's just a reporter," he blurted out. "I've known him since I was a kid."

"Easy there, private. He must have been following a lead. Crazy to get out of the car. Come with me. We need to get you back to the barracks and have a doctor examine you. You're in shock."

CHAPTER 53

MAY 1951

HELEN SAGGED IN her chair unmoving, hollowed out by grief. Two hours had passed since Harry's phone call. Dizzy with exhaustion, she crawled into bed but in the overwhelming silence she could not stop visualizing Kenneth's shattered body.

Harry's words circled endlessly in her head. *Kenneth mistaken for a rebel. Died in Alex's arms.* She groped for the sleeping pills on the bedside table. How easy to swallow the lot, and escape her anguish. A harsh wind rattled the shutters, and she hurled the bottle from her. To lessen her pain, she threw off the sheets and swung her feet to the floor. What torment was Alex feeling? Thank heaven Harry had been asked to come. *In time, Alex will accept that he could not have stopped the tragedy. Kenneth was an investigative reporter.*

Suddenly, the stark enormity of that thought sent her stumbling to the bathroom where she dry-retched. If she had not fed her curiosity and blurted out her information, Kenneth might still be alive. Images of Kelsey fluttered like moths in the dark. How to soften the blow to her? After the stomach cramps subsided, Helen took refuge under the bedclothes again, but this time, as night inched towards dawn, she pushed down her emotions. Kenneth's death must not engulf her. Slowly, reason entered her chaotic thoughts.

Next morning, she woke to a steady tapping on her door. "Sweets, it's me. May I come in?" Helen slipped on her bathrobe.

Jill's face relaxed from relief at seeing her. "It's heartbreaking, Helen, I'm so sorry. Lawrence phoned and asked that I check you were all right. He arrives this evening. Get dressed, love. You need to eat."

She appeared ten minutes later, hair tied back and lips smudged with coral lipstick, but her green silk dress offered no warmth. Kenneth's gold shamrock dangled from a chain on her wrist. At Jill's urging, she gnawed on a piece of dried toast and sipped milky coffee.

"It's such agony, Jill. I wanted to die after Harry phoned, but I'm over that. There's Kelsey and Alex to think of." Her voice faltered. "I can't even cry."

§

Rain beaded the windshield of Lawrence's rented car as he parked in front of The Hermitage. He flicked on the wipers and sat listening to their monotonous *whap-whap* against the glass. When Harry phoned, with a sketchy outline of what had happened, he had stayed awake throughout the night, trying to jig-saw the missing pieces together.

"Don't call Helen," Harry had cautioned. "She needs privacy. Jill will comfort her. I'm with Alex. He's in shock and under observation. I'll reach you later."

Pain enveloped Lawrence's neck and shoulders. How could things have gone so wrong? Richardson's damnable old-boy voice when he tried to explain away the fuck up made him squirm.

"None of us is a perfect mind-reader, Lawrence. No one could have predicted such a personal twist. The military chose your son as the marksman, not me. It's a tragedy, but you should be proud of Alex. He put an end to Cooper—a ruthless IRA man with personal vengeance on his mind. As to Inglis, *the mind of man plans his way, but the Lord directs his steps*. It seems to me—" Lawrence hung up.

Guilt infested him. Harry's mistakes arose from gambling and misguided choices, but those paled in comparison to his. His stemmed from cold, calculated ambition, and if that meant deceiving those who trusted him, he did. A deep shame enveloped him.

He endured Jill's condolences when he entered, and then followed her upstairs to Helen's suite. "Helen," Jill called, "Lawrence is here." Once the door opened, she retreated quietly.

§

He looks desolate, Helen thought, his face grey and sunken. She could only guess as to his personal hell. She felt oddly displaced seeing him in her room, as if part of her was absent.

"Don't sit down. What I have to say won't take long." But he shook his head and sat on the chair nearest the door.

"Please, Helen, before you speak, let me explain. What happened was tragic and unforeseen. I repeat, unforeseen. I disliked Kenneth Inglis; he was my rival, but I respected his intellect. He was not an innocent bystander. He was looking for a story. It was a military operation. He must have known the dangers. As to Alex, he's young; he will pull through. As I told him, he must deal with the consequences of the choices he's made and the career path he's chosen."

There was a freighted silence before she spoke. "Stop the charade and don't shift one smidgen of fault of this tragedy to your son. You've been a controlling man your entire life, Lawrence—enforcing your point of view, your methods, your beliefs—but you have *never* been a careless or absent-minded one." He opened his mouth to speak, but she silenced him with her hand. "You didn't leave your briefcase in my room because it was a nuisance, any more than the lock was faulty. I should have known. You're too fastidious." She perched on the sofa with anger tingling like acid on her tongue. "How well you and your fellow pariahs played me—my curiosity, my vanity, my insecurities. What a list I could make of my faults. But you knew them, and gambled on them. You're contemptible."

His eyes refused to meet hers. "I can't undo the harm that's come our way, Helen, but I won't take responsibility for all that's happened. In my grim world, we use human weaknesses to advantage. My fault is hubris—an excessive pride of self and family. I can see now how it has harmed most of my close relationships and—"

"Don't. Don't acknowledge a few of your faults now. It doesn't vindicate you. Did that toad Richardson have something over you?"

Lawrence heaved a deep sigh. "The Intelligence Service *always* has something over you. But power is addictive, and working for Intelligence changed me. Can I lessen this crisis in some way?"

"Yes. There is something." Unbelievably, his eyes met hers as though deliverance might be at hand. She stood up, strangely calm. "First, do not dishonour Kenneth by showing your face at his funeral. Do nothing to remind me of your part in his death. Second, support Alex. Do not detract from him, and respect his individuality.

Third, I want a divorce which allows me to live in Ireland with Kelsey. Respect my wishes. In return, neither Kelsey, Alex, nor Harry will ever know from me that Kenneth's death resulted from your treachery. If you falter, remember a tendency for blackmail resides in all of us. Be thankful that your relationship with Margaret remains unharmed." She crossed her arms. "Do we have an understanding?"

Already sunk deep in his chair, he nodded. "We do. I'm resigning from the service, and plan on establishing a small architectural practice near Margaret and Robert." He levered himself upright and went to the door. "You will never know how much I regret our life coming apart. I hope one day you will forgive me, though I doubt I shall ever be able to forgive myself. I will have your wishes confirmed in writing by my lawyer, and furthermore, guarantee you are financially secure. Knowing your capabilities, I can't imagine you not taking up some endeavour in the hospitality business. If you do, my architectural services will be at no expense, should you need them."

She nodded. With a surreal sense of detachment, she crossed to the window after he left and watched him walk to his car. He did not look up, nor did she expect that of him. Their chapter together was finished.

CHAPTER 54

MAY 1951

THEY BURIED KENNETH in the grounds of Enniscrone's oldest church, with a view from the cemetery which overlooked Killala Bay. Father Gareth presided over the private burial service.

Helen comforted Kelsey and Alex beside her, glad that Harry and Rhoda stood nearby. Ryan, Kenneth's Dublin colleague, was there too. Several gypsies from the camp also gathered, dressed in their funeral colours of red and white—including Sorcha in a white skirt and her hair tied back in a red ribbon. When Kelsey saw her, she ran across the grass and sobbed in her arms.

At the close of service, Kelsey, holding Helen's hand, dropped bluebells onto the coffin. Helen had chosen the headstone inscription. *Kenneth Inglis. Born 1904, Died 1951. A life well-lived. A life well-loved.* A decade of knowing and loving him, had not dimmed the 'shining core' he had spoken of so long ago. She blew a kiss into the air. "You will always be in our hearts."

§

The formal reading of Kenneth's Last Will and Testament took place in a Ballina law firm two days later. Being the executor of Kenneth's estate, Harry knew the contents and insisted Helen attend. "You need to be there," he said. They left Kelsey in Rhoda's care, and drove the half-hour to town.

"Everywhere I go reminds me of him, Harry. Kelsey and I were coming to live with him. He'd even registered her in a Ballina day school and built an addition to Benevolence. I've no idea what to do now."

"Don't worry. You're forgetting that Kenneth and I were very good friends. I notice you've been silent about Lawrence."

"I needed to keep things to myself for a while, but we're getting divorced. He has agreed to my conditions, and they are now binding. I know the monetary settlement will be fair, and he said I can call on his architectural skills at no cost, should I move ahead with some project or other."

Harry nodded. "My brother's pride will guarantee that. I sense there's much more you could tell me, but I respect your silence. How did you break the news of Kenneth's death to Kelsey?"

"An elephant helped," she said, smiling at his puzzlement. "I phoned the school to inform them we that were moving to Ireland at the end of the term. They suggested, because of Kenneth's passing, that it would be less disruptive for Kelsey if she skipped the last six weeks of term. Her grades are excellent. By the time I arrived, they had her possessions packed."

"And the elephant?"

"I took her to Edinburgh Zoo before we caught our flight to Dublin. She and Kenneth shared a fondness for elephants. When we arrived, I told her a white lie—that Uncle Kenneth had died from an accident at work. She cried, but when she stood near the elephant, it must have sensed her grief, because it explored her face with its trunk, and then hung it around her shoulders. She found the encounter of great comfort, and when we left, she told me that when she leaves school, she wants to look after animals."

"So, it's possible we'll have a veterinarian in the family one day."

Helen rolled the window open and breathed in the rush of cool air spiced with the first cut of hay. Their discussion of Kelsey's future brought to mind Alex, and what he had shared with her the night before at the farm.

"I'm being deployed to Singapore next month, Mum. Korea is a long way off. I want to stay in the army the full five years, and then start farming."

"I'm glad. I'm sure staying is like getting back on a horse after being thrown. Don't be in a rush. The farming life will be here when you return."

The law firm on Barret Street looked across the River Moy to St. Muredach's Cathedral. Kenneth had taken her to see it on one of their outings. The formalities of reading Kenneth's Will were soon over. After settling debts, and leaving a sum of money to Harry, and to a woman's shelter, it stated that ten thousand pounds be held in trust for Kelsey's education, and 'with my love and affection, the residue of my estate, including clear title to Benevolence, go to Helen McKellan.'

Helen sat in stunned silence. *Don't,* she lectured herself. *Don't fall apart now.*

That evening, the Brown Cow owners followed Irish-wake tradition and stopped the clocks, turned the mirrors to the wall, hung white sheets at the windows, and lit candles. Beyond the usual food and alcohol and small dishes of snuff, the men passed clay pipes filled with tobacco amongst themselves. Alex explained to Helen that, although the gathering was not a true Irish wake, every male must take a puff to ward off evil spirits.

The pub rang with the voices of locals recalling their best Kenneth encounters, and their stories brought Helen comfort. Many paid her their respects, and lingered to admire Kelsey's smile, the chestnut gleam in her hair, and the touch of her hand. *They must see Kenneth's likeness,* Helen thought.

She noticed Mary approaching with a dolorous Murphy at her side. "Are you holding up all right, Ma'am? It's a sad day that brings us together."

"It is, Mary, but everyone being here for him this evening helps us."

"Our Mr Kenneth never lost sight of his humble beginnings," Murphy said. "That's why his writing will always speak to us."

"Did you know his da was a teacher in Castlebar, and Mr Kenneth helped at the school until he was of an age to work?" Mary added. "Not that he was a total saint, but he respected Catholic values. Tragic about his sister."

Aware of Mary's prattling tongue, Helen patted the woman's hand. "We are here to share good memories, Mary, not woeful ones."

Annoyance with Mary flashed in Murphy's eyes. "I'm hoping, Ma'am, that you and Kelsey will visit me and Mary at our tea-shop."

"We'll look forward to that; we will not be living far from here."

"Is that a fact? Where might that be, Ma'am?" Mary asked, knowingly.

"Quit with the questions, Mary," Murphy said, and steered her away.

To Helen's relief, Rhoda arrived with Brigid. "Welcome home, Ma'am," Brigid said, and kissed Kelsey. "I'm looking forward to you and your mammy visiting me and my family when you're settled."

Helen glanced across to where Harry stood, surrounded by friends and latecomers. After a round of songs, he tapped his glass with a spoon. "Attention everyone. Alex McKellan wants the floor."

Helen knew that none in the room realized Alex was the last to see Kenneth alive—only a slight tic above his eye betrayed his nervousness. "For those of you who have not read the *Daily Leader*, Kenneth died in a border incident," he said. "We'll never know the full story, but he took many risks to bring us the news, and he shone an unwavering light on injustice. Kenneth was a learned man—ask my uncle Harry. Kenneth never gave up on arguing history, politics, or anything else on which you cared to challenge him."

"Except for horse racing!" someone joked. Someone else added, "That's because he didn't heed Harry's tips!"

Alex visibly relaxed with the laughter, and waited until it subsided. "Kenneth always had a story and a song on his lips. He also loved to fish, provided he cast from a river bank. 'Turns me greener than a shamrock to think about boats,' he claimed, but he reeled in many a big one." Knowing nods came from the journalists. "Please join me in toasting a man Irish to the core, and whose stories few can match."

Helen felt Rhoda's arm slip around her waist, and leaning against her, knew she and Rhoda would become good friends. After the raising of glasses, a fiddler struck up *The Dear Little Shamrock*—one of Kenneth's favourites—and the crowd sang along until Harry tapped his glass again. "Now it's time to meet two special ladies. Helen and Kelsey, will you step forward please?"

Holding Kelsey's hand, Helen approached and thanked everyone for their kindness and good wishes. "How many know Kenneth wrote children's stories? Ireland's myths and legends fired his imagination, and his stories are prized by both Kelsey and me. Kelsey has one of his books with her; don't you?"

Kelsey nodded, and held it up for all to see, then gave the book to Harry to pass around before she ran and stood with Rhoda. Helen continued to speak. "Kenneth was not one for talking about eternity, but let me share something else he wrote a few years ago," and smiling, produced a sheet of paper

> *"I've never subscribed to the idea we are the entirety of our experiences and the people in our lives. If that were true, we'd be reeds in the wind, victims of whatever external influences came our way. Where's the mystery in that? I believe we are each unique, maybe born to a calling beyond our ken, but in the here and now, our greatest duty is to offer love and kindness. Sometimes that means giving those you love time to discover themselves, to even drift away—but when it's time, they will find their way home."*

She looked up. "Although Kenneth is not with us in person, he *is* home, as are many of us in this room tonight."

Someone started singing *The Rare Ould Times* but in the middle of the second verse, the pub's door flew open. Two dishevelled men burst in, shouting, "Help! The hotel is on fire! We need buckets, and volunteers!"

§

By the time Harry's truck screeched to a halt near Helen's old studio, the hotel had flared the night sky to a fierce orange. Armed with buckets from the Brown Cow, Harry and Alex sprinted to where a line of people hauled water from the estuary. Above the steady roar and crackle of the fire devouring the hotel, smoke spiralled upwards in black clouds. Helen knew saving it was hopeless.

"Are those dragon tongues?" Kelsey asked, holding a hand to her mouth.

"No, darling, they're wild flames fanned by the wind. Stay close."

"Look! Here come the fire trucks!" Rhoda shouted, as two raced past them.

Thick smoke clawed at Helen's eyes. She ripped her scarf into pieces and soaked them in a bucket. "Kelsey, Rhoda, wipe your eyes," she said, "but remember it's salty." She made a cover for Kelsey's nose and mouth.

The wind increased and flung sparks and debris in all directions. Chunks landed on the new boathouse opposite the pub. "Run!" Alex yelled, "The fuel tanks will catch." Within seconds, they exploded, and hot fragments hit the driveway.

Helen searched for Harry, then saw him in the paddock. Grabbing Rhoda's arm, she pointed, and together with Kelsey, they raced towards him, waving their arms to hold the animals back until he roped and led them to higher ground. When he returned, he crouched next to Kelsey and comforted her. "Don't cry. The horses are safe." He looked up at the two women. "I'm not so sure if everyone in the hotel escaped, but we'll know soon enough."

The firefighters were too late to save the hotel, but they doused the last of the flames and started the work of breaking up pockets of glowing embers. Helen gulped. "Months to build and ravaged by fire in hours. Where are the owners?"

"Out of the country" a man said. She turned and looked into the familiar face of Seamus. "The fire will raise plenty questions, so it will."

"What are you suggesting?" Helen protested, her nostrils flaring as Alex arrived stinking of smoke.

"Money troubles, I'm thinking. Seeing as the owners over-insured the hotel, it don't take much to puzzle out."

"You mustn't start rumours, Seamus," Helen said, clearing her throat. "More than likely it was kitchen carelessness. Were there casualties?"

"None," he growled. "The owners closed the place for renovations. The caretaker and wife escaped. Convenient the fire happening late on a windy night."

"Well, the insurance people aren't fools," Harry said, and lowered his voice to Helen. "Kenneth would say, 'Don't mourn the building; it's the memories of the good times that matter.'"

"Yes, but the best part of my life was in the hotel, and now it's gone."

"The best part is right here. You have Kelsey, and you are here with us. It was never the hotel. It was you that gave the locals life and gaiety. Remember the Friday-night singsongs? Where else could I have forgotten my troubles in making my way in this cruel world?" Clutching his hands, he looked piously up at the sky.

She laughed. "You are such a clown, Harry." She hugged Kelsey closer. "Sometimes you are very wise though. Thank you. I lost my perspective."

Rhoda smiled at them. "Let's go back to the farm for a nice cup of tea. You too, Seamus."

"Or something stronger," added Harry, winking at Helen.

ACKNOWLEDGEMENTS

THIS IS A song of gratitude to all those who gave their encouragement and support in the creation of *The Irish Affair.*

First and foremost, to my parents, for the years I lived in Ireland.

To Matt Hughes who mentored me during the early stages, and told me a book is only a thought until you start to write.

To Jozefina Maria Kollee (Jos) who gave me her unbridled encouragement from the first word to the last.

To Diane Davis who championed my writerly dreams from the moment we met on Denman Island.

To the members of my first writers group who came to my home and lent their ears and minds to my earliest draft: Matt Hughes, Susan Ketchen, Michel Gauthier and Danny Zanbilowicz.

To Bernice Friesen, Michael Lalonde and Jim Saunders for their helpful critiques.

To my Facebook friends who participated in a 'title' poll.

To Nico teWinkel who vanquished my computer dragons.

To Evelyn Gillespie of the Laughing Oyster Bookshop who showed me the intricacies of book searches.

To Andrew Lorimer of Lorimer Productions who contributed to the design of the book cover, and created my website.

To Astra Crompton, my Publishing Specialist, for her constant patience and guidance throughout the publishing process.

To the FriessenPress team who followed through so diligently.

THANK YOU

AUTHOR'S NOTE

THE SEEDS FOR the Irish Affair were inadvertently planted by my father. In my early teens, he shared stories of how he met my mother, his life as a student at Oxford University, and his fascinating descriptions of his underground office at the Admiralty in London during World War II. One evening, after we had seen the film, *The Man Who Never Was,* he admitted to his involvement in the MI5 operation which inspired the film. I was hooked, but no pleading or begging coaxed another war story from him.

Many years later, after I emigrated to Canada, I met and married David Diver. Once again I was treated to first-hand recollections. This time of a young boy's experiences in London during the Blitz—watching aerial dogfights, hiding in Anderson air-raid shelters, and being one of the thousands of children evacuated from the city.

On a trip to London, I visited the Royal Air Force Museum at Hendon. Here, I saw the World War II Westland Lysander, The Bristol Beaufighter and Hitler's 'terror weapons'—the Flying Bomb VI, known as 'the doodle bug,' and the stratosphere V2 rocket.

The reference book, *Atlas of World War II* by David Jordan and Andrew Wiest, gave me valuable insight into the Battle of the Atlantic and U-boat wolfpack tactics, as well as The Normandy invasion. The Internet also provided a wealth of information on Irish politics, Bletchley Park and Blenheim Palace.

As for Irish folklore, my nanny filled my young ears with many a scary tale at bedtime!

With award-winning short stories and poems that have been showcased in a number of anthologies, Linda Christian Diver enjoys honing her craft through reading, research, and workshops, and is a member of several writing groups. She and her husband, David—a professional jazz and classical pianist—live with their dog in the Comox Valley of Vancouver Island, ringed by mountains and near the swell and chop of the Georgia Strait. Together, they enjoy geo-politics and healthy debate, as well as the best that lively company, and good music offer.

Printed in Canada